FIERY KISSES

Tara clung to Sloane, her trembling lips parting beneath his devouring insistence. His arms tightened around her as if he would crush her into him, but Tara didn't notice. She welcomed his fierce embrace, the solid male weight that moved against her. Tara gasped in wondrous pleasure as he rained kisses along her shoulder, setting the tantalizing rhythm with which she swayed and then finally lost her grasp on reality.

Sloane caught her cry of joy and pleasure within his mouth, his kiss savoring the sweet taste of her while his body delighted in total, exquisite passion. They were one, their hearts thundering at the same frantic pace, their souls soaring above each breathtaking plateau of pleasure to reach an ultimate pinnacle . . .

LONE STAR SURRENDER

CAROL FINCH

ZEBRA BOOKS
KENSINGTON PUBLISHING CORP.

ZEBRA BOOKS

are published by

Kensington Publishing Corp.
475 Park Avenue South
New York, NY 10016

First printing: October, 1988

Printed in the United States of America

This book is dedicated to my children,
Christie, Jill and Kurt
and to my husband, Ed . . . with much love.

Chapter 1

Texas, 1885

Biting back a self-satisfied smile, Tara Winslow squirmed to settle herself more comfortably on the wooden seat of the passenger car. Things had worked out so splendidly that she could scarcely believe it. After receiving the letter from her father, Terrance Winslow, inviting her to spend the summer with him, Tara had caught the train from St. Louis with not a minute to spare. When she'd reached Dallas she had sailed into a store to purchase suitable clothing for her stay in Texas.

Although she had suffered one minor mishap with a dusty cowboy who smelled more like a horse than a man, she had persuaded the drunken galloot to keep his hands to himself or risk having them chopped off in a most unpleasant manner. The cowboy had backed off when Tara rammed her derringer in his belly, and he had become a great deal more polite than he had been when they first chanced to meet.

Traveling alone to the sprawling plains of Panhandle Texas would not lead her into disaster, but to adventure, and to her beloved father, Tara told herself confidently. What could possibly go wrong? Besides a conflict with a drunken cowboy, she stipulated. She would simply follow the train to the end of its tracks and take the stage the remainder of the distance to Clarendon, or "Saints' Roost," as Terrance had fondly referred to the frontier town where he made his home.

Once she reached Clarendon she would assist her father with setting the type for his newspaper. It had every indication of being a pleasurable, educational summer, Tara decided as she stared across the wide-open plains that stretched toward the horizon. Besides, the eyes of Texas were upon her. Soon she would be nestled in her father's loving arms.

Tara propped her chin on her hand, her violet eyes focused on the flat Texas countryside that rushed past her. The same excitement that had claimed her when she had fled from her grandfather's mansion in St. Louis still sizzled through her veins, and it was becoming increasingly difficult to contain herself. Three long years she had waited to be reunited with her father! The image of Terrance Winslow rose above her. Ruefully, Tara recalled the last time she had seen Terrance and the emotional upheaval surrounding his departure. But that was all behind her. She and her father would compensate for the years they had spent apart.

"Señorita?" A soft male voice filtered into her pensive contemplations. Instinctively, Tara clutched her purse, which contained her derringer.

Her thick, long lashes swept up to survey the wrinkled, weatherbeaten features of a man of Spanish descent who looked as old as Father Time. Tara arched a quizzical brow as she assessed the aging man. He was dressed in Spanish-styled breeches, a jacket, and a large sombrero that partially shielded his graying hair. She had seen him watching her from a distance as she boarded the train in Dallas, but he had never approached her until now.

"May I join you, señorita?" he asked, producing a polite smile.

8

Why? There were plenty of empty seats in the passenger car. Why did the one beside her appeal to him, Tara thought suspiciously.

As if the old man had read her mind and plucked out the thought, he grinned down at her. *"No hay porque afligirse.* I wish you no harm, *uno cauto,* only conversation. It is a long ride to Clarendon."

Two attractively arched brows shot straight up. "You are traveling to Saints' Roost?" she questioned incredulously. It seemed too great a coincidence.

"Si." Don Miguel Chavez eased down beside her and then heaved a weary sigh. "It will prove a profitable journey, though the long hours I have spent on the train are tiring to these old, brittle bones."

"What kind of business are you in that finds profit in train rides, señor?" Tara questioned, true to her inquisitive nature.

A wry smile pursed Don Miguel Chavez's parched lips as he absently patted the gold locket that was stashed in his vest pocket. "I am presently in the business of uncovering buried secrets, among my other obligations to one of the good citizens of Clarendon."

My, but the man talked in riddles, Tara thought to herself. Her curiosity piqued, she prodded, "And this citizen's name? Is he expecting you?" She allowed her perceptive gaze to slide over the old man's features, not at all certain she should trust him.

Another grin rippled across Don Miguel's lips. "Did I say it was an *hombre,* señorita?"

There was a merry twinkle in his dark eyes as he assessed the bewitching young woman with hair of spun silver and gold.

It seemed the crusty vaquero delighted in remaining mysterious and vague, but Tara was eager to accept the challenge of prying information from him in a manner that would make her newspaperman father proud.

9

"Is it then a lovely señorita's obligations that return you to the High Plains?" she queried

One graying brow raised slightly and then returned to its normal arch as Don Miguel laughed deep in his chest. "You are determined to learn my mission. But what of you, *querida?* What brings you West without a companion? Haven't you been cautioned not to travel alone? Perhaps I should offer my services as an escort, since we seem to have a mutual destination."

Tara had the odd feeling that Don Miguel's presence was not coincidental. But that was impossible, she told herself, checking her overly suspicious nature. And if she wasn't careful, Chavez would steer her off course and she would never discover anything about him.

Her violet eyes flared with mischief as she regarded him with a smile. "Perhaps I would consent to that if I knew your true purpose. Thus far, you have tactfully managed to tell me nothing."

"And you have allowed me an equal understanding of your reasons for venturing West," he countered, his voice heavy with a Spanish accent. "Have you a friend or acquaintance in Saints' Roost?"

Tara regarded the vaquero for a long, calculating moment, undecided. There was something very mysterious about this man. And yet, there was a subtle warmth in his dark eyes, something that suggested that he was harmless. Finally, she decided to divulge her name and the reason for her journey to Texas.

"I am Tara Winslow, and I am on my way to visit my father," she confessed. "And what is your name, señor?"

He swept the sombrero from his tuft of gray hair. "My name is Don Miguel Chavez. Your *padre* requested that I keep an eye on you during your journey. He knew you would find a way to join him, and he did not wish to insult you by forcing an escort upon you. But I see no shame

10

in the fact that a father wishes safety for his lovely daughter."

Tara managed to steady her rattled composure. Her father had known she would find a way to escape her grandfather's domination and her mother's overprotective smothering. It had not been as easy as Terrance might have speculated. Nor had it been the first time Tara had tried to leave the estate to seek out her father, only the first *successful* attempt. And when her mother and grandfather read the note explaining her intentions, Tara wondered if they would send the cavalry after her. But at twenty-one she had the right to come and go as she pleased, she reminded herself stubbornly.

When her wandering thoughts converged, Tara interrogated Don Miguel about his mission. He had piqued her curiosity, and Tara was determined not to be sidetracked. "Just what is this secret you have uncovered?" she pressed.

Don Miguel chuckled heartily at the spirited beauty with wide violet eyes. "Señor Winslow has spawned a very persistent *hija* to follow in his footsteps. When he suggested that you might be traveling alone, I thought it odd. But there is a rare quality about you. . . ." Nodding thoughtfully, Don Miguel assessed the golden-haired lass. Cautiously, he lifted his hand, as if he were afraid he might frighten her, and then brushed his index finger over her creamy cheek. "You remind me of my own daughter," he sighed. "She was also a vision of loveliness. But like a splendid butterfly, her life span was all too short. I still despair that I have lost her." Don Miguel stared deeply into Tara's eyes and then smiled gently. "But you are blessed with an inner spirit, and your eyes are the mirror of your soul. I see much strength within you."

Tara found herself strangely drawn to this soft-spoken

11

man. An easy smile caught the corner of her mouth, giving her a radiant appearance that made Don Miguel catch his breath.

"My mother considers my wild spirit a fault," she admitted. "But my father has always approved of it." Before Don Miguel could derail her thoughts once again, Tara circled back to her previous question. "You still have not told me your secret. If I am to trust you, I would ask you to divulge something about yourself."

Don Miguel squirmed on the bench seat and took a moment to survey the scenery as the train sped across open range. "It will come to your attention soon enough, I suppose," he sighed and then cast Tara a fleeting glance. "Your father and a close friend of ours . . ."

"Who shall remain nameless," Tara assumed, since Don Miguel had shown himself to be very evasive.

"*Que sera*," he admitted. "Forgive me, señorita, but it is as it must be."

"Continue," Tara insisted, sitting on the edge of her seat. She loved an intriguing story, and she had the tingling feeling that this was to be one.

"Your *padre* and his *amigo* are interested in the legend that haunts Palo Duro. For more than a score of years a phantom has appeared along the mesa to torment one of the prominent ranchers. Merrick Russel is often visited by the ghost known as the Night Rider."

The color seeped from Tara's cheeks. The name Merrick Russel was a familiar one. The previous summer Julia Russel and her father, Merrick, had visited them in St. Louis. Tara and Julia had taken an instant liking to each other. Although Tara would eagerly have accepted Julia's invitation to travel back to Texas, her mother would not permit it. And so Julia and Tara parted, hoping one day they would chance to meet again.

Tara tossed aside her musings, contemplating Don

Miguel's comment. Julia had never mentioned anything about a ghost haunting their ranch. Tara had heard tales of haunted mansions in the South after the tragedies of the Civil War, but no one had said anything about Palo Duro Canyon being plagued with specters. Sweet merciful heavens! What was she letting herself into?

"Many years ago, when the comancheros prowled this deserted region of Texas trading with the Indians and hunting the buffalo, two young brothers came West with their dream of establishing a cattle empire. They had planned to graze the fertile valley of Palo Duro Canyon. But one night Merrick's brother was trampled by stampeding cattle." Don Miguel's eyes took on a faraway look as he peered back through the window of time. "Some say it was the work of the ruthless comancheros. Others claim it was merely a frightened herd that caused his death. And there are those who swear Merrick himself brought about his brother's death because of his greed."

Tara shuddered at the thought of being caught amidst a herd of stampeding cattle. The vision was a grizzly one, and she quickly dismissed it, anxious for Don Miguel to continue.

"Through the years there have been occasional sightings of this ghostly specter who sits astride his glowing white stallion, keeping constant vigil over that which should have been his." His shoulder lifted and then dropped in a lackadaisical shrug. "Some swear it is only the tumbleweeds that sweep the range that were seen by the night herders, and others are certain the vision is some supernatural spirit from another world." Don Miguel darted Tara a sidelong glance, aware that she was spellbound at the tale. "Even Señor Russel believes that his brother has returned to frighten the herd and to place a lifelong curse upon him, causing his profits to dwindle and the stockholders to question his management abilities."

"Julia's father relies upon that excuse for his woes?" Tara blurted out. How could a grown man claim to believe a spell had been cast on him? Were all Texans the backward sort, with uneducated minds that conjured up phantoms to explain what they didn't understand? Her mother would heartily have answered yes, but Tara was not about to fall into the trap of judging these cattlemen until she knew more about them. After all, she had only met Merrick Russel once, and she knew very little about him.

A devilish smile parted Don Miguel's lips. "Indeed, Señor Russel does believe it, and it leaves one to wonder why," he answered in belated response to Tara's bewildered question. "Your *padre* has kept the legend alive with his newspaper, following up the reports of strange happenings by Merrick's ranch hands. Señor Russel is much distressed by the attention his ranchero has been receiving. But he will openly admit that unexplainable stampedes always occur on Mesquite Mesa, the very place where his brother perished."

Was Don Miguel implying there was dissension between her father and Merrick Russel? Undoubtedly, Tara mused pensively. Terrance Winslow was like a bloodhound when it came to sniffing out a story. He would never be satisfied until he had distinguished fact from fallacy. But why was Terrance so intrigued by this legend?

"And what exactly is your interest in this legend?" Tara questioned pointedly.

"*Si*, there is much of the father in the daughter," Don Miguel smiled. "He is determined to uncover the truth, just as you are. But you must forgive a stubborn old man, *querida*. I have been sworn to secrecy. I cannot divulge what I have discovered to anyone, except him who sent me."

14

"My father?" Tara relentlessly prodded.

Don Miguel flicked the end of her upturned nose. "You are much too persistent, *chiquita*. It makes me wonder if there was yet another reason why your father sent for you at this particular time. Perhaps our clever reporter has left nothing to chance."

Tara frowned. My, but Don Miguel talked in confusing riddles, revealing just enough to drive her mad with curiosity. Everyone had vices, and excessive inquisitiveness was Tara's downfall. She would never be satisfied until she knew exactly what Don Miguel was babbling about.

The smile that hovered on Don Miguel's lips evaporated, his expression becoming somber. "But I feel I must warn you, *mi niña inocente*. Things may not always be as they appear. Do not be quick to trust just anyone. Make them earn your confidence."

"Even you?" Tara could not help but say, wondering what the devil she was about to get herself into.

"I am but an old man obeying a loved one's dying request," Don Miguel told her softly, his hand absently brushing over the locket he carried in his pocket. "I have no other purpose left in life but to see justice served. I mean no harm. I consented to escort you to your *padre* so as to come to know the young woman of whom he so often speaks." He reached into his pocket to extract the picture Terrance Winslow had presented to him before he left Clarendon. "I waited in Dallas after completing my business at the mission of Valquez, hoping to catch sight of this lovely young woman at the depot." He turned the portrait to allow Tara a glimpse of her own picture. "I had almost given up on you, señorita. But when I saw you returning to the passenger car, there was no mistake of your identity, except that your picture did not capture your true beauty."

15

Her long, thick lashes fluttered against her cheeks in response to his generous compliment. Tara found it impossible not to trust this gentle vaquero. There was a certain compelling warmth about him, and yet there was also a strange sadness in his smile that intrigued her. Her hand moved gingerly toward his, feeling his leathered skin beneath her palm.

"I have no fear of you," she told him honestly. "If you are a friend of my father's, you are my friend, as well."

"*Gracias*, señorita." His dark eyes danced with mild amusement. "There is one other I would have earn your trust, one you are destined to meet." A grin rippled across his parched lips as he scrutinized Tara's oval face and satiny complexion. "But I think you will make him *earn* your respect and friendship, as well he should."

Now Tara was thoroughly confused. Don Miguel talked of legends and phantom stallions, suggesting that her father was on the trail of some mysterious specter and that he had enlisted the assistance of a friend. Now he was suggesting that she would meet another mysterious stranger. What did he have to do, if anything, with the legend of the Night Rider and Don Miguel's obligation to a "loved one"? And what about her father? What was his interest in the legend? Had he changed these past three years? Could her mother's opinion of Terrance be closer to the truth than the one Tara carried in her heart? And if it were, why the devil was she trouncing off across Texas to find him? She might have been better off where she was and never realized it!

Don Miguel peered out the window and then eased from his seat. "I think we have reached the end of the rails. Wait here for me until I check the stage line, which will take us the remainder of the way to Clarendon."

As the train screeched to a halt, Don Miguel disappeared out the door and Tara stared after him, her

16

violet eyes wide with questions. It seemed Texas held more surprises than she had anticipated, and yet . . . Memories of the restless days she had endured in St. Louis, pining for her father, wanting more from life than her grandfather's money could buy, filled her mind. No, she wasn't turning back now. She had come too far, and she was determined to see her father and satisfy three agonizing years of curiosity. Perhaps then she would be prepared to return to wed Joseph Rutherford and accept the lifestyle he offered.

"The stagecoach will not leave until tomorrow afternoon, so I have taken the liberty of renting a carriage for our journey," Don Miguel informed her when he returned to the passenger car.

"The sooner we reach Clarendon the better," Tara assured him as she placed her small hand in his and followed him down the aisle.

As the carriage rumbled down the dirt streets of Harrold, past the empty cattle pens near the depot, Tara drank in the view of sprawling range lands that stretched as far as the eye could see. The wide-open spaces of Texas, she said to herself as she settled herself on the seat beside Don Miguel. This was a land where a man could ride into the sun without ever losing sight of his destination. An exhilarating sensation channeled through her body as her acute gaze swept the surroundings, which were unlike anything she had ever known. There was something fascinating about Texas, and she was anxious to become a part of it, if only for a time. If her father was in the business of chasing phantoms, then she would accompany him, at least to satisfy her curiosity, she told herself as she cast Don Miguel a sidelong glance, wishing he would have been more explicit in his explanation. But the aging vaquero was tight-lipped as a clam, and Tara suspected it would take a crowbar to pry information from Don Miguel Chavez. But Don Miguel had dropped the subject and refused to reopen it once they set out in the carriage.

As the orange ball of fire drooped lower on the horizon, Tara pulled her jacket more closely about her to ward off the evening chill. Then she sighed, thinking how much she would enjoy a warm, relaxing bath. Her body was stiff and sore from the long days she had spent aboard the train. But soon she would be reunited with her father, she reminded herself. It would be worth the long hours of traveling. Then she would soak to her heart's content.

Don Miguel had told her of the days when he had brought his family from New Mexico, following the trails the comancheros had blazed into the unclaimed land of the Panhandle, herding their large flock of sheep. His life had been uncomplicated and peaceful until cattlemen came into the rich grazing lands and began buying up the land. Don Miguel was forced to pack up and move his family farther east or return to New Mexico. He had chosen to remain on the land he had come to love, resettling on the part of the Texas range still unclaimed and unleased by cattlemen.

Before Don Miguel had finished narrating the story of his past, a story that Tara hoped would eventually lead to his dealings with her father and the mysterious obligation he had hinted at, the sound of an approaching rider caught their attention, and Don Miguel tensed beside her. He squinted in the darkness to make out the form of a man on horseback. A muffled curse burst from his lips as he whipped the horse, sending it racing at its swiftest pace. Tara clutched the side of the carriage and held on for dear life as they careened around the curving road and left a cloud of dust behind them.

Her wild eyes settled on the dark silhouette that

pursued them, and then she gulped air as a pistol shot rang out, the bullet sailing dangerously close to Don Miguel's shoulder. Although Don Miguel made a valiant effort to elude the rider, he quickly closed the distance between them, reaching out to grasp the reins, forcing the carriage to a halt.

"Get out, Chavez," a gruff voice demanded, the order backed by a revolver that was aimed at Don Miguel's chest.

When Tara clutched at her purse to retrieve her derringer, Don Miguel's hand closed over hers. Her lashes fluttered up to catch his warning glance, and then her gaze darted to the rider who swung to the ground. His Stetson was pulled down around his ears, disguising his facial features, and a red bandanna further concealed his appearance. His body was camouflaged by a long gray coat that descended to the top of his worn boots. All Tara could tell about the man was that he was ominous and threatening. When he reached up to grab a fistful of Don Miguel's jacket and roughly yanked him to the ground, Tara's heart slammed against her ribs and very nearly popped out of her chest. He shoved Don Miguel backwards. Tara clutched at her purse when the masked rider grabbed her arm, uprooting her from the spot and pushing her toward Don Miguel.

"What is it you want from us, *hombre?*" Don Miguel questioned as he pulled himself up off the ground. "I have no money, nor does the señorita."

"What errand are you running this time, old man?" came the harsh, muffled voice behind the bandanna.

"Errand?" The rider was met by Don Miguel's carefully blank stare. "I have only come to escort the señorita to her *padre,* nothing more."

A sardonic laugh exploded from the man's bulky chest. "Spare me the lies, *amigo.* I know you intended . . ."

The sound of a second horse thundering toward them

19

slashed through the stilted silence and Tara glanced up to see a white stallion glistening in the moonlight. It was like a flash of lightning streaking across the horizon, weaving through the chapparal and then disappearing momentarily as it floated ever closer. Upon its back, silhouetted against the black sky, was a rider shrouded in white, the wind whipping through his cloak. To the discerning eye it appeared as if wings were attached to his shapeless body. The image had an incandescent appearance in the starlit darkness, and Tara went rigid, wondering if she dared trust her eyes. Was it a *man* that seemed to float about the silver-white steed that appeared to be as swift as the wind?

A furious exclamation burst from the man's lips when he caught sight of the ghostly vision that had interrupted him. Tara took advantage of his hesitation, fishing into her purse with trembling hands to retrieve her weapon. And then it was as if everything happened at once. Two pistols exploded to shatter the dark silence. The horses' shrill whinnies pierced the air and Tara's scream of terror echoed about them. Don Miguel clutched at his chest and stumbled back against Tara, knocking her off balance. Another frightened shriek burst from her lips as she and Don Miguel tumbled to the ground. The horrifying image of Don Miguel being shot at close range vanished from Tara's paralyzed mind as her head slammed against a rock. She surrendered to the swirling darkness, welcoming the silence with open arms, a silence that could not be invaded by the vicious man whose face was hidden behind a red bandanna and a specter that sailed on the wind. There was nothing but the black abyss of unconsciousness as her body became a lifeless heap beneath Don Miguel's.

The old vaquero's pained eyes fluttered open and he grimaced as he reached into his vest pocket to retrieve the locket. Calling upon his last bit of strength, he twisted slightly to drop the gold pendant inside the bodice of Tara's gown. Desperately, he tried to drag his body from the unconscious young woman who was sprawled beneath him.

"*Vaya con Dios. . . .*" he breathed as his gaze lingered ruefully on Tara's shadowed features. And then his eyes closed for the final time. The trace of a smile seemed to hover on his lips as his murderer leaned down to hurriedly rummage through his clothes, finding nothing for all his efforts. Somehow, Don Miguel knew that he had fulfilled his part of the obligation and that his secret would remain safe until it fell into the right hands.

Chapter 2

"Damn," came from beneath the white hood Sloane Prescott wore over his head as he knelt beside Don Miguel. His stormy blue eyes sparkled with anger, watching with barely contained fury as the assailant vanished into the darkness. Sloane cursed himself for arriving too late to save the old man's life.

His gaze shifted to the woman who lay lifeless beneath Don Miguel. Bloodstains colored the front of her jacket and gown. Anger and resentment flashed beneath the crumpled white hood as Sloane slung the poncho over his shoulder to free the gloved hand that moved instinctively toward the young woman's face. Sloane's keen eyes surveyed Tara's bewitching features. The moonlight glistened in her silver-gold hair, lustrous tendrils that sprayed about her like a shining cape. Another muffled curse caught in the wind when Sloane had to remind himself that this distracting beauty was in need of medical attention. After crouching close beside Tara, Sloane laid his head against her breast, searching for a sign that she had not already followed Don Miguel to his senseless death. A sigh of relief tumbled from his lips as he withdrew, satisfied that the young beauty still lived. His eyes narrowed once again on the blood-red stains just above her heart.

Sloane quickly surmised that the second shot he

had heard echoing in the night must have been the one that had left this comely blonde unconscious and near death. Carefully, he scooped Tara's limp body into his arms and carried her to the white stallion. There, Sloane paused, his misty eyes sliding back over his shoulder to linger on Don Miguel for the final time. Then, another thought struck Sloane and he muttered under his breath. When he had eased Tara back to the ground, he reversed direction to return to Don Miguel. Sloane had been so overwrought with anger and grief that he had neglected to search for the locket of Valquez.

Damnation, wasn't it enough that the vicious bastard had murdered this innocent old man? Sloane swore bitterly. Had the assassin absconded with the locket, or had Don Miguel been unable to locate it? Scowling sourly at the disastrous turn of events, the Night Rider gathered his feet beneath him and moved swiftly back to hoist Tara into the saddle.

Nudging the silver-white steed, the phantom of Palo Duro Canyon propped Tara back against his shoulder and watched her long, silky hair cascade over his arm. Where had Don Miguel found himself such a captivating companion? No doubt the lass had been irresistibly drawn to the soft-spoken man with the winsome smile. Yes, Don Miguel had had the gift of gentleness, Sloane mused ruefully. While Don Miguel took his life in stride, Sloane had spent his last few years harboring suppressed anger and a maddening hunger for revenge. He had been void of all other emotions until tonight. The loss of Don Miguel left an aching emptiness in the pit of Sloane's belly. He had often warned Don Miguel to carry a revolver, but the old vaquero had refused. His theory that gentleness could curb violence had proved to be wishful thinking. If Don Miguel had been carrying a weapon he would still have been alive. Or at least, he would have stood a fighting chance, Sloane thought

23

resentfully. And now those whom Sloane had truly cared about were gone—a woman whose life had been filled with torment, an old man who had endured more than his share of tragedy. The only affection Sloane had ever felt withered inside him like a fragile spring blossom stung by a late frost.

Hard, bitter eyes peered through the ragged holes in the incandescent white hood, intently focused on the woman he cradled in his arms. Was he now carrying this lovely innocent victim away from the scene of a dastardly crime only to watch her die a slow, agonizing death? Sloane scowled disgustedly. Was there no justice to be found in this cruel world? He would do his best to save the lady's life, and, hopefully, she would be able to identify the ruthless *hombre* who had murdered Don Miguel and attempted to kill her, as well.

Sloane's only chance of saving the girl was to dig out the bullet himself. He prayed it had not lodged too close to her heart. The ride into Clarendon could prove fatal. Sloane couldn't risk having her die in his arms. Although he could not bring Don Miguel back, he would do his damnedest to revive his attractive companion.

As the moon-eyed stallion neared the caprock of Palo Duro Canyon, Sloane spoke softly, urging Diablo to guard his steps along the old Comanche trail that wound along the rock ledges of sandstone that cut through the High Plains. His muscular arms tensed, keeping a secure hold on Tara when she roused momentarily and then became as limp as a rag doll. Her full breasts crushed against Sloane's restraining arm and he winced uncomfortably, unwillingly aroused by the feel of her womanly body pressed so tightly to his. His astute gaze focused on her heart-shaped lips, lips so pale and soft that they invited him to press his mouth to hers, if only to revive this dazzling beauty with his kiss. At least he knew she was still alive, Sloane reminded himself, casting aside his

24

lusty thoughts.

Sloane squinted in the darkness to see the shack that was nestled beneath the jagged ridges of the canyon. If only the young woman could cling to life for a few more minutes, he might have the chance to save her. When Diablo paused in front of the cabin, the Night Rider maneuvered himself from the saddle without jostling Tara. Bracing his shoulder against the door, he strode inside, his white cape rustling quietly about him. Gently, Sloane eased Tara onto the cot, and without delaying a moment, stirred together a concoction of peyote and wild herbs that would leave her numb while he performed primitive surgery.

After forcing the potion down her throat, Sloane stoked the coals in the hearth, boiled water, and sterilized his hunting knife. He set both lanterns on the shelf behind him, providing meager light for the operation. After chugging a glass of whiskey to steady his shaking hands, Sloane expelled a frustrated breath. He had cut on various four-legged creatures in his life, but never had he dared what he was about to do. The mere thought of it had him cursing the miserable bastard who had forced him into this unpleasant situation.

His jaw tensed nervously as he paced the floor, sparing as much time as he could to allow the drugging potion to take effect. Heaving a determined sigh, Sloane held up the sharp-edged knife for inspection and then bent his gaze to the bewitching creature he was about to carve into. It seemed a sin to mar such a flawless young woman. Sloane quickly reminded himself that the bullet she carried near her heart left him with no choice. The damage had been done, and he had to remove the bullet and cleanse the wound.

A strange sensation blossomed somewhere in the depths of his soul as the lantern light splattered over the young woman's alabaster skin. Impulsively his tanned

25

finger brushed over her pale cheek, finding its texture as soft and velvety as a rose petal. The shards of golden light sprayed across her skin, and he found himself staring helplessly at her. Finally, he shook his head to shatter the strange spell that clouded his mind and harshly reminded himself that this captivating damsel would be in further distress if he didn't remove the bullet.

His probing eyes peered through the hood, focusing on the scoop-necked gown. His hand glided down her swanlike throat to investigate the creamy flesh of her breasts, which rose and fell with each shallow breath she took. Gritting his teeth, the Night Rider reminded himself that there was naught else to do but rip open the bodice of her dress and attend the wound that lay beneath her blood-stained shoulder.

Crouching above her with his legs braced against her arms to hold her in place in case the prick of his knife caused her to writhe in pain, he slid his hand inside the stained fabric. Prepared to tear open the gown and immediately set to work, he gripped the knife and aimed it at Tara's chest, intent on his task, yet feeling terribly inadequate.

Through a haze of sensations that tapped at her consciousness and the foggy, distorted images that had haunted her, Tara felt herself drifting somewhere just beyond reality. Gentle hands were gliding over her skin, and her muddled impressions of what was happening eluded her before she could make any sense of them. With tremendous effort, Tara forced her eyes open, vaguely aware of the painful throbbing at the base of her neck where she had slammed her head against the rock.

A shocked gasp escaped her lips as her blurred eyes tried to focus on the wrinkled, hooded face above hers. The specter was shrouded in white, and he was poised above her with a knife that glistened in the golden light. She became aware of his fingers lying familiarly against her breast, and she instinctively shrank away, unsure of what she was seeing. Was she staring death in the face, the ghostly spirit that had come to cut out her soul and send it on its journey to the final resting place? Had the Night Rider of Palo Duro been sent to accompany her into *his* world? But she was already there, wasn't she? Tara couldn't swear that she was dead or alive. Her senses were dulled by the potion, and she felt as if she were moving in slow motion, wanting to fight for her life if she had one left, but without the strength to do so.

"No!" Tara's tormented voice sounded a thousand miles away and very unlike her own, as if she were calling through a long tunnel somewhere on the other side of reality.

A surprised squawk erupted from the Night Rider's lips as Tara roused enough to voice a protest. He had been so intent on beginning his distasteful task that he was caught off guard. When her trembling voice sliced through the tense silence, he very nearly jumped out of his skin. The knife toppled from his hand, but he managed to grasp it before it plunged into . . . he shuddered to think where it might have struck if he hadn't regained his shattered composure in the nick of time.

"Relax, *querida*," he coaxed, his voice no more than a whisper. "The bullet must be removed if you are to live."

As his steady hand folded around the neckline of her dress to rend the cloth, Tara sucked in her breath and attempted to push him away. Her clumsy movements only served to bring his fingertips in firm contact with her heaving breasts.

"No!" she shrieked, shocked by the feel of a man's hands resting familiarly against her skin.

The Night Rider swore under his breath. Why couldn't this gorgeous creature have waited another hour before she awoke, he thought disgustedly. It was distasteful enough to butcher her lovely body without having to fight his way to the blasted wound!

"Don't kill me!" Tara whimpered, her wild eyes trying desperately to focus on the hooded face that towered above her like the cloud of impending doom. "Papa! Save me! Please. . . ."

Christ! He had his hands on a wildcat! She had come back from the near-dead and fought like a wounded mountain lion. He plopped down on her abdomen, his arm stiffly braced on her breast to prevent her squirming away, and gnashed his teeth together to stifle the angry urge to shout at this violet-eyed tigress. But the woman was on the verge of hysterics and he feared one harsh word would set her into a frenzy.

"You must relax," he urged in the tenderest voice he could muster, considering Tara was floundering beneath him in such a wild manner that he came dangerously close to toppling from his perch and landing facedown on the dirt floor. "My intention is not to kill you, but to save you. Will you *hold still!*" The last two words were a gritted growl as he gripped the bodice of her gown. With the quickness of a jungle cat clawing his prey, he ripped the dress away and braced his knees against her shoulders to keep her in place. "My God!" He swallowed a shackful of air when his eyes fell to her exposed breasts. There was no wound! Not even a scratch! But the blood stains . . . ?

While he was frantically trying to comprehend the reason why her dress was saturated with blood and she had been unconscious, his wide eyes were flooding over the creamy mounds of skin that lay bare to his all-consuming gaze, leaving not one inch of satiny flesh untouched by his bold assessment. Could it have been Don Miguel's mortal wound that had caused the stain that had led him to believe she had been shot, as well? Before he could pursue that train of thought, he caught sight of the locket that had tumbled across her belly and

28

lodged against his thigh. His breath froze in his throat as the tarnished gold pendant brought a sea of painful memories splashing over him, further crumbling his composure. How had she gained possession of the locket? Who was she? Why was she traveling with Don Miguel?

"Let me go!" Tara railed hysterically as his hand slid against her ribs to retrieve the locket.

"Be quiet," the Night Rider demanded gruffly as he tucked the pendant beneath his poncho and then clamped his fingers into the ivory skin on her shoulder to push her back to the cot.

When Tara screamed bloody murder, his mouth descended onto hers to shush her, but his original purpose flew out the window as his lips found her soft mouth. His body moved instinctively closer to hers as his kiss deepened, savoring the sweet taste of her and inhaling the feminine fragrance that swarmed his stunned senses. His wayward hands glided over the slopes of her shoulders to cup her full breasts, feeling her silky skin quiver beneath his intimate touch. Trickling drops of sensation became a raging waterfall of passion. So much had happened that night that the Night Rider could only respond to the primitive needs that overshadowed better judgment. He wanted to lose himself in the feel of this shapely nymph, to forget the tormenting thoughts that plagued him, to ignore the chaotic emotions that whipped through his mind. He wanted to respond without thinking, rolling with the flow of wild, tantalizing urges that flooded over him.

Strange, erotic sensations replaced the stark fear that had plagued Tara, and she found herself melting in a man's arms. He was weaving mysterious dreams about her, and she felt oddly content and protected in his embrace. She responded to his gentle touch, her inhibitions mellowed by the strong potion that had numbed her senses. The hardness of the man's thigh guided her legs apart, fitting their bodies intimately together. Tara was being drawn into the web of wild abandon, one that clouded her already hazy thoughts. Someone was tenderly touching her as no man ever had, but who? Her eyes were so heavy that it was next to impossible to open them.

For what seemed an eternity, his sensuous lips played against hers. She could hear his soft words and feel them against her skin as his mouth languidly whispered over her, but their meaning escaped her. Tara was sinking deeper into the arms of a rapturous dream, suspended in a time and space she could not comprehend. When his mouth returned to hers, his darting tongue intruded to investigate the hidden recesses of her mouth, savoring the honeyed kisses she offered in return. His hands tracked across her breasts and then curled around her ribs to massage away the last bit of tension that claimed her, leaving Tara feeling like a mass of quivering jelly that was being heated from inside out.

This wasn't really happening. It couldn't be happening. She was tangled in the arms of an erotic dream, one that defied anything she had experienced. This simply couldn't be reality, Tara told herself drowsily. These incredible sensations were distortions caused by her boggled mind. Her thoughts were garbled. She was in a trance, drifting . . . melting . . . soaring . . . diving. . . .

"Who are you? Tell me your name, *querida*," the Night Rider whispered again, having received no response when he had posed the question a few moments earlier.

A groggy moan floated free, and Tara attempted to pry open one heavily-lidded eye, but the drugging potion had taken full effect. She was flowing with the waves that lifted and curled, towing her farther from reality's shore. It took forever for his question to soak in, and once it did, it took an eternity for her to decipher it.

30

"Your name. Give me your name," he commanded as his hand investigated the shapely curve of her hips and then crept beneath the hem of her dress to explore the silky flesh of her thighs.

She sighed drowsily, grappling with his question. Her body was like putty beneath his skillful hands, and her mind was groggy. His caresses left her weak and senseless, stirring unfamiliar sensations that coiled in the pit of her stomach and then unfurled, flowing like a meandering river through her blood, triggering strange, arousing tingles somewhere deep inside her.

His body caught fire and burned as he intimately touched this captivating young beauty with eyes the color of amethysts and hair that was an intriguing mingling of sunshine and moonlight. It had been more than a month since he had been with a woman, and the feel of this sleepy-eyed seraph's curvaceous flesh molded to his inflamed passions. Instinct crowded out reason, and he could do nothing but respond to the wild urges she instilled in him.

His hands had developed a will of their own as they roamed over her, worshipping the softness of her skin, discovering each tantalizing curve and swell by touch. The feel of her body was branded on his mind, and he closed his eyes to revel in the exquisite feelings that blocked out the tragedy he had experienced earlier that night. His lips skimmed the trim column of her throat as his senses were invaded by the sweet scent of her, an aroma so compelling that it fogged his mind. She had made him forget there was a cruel, bitter world outside the silky circle of her arms.

A groan of unholy torment bubbled in his laboring chest as he dragged the hood from his head, not caring whether she roused enough to see his face. He hungered to feel her velvety skin against his cheek without being hindered by the ghastly hood. He hungered to brush his

31

lips over her breasts, to make wild, sweet love to this vision of loveliness, even if she wasn't in full command of her senses, even if she was so heavily drugged with peyote that she would barely recall this night.

As his butterfly kisses skimmed over each pink peak, Tara instinctively arched against him, her arms wandering over his shoulders to draw him closer, reveling in the splendorous sensations that spilled over her quaking body. And then his warm mouth returned to hers as he tilted her head to his devouring kiss, a kiss that stole the last of her breath and left her aching for a dozen more just like it. She was helplessly drowning, swept into the crosscurrents of pleasure, struggling to grasp the question he had asked of her before he assaulted her with these wild torrents of joy.

Tara could feel the hard masculine length of him pressing closer, leaving her yearning to satisfy a need she did not understand. It was a craving so alluring and devastating that her entire body quivered uncontrollably as she moved toward the compelling flame that had set her afire.

"My name is Tara. . . ." she finally whispered in belated response when his lips abandoned her to allow her a small breath of air.

And then she was lost to the erotic sensations that toppled over her like bubbly champagne overflowing the rim of a goblet, taking logic and reason into the trickling streams of ecstasy and sending them wandering off in a thousand different directions.

The Night Rider froze, bewildered by her thick, husky words. His breath lodged in his throat, nearly strangling him, and it took tremendous effort to choke out his question. "You are Tara Winslow?" he croaked in astonishment.

The slightest nod of her silver-blond head sent him bolting away from her as if he had been snakebit. His wild eyes bulged as he glanced down at his fingertips that had been curled behind her neck. There were bloodstains on his hand!

Fumbling with the discarded hood, the Night Rider yanked the disguise over his head and cursed himself for getting so carried away with a woman he had only met, one so heavily drugged that she couldn't possibly have realized what she was doing. And what the sweet loving hell did *he* think he was doing, the Night Rider asked himself. His agonized gaze fell to the ripped gown that was draped about Tara's waist, now riding high on her thighs after he had intimately caressed her.

Scowling at his stupidity, he snatched up the quilt from the foot of the cot and laid it over Tara's barely concealed body, a body he had familiarly touched, kissed, and very nearly . . . He muttered several epithets to his own name and then thanked his lucky stars Tara had finally fallen into a deep sleep.

He strode across the cabin to find an antiseptic to cleanse the wound on the back of her head. Twisting her silky hair around his hand like a rope, he resettled the silver-gold mane across his pillow and then inspected the gash.

This stunning minx must have been knocked unconscious during the scuffle, he concluded. And if Terrance Winslow ever learned that he had taken privileges with his daughter . . . sweet merciful heavens! He didn't want to be within ten miles of the man when he started raving like a banshee. Terrance had boasted about his sophisticated young daughter the moment he'd set foot in Texas and hadn't stopped talking about her since. He had made her out to be a saint. Even a lynching would be too good for the man who laid a hand on Winslow's prized possession.

"Lord, I hope you don't remember any of this," the Night Rider muttered to the sleeping beauty as he lifted her head in his hand and wrapped a bandage around the wound.

When he had finished his ministrations, he rose to his feet to work the kinks from his back. His eyes settled on Tara, and for a moment he could only peer helplessly at her. Now what the hell should he do? Running several plans of action through his head, he paced the confines of his shack and then expelled his breath in a rush. Damn, he was between a rock and a hard spot. He couldn't very well allow her to recuperate here, and it would take the remainder of the night to return her to Clarendon.

Finally, he made his decision and scooped Tara into his arms. Long ride or not, he would be forced to take her to Terrance. He grumbled as he strode toward the stallion. After he maneuvered Tara in his arms and took up the reins, the Night Rider heaved an exasperated sigh. God, this night had been a diverse web of disaster. Don Miguel was dead. Tara had been injured, and the murderer . . . hatred clouded Sloane's thoughts. It was not difficult to guess who was behind the killing. But, as usual, the assassin had covered his tracks and would, no doubt, have an alibi. For more than a year the Night Rider had kept a constant vigil on Palo Duro, watching and waiting for Merrick Russel to make a careless mistake and expose himself for what he was. Perhaps the locket Don Miguel had managed to stash in Tara's gown would bring him closer to the truth, he mused.

Tara had made him forget the anger and resentment that boiled through his veins, but now cruel reality crowded into his thoughts. The tenderness he had displayed toward Tara gave way to frustrated bitterness. Sloane had had but one purpose in coming to Palo Duro Canyon, and he could not rest until he knew the truth about the Diamond R Ranch.

His mouth was set in a grim line as he urged Diablo along the narrow ledge that led up the sandstone walls of the canyon, taking the dangerous short cut to Clarendon to save valuable time. Sloane's eyes were cold and hard, squinting into the darkness as he cradled the sleeping beauty in his arms. As far as both he and Tara were concerned, this night didn't exist. He would have no more association with Tara Winslow. It would be Terrance's duty to learn what had happened on the road from Harrold. Hopefully, Tara could identify Don Miguel's assassin, Sloane mused, and then braced himself as the silver-white steed lunged forward to make the last steep climb to the caprock of Palo Duro.

Chapter 3

At the darkest hour before dawn, the Night Rider swung from the saddle and carried Tara to the door of Terrance Winslow's small cottage behind the newspaper office. But as he raised a gloved hand to knock, his arm dangled in midair. How the devil was he going to explain the fact that Tara's clothes had practically been ripped off her luscious body? Gritting his teeth, he wrapped the blanket more tightly about her and then knocked on the door. After he had waited several anxious moments, Terrance appeared on the step and then half-collapsed as his wide, disbelieving eyes fell to the young face that was nestled against the Night Rider's incandescent white poncho.

"Oh my God, Tara!" Terrance croaked as his alarmed gaze landed on the bandage that was draped around his daughter's head. His face washed white as his haunted eyes lifted to meet the Night Rider's ghastly hood. "Where did you find her? What happened?"

"She was knocked unconscious when someone took a shot at Don Miguel," the Night Rider mumbled.

Sickening dread darted through Terrance. "Where is Don Miguel?"

"He's dead," the Night Rider scowled as he pushed past Terrance and aimed himself toward the spare bedroom. "Your daughter was unconscious when I found her. I don't know if she can identify the murderer, but it will be up to you to find out. She has been too groggy from her head wound to offer any information other than her name and even that was slow in coming."

"Don Miguel is dead?" What little color that had managed to creep back into Terrance's cheeks ebbed when he heard the distressing news. "Damn, I never thought he would go that far."

"Didn't you?" The Night Rider's voice was brittle with bitterness. "The moment Don Miguel began snooping around Palo Duro Canyon, Merrick was on edge. I'm sure he thought Don Miguel knew too much and would become a threat to his existence." Another frustrated growl erupted from his chest. "I should have known better than to send for Don Miguel. It was my fault for bringing him here."

Terrance was also feeling a twinge of guilt. "I am just as much to blame. And look what my own daughter has been forced to endure," he breathed in torment.

"I need some hot water and fresh bandages," the Night Rider ordered as he paused beside the bed.

As soon as Terrance wheeled away to fetch the necessary supplies, the Night Rider tossed the quilt aside, pulled the torn gown from Tara's body, and then stashed it beneath his poncho. His eyes made a slow, deliberate sweep of her curvaceous figure before he dragged the sheet up to her neck. A wry smile pursed his lips as his hand absently trailed over her delicate features. She was exquisite, every silky inch of her. His body was becoming aroused, just as it had when he found himself impulsively kissing and caressing her to erase the pain and torment that had plagued him that night.

When the door whipped open, his back stiffened and he smothered the titillating thoughts that were dancing in his head. This was no time to be reliving a dream, he scolded himself.

37

Terrance pulled up short, his mouth gaping when he saw Tara's bare shoulders protruding from the sheet. "What the hell did you do to my daughter?" he growled.

"I was making our patient more comfortable," Sloane said matter-of-factly, but he inwardly flinched at the horrified expression that was plastered on Terrance's face.

Terrance's glare cut a few more holes in the white hood that disguised the Night Rider's visage. "You've got your nerve! How dare you. . . ."

"Her gown was soiled with blood and caked with dirt," Sloane cut in, giving quick death to Terrance's ranting. "Would *you* have preferred to disrobe your own daughter?" he queried as he twisted around to dip the cloth in the bowl of hot water Terrance held clenched in his fists.

He stammered like a tongue-tied idiot, cursing the catastrophic chain of events that had led to this. "Well . . . no . . . but . . . uh . . . I . . ."

"Someone had to do it," the Night Rider managed to say in a bland tone. "Who better than a faceless ghost?"

"At the moment I would feel much better about the entire incident if that was indeed what you were," Terrance grunted disgustedly. "If she ever learns that you—"

"Do you intend to tell her?" One thick brow arched beneath the hood as Sloane leaned over Tara to unwind the bandage he had hurriedly wrapped around her head.

"Hell no! Tara would be humiliated if she knew. I would spare her that. She has already been an eyewitness to a murder!"

The thought soured Sloane's disposition. "You had better notify the mortician. When I finish with Tara I'll collect her belongings from the carriage and leave them on the edge of town. There is no reason for anyone else to know she witnessed the killing. The one man who knows about it will pose enough danger for her as it is."

Terrance gulped hard. He had been too flustered to consider that. Don Miguel's murderer would not be pleased to have a witness. "What are we going to do?" he breathed weakly.

"It was dark," Sloane reminded him. "The chance that your daughter even saw the assailant's face is remote." Peering over his shoulder, he fixed steely blue eyes on Terrance's apprehensive expression. "You print the news. I suggest you make it known that no one knows who is responsible for Don Miguel's death and make no mention that he was traveling with a companion."

Terrance nodded mutely and then expelled a heavy-hearted sigh. "I am sorry about Don Miguel. He deserved better than this. He was a good man."

"Yes, he was," the Night Rider quietly concurred, his voice cracking, despite his attempt to control his emotions. When he had replaced the bandage on Tara's head, he rose to full stature and strode toward the door. "Keep your daughter in bed and don't tell her any more than necessary. The less she knows, the better."

"Guard your step, Sloane," Terrance warned, clasping his hand on the phantom's shoulder. "You took a great risk by bringing Tara to me."

"I only wish I could have safely delivered Don Miguel, as well," the Night Rider murmured before sailing toward the door.

Terrance watched the cloaked figure disappear around the corner and then cursed himself for putting Tara through this nightmare. Why couldn't he have been content to let Tara remain in St. Louis? Lord, he had taken a terrible risk when he'd urged her to visit him, knowing how fiercely her mother would object, knowing the dangers that lurked in Palo Duro Canyon.

But dammit, it had been three years since he had seen his little girl. His misty eyes lingered on Tara as he paused at the bedroom door. Now she was all grown up. Tara had blossomed into a breathtakingly lovely young woman. And if the Night Rider didn't have a heart of rock, he would surely have noticed, Terrance thought to himself.

Quietly he walked over to the bed and bent to press a fond kiss to Tara's pale cheek. "Forgive me, Tara. Perhaps I was a fool to send for you," he whispered regretfully. "But I have waited an eternity to see you."

Heaving a sigh, Terrance withdrew and shrugged on his coat. There was much to be done before dawn, and he prayed Tara would sleep through the worst night of her life. Terrance would have given almost anything if he could have turned back the hands of time and altered the drastic course of events. But the disaster only served to make Terrance more determined to help the Night Rider uncover the skeletons that were hanging in Merrick Russel's closet. Surely time and patience would effect success. Their crusade against the powerful rancher would one day expose Merrick Russel for the ruthless, deceptive man he was. Terrance had kept the legend of the phantom of Palo Duro alive with his newspaper articles, feeding on superstition, clouding the good citizens of Donley County with doubt about their influential neighbor. Rumors of the phantom that haunted Palo Duro Canyon had spread like a prairie fire, and Merrick had difficulty keeping good help. There were only a few cowboys who had stood by him; most came and quickly left when they were visited by the ghost on his silver-white stallion. Yes, one day the Night Rider's tormented soul would find the peace for which he searched, Terrance assured himself. And Tara was going to help him, whether she realized it or not. She could learn valuable information during her stay at the Diamond R Ranch, and sooner or later Merrick would trip himself up. The swindling bastard, Terrance mused disgustedly. Not only did Terrance long to be reunited with his daughter, but he knew she could help solve the mystery that clouded the Diamond R Ranch. Tara was an inquisitive young woman, and once she heard of the specter that kept a constant vigil over Palo Duro, her father was sure, she would be sniffing out information that could aid them in unraveling the events of the past and present that kept the suspicion brewing around Merrick Russel.

A doleful groan echoed in the silence as Tara lifted sleep-drugged eyes to the bright sunlight that filtered through the window. A muddled frown knitted her brow as her foggy gaze circled the unfamiliar room. Where was she and how had she come to be here?

Tara attempted to prop herself up on her elbow, but stars were spinning in front of her eyes like a revolving carousel. Every muscle rebelled against movement, and she sank back on the bed to sort through her hazy thoughts, thoughts so confusing that she didn't dare trust them.

"Tara?" Terrance poked his head inside the door the moment he heard her raspy voice. "Thank God, you finally woke up. I was beginning to wonder if I should send for the doctor."

The faintest hint of a smile found one corner of her mouth as she focused on her father's concerned face. She was certain he would look the same as he had the last time she had seen him, if only she could see him clearly.

Terrance sank down on the edge of the bed and stroked a renegade strand of her golden hair into place and then blessed her with a loving smile. "How is your head? A mite sore, I expect."

She nodded slightly as her fingers inspected the knot. A hauntingly distorted thought flashed through her eyes, a memory that stabbed her like a knife. "Don Miguel . . .

where is he?" She hated to ask, but she had to know.

Terrance's face fell like a rockslide. "He is dead, Tara."

Tara bit her trembling lips as the tears streamed down her cheeks. "I had only just met him, but he was a kind, gentle man. I hope his murderer swings from the tallest tree in Texas," she choked out bitterly.

"Can you identify his murderer?" Terrance's voice was soft and hesitant. She would be in far less danger if she hadn't seen the assassin's face, but Terrance was itching to know if his suspicions were correct.

Tara racked her brain to piece the jostled thoughts into place, but the terrifying experience had stirred a deep-seated fear, one that subtly urged her to forget the nightmare. A perplexed frown tugged at her weary features. "It all happened so quickly that I cannot quite sort it out." Another bemused expression settled on her face. "But I recall having the strangest dream, Papa. It must have been caused by the story Don Miguel told me about the ghost that haunted the canyon. I could swear I saw him myself, and yet I cannot even imagine that such a phantom exists. When I opened my eyes the specter was poised above me with a knife, prepared to plunge it into my heart. I fought against him, but it was as if I were strapped down and I couldn't escape the ghastly vision. I called out to you, but you were so far away. And then . . ." Her voice trailed off as another strange, unexplainable memory seeped into her mind. It was as if someone had taken her in his arms, comforting her, kissing her, stirring sensations Tara had never experienced. They couldn't have been real, she told herself. Surely she was confusing those feelings. Perhaps she vaguely remembered her father bending over her. Finally, she shrugged away the entangled memories, certain each separate incident had converged to form one of the wildest dreams she had ever conjured up in

42

her sleep.

"And then?" Terrance prodded.

Tara massaged her aching temples and heaved a tired sigh. "I don't know how I came to be here. Did someone come upon us and bring us to Clarendon?"

"A shiftless cowboy who was passing through town," Terrance lied, following the Night Rider's advice to tell her as little as possible.

"I am most thankful he did," Tara breathed as she eased back on the pillow. "I hope to see him again, so that I may convey my gratitude. I shudder to think what might have happened if I had been left unconscious on that abandoned road."

"The trail herder has come and gone, but I graciously thanked him for delivering you to me," Terrance murmured, a tender smile grazing his lips. "I will fetch something for you to eat, and then you must rest."

Tara nodded agreeably and then dozed off, only to be hounded by the same ridiculous dream that had plagued her before.

She was not a superstitious soul, and she could only contribute her wild nightmare to the harrowing experience she had endured and the eerie tale Don Miguel had spun about her. But she *had* seen a ghost, hadn't she? And the murderer? There *had* been another man on the road with them, Tara told herself as she roused from the arms of her nightmare. Pistols had exploded about her and she . . . Tara choked on a sob when the fragment of the memory pierced her soul. *She* had caused the gunfire. Don Miguel had warned her to keep her derringer concealed. But like a fool she had fished it out of her purse. Their assailant had seen the weapon and . . . tears scalded Tara's eyes as the tormenting vision of Don Miguel falling back against her shot through her throbbing head. *She* was responsible for Don Miguel's death, just as surely as if she had aimed her derringer at

' God forgive her. Her rash actions had cost Don Miguel his life.

Tara sobbed hysterically into her pillow, cursing her stupidity. And then another maddening thought seeped from the corners of her mind, a vision that kept contradicting itself. She didn't want to think about that ghastly face, the riptide of sensations it had stirred within her. She didn't want to remember. . . .

After allowing Tara a week to recuperate, Terrance finally agreed to show his daughter around the frontier town in Donley County. Their first outing was no more than a buggy ride around the community, but Tara was delighted to be anywhere out of the confines of her room.

"The Comanche Indians who once roamed this area of Texas were removed to a reservation in Oklahoma Territory," Terrance explained. "Clarendon is a Christian community of highly educated immigrants who are well versed in law and the fine arts. Many of the four hundred citizens have graduated from such noted colleges as Harvard and Yale."

"But how did the town come by the name of Saints' Roost?" Tara questioned curiously. "It seems an odd name for Harvard and Yale graduates."

Terrance gestured toward the frame church-school structure. "The town was founded by a young minister who called upon his flock to aid him in developing a prospering community on the prairie. Clarendon doesn't have the brothels and saloons that other towns have." He called Tara's attention to the large stone hotel, the blacksmith shop, and the various offices that lined the street. "All town property was sold with the provision that liquor would not be sold in this town. Saints' Roost boasts of hospitality and refinement." A wry smile pursed his lips as he shot Tara a quick glance. "But I

44

don't suppose Libby would believe civilization could exist on the High Plains of Texas. Your mother has her mind set on thinking this country is plagued with savages and heathens."

"She refers to all Texans as illiterate cow servants and unrefined cottagers," Tara snickered. "I'm sure Mother is beside herself with worry, certain a three-month stay in Texas will cause me to forget everything I learned at those sophisticated finishing schools she and Grandfather forced me into."

The smile evaporated from Terrance's features. "You haven't told me how you managed to escape Ryan O'Donnovan's clutches," he reminded Tara. "I knew it wouldn't be easy, but I prayed you would find a way to come. If Ryan had his way, you and I would never have seen each other again."

How well Terrance knew his father-in-law, Ryan O'Donnovan, Tara mused pensively. That day, three years ago, when Terrance had strode into the elaborately decorated parlor and struck a pose before his wife and family, Tara thought the world had come to an end. In a strained voice, Terrance had declared that since he could never satisfy his father-in-law, he was leaving St. Louis. He had also insisted that since his wife, Libby, was so heavily influenced by Ryan's tyrannical reign, she would probably be happier without a husband. Terrance had spouted off his rehearsed speech, claiming he could not fight both Ryan and Libby and ever hope to win. When he had pivoted on his heels and walked away, stunning Libby and delighting Ryan, Tara had cried her eyes out.

Ryan had tried to console Tara, assuring her she would be better off without the influence of her reckless, irresponsible father. But Tara thought nothing of the kind. She adored Terrance and his zest for living, his unquenchable thirst for adventure. Libby had frowned upon Terrance's desire to open a newspaper office on the edge of the frontier when he had a prospering paper in St. Louis. Tara's mother thought it ridiculous to leave the lap of luxury, unless she were to be forced out of it. And although Ryan had constantly ridiculed Terrance for even suggesting the idiocy of carting Libby and Tara off to the wild, uncivilized plains of Texas, Tara would gladly have accompanied her father the day he left. But Ryan would never have permitted it. He and Terrance had always been in constant conflict, and Tara had been well aware that her grandfather was elated to have Terrance out of their lives.

"I did not wait around for Mother and Grandfather to accept or reject my decision to come to Texas," Tara informed Terrance, her gaze drifting over the sod, adobe, and stone homes that were clustered about the area. A mischievous smile bordered her lips. "As a matter of fact, I wrote a short note that said, 'Gone to Texas. Will return at summer's end.' Then I gathered my belongings and funds for the trip and escaped through the window."

Terrance chuckled, imagining how upset Libby and Ryan must have been when they discovered Tara had finally fled the prison of refinement. "I can hear Ryan ranting that you inherited a generous share of your father's bad blood," he scoffed. "That old buzzard never did think I was good enough for Libby."

Tara could not argue that point, and so she didn't. For three years she had listened to Ryan belittle Terrance. But his snide remarks had never changed Tara's opinion of her father. They shared a common craving for adventure. Although her journey had been plagued with disaster, Tara was glad she had come to Texas. She was her father's daughter, and all the sophisticated schools and social affairs she had attended at her mother's insistence could never change that.

"Shall we try the restaurant at the hotel?" Terrance suggested, bringing the buggy to a halt. "I, for one, would like to eat something other than my own cooking. How you survived it while you were recuperating is beyond me."

"Just being here with you is nourishment enough," Tara assured him with gay laughter.

Terrance glanced up to see his daughter peering down at him from the carriage seat, and he melted in the warmth of her radiant smile. God, how he had missed Tara. Leaving her had been one of the most difficult things he had ever done. But the strain between himself, Libby, and Ryan had taken its toll. They could not have continued on the same rocky course, not when he constantly rebelled against Ryan's rule while living on Ryan's grand estate, resenting the powerful influence Ryan had over Libby.

When Tara had written to inform him that Ryan had selected her fiance from among his circle of friends, Terrance feared his daughter would die of boredom married to Joseph Rutherford. The Rutherfords, though wealthy and respected in St. Louis, were among the flock of stuffed shirts that Terrance could barely tolerate. Terrance had his own opinion of the kind of man Tara should marry, and that man in no way resembled the spindly-legged, polished-mannered Joseph Rutherford. Indeed, the man Terrance hoped would catch Tara's eye was everything Joseph was not!

Taking Tara's arm, Terrance steered her toward the hotel. "Ah, Tara, having you here with me is like a glimpse of sunshine on a gloomy day. I've missed you more than you will ever know."

Tara gave her father a loving squeeze, right on the main street of "Saints' Roost." "And I expect this will be one of the most enjoyable summers I have ever spent." Except for that one catastrophic incident, Tara tacked on. If only she could forget that horrible night, she mused as she entered the hotel on her father's arm.

Being in Terrance's delightful company would ease the pain and dim the memory, she assured herself. Looking back was depressing, and she had waited too long to see her father to dwell on an incident she could not change. Tara still mourned Don Miguel's passing and blamed herself for the tragedy, but her father insisted that the fault lay with the unidentified man who had fired the shot that had taken Don Miguel's life.

Tara was disappointed to learn that the murderer was still at large, and she wondered if she would ever have a clear recollection of the assailant. Terrance had been very patient with her, never forcing her to face the tormenting memory until she was prepared to deal with it. For that, Tara was thankful. The encounter was still a jumbled haze of confused images, very nearly impossible to sort out in her mind.

Forcing aside her pensive deliberations, Tara focused her full attention on her father, listening to him ramble on about the early days in Clarendon. Texas was a welcome change from the life she had known. It was a world she had only read about in books, until she had dared to take flight from St. Louis and see the wide-open country with her own eyes.

Cobalt-blue eyes considered the rising walls of Palo Duro Canyon with a mixture of contentment and a strange, disquieting restlessness. Sloane had been listless of late, going through the motions of living, playing his charade by night. Heaving a frustrated sigh, he guzzled his glass of brandy and then promptly poured another. He had never been a drinking man. Well, at least not a compulsive lush, he amended. But lately, he had leaned heavily on the brandy bottle to chase down a memory that granted him no peace.

The visage of an enchanting blonde with amethyst eyes

kept interrupting his thoughts, arousing his male body in quick response. His gaze strayed back to his cot, seeing her exquisite face and shapely body bared to his appreciative gaze.

Sloane snapped back to attention, chiding himself for dwelling on his fantasy. "This is ridiculous," he growled, downing another gulp of brandy. "Tara is Terrance Winslow's daughter, for God's sake."

How many times had he reminded himself of the fact, Sloane mused sourly. Craving a woman and hungering for Winslow's daughter had become one and the same. Try as he might, Sloane could not get Tara off his mind. She had taken up permanent residence in his thoughts, and Sloane had tried desperately to rout her.

"She probably doesn't even remember what happened that night," Sloane scolded himself and then plopped down in his chair. "And lucky for you she doesn't." Rolling his eyes, Sloane laughed bitterly at the realization that he had begun to talk to himself. But that wasn't the worst of it. Now he was answering himself, and all because of a woman! Forget her, came the firm voice of reason. He had enough on his mind without conjuring up fantasies about a woman who probably didn't even know he existed and could have cared less.

Heaving another exasperated sigh, Sloane grasped the brandy bottle and drained the last of its contents into his glass. Why was he carrying on like a lovesick pup? He knew nothing about the girl, for Christ's sake! It was unlike him to be distracted by a woman. Those feminine creatures had walked in and out of his life for the past several years, and he had never regretted watching them go . . . until now. Growling at the ludicrous obsession for a woman he hardly knew, Sloane bolted to his feet to survey the shadowed valley. *Forget her. You will never see her again, and it's just as well. You have no place in your life for amorous entanglements.* Determined to follow his own good advice, Sloane ambled over to sink down on his cot. But while he wandered through the no man's land of his good intentions, Tara's bewitching face materialized above him. Sloane could almost smell the alluring aroma of her perfume, feel her full lips melting beneath his. . . .

"Dammit, you really are going mad, Prescott," Sloane preached to himself. "You've consorted with ghostly spirits so long that you have eroded your brain."

Sloane had lived with a single purpose for more than a year, living and breathing, *thriving* on the hope that one day he could expose Merrick Russel for the bastard he was. Progress had been slow, but Sloane had been patient, plotting and planning to keep Merrick's life in turmoil until the moment was ripe. And he had accomplished that, Sloane reminded himself as he restlessly flounced on his cot. But now his thoughts had begun to wander, dwelling on a creamy oval face and spellbinding violet eyes that were fringed with long, thick lashes. If Terrance knew what lurid thoughts were whirling in his head, he might well decide to withdraw his support of Sloane's ultimate cause.

And just what the hell was Tara doing in Texas? Sloane asked himself. That question kept popping into his mind, followed by not one speculation. Had Terrance sent for his long-lost daughter, or had she come on her own accord? And why now?

Forcing the questions from his mind, Sloane tried to catch a nap before he straddled his white stallion and set out on his nightly ride. Thus far, he had frightened off several of Merrick's ranch hands, leaving the cattle baron short-handed and cursing the phantom who prowled Palo Duro Canyon. His purpose was enough to sustain him, Sloane assured himself. He would have no further association with Tara Winslow. Besides, she would be safely tucked away in Terrance's home in town, where the sheriff could keep a watchful eye on the citizens of Clarendon. Don Miguel's murderer wouldn't bother her, especially if she had no recollection of the events that had taken place that night. But what if she remembered? Sloane frowned pensively. That curvaceous blonde would be in harm's way if she could offer a description of the assailant.

Although Sloane was curious to know how Tara was faring after the incident, he had avoided traveling to Clarendon. He needed to speak with Terrance, but he had mixed emotions about confronting Tara again.

"Go to sleep." Sloane grumbled at himself. The nights were short enough as it was. If he spent his time mooning over a woman, he would be less than successful in digging up evidence to incriminate Merrick Russel. Sloane had made a vow to seek revenge on the powerful rancher, and that was one promise he intended to keep, no matter what personal sacrifice it required.

For more than two weeks, Tara puttered around her father's home and reacquainted herself with the workings of his newspaper office, one much smaller than he had had in St. Louis. She and her father spent long hours reminiscing about her childhood, and Terrance quizzed her about her life with Libby and Ryan. When Tara confided her reservations about wedding the man Ryan O'Donnovan had selected for her, Terrance heartily agreed that she should have been given the choice to accept or decline the proposal.

That was what she adored most about her father, Tara thought as she helped Terrance lock the forms into the two chases that sat before them. He always insisted that she should follow her instincts and her heart, rather than be pressured by Ryan's overbearing tyranny.

"I shall be sure to tell Grandfather that you strongly

51

disapprove of the match," she chortled, knowing that would ruffle Terrance's feathers. And it did.

"It will come as no surprise to that Scotch-Irish billy goat," Terrance snorted derisively. "We butted heads over so many issues in the past that Ryan O'Donnovan would swear I took the opposite side in every debate just to infuriate him."

"Didn't you?" Tara teased, flashing her father a wry smile. "I thought you delighted in playing the devil's advocate. The more thorns you could stick in Grandfather's side, the better you liked it."

"He invited controversy," Terrance defended himself as he gestured for Tara to grasp the other end of the chase. They moved toward the large hand press in the corner of the office. After inking the pages, Terrance dipped a sheet of paper in the water trough and then placed it over the type. "But I suppose I *was* a bit ornery, since I enjoyed riling the old man. He is and always has been a stubborn old man, and I could not resist throwing obstacles in his path."

"And now it is I who lock horns with Grandfather," Tara admitted, grinning mischievously as she turned the lever of the press to make the impression on the newspaper.

"A lady after my own heart," Terrance smiled proudly as he came around the newspaper press to flick the end of Tara's dainty nose. "If Ryan wasn't so fond of you, he might have suggested that you leave with me. But I suppose Libby would never have permitted that." His voice took on a strange resonance when he mentioned his estranged wife's name.

"Do you miss Mother?" Tara questioned, her sharp gaze probing her father's pale blue eyes.

Terrance wiped the ink from his hands and then blotted away the stain he had smeared on the tip of Tara's nose. "I suppose I always will," he admitted with a slight shrug. "But sometimes loving someone isn't always enough. Ryan held too much influence over her, and I thought it best to leave before I spoiled the memory of the love we had once shared. I can only hope one day you can find that special someone, and that your life won't be interrupted by an outsider." A merry twinkle lightened his blue eyes as he bent his gaze to Tara. "I ruined every chance of ever going back. Don't you make the same. . . ." His voice trailed off as Julia Russel burst into the office with her father following at a less energetic pace.

"Tara! When I heard you had come to Clarendon, I insisted that Papa bring me into town." She gave Tara a loving squeeze and then flashed Merrick a condescending frown. "But I thought he would never get around to making the trip."

Tara stepped back to admire the comely young woman with the vibrant smile and shimmering red-gold hair that was neatly tied in a bun at the nape of her neck. "You look as lovely as ever," she complimented Julia. "But whatever has become of your bubbling enthusiasm?" she teased, her violet eyes sparkling with amusement.

Julia laughed at the taunt as she silently admired Tara's exquisite beauty. She was the essence of poise and grace. Her feminine manners and subtle wit had drawn Julia to her the first moment they met. Tara claimed that natural sophistication and charm that Julia envied. Tara seemed to have it all, and if she did lack something, Julia couldn't imagine what it might have been.

"And I see you haven't lost your dry sense of humor," she tossed back at Tara, who accepted it with a casual shrug.

"I could not afford to misplace it," she insisted with an easy smile. "After all, what would life be without it?" Her gaze lifted over the top of Julia's strawberry-blond head to meet Merrick's deadpan expression. "Good

53

morning, Merrick."

Merrick mumbled a greeting and then shifted uneasily from one leg to the other. Tara sized up the tall, lanky man with his coarse, ruddy features. The man must have been born with that severe expression glued on his face, she thought to herself. His mouth turned down at the corners, and even when he did shoot forth a smile it was difficult to refer to the gesture as pleasant. Julia and Merrick were as different as day and night. Tara's eyes ran the full length of Merrick's thin stature and she instantly concluded that he looked appropriately like a man haunted by a ghost. It was a wonder to Tara that Julia could have been blessed with even the meagerest amount of personality with her father as her example.

"I have come to ask you to visit our ranch," Julia commented, stirring Tara from her pensive deliberations. "And of course, you are welcome to come to Palo Duro when you can spare the time, Terrance. Isn't he, Papa?"

"Of course," Merrick chimed in, his tone less cheerful than his daughter's.

Masking his feelings behind a polite smile, Terrance nodded agreeably. "I'm sure Tara has been awaiting the opportunity to visit the canyon, since I have been raving about its beauty. And I could not very well ask Tara to travel all the way across Texas without enjoying the breathtaking sight."

"I'll help you pack," Julia offered as she grasped Tara's arm and whisked her toward the back door of the office.

When the young women disappeared from sight, Merrick peered grimly at Terrance who had busied himself at the press. "I was sorry to hear about Don Miguel. I know how fond you were of the old man," he said.

"It was a tragedy," Terrance muttered without looking

54

up from his proofreading of the front page. "Unfortunately, the sheriff has no clues as to why Don Miguel was set upon."

"I know. I read your article in the paper," Merrick remarked as he strolled up behind Terrance to read over his shoulder.

"It will be the first of many articles," Terrance said. "No matter how distasteful the truth might be, I will not be satisfied until the assassin is apprehended."

Silence hung in the office like an invisible partition. "You think I am responsible, don't you?" Merrick growled irritably.

"The thought has crossed my mind," Terrance grunted caustically. "Just why did you have so little use for Chavez? I have never heard an unkind word against him . . . except from you."

Merrick's weathered face was taut with annoyance. It irked him that Terrance claimed the power of the press and that he refused to be swayed. "Newspaper reporters are far too snoopy for my tastes, Winslow, and I will not tolerate being interrogated by you or anyone else," he snorted, avoiding the question Terrance had posed. "I was nowhere near the road to Harrold the night Don Miguel was brutally slain, and I resent your subtle accusation."

"I'm sure you do," Terrance grumbled under his breath, wondering why he was being polite enough to fling only one sarcastic rejoinder when there were a dozen on the tip of his tongue. "And one more thing, Merrick." His brooding gaze pinned Merrick to the wall. "Just in case you are curious, Tara doesn't remember much of anything about the incident. Did you think she might recognize you?"

Merrick looked as if he had been slapped across the face, and Terrance muttered to himself, unable to determine whether Merrick was aware that Tara had been involved in the incident. But Terrance would have bet his right arm that Merrick knew exactly what had happened that night, and he was not about to risk Tara's safety by allowing the conniving bastard to think his daughter posed a threat, as Don Miguel had. He was not sending Tara into the jaws of hell if the devil was waiting to pounce on her.

"Tell Julia to meet me at the dry goods store," Merrick hissed as he spun on his boot heels and stalked toward the door. There he paused, putting a stranglehold on the door knob and then glaring holes in Terrance's striped shirt. "And for your information, I don't know what the hell you meant by that remark."

"Don't you?" Terrance's graying brow climbed to a mocking angle as he raked Merrick with scornful mockery. "Nothing moves in Panhandle Texas without your knowing it, Russel. I have been here long enough to know that." His intense gaze drilled into Merrick who looked angry enough to explode like a keg of gunpowder running on a short wick. "And if some calamity should befall my daughter while she is under your guardianship, I will hold you personally responsible, even if she sustains a mere scratch. Do we understand each other, Russel?"

"We always have, Winslow," Merrick gritted out as he whipped open the door and then slammed it shut behind him, causing the newspaper office to rattle as if it had been besieged by an earthquake.

Terrance frowned disconcertedly as he watched Merrick stalk away. Was he a crazed fool for sending Tara to the Diamond R Ranch? Would Merrick dare harm her? A frustrated sigh broke loose as Terrance raked his fingers through his graying hair. Merrick was many things, none of which Terrance approved of, but surely he wasn't a moron. Merrick wouldn't dare allow anything to happen to Tara. It would confirm his guilt, and the man had spent most of his life proclaiming his innocence. No, Tara would be safe, Terrance assured himself. The Night Rider would be watching over her. To Merrick Russel the haunting phantom was a disturbing link to the past, but the Night Rider would become Tara's guardian angel, watching her from afar, keeping her safe until she returned to Terrance.

Clinging to that encouraging thought, Terrance strode through the office to bid farewell to his daughter.

Chapter 4

"Oh Julia, it's beautiful," Tara breathed in awe as
Merrick pulled the wagon to a halt on the caprock
overlooking Palo Duro Canyon. Now she fully understood why her father had insisted that she witness this
magnificent view. It was like peering into heaven.

The canyon appeared out of nowhere, amidst the flat
plains of Panhandle Texas, sprawling out a thousand feet
below them. The sheer rising walls displayed a spectrum
of pastel-colored rocks and jutting hills within the rim of
the canyon. Dark green cedar trees were splattered
against the walls, as if an artist had dabbed his paintbrush
here and there to add another entrancing hint of color to
an already spectacular scene. Tall cottonwood and berry
trees clung to the bank of the river that meandered
through the grassy valley below them. In the distance
Tara could see the forks of the stream spreading like slim
fingers of sparkling blue water on the canyon floor.

Shades of purple, orange, brown, and white were
woven into the sandstone slopes and ridges that lined the
towering canyon walls. Tara marveled at the natural
beauty of the landscape that was spread before her. Never
had she seen such a majestic valley. It held her so
spellbound that words escaped her.

The rushing sound of a waterfall wafted its way up to
her, and Tara turned in her seat to see the Prairie Dog

Fork of the Red River tumbling over the rock ledges. It was like a heavenly paradise carved into the wide plains, and for a moment Tara was content to sit and view the exquisite sights.

"The river is always clear and blue, and rarely more than ten feet deep, except when it swells with heavy rains," Julia informed her.

Tara's wide eyes took in the breathtaking scenery, following the crystal-blue river, noting the herd of cattle that dotted the lush pasture of Palo Duro. "I can see why you are so fond of your ranch, Merrick." Tara glanced at the man who sat silently perched on the wagon seat, but her eyes were magnetically drawn back to the fertile valley below her. "I have never seen anyplace as lovely as this."

"And I intend to keep it in my family for the next century," Merrick assured her gruffly as he popped the reins over the horses' rumps and urged them down the steep winding road that led to the canyon floor.

Tara was too taken with the view to have her spirits dampened by Merrick's sour tone. The man was behaving as if he were chewing on a lemon rind, but Tara hardly noticed, so distracted was she by the breathtaking scenery.

"Charles Goodnight was the first cattleman to drive the buffalo from the canyon and establish a ranch in the valley, and Papa was not far behind him," Julia explained, and then indicated the canyons to the south. "Papa has never once regretted building a home here. I hope you will be impressed with our headquarters and that you will want to spend several weeks with us."

Tara was thoroughly delighted to be in Palo Duro Canyon. If she were forced to wed the dull, stuffy Joseph Rutherford, at least she would have one summer to cherish in memory. And the next few months would undoubtedly provide a mountain of enchanting memories to overshadow the initial tragedy of her coming to Texas. When the painful reminder of that night crept out of the corner of her mind, Tara shoved it back into the shadows. She didn't want to think of it, not now or ever again.

When they paused in front of the Russel mansion, Tara's mouth gaped. Before her sat a Victorian style home of natural stone. Julia informed her that a freight wagon from Dodge City had hauled the nails, lumber, and window glass to the Panhandle to add this look of elegance to West Texas, at Merrick's request. Tara's wide eyes assessed the towering Gothic arches above each window as she strolled into the mansion, amazed to find that the Diamond R headquarters had been spared no expense. The seven-bedroom home also boasted a huge parlor, banquet hall, kitchen, dining room, and basement to store supplies. Ornate draperies covered the windows, and furniture shipped from New England lined every huge room. Tara felt as if she had walked into a palace filled with luxuries she had never expected to see on the plains of Texas. She was certain Libby would never believe Camelot could exist in Texas, since she considered the entire state to be infested with marauders and ruffians.

After Tara had been shown to her room to unpack her belongings, she descended the stairs beside Julia, who insisted that they make a tour of the headquarters.

Tara felt she had stepped into another world, one unlike anything she had ever known. The Diamond R Ranch was indeed an entity unto itself, an enchanting kingdom set in a spectacular valley in which the pastel-colored walls of Palo Duro served as natural fences, a self-sustaining empire over which Merrick ruled like King Arthur reigning over his court.

Julia pointed out the mess house where the ranch hands took their meals. Adjacent to that timber structure was the dairy where butter and milk were kept in sizable quantities to last the entire year. A poultry house sat to the east of the dairy, and a stone's throw away was the blacksmith's shop, where wagons were mended and horses were shod. The number of employees required to keep this enterprise functioning efficiently must have been staggering.

An amused smile pursed Julia's lips when she glanced at the attractive silver-blonde, who was all eyes. But before she could tease Tara for gawking at the strange new world she had entered, Julia caught sight of Sloane Prescott strolling out of the mess house, and her heart melted all over inside of her chest. She tugged on Tara's arm and dragged her across the yard to introduce her to the man who had become the object of her attention the past few months.

"Sloane! I have someone I want you to meet," Julia called to the tall, darkly handsome horse trainer. He had caught her eye the first day he rode into headquarters to sell them a string of expertly trained horses. Her father had been so impressed with Sloane's abilities with horses that he had offered him a job. Sloane had accepted after making a few stipulations, which Merrick accepted without complaint.

Sloane broke stride as he glanced past Julia to see the shapely blonde whom he had come to know by touch. His breath caught in his throat when his eyes traced Tara's tantalizing figure, knowing full well what lay beneath the attractive garb. For more than two weeks he had been visited by a forbidden dream that roused him from sleep and had him restlessly pacing the floor of his cabin. Ah, how distinctly he remembered the feel of her satiny flesh beneath his inquiring hands, the taste of her kisses, more potent than cherry wine.

Sloane had seen his share of beautiful women, but this curvaceous blonde left all others a dim memory in his mind. After the night Sloane had spent with Tara, he had been hungering to appease the craving he had been unable to fully satisfy. But how the devil could he approach this sophisticated lady when he was posing as Merrick's backward, uneducated ranch hand? He couldn't allow Tara to know he was the mysterious phantom of Palo Duro Canyon who had very nearly stolen her innocence. Did she remember that night? Did she wonder whose face had been behind that grizzly mask? Sloane had made no contact with Terrance after that fateful night, deciding it best to leave bad enough alone. God, if Terrance ever learned what had transpired, Sloane would indeed be a ghost whose sinful soul roamed the canyon seeking salvation.

After regathering his composure and resuming his role, Sloane asked himself why Terrance had dared to send his lovely daughter to the ranch. But before he could speculate further, Julia's voice interrupted his contemplations.

"I want you to meet my dear friend from St. Louis." Julia took advantage of any and every excuse to be within ten feet of Sloane. The mere sight of his virile physique made her knees go weak. "Sloane Prescott, this is Tara Winslow." She introduced them in a noticeably breathless voice.

Tara's long, sooty lashes swept up to meet a dazzling pair of cobalt-blue eyes that pierced right through her. She winced uncomfortably as his bold gaze raked her up and down, missing nothing in between.

There was something about the lazy smile that dangled on the corner of his sensuous mouth that disturbed her. Tara couldn't quite define the feeling that gripped her when she met his impudent grin, but she immediately took offense. His ruggedly handsome features were framed with unruly black hair, which was partially hidden by the broad-brimmed hat that sat low on his forehead. A neckerchief hugged the tendons of his neck. As her scrutinizing gaze slid lower, Tara found herself unwillingly admiring this cowboy's broad shoulders and narrow hips. Tight blue breeches clung to his legs and leather chaps disguised what Tara guessed were well-muscled thighs, judging by the rest of his virile physique.

When Sloane Prescott struck a nonchalant pose and didn't bother to tip his hat, remove it, or make any gesture befitting a man who had been introduced to a lady, Tara flashed him a condescending frown. And when those probing blue eyes flickered down her torso in blatant appraisal, Tara bristled like an angry cat. The man was looking right through her with his penetrating gaze, and she had the uneasy feeling he knew exactly how she would look in the altogether. Even though she felt an odd physical attraction to this stranger, she took an instant disliking to the philistine who boldly raked her as if she weren't wearing a stitch.

"It's a pleasure to meet you, ma'am," Sloane said in his slow, lazy southern drawl.

The timbre of his baritone voice left her skin tingling, as if he had murmured the words against her neck. Her chin tilted a notch higher, distressed as she was by her unwarranted reaction and the involuntary need to appear cool and aloof. How could this handsome stranger touch off two distinctly different instincts in a matter of minutes? She was intrigued by this rugged breed of man who resembled no one she had ever met, but she could not help taking offense when those cobalt-blue eyes reached out and touched her.

"How do you do, Mr. Prescott," she replied in a tone that implied she had no particular interest in how he was doing as long as he didn't do it near her. Tara pirouetted and would have walked away if Julia hadn't clasped her arm to keep her rooted to the spot.

"How is Papa's prize stallion coming along?" Julia

questioned, groping for conversation, anything to allow her a few more minutes with her ruggedly handsome raven-haired, blue-eyed rogue.

His shoulder lifted and then dropped lackadaisically as his mildly amused gaze worked its way across the full bodice of Tara's white chemisette and gaping blue bolero. "He's a feisty one." Sloane's husky voice could have lulled a crying baby to sleep. It was low and soft and altogether irresistible. "But Vulcan is beginnin' to come around. He still resents a man's touch. . . ." His cobalt-blue gaze anchored on Tara, who shifted skittishly beneath his probing regard. "Some wild creatures need more coaxin' than others." Slanting a smile in Julia's direction, Sloane nodded slightly and then backed away when Julia sidled closer. "S'cuse me, ladies. Merrick is payin' me a handsome sum to tame Vulcan, and the contrary stallion still lacks several manners."

As did his trainer, Tara thought to herself, frowning as her eyes followed the powerfully built cowboy who ambled toward the corral. There was something about Sloane Prescott that Tara didn't like, but there was even more about him that fascinated her. She didn't appreciate the fact that she liked what she saw. The frown settled deeper in her exquisite features. Did that make any sense? Tara was certain the blow to the back of her head had scrambled her brain. How could she be feeling such a potent crosscurrent of conflicting emotion about a man she had only met?

A forlorn sigh tumbled from Julia's lips as her gaze followed Sloane's footsteps from the dirt path to the stock pens. "Isn't he the most attractive, devastating man you have ever laid eyes on? I have done everything I can think of to get Sloane to notice I'm alive, but I swear he is more interested in four-legged critters than he is in women."

And that was most fortunate for women, Tara mused,

considering the way he had stripped her naked with those penetrating blue eyes. He might not have had much use for women, but he had made no pretense about giving her the once-over—thrice! Sweet merciful heavens, she could have slapped his handsome face for thinking what she *thought* he was thinking. And unless she missed her guess, it had nothing to do with horses! Lord, why was she stung by the overwhelming urge to retaliate when he had *said* nothing to offend her? Because she had been on the receiving end of some very sensual glances, she reminded herself. She was not so naive that she didn't know when a man was undressing her with his eyes, and for the life of her she couldn't imagine why. Julia had just pointed out that Sloane Prescott had little time for women.

Although Tara had her heart set on disliking Sloane, she reluctantly agreed that there was something magnetic about the tall, muscular cowboy. There was a strange aura hovering about him, an inner confidence that bordered on arrogance, a subtle message in his eyes that implied that Sloane Prescott did what he damned well pleased and didn't give a fig about what anyone else thought. He was his own master, Tara guessed, and she seriously doubted that even grumpy Merrick Russel had much effect on Sloane. How could he? Sloane was as big and hard as the Rock of Gibraltar, she thought to herself.

"I have been trying to work up enough nerve to invite him to escort me to the ball Papa is giving in a few weeks," Julia went on to say, dragging Tara from her contemplative deliberations. "But Papa thinks Sloane is a little rough around the edges."

"Amen to that," Tara chortled, her violet eyes flaring with mischief. "Not good enough for Merrick's precious daughter, is that it?" She raised a mocking brow and then slid Julia a wry smile. "What you need, my lovesick friend, is a tutor for your ill-mannered Mr. Prescott,

65

someone who could groom him in the art of gentlemanly behavior and teach him some proper etiquette befitting a man who might court the rancher's daughter." Tara sized up Sloane as he swaggered through the gate and called softly to the coal-black stallion that had been pacing the corral searching for a means of escape. The magnificent steed quieted immediately and then answered Sloane's whistle, following him into the shed like an obedient pup. "If your Mr. Prescott had the same way with women that he seems to have with horses, you might find yourself in serious trouble."

"You would hear no complaint from me," Julia murmured dreamily and then spared her comely companion a thoughtful glance. "And I think I know just the person to teach Sloane the proper techniques of courting and gentlemanly behavior. With a little coaxing and guidance, Sloane could win my father's affection, especially since Papa already has the utmost respect for his ability with the livestock."

"Then I suggest you immediately enlist the assistance of your tutor. Since Mr. Prescott is cut a little rougher than most, it will take several weeks to instruct him on how to behave when he is in the presence of a lady," Tara smirked as her critical gaze flowed over Sloane's broad back. "And you may have waited too long as it is."

"You can begin right now," Julia suggested, beaming radiantly at the possibility of attending the party on Sloane's arm. "Papa asked me to ride over to the Simpsons' and Palmers' to offer personal invitations to his party, and you can be alone with Sloane."

"Me?" Tara chirped like a sick sparrow. "I'm not at all sure I like the man, and I certainly have no interest in becoming better acquainted."

"Well, of course, you." Julia giggled at the stunned expression that was glued on Tara's face. "You are safely betrothed to another man. You are sophisticated, poised, and knowledgeable. Who could possibly fit all those qualifications around here besides you?"

"But . . . I . . ." Tara sputtered, her face white-washed.

"Bargain with him," Julia insisted. "Ask Sloane to instruct you in riding and you can subtly point out ways to improve his manners. And then you can teach him to dance, court a lady, and . . ." Her voice trailed off as she watched Sloane swing upon Vulcan's back, forcing the high-spirited steed to respond to the rein against his neck.

"But I already know how to ride," Tara protested, groping for any excuse to decline the outrageous favor Julia was asking of her.

"Sloane doesn't have to know that." She stared at Tara as if she were addle-witted. "Pretend ignorance." Julia gave Tara a gentle shove toward the corral and then wheeled toward the house. "I will ask Papa to give Sloane the remainder of the afternoon off so he can acquaint you with the ranch while we are away."

Tara half-collapsed when she found herself abandoned. This was preposterous! Groom Sloane Prescott for his social debut? She would have preferred to groom the horses. Resigning herself to the fact that she had stuck her foot in her own mouth by planting the seed in Julia's head, Tara aimed herself toward the corral and the incorrigible Sloane Prescott. Since love was blind and Julia fancied herself in love with this philistine, Tara could only conclude that Sloane had *no* manners at all, if Julia admitted that he needed some sort of instruction. Lord, what had she gotten herself into this time?

Sloane's hawkish gaze slid over Tara's voluptuous figure as she leaned against the corral fence and hesitantly glanced at him. Her silver-gold hair glistened in the sunlight, giving it such a lustrous appearance that he longed to comb his fingers through the silky strands.

Her oval face was the picture of perfection, and her sensuous, heart-shaped lips seemed to beg for his kiss. Sloane swallowed hard as his eyes languidly slid over her full breasts and lingered on her trim waist. The black Merino skirt disguised the shapely curve of her hips, but he knew that beneath the folds of the gathered skirt and thin white chemisette and bolero was what dreams were made of—and he was having one!

Tara knew what that insolent cowboy was thinking, as if the words were printed on his brow. Confound it. There it was again, that all-consuming gaze that made her want to wrap herself in a saddle blanket. The man *did* need to learn a thing or two about manners, and she was woman enough to teach him, she told herself.

"It is not polite to stare so boldly," she reprimanded him, casting him the evil eye. "A gentleman would never stare at a lady the way you do, Mr. Prescott."

"More the pity for him," Sloane drawled as he effortlessly swung from the saddle and stalked toward her like a jungle cat cornering his prey. "I see no fault in admirin' beauty when it glides across my line of vision."

Tara was most thankful for the sturdy corral fence that separated them. Sloane looked faintly dangerous as he approached her, and she forced herself to stand her ground.

"Just how would yer prim and proper gentlemen from St. Louie stare at you, Tara?" he questioned, his baritone voice glazed with sticky-sweet sarcasm.

"With a great deal more respect than you offer," she sniffed distastefully, finding herself now raking *him* up and down with *her* eyes, wondering why they had gotten off to such a rocky start. Because Sloane's leers were downright rude, she reminded herself huffily. The man had as much charm as a rattlesnake, and Tara detested the slithering creatures.

Sloane was quick to sense that he had riled her, and it

amused him to realize that the lady could become a tigress when her temper got the best of her.

"It ain't against the law in Texas for a man to admire a beautiful woman. I always consider the stature and temperament of a horse before I walk up on one," he drawled lazily, intending to annoy her. And he did.

"I do *not* appreciate being compared to a damned horse!" Tara snapped back at him. "Your manners would not fill a thimble, Mr. Prescott."

When she spun on her heels, deciding that the task Julia had requested of her would involve more patience than she could collect in a lifetime, his hand snaked through the rails of the fence to snag her before she could make her escape.

"The name is Sloane," he insisted as his fingers bit into the tender flesh of her arm, cutting off the circulation as he flattened her against the fence, her face only a few inches from his mocking smile. "And I'm beginnin' to think the term *lady* more aptly applies to the mare I broke to ride this mornin', instead of you."

Tara puffed up indignantly, and it was all she could do to refrain from smearing that intimidating grin all over his face and rearranging a few of his features. Never had she been insulted so many times in the span of a few minutes. He had his nerve, that sidewinder!

"Give me back my arm," she gritted out as she tried to pry his long, bronzed fingers from the sleeve of her bolero. "I don't want your filthy hands on me."

Sloane delightedly watched the violet-eyed minx come apart at the seams. Her behavior shattered the image of the quiet, reserved debutante Julia had introduced him to. His first impression had been that this delicate rose was out of her element at the Diamond R Ranch, but this was no fragile flower. Tara Winslow was a wildcat!

Laughter rumbled in his massive chest as he dragged her closer, peering into her flushed face at close range. "I always do as I damned well please, Tara," he assured her, his voice crackling with amusement. "And I don't need some high and mighty sophistikit from St. Louie tryin' to change me."

Tara had always been one to stare a challenge in the face, and suddenly she found herself determined to make a gentleman out of this crude-mannered cowboy. If Julia wanted Sloane Prescott dressed and stuffed for Merrick's grand party, then, by damn, she would serve him up to Julia on a silver platter! Sloane Prescott might be as rough as rawhide and as tough as leather, but she was going to smooth his ragged edges if it was the last thing she ever did!

A daring smile found the corners of her mouth, curving them upward as she ceased her struggling and met his taunting grin. "I contend that we both have a great deal to learn from each other, Mr. Pres . . . Sloane," she corrected herself in the most civil tone she could muster. "You can teach me to be more tolerant of your breed of men, and I will instruct you on the type of gentlemanly behavior that lures a lady."

His dark brows shot straight up as his grasp on her arm relaxed. "You want the two of us to exchange bits of knowledge?" he croaked, bug-eyed. "I could have sworn you had taken an instant dislikin' to me." He dragged out the words with his lazy drawl, as if they were tangled on the end of his tongue.

Tara massaged her arm, straightened her blue bolero, and then tossed him another smile. "Perhaps if you could climb down from your high horse I could bring myself to like you. . . ."

"Providin' I polish my manners," Sloane finished for her. "And maybe, just maybe, I could tolerate you if you stepped down from *yer* pedestal, little princess."

Gritting her teeth, determined not to rise to another taunt, Tara thrust her hand between the fence railing.

"Shall we shake hands and try *not* to come out of our corners fighting, Sloane?"

His large, calloused hand swallowed hers, and Tara winced uncomfortably, feeling as if she had just latched on to a lightning bolt. Shocking sensations darted up her arm, and it was with dedicated concentration that she ignored them. My, but the man had a strange effect on her—and she was not particularly proud of her reaction. She did not like being physically attracted to this brawny cowboy. Their pupil-instructor relationship could get out of hand, and Tara didn't dare risk that. With a gulp, she met those shimmering pools of blue, fighting the unsettling emotions that swirled and crested like waves on a stormy sea. At least Sloane would preoccupy her, she told herself shakily. He could help her forget the tormenting memory of that frightening night when she had effected Don Miguel's death, a hazy memory that tugged at her thoughts when she wasn't guarding them closely.

While Tara was attempting to ignore the churning feelings within her, Sloane was lost to an enchanting fantasy. He could see wild violets waving in the wind when he stared into her eyes, eyes that were surrounded by a fringe of long, thick lashes. His gaze glided over the creamy texture of her cheeks, knowing they would feel like velvet beneath his touch. His attention focused on the sensuous curve of her heart-shaped lips, lips so soft and inviting that Sloane had to fight the battle of self-conquest to keep from taking her sweet mouth. But then a movement behind Tara caught his eye, and he jerked up his head to see Loren Marshall walking toward them, shattering the mystical dream that was playing havoc with his thoughts.

"Merrick wants me to drive him and Julia over to the neighboring ranches this afternoon. The boss asked if you would show Miss Winslow around the canyon while

71

we're away."

Loren was delighted to see Sloane with Julia's lovely guest. He had turned envy green each time Julia hovered around Sloane, angling for his attention. Nothing could have pleased him more than for Sloane to show an interest in Tara, allowing Loren to monopolize Julia's time.

An ornery smile dangled from one side of Sloane's mouth as his gaze shifted from the ranch foreman to the shapely blonde, with her sparkling amethyst eyes. "Tell Merrick I will tear myself away from my duties only at his request, and that I have personal matters to attend later this afternoon. I won't be back at the ranch until Wednesday."

Tara could enthusiastically have strangled Sloane's sturdy neck for his insulting remark, but she clamped an iron will on her temper and swallowed the barb she came dangerously close to hurling at the miserable rat.

When Loren wheeled around and aimed himself toward the ranch house, Tara raised a perfectly arched brow. "Well, Sloane, will you consent to teaching me to handle a horse this afternoon, if I agree to show you how to behave in the presence of those of us of the female persuasion?"

"I can think of nothin' more entertainin', ma'am," he drawled as he swept the Stetson from his crisp, wavy hair and bowed mockingly before her.

Tara longed to yank the wooden rail off the fence and club him over the head with it, but again she restrained herself from violence, having learned a valuable lesson during her confrontation with Don Miguel's assassin. She would bide her time until they rode along the river. Then she would shove the lout from his saddle and let him drown. One should always depend on the element of surprise, she reminded herself. Julia could find herself another escort to the party, one who deserved her affection, someone who wasn't as infuriating and stubborn as this jackass.

"Please select a gentle mare for me to ride," she cooed, gloating over the fact that she was about to make a fool of this strutting stag. Let him think she didn't know the first thing about horses, she thought wickedly. She would have the last laugh on Sloane Prescott.

Cobalt-blue eyes skimmed the *remuda* of horses adjacent to the training pen. "I'll see what I can round up for you, ma'am."

Tara watched in amazement as Sloane whistled like the pied piper and brought the entire herd of forty horses to attention. They stood stock-still as he ambled among them to make his selection. Perhaps the man had a way with horses, but he didn't know a blasted thing about impressing women. Tara smiled in smug satisfaction. Before she was through with that cocky cowboy she would have him hobbled with his own lariat and he would be eating out of the palm of her hand. She would allow herself a week to transform this ill-mannered toad into a charming prince. Tara seriously doubted she could tolerate this rough-edged man for more than seven days, so she would have to work fast and furiously to smooth his ragged edges. If Julia wasn't satisfied with the change, she could take him as he was or find herself another beau. And if Julia had any common sense she would choose the latter course of action. Surely there was a better match for a wealthy rancher's daughter than a man who barely offered Julia more than the time of day, Tara mused as her critical gaze flooded over the powerfully built cowboy, searching for some physical defect and finding not one flaw on his masculine form to ridicule, much to her chagrin.

Chapter 5

"Here you are, Miss Winslow." Sloane extended the reins and then dropped them into Tara's hand. "Hazel has the sweetest disposition of any of the Diamond R stock." A devilish grin carved deep smile lines in his bronzed features. "Maybe you could learn somethin' from this even-tempered mare," he suggested, his drawling voice laced with an undertone of taunting sarcasm.

"Damn you and your blasted insults!" Tara spewed, forgetting she had intended to hold a tight rein on her temper in Sloane's presence.

One dark brow raised acutely and then slid back to its normal arch. "I didn't know it was proper for dignified ladies to spout vile words," he teased.

"It is permissible when she is assaulted by such a crude, overbearing, insolent excuse for a man." Tara wrapped the words around her tongue and hurled them at him. "I am beginning to think you have already been educated far beyond your intelligence. It is little wonder that you work so well with four-legged beasts, since you seem to share their level of mentality."

Her stinging jibe bounced off his tough hide, leaving no mark. Tara had fully intended to anger him, just as he had infuriated her, but the remark seemed to have the opposite effect. Sloane's blue eyes danced with mirth, and then he burst out laughing.

"You've got a nasty temper, Tara. Maybe this arrangement we made *will* benefit the both of us." A suggestive grin pursed his full lips as his gaze slid over her curvaceous figure. "You can teach me to be less of a man, and I will teach you to be more of a woman, one who doesn't take offense at every teasin' comment."

Teasing? Tara eyed him skeptically and purposely ignored the seductive gleam in those pools of liquid blue. Sloane was intentionally trying to get beneath her skin, and she could not fathom why he delighted in annoying her. Perhaps they just brought out the worst in each other. They had been at each other's throats since they first met, and it was going to require tremendous effort to overlook his intimidating rejoinders. In the future she would rely on self-discipline, she lectured herself. If she didn't retain her composure, she might find herself snatching his revolver from his holster and blowing him to smithereens. A wicked smile surfaced on her lips when she gave way to that thought. It would serve him right after the way he had treated her, she thought spitefully.

A wary frown settled on his tanned features. "I don't know what yer thinkin', woman, but I swear it ain't the kind of vision that supposedly dances in a young lady's head."

"No, it isn't," Tara assured him saucily as she intentionally strutted around to the wrong side of the mare and clumsily dragged herself into the saddle. "As a matter of fact, it was positively wicked."

Her awkward maneuvers were so comical that Sloane laughed out loud. Although Tara was a dazzling beauty with a feisty temperament, she was also a source of constant amusement. Sloane hadn't laughed and smiled so much in years. He adored taunting her until that hellcat emerged from beneath that controlled exterior.

"How do you make this nag go?" Tara questioned as

she grasped a rein in each hand and rocked back and forth on Hazel's back, her legs jutting stiffly out on either side of the mare's ribs.

Sloane choked on a laugh. He had seen his share of tenderfeet in Texas, but Tara looked ridiculous when she played her role to the hilt. With a great deal of effort, Sloane managed a deadpan expression, certain his facade would crack if she pulled another silly stunt. "Press yer knees against Hazel's flanks, and for God's sake, take both reins in yer right hand. You look as if yer steerin' two horses that are runnin' off in opposite directions."

Nodding agreeably, Tara complied with his command, making an effort to bounce in the saddle and sway sideways when Hazel veered off to the left.

When Sloane growled behind her, Tara twisted around to cast him a glance of feigned innocence, as if she couldn't imagine what could possibly be wrong with the way she was handling the mare.

"Whoa, Hazel," Sloane ordered in that soft, coaxing tone that he reserved for four-legged creatures.

Hazel didn't move a muscle as Sloane swung up behind Tara. Her back stiffened as his male contours molded themselves to hers. His hard thighs crowded her hips, and Tara was jarred by the exciting tingles that shot up and down her spine. She resented her reaction to this exasperating cowboy, but she was helpless to defend herself against it. She was attracted to this masculine mass of rawhide and leather simply because it was impossible not to be.

"Move with the horse," Sloane murmured in instruction, his warm breath caressing her neck as he took the reins from her trembling hand and urged the mare forward. "A light touch of leather will make her respond. You needn't twist her head off if you want her to turn."

Tara feared she would melt like butter sitting too long on a hot stove as Sloane's rock-hard chest fitted itself to

76

her back. The feel of his sinewy arms holding her captive had her heart doing back somersaults. As Hazel trotted off, Tara tried to inhale a ragged breath and recollect her shattered composure, but she was plagued with the uneasy feeling that Sloane Prescott was more man than she could handle. Her confidence drooped another notch when his left hand settled casually on her thigh and his chin rested on her shoulder.

"Stop that," she squeaked, slapping at his adventurous hand. His nearness was suffocating her, and she could barely draw a breath without having her senses swarmed by his manly scent.

A low rumble echoed in his chest as he bent even closer to whisper in her ear. "Must a gentleman ask permission of a prim and proper lady before he touches her?" he taunted unmercifully.

"Touching and groping are two entirely different matters," Tara choked out as his wayward hand glided upward to investigate the curve of her hip. "And you are groping!" She shifted away from his muscled torso and then squealed when she very nearly toppled from her perch.

Sloane's left arm curled around her waist, drawing her back against him, branding her with fire each place he touched. Tara felt as if she were going up in smoke. Sloane was causing volcanic eruptions, leaving every nerve and muscle smoldering in the wake of his close physical contact.

"Please let me . . ." Tara stopped in midsentence when she glanced up to see that Sloane had paused before the cascading waterfall. She was greatly relieved when he hopped from the saddle, allowing her overworked heart to return to its normal pace.

"It's beautiful, ain't it?" he questioned as he lifted her from Hazel's back and urged her toward the riverbank. "It also makes a most enjoyable bath. Would you like to

77

take a swim? I will be only too happy to ensure there ain't no Peeping Toms hidin' in the brush," he drawled, his tone laced with seduction.

Tara eyed him cynically. "Do you honestly expect me to believe *you* wouldn't be one of them if I decided to shed my clothes and dive in?" she sniffed distastefully. "That would be like asking a wolf to stand watch over a lamb. No thank you, sir. When I take to the water I will be *completely* alone."

Sloane's soft laugh whispered in her ears. Absently, he lifted a strand of silver-gold from her shoulder and brushed his fingertips over the silky tendrils. "You can never be completely alone in Palo Duro," he murmured, preoccupied with the feel of her spun gold hair trickling between his fingers. "Haven't you heard there is a phantom who prowls this canyon?"

He could not help but wonder if Tara recalled anything about the night they had spent together. Did she remember how intimately he had touched her? Had she experienced any of the sizzling sensations that had boiled through his veins? The memories of that night were crowding in from the four corners of Sloane's mind, and he felt the slow rise of desire clouding his thoughts.

Her violet eyes strayed back to the waterfall. Tara ambled away to follow the bend of the river, letting the misty breeze cool her flushed face. Sloane's remark dampened the pleasure of her surroundings, and Tara had to force herself to deal with the legend Don Miguel had mentioned, one that had come dangerously close to reality and yet still remained in her thoughts like a hazy dream.

"I have heard the legend, but I am not at all certain such a spirit exists. I cannot imagine intelligent men and women believing this canyon is haunted."

"There are a great many who swear the Night Rider exists," Sloane insisted, falling into step behind her.

Pausing, Tara turned to face him, her wide eyes searching the depths of his. "Do you believe Merrick's dead brother's ghost is standing watch over this valley?" she questioned point blank.

His shoulder lifted in a shrug and then he knelt to scoop up a rock to skip across the river. "Mostly I just mind my own business," he replied evasively. "I've seen the vision, but I figure it's the boss's problem, not mine."

Tara thoughtfully chewed on her bottom lip, straining to untangle the nightmare that seemed just beyond her grasp. "I don't believe in things I cannot touch or feel, and it seems odd . . ."

Sloane's low chuckle interrupted her train of thought. "And if the Night Rider galloped past you and voiced a greetin' then you would swear he *did* exist?" he smirked.

She was in no mood to become the brunt of another of his jokes. The thought of a phantom rider upset her more than he could know. But Tara didn't want to believe in specters, especially when she was trying so hard to forget that horrible night.

"I am only saying that I am skeptical of phantoms," she said dismissively as she moved away from Sloane. "Can we talk of something else? Tell me about yourself."

Sloane studied her thoughtfully for a long, quiet moment and then allowed the subject to die a peaceful death. "What do you want to know about me?"

"Julia informed me that you aren't the usual ranch hand who rooms in the bunkhouse and works the normal hours Merrick demands of his other hired hands." Tara pivoted to appraise Sloane's virile form, her eyes wandering at will. "What personal matter must you attend tomorrow?"

"Is it unladylike to meddle?" Sloane's dark brow slid to a mocking angle. "You have assured me that I ain't a gentleman, but I ain't asked you such pryin' questions . . . yet."

"I was only trying to make conversation," Tara defended herself.

His features mellowed in a smile. "I am paid for my services, and I work for Merrick when I please," he told her. "Since I own a few acres and run my own stock in the valley, I have my own affairs to attend. Merrick knows I have no ties to him and that I consent to his orders only when they suit me."

He was very much his own man, Tara mused pensively. But then, she expected as much from this tumbleweed. No doubt, one day he would yearn for greener pastures and he would pull up stakes and leave. No one would stop Sloane Prescott. He would go where the wind took him and leave no memories behind. Julia was a fool for thinking she could soften this man's heart, for it was surely carved from solid rock.

"You've forgotten somethin'." Sloane's deep, lazy voice sliced through her contemplations.

Tara arched a quizzical brow and lifted her face to his, causing Sloane to melt in his boots as he studied her from such an arousing angle. Lord, she was breathtaking. Her eyes sparkled like priceless amethysts, her skin seemed as soft as satin, and her shapely figure invited his caress. Being alone with Tara stirred him, and he had never been one to deny himself when he was in the company of a beautiful woman.

"Have I?" she questioned innocently.

"You were goin' to teach me the gentlemanly art of courtin'," he prompted as he closed the distance between them. "Just how is a man supposed to approach a dignified lady? Like this . . . ?"

He came on like an invading army, and there was not one ounce of gentlemanly reserve in his tactics. His arm roughly hooked around her waist in a crushing embrace, knocking her off balance, bending her into the hard contours of his body, forcing her to cling to him or fall flat on her back. His dark head came deliberately toward hers, his penetrating gaze focused on her lips as if they were the first pair he had ever laid eyes on, as if the sight of them fascinated him.

Tara couldn't breathe, and Sloane didn't have the decency to prop her upright before his greedy mouth took bold possession of hers. Shock waves of pleasure sizzled through her as his tongue skimmed her trembling lips and then intruded to explore the dark recesses of her mouth. His arms were like bands of steel mashing her breasts into the muscled wall of his chest. Her whole world was tilting precariously, and she was sure it was about to slide out from under her as his wandering hands mapped the gentle curve of her hips, burning her with a white-hot fire that spread over every inch of her body.

When he finally dragged his lips from hers, a provocative smile hovered on the corners of his mouth. "Or like this, Tara?" he questioned huskily.

Sloane twisted, allowing Tara to stand on her own wobbly legs. His hard male body pressed full length against hers. Before she could catch her breath or utter a word, his lean fingers speared into her silky hair, holding her head in his hands as his sensuous lips fitted themselves to hers with such heart-stopping tenderness that Tara thought she was going to melt all over him. A blaze as hot as a raging prairie fire leaped across her skin as his hands splayed across her back and then curled around her ribs, roaming dangerously close to the undercurve of her breasts. Her small gasp broke loose and then died beneath his kiss as he savored and devoured her. His wandering caresses moved upward, his thumbs brushing over the soft fabric that covered the peaks of her breasts, and Tara caught fire and burned. Her senses were reeling in astonishment. She had been kissed before, but never with such thorough devastation! Sloane Prescott was teaching her things she had never known about kissing, and she was left to wonder who was instructing whom. Sweet merciful heavens! This cowboy had swept her right off her feet, leaving her no direction to retreat, forcing her to respond to the arousing sensations she had never realized existed.

A forbidden memory tripped across her mind, confusing her. Somewhere within the traumatic nightmare that haunted her was a recollection that disturbed her. She vaguely remembered these sensations obviously triggered by her tormented mind. What she was experiencing were shades of a cloudy dream, she rationalized, and then frowned at her own twisted logic. She wasn't making any sense, even to herself. Sloane was awakening a need, unknown sensations, needs closely related to passion—but how could she have known that, unless she had been a trollop in a previous life? Sweet mercy! What was she saying? Sloane's skillful embrace had her so confused she didn't dare trust her own mind! He was tampering with her sanity and she couldn't even decipher her own thoughts without becoming entangled in them!

Like the morning sun, ever so slowly ascending into the azure sky, Sloane lifted his raven head to break the spellbinding kiss. But Tara's lips continued to tingle with the arousing aftereffects of his embrace, leaving her feeling as if the earth was moving under her feet.

"Which approach does the lady approve of?" Sloane queried, his voice ragged with disturbed desire.

Tara's tangled lashes swept up and she blinked bewilderedly. Her heart was still hammering so furiously that she wondered if it meant to beat her to death before she could respond to his question.

"I think you are much too bold," she said in a half-strangled voice. "The first kiss should offer a token of respect, not ravishment."

Tara reached up on tiptoe, curled her finger beneath

his stubbled chin, and then timidly pressed her lips to his before retreating a safe distance away.

One heavy eyebrow slanted downward in strong disapproval.

"Beggin' yer pardon, ma'am," he drawled. "But I can't imagine even a gentleman bein' satisfied with such a meager treat. I think my way is best."

And without further ado, Sloane again demonstrated his technique of kissing her senseless. His lean fingers clamped into the small of her back, forcing Tara to collide with his hard male body. His muscular thigh pressed into her. His free hand slid behind her neck, tilting her head back to his fiery kiss, a kiss so potently intense that Tara felt as if she were being cremated in an inferno of flaming desire. He was feeding an already incredible hunger that wouldn't go away. Suddenly, Tara wasn't certain she wanted it to. Sloane was making a mockery of Joseph Rutherford's brand of kisses, assuring her that she could never be satisfied with a man like Joseph. Sloane had taught her things she hadn't known about herself, things that frightened and shocked her. Tara had a weakness for passion, it seemed, and Sloane had instilled a need in her that blossomed and grew until it consumed every part of her being.

His virile body moved suggestively against hers, as did his roaming caresses. And Tara could have sworn he had sprouted an extra pair of hands. He took his Texas time about investigating every curve and swell she possessed, leaving her vividly aware of the spark of passion that had been created between them. His mouth devoured hers, stripping her breath from her lungs, making her feel like a drowning swimmer on her way down for the third and fatal time. And the most baffling thought that skipped across Tara's malfunctioning brain was that she didn't particularly care if she were rescued, at least until these exquisite sensations eased their grasp on her.

83

For what seemed forever, his lips clung possessively to hers, and Tara drank freely, offering a willing response that she was helpless to control. Sloane was unchaining wild, delicious feelings in her, feeding the fires of passion that Tara feared even a blizzard couldn't cool.

The feeble voice of reason warned her to compose her emotions before she lost all control. Lord, it was next to impossible to think and react when Sloane's skillful kisses and caresses turned her mind to mush. Attempting to cling to better judgment, Tara threw herself away from his potent embrace, hoping to put a safe distance between herself and the powerful mass of brawn and muscle who had very nearly turned her wrong side out, exposing emotions she usually kept under tight rein.

But when she did push away, she tripped over the driftwood behind her. Tara squawked and flapped her arms in an attempt to regain her balance. Her boot heel caught on the hem of her skirt and she shrieked when she found herself teetering. Like a snake uncoiling to strike, Sloane lunged for her, and Tara instinctively reached for his hand. The sudden tug on his arm, while he was off balance, launched him forward, and Sloane's eyes locked with Tara's wide ones as they both plopped into the river in an unceremonious heap.

Fear spurted through her as Sloane's bulky weight forced her under before she could grasp a precious breath of air. Scratching and clawing to fight her way upward, Tara burst to the surface, sputtering and choking after having swallowed half the water in the Prairie Dog Fork of the Red River.

Sloane chuckled as Tara climbed all over him, cursing a blue streak as she struggled toward shore. He twisted away from the bedraggled she-cat and then hooked his arm around her waist to haul her to the riverbank. When he set her to her feet she was furious with him for the way he had toted her under his arm like a feed sack. Hadn't she suffered enough humiliation at his hands? He had insulted her, taken outrageous privileges, nearly drowned her, and then he laughed at her. Her violet eyes blazed like torches as she turned on him, her wet hair dangling wildly about her, her breasts heaving with every agitated breath she took.

"Damn you, Sloane Prescott. You are the most exasperating man I have ever met. There is a certain young lady hereabouts who wanted to invite you to Merrick's party, but you would find a way to make a disaster of it. I swear, you are a lost cause!"

"A lost cause, am I?" he echoed, having difficulty keeping a straight face when this dainty beauty closely resembled a wet mop. It baffled him to realize he still found her appealing when she looked her worst. There was no way around it. Tara aroused him, and as much as he would have preferred to deny it, he couldn't, not without lying to himself. Her garments clung to her curvaceous figure, accenting her luscious swells and contours and Sloane had willfully to ignore the enticing display in hopes of maintaining his self-control. He gestured toward her dripping clothes, dragged his hawkish gaze from the taut peaks of her breasts that pressed against the wet fabric, and then flung her a mocking grin. "It seems to me the pot is callin' the kettle black," he drawled so sarcastically that Tara glared murderously at him, spitefully wondering how he would look with a noose tied around his neck, stretching it to its limit. "I think *you* need to brush up on yer rules of etiquette, duchess. I can't imagine that proper ladies go 'round cursin' and swearin' a blue streak the way you've been doin'."

"I wouldn't be if you hadn't knocked me into the river, you clumsy ox!" she sputtered furiously.

"Me?" Sloane hooted in protest. The expression that was plastered on his face was so mockingly innocent that

Tara seriously considered pounding him flat and floating him so far down the river he could never chart his way back. "Yer the one who tripped over yer feet and dragged me down on top of you. I was only tryin' to help, like any considerate gentleman would do," he tacked on to further infuriate her.

He did. "I can most certainly do without your kind of assistance!" Tara was all but yelling in his grinning face, and the glower she leveled at him carried enough heat to scorch a desert.

"That suits me just fine," Sloane grunted as he barged ahead of Tara to swing into the saddle and then reached down to hoist her up behind him. "You best hold on to me, unless you want to be bounced off Hazel's rump. *Ladies* like you don't deserve much consideration, and I'm not prone to give it in the first place. If you fall I ain't stoppin' to retrieve you."

Tara gasped in alarm when Sloane gouged his boot heels into the horse's ribs, sending the mare lunging forward. Hazel lowered her head, her nostrils flaring as she bounded across the pasture in answer to her trainer's command. Gnashing her teeth together, Tara wrapped her arms around Sloane's muscled midsection and held on for dear life as the steed thundered through the valley at breakneck speed.

When the steed began to labor, Sloane tugged on the reins, slowing Hazel to a walk.

"The Sad Monkey," Sloane said abruptly as he indicated a rock formation in the canyon that resembled the facial features of an ape. Then his arm swung to the northwest. "Lighthouse Peak." He gestured toward the towering buttes that jutted upward from the high rim of the canyon. "Hard rock is the Indian translation for Palo Duro. The Comanches named the canyon for the hard cedar trees found here. They made their bows and arrows from 'em. For decades the Indians and buffalo roamed this plush valley. Then the Comanches were driven north to the reservations in Oklahoma." After his brief history lecture, Sloane touched the reins to Hazel's neck, urging her back in the direction they had come.

Tara sighed appreciatively at the grandeur of the canyon that slit open the High Plains. Sloane had managed to distract her, and she had no inclination to strike up another argument. She was content to ride behind him, spellbound by the magnificent scenery.

"I can understand why Merrick clings so fiercely to this ranch," she mused aloud.

"A ranch bought and paid for with his own brother's blood, the way I heard it told," Sloane snorted gruffly. "Greed does strange things to men. Merrick would kill to keep this ranch intact."

She frowned. "Do you truly believe Merrick murdered his own brother just to have the ranch all to himself? Why would you work for him at all if you dislike him?"

"Greed," Sloane laughed bitterly as he tossed Tara a backward glance. "I wanted forty acres of this valley, and Merrick wanted my services badly enough to sell them to me. I tolerate him because he pays me well, and he tolerates me because he wants to boast that he raises and trains the best horseflesh in all of Texas."

"But Julia said Merrick has a great deal of respect for you," Tara interjected. "Why . . ."

"And I have a great deal of respect for Merrick," Sloane told her flatly. "But that don't imply that we particularly like one another. You can respect a man's capabilities without admirin' him as a man, and that's the way I regard Merrick Russel."

Tara studied his broad back, grappling with his remark. Sloane Prescott was straightforward. He minced no words. He wanted something from Merrick, and Tara silently wondered if Sloane's long-range plans included taking over the Diamond R Ranch, bit by bit. If Sloane showed an interest in Julia, he could wedge his foot in the door with little difficulty, she predicted. Surely he was intelligent enough to figure that out all by himself. But he hadn't taken the direct approach in that particular matter, and that seemed slightly out of character for Sloane.

Julia had made it clear that she enjoyed Sloane's company, and she *was* a very attractive young woman. No man in his right mind would ignore the affection and wealth Julia Russel had to offer. Giving way to that leery thought, Tara pushed away from Sloane's muscular body, wondering if he weren't just a little mad not to take what Julia would have handed to him on a silver platter.

She had never dealt with a man like Sloane before, and she was wary of him. He was a rough breed of man, one so hard and tough he could probably survive on a desert without food and water. He was set in his ways and very difficult to maneuver. He seemed callous and uncaring, she thought to herself. She was certain his foremost concern was Sloane Prescott. Everyone else ran a distant second, and Tara seriously doubted he would go out of his way to help someone who found himself in distress. In Sloane's world it was every man for himself, and women were given even less consideration. She was sure he was the type who would allow a door to slam shut in a woman's face and never give it a thought that he should have held it open for her.

Tara was bumfuzzled by her reaction to this handsome mass of brawn and muscle. He could release the uninhibited woman in her who lurked just beneath the surface with his practiced caresses and tantalizing kisses. He left too many conflicting emotions churning within her, ones she deemed dangerous. Suddenly, Tara found herself anxious to return to headquarters and put a safe distance between her and this bold cowboy. She didn't trust him, and she could no longer trust herself when she was alone with him. He was like a magician who could entrance her, making her react and consider possibilities that should never have entered her mind in the first place.

When Sloane paused beside a clump of cottonwood trees, Tara eyed him skeptically. "Is there something of scenic importance here?" she questioned.

Sloane clamped his hand around her arm and pulled her from the saddle, a devilish smile hanging on his lips. "I thought you might want to do somethin' about yer appearance. If I drag you back to headquarters like this, someone might think you and I were doin' somethin' besides tourin' the canyon." His blue eyes slid over her curvaceous figure, not missing even the smallest detail. "If I wasn't such a gentleman, I wouldn't be considerin' yer reputation."

Tara flung him a withering glance. Sloane a gentleman? That was a contradiction in terms if she'd ever heard one.

Since Tara simply stood there scrutinizing him, Sloane ambled forward to comb his fingers through the tangled mass of her spun gold hair, smoothing the renegade strands back into place. Tara was amazed by the gentleness he displayed as he turned her around to continue his ministrations on the unruly tendrils that cascaded over her shoulders. When he had completed his task, he stepped back to survey the transformation. His keen eyes assessed her clothes before his gaze fell to the top two buttons of her chemisette, which had come undone. Her heart fluttered wildly as his fingers brushed lightly against her skin to fasten the buttons. With the second task completed, Sloane gave her the once-over, his heated gaze like a warm iron smoothing away the wrinkles on her garments, and Tara felt the heat of his cobalt-blue eyes as they cruised over her.

His stamp of approval was a butterfly kiss that

skimmed over her lips, and Tara could scarcely believe this was the same callous rakehell who had escorted her on a tour of the canyon. Sloane Prescott was an enigma, she thought to herself. Beneath that tough rawhide exterior was a man with gentle tendencies, ones that could be polished if a woman had the time and inclination to groom him.

She blinked bewilderedly, realizing she was oddly discontent with his feathery kiss. What he had taught her to crave was one of those fiery kisses that could melt her into liquid desire. Was she mad? This was the man *Julia* had her heart set on, for heaven's sake! She could not risk becoming involved with Sloane.

His all-consuming gaze traced her petite figure, mesmerized by the way the waning sunlight splattered through the trees and sprayed across her alabaster skin. Damn, why was he so captivated by this stunning minx? He had had his share of women, women who had come and gone with no strings attached. But Tara was a lady . . . in a certain sense of the word, he amended. He would have bet she knew little about passion, judging from her reaction to his bold advances. He couldn't appease himself with a woman like Tara and then cast her aside when his passion was spent. If he had any common sense at all he would avoid her like the plague.

His eyes retraced their devouring path over every curve and swell she possessed, and he felt the stirring of primal needs as his gaze lingered where he yearned to touch. There was something intriguing about this violet-eyed, silver-blond beauty who had the face of a seraph and the temperament of a tigress. She was far more than the eye beheld, and Sloane felt a strange obsession for her, a craving that had gone unsatisfied. She was so close and yet she was so maddeningly far away. He wanted to know her as a man knows a woman, and he couldn't shake the thought of holding her exquisite body in his arms without confining garments to inhibit them.

One long, tanned finger gingerly traced the delicate line of her jaw. When he met those enchanting amethyst eyes that burned with living fire, Sloane felt himself losing control.

"To hell with bein' a gentleman," he growled, his voice heavily laden with desire. "When in Rome, one does as the Romans do, but when a man is on the frontier, he does things his own way. . . ."

A gasp broke from her throat as he yanked her to him, lifting her from the ground, holding her so tightly to him that his hard, muscular body was imprinted on hers. His mouth crushed into hers with rough, devouring impatience. It was as if he could not get enough of her, and she was shocked to find that she was just as hungry for him. The manly scent of him and the feel of his male torso molding itself intimately to hers sent her senses reeling in wicked delight. When his free hand wandered familiarly over her breasts, Tara moaned, amazed at her own abandon. Good God, this man was the devil's own temptation. Never in her life had she been forced to deal with the feelings that were now spreading through her entire body.

She could feel desire flooding through her, washing away reasoning, crumbling each barrier of resistance she had sought to construct. There was something frightening about her compelling attraction to this rough-edged man, something as potent and vivid as the dream she had experienced the night she had been injured. That mysterious mixture of sensations brought Tara back to her senses, and she writhed for freedom before she found herself in a compromising situation. She had never been so reckless in a man's arms, and she berated herself for allowing her defenses to crumble so easily when Sloane captured her in his powerful embrace.

"I think we had better return to the ranch before . . ."

91

Her breathless voice skipped along with the breeze as her gaze darted away from those glistening pools of blue that could entrance her.

"You don't trust me, do you?" Sloane queried hoarsely, clenching his fists at his sides to prevent clamping them about her.

Slowly, she turned back to him, regarding him cautiously. "You are a very forceful man, and I . . ." Tara bit her lip, wondering if she should be honest with him on such a delicate subject. But perhaps if she were truthful with him he would show more respect, she reasoned. Deciding that honesty was the best policy, Tara blurted out the words that waited on the tip of her tongue. "I have never been intimate with a man, and I think you expect too much. I cannot know what type of relationship you usually have with women, but I would guess you are accustomed to taking far more than I am in the habit of giving. You and I are as different as midnight and dawn."

His heavy brow lifted as he regarded her with mild amusement. "And you think what I want from you has nothin' to do with learnin' the rules of etiquette," he predicted with a chuckle.

Tara glanced down at the toes of her boots, as if something there demanded her undivided attention. "It would certainly seem so. I am not accustomed to having the stuffing squeezed out of me each time I come within ten feet of a man. You are much too bold."

Sloane moved deliberately closer, his face only inches from hers. He curled his index finger beneath her chin, forcing her to meet his penetrating gaze, which probed into her to search out the dark secrets she preferred to keep concealed. "But you didn't complain when I kissed you," he reminded her huskily.

No, she hadn't, and Tara could have kicked herself for that. But she was drawn to Sloane because he was different from any man she had ever known. This bold, rugged breed of man drew her like metal to a magnet, even when her instincts urged her to run before she was caught up in something she didn't quite understand and was helpless to control.

Tara reached up to mold her hands to the sides of his tanned face, drawing his raven head to hers. Her kiss whispered over his eager mouth. "I do not object to being kissed," she admitted. "But what follows in the wake of your kisses disturbs me."

Sloane was certain he had died and gone to heaven. Lord, this dainty nymph could have turned him into melted butter. But if she thought her tactics could mellow him enough to settle for a tender kiss, she had sorely misjudged him. He was a man with a man's appetite, and she knew that as well as he did. Impulsively, his arms slid around her, letting her feel his bold manliness against her thigh.

"Don't think to tame me, minx," he rasped. "I will never be like the men you've known in St. Louie. I'm cut from a different scrap of wood, and I have no desire to change my ways."

He was as hard as cedar, Tara thought as the taut muscles of his thighs moved familiarly against hers. It was apparent that Sloane Prescott was more man than she could handle. He wasn't about to budge an inch, and she had the uneasy feeling that *compromise* was an unlisted word in his limited vocabulary. Perhaps Julia could handle a man like Sloane, since she was accustomed to his kind, but Tara was beginning to doubt her own abilities. She had no difficulty keeping Joseph Rutherford at arm's length, but Sloane Prescott was an entirely different matter. If she didn't guard her step, she might find herself . . . Tara didn't dare imagine what it would be like to share Sloane's bed. The mere thought was suicide. He would devour her.

She wiggled from his embrace, stilled the accelerated beat of her heart, and then struggled to breathe a normal breath. "I would like to return to the house," she said in a shaky voice. "I think we both have had enough instruction for one day."

When she pivoted on her heel to put a safe distance between them, Sloane grasped her arm, swinging her back around to face his somber expression. "You know what I want from you, don't you, Tara? You and I are playin' with fire. I knew it the moment I laid eyes on you. And if a certain young lady plans for me to escort her to Merrick's party, she may as well know what I expect in return for dressin' up in fancy clothes and waltzin' her across the ballroom."

Tara was too stunned to respond. Her mouth gaped open, staring up at Sloane as if he had sprouted another head, one equipped with devil's horns. Sweet merciful heavens! Julia didn't know what she was getting herself into. Sloane wanted a woman's body, not the personality that went along with it. He was a coarse, coldhearted man who had no time for love or meaningful relationships. No doubt, a quick tumble in the grass would satisfy this barely civilized brute, she thought acrimoniously. Once he had conquered a woman, he would be content to search out another to ease his lusty cravings. Well, he could take his rude suggestion and stuff it in his saddle bags! Tara would never surrender to this rough-edged cowboy, not even if he were the last man on God's green earth, and if Julia had any sense, she wouldn't either.

Her violet eyes flared furiously as she yanked her arm from his grasp. "You have your nerve, Sloane Prescott!" She hurled both barrels at him, intent on blowing wide holes in his male pride. "Do you think every woman will wilt in your arms, just because you have decided to *honor* her by allowing her to appease your voracious appetite?" Her voice was getting higher and wilder by the moment.

Tara felt more at ease when she was shouting at Sloane. It was safer than being caught in the tight circle of his arms, fighting the tug-of-war of emotions that his kisses and caresses evoked. "I resent your speaking to me as if I were some common trollop who is not particular who she sleeps with, and I delight in giving you a piece of my mind, you arrogant lout!"

"Do you think you can spare it?" Sloane smirked caustically, taunting her and loving every moment of it.

Tara reacted impulsively and flesh cracked against flesh, leaving her handprint on his left cheek. "I hope I have made it clear that I do not fall into bed with every man I meet. And if I did, I wouldn't get around to you until the turn of the century!" She glared at him with scornful mockery, intently searching for something about his virile physique to criticize, annoyed that he was all brawn and muscle. "Why don't you go seduce your precious horses, cowboy!" she suggested flippantly. "You show them more respect than you offer to women. Good day and good riddance."

With her usual agility, Tara snatched up Hazel's trailing reins and bounded into the saddle as the mare trotted away. Sloane's jaw sagged on its hinges and he stared bug-eyed as Tara, with her skirts billowing about her, thundered across the pasture as if she had been born riding. That little termagant could manage a horse as well as he could! She had been toying with him, leading him to believe she didn't know the first thing about horses.

Growling in irritation, Sloane stalked off after her. But his anger dwindled with each step he took. As he watched Tara disappear in the distance, a reluctant smile skimmed his lips. He had been very bold and abrupt with that little spitfire, he reminded himself. Perhaps she deserved the last laugh . . . this time. After all, he was harboring a secret that would have her blushing up to the roots of her silver-blond hair. But next time he would know for certain that he wasn't dealing with some delicate, defenseless lady from the East.

Armed with that knowledge, Sloane strode across the pasture, chuckling at the compelling image that fluttered just beyond his grasp. If Tara Winslow thought she had seen the last of him, she had another think coming. He had come dangerously close to making love to her, and he had the uneasy feeling that that foretaste of heaven would torment him until his compelling dream collided with reality. That hellcat couldn't sashay into his life, turn him wrong side out, and then flit back to St. Louis. It wasn't that simple anymore.

Little Miss Prim and Proper Winslow had met her match, Sloane mused determinedly. He was going to make a lasting impression on that minx, one way or another. That feisty witch would be begging for his touch when he finished with her, he promised himself. And Sloane was prepared to bet his forty acres that she would not voice one complaint about his being something other than the sophisticated gentlemen she was accustomed to dealing with. Besides, a gentleman couldn't handle a woman like Tara. Bowing and begging permission would never get a man anywhere with that hellion with the angelic face and round violet eyes. Tara would walk all over a man if he wasn't careful, and Sloane had never warmed to the idea of having footprints on his back. Tara would come to him on *his* terms, he told himself confidently. A woman was like a flighty colt. She could be hobbled and gentled if a man relied upon the technique that suited her disposition.

As his thoughts continued to wander, Sloane frowned disconcertedly. For the life of him he couldn't imagine why Terrance had permitted his precious daughter to associate with a man like Merrick, knowing how ruthless the man could be at times. Had Terrance sent for Tara or had she come on her own? Just why was she vacationing on the Diamond R Ranch? Terrance could very well be inviting trouble by tossing Tara in Merrick's path. Did Terrance expect the Night Rider to keep constant vigil over her? Sloane scoffed at the thought. After watching that blond-haired she-cat thunder off, riding as if she were born in the saddle, Sloane doubted Tara needed a guardian. If Sloane tried to keep a watchful eye on her he could very likely get himself trampled by that hot-tempered tigress.

Chapter 6

When Tara thundered back into headquarters, relieved that she had left Sloane in a cloud of dust, Cal Johnson ambled over to assist her from the saddle. A curious smile pursed his lips as he peered off into the distance.

"Where did you leave Prescott?" he questioned as he unfastened the girth and dragged the saddle from Hazel's back.

Tara glanced up at the plain-faced cowboy with wiry brown hair and a lanky frame. It seemed a pity the Lord had thought to dish out handsome features to Sloane and offer Cal the leftovers. There was not one thing attractive about the man and the flash of wild recklessness in his eyes disturbed her.

"I left Prescott where he belongs," Tara muttered as she smoothed the unruly strands of silver-blond hair back into place. "He is in the pasture grazing with the rest of the undomesticated creatures."

Cal chuckled in amusement as he assessed the violet-eyed beauty. He had admired Tara from a distance and was disappointed Merrick hadn't asked him to show Tara around the ranch. It delighted him to learn that Sloane had not fared well with the comely blonde. On a number of occasions when he had accompanied Sloane to Tascosa, he had found himself taking Sloane's leavings. It galled him, and now he had the opportunity to devote himself to a woman who apparently wanted nothing to do with Sloane Prescott. It must have been a first for him, Cal mused. Women usually trailed after Sloane like kittens on the trail of fresh milk.

"If you want another escort, I'd be happy to show you around," Cal offered, flashing her a hopeful smile.

"Another time perhaps," Tara murmured before she aimed herself toward the house for a refreshing drink to cool her irritation with that infuriating man who had made mincemeat of her emotions in one afternoon.

When Sloane finally strolled toward the pens, Cal flashed him a mocking grin. "Did you and Miss Winslow have an enjoyable tour?"

A sour frown plowed Sloane's brow. He had little use for Cal Johnson. The man seemed all too eager to please Merrick Russel, and Sloane was quick to find fault with any hired hand who catered to Russel as if he were the reigning king.

His reply was a disgusted grunt as he brushed past Cal, who was not about to let the matter drop until he knew what had happened.

"Doesn't the lady appreciate the straightforward approach?" he taunted as he followed at Sloane's heels. "Maybe I can learn something from your blunderin'."

"She ain't yer type, Cal," Sloane muttered as he strode toward his horse and tossed a saddle on the bay gelding's back. "I doubt she will be interested in you, either."

"I can be very persuasive," Cal insisted, a rakish grin spreading across his thin lips.

Sloane swung into the saddle and then studied the lanky cowboy for a long moment. "I heard you were abusive with your women," he said with a gruff snort. "Don't lay a hand on Tara or I'll see that you regret it."

Cal puffed up indignantly. "You ain't got no claim on the lady, Prescott. And what I do with women is my business."

"I'm making Tara my business," Sloane told him in a deadly tone and then nudged the gelding, sending him off in a trot.

Cal glared holes in Sloane's departing back. Why Merrick tolerated Prescott's insolence was beyond him. But Merrick had given Sloane the run of the ranch, allowing him to come and go as he pleased, as if *he* ruled the roost. That annoyed Cal. He had spent the past few years catering to Merrick, hoping for special privileges, but he had yet to earn the amount of respect Sloane had gotten this past year. A dark scowl settled on Cal's weather-beaten features as he stalked back to his duties. He would have his way with Tara Winslow whether Sloane liked it or not. He had spent too long walking in Sloane's shadow, he reminded himself bitterly. He envied Sloane's position and his way with women. One day he would have the world in the palm of his hand, and Sloane would have nothing more than the forty acres Merrick had consented to sell him. And why Merrick had parted with his precious land in the first place was beyond him. No doubt, Merrick would sell his soul if it would help him obtain what he wanted. And he wanted to become known as the best stock breeder in Texas. Sloane had made him a fortune, training his prize horses and selling them at prime prices. Cal would have given most anything to have Sloane's way with animals and his uncanny knack of maneuvering Merrick.

An anxious smile formed on Julia's lips as she poked her head into Tara's room. "Well, how was your afternoon with Sloane? Did he teach you anything you didn't know about riding? Did you teach him some manners?"

"The entire incident proved disastrous," Tara muttered, her mood soured by the mere mention of Sloane's name. "It was a mark of heroism that I even tolerated his presence. He made me so furious that I jumped on Hazel's back and galloped off, forgetting that I was pretending to be ignorant of horses." She sliced Julia a disgusted glance. "I think it would be wise for you to invite someone like Loren Marshall to the party and leave Sloane to his four-legged beasts. The man is so rough around the edges that it would take forever to smooth him out. I don't have the time or the patience."

Julia plopped down on the edge of the bed and sighed heavily. "I thought I was in love with Loren until Sloane came to work here. Then I wasn't certain, and I have never been able to spend enough time with Sloane to know if it's infatuation or love."

"Take my word for it." Tara sniffed distastefully. "Sloane Prescott is better left with the mavericks and mustangs, since he seems to prefer to remain as wild and free as they are. The man is too uninhibited and unrefined to behave like a gentleman, even for one night."

"But that is what makes him so intriguing," Julia argued.

"Then I suggest you admire him from a distance, unless you want to risk being trampled," Tara countered in a caustic tone.

"You don't like him very much, do you?" Julia surmised.

"Don't like him?" Tara hooted. "That is putting it too mildly. I detest his rude manners. It makes me cringe to hear him mutilate the English language with his poor grammar and slow, lazy drawl. And I detest his magnificent arrogance."

"But I happen to like him, and I want him to accompany me to the dance." Julia thrust out a stubborn chin. "Is it asking too much that you teach him a few dance steps and instruct him in behaving like a gentleman? I thought friends enjoyed doing favors for each other."

"I hardly consider grooming Sloane Prescott for his social debut a favor!" Tara snapped more harshly than she intended. "The man is beyond help, and you are asking the impossible. It would be easier to tame a mountain lion and bring him to the party on a leash than to waltz around the ballroom in that uncivilized heathen's arms."

"If you asked a favor of me, I would see it done," Julia insisted.

"Good. I would ask you to drop the subject . . . permanently. The man has given me a hellacious headache," Tara grumbled as she massaged her throbbing temples.

Julia complied with a wry smile. "Very well, I won't mention him again, but I remember once in St. Louis when a certain gentleman came to call, and I lied right through my teeth and told him you would be unable to accompany him that night or any other night for the following week because you were traveling with me to visit relatives. And as I recall we went nowhere at all." She sighed melodramatically. "But I was only too happy to do the favor, since you had little use for the man at the time."

"And now I find myself engaged to him," Tara bit off and then tossed Julia a disgruntled frown, annoyed that her younger friend had her sprawled over a barrel. "Oh, all right, I will tolerate your Mr. Prescott for the duration of my sojourn at your ranch. But don't expect miracles. Contrary to superstitious beliefs, it is impossible to transform a lizard into a charming prince."

Julia chuckled at the vexed frown that was plastered on Tara's lovely face. "Thank you, Tara. I realize what a great personal sacrifice this is for you. But even if the two of you have a personality conflict, you must admit he is a very attractive man."

"Attractive, perhaps, to one of his own kind," Tara smirked as she stomped over to fetch clean clothes that had not absorbed the musky fragrance of Sloane Prescott.

"Are you suggesting that *I* am kin to lizards and snakes?" Julia flung at her, feigning indignation.

"I said nothing of the kind," Tara denied. "I only implied that we are judged by the company we keep. I still think you would be happier with Loren. He seems very fond of you, while Sloane has more use for horses than women. What he wants from women has nothing to do with love." She stared pointedly at the strawberry blonde, who was two years her junior. "It is best to let sleeping dogs lie."

"Sloane has potential." Julia defended him. "You can teach him to become respectable and courteous to women."

"He has *raw* potential, and it would take countless hours to perfect it," Tara amended.

Julia's shoulders lifted and then dropped nonchalantly. "Perhaps," she sighed. "But if any woman can assume the task of molding Sloane into the type of man she would be proud to call her husband, *you* can. You have a way with men. They naturally flock to you."

After Tara wiggled into her yellow satin gown she glanced over at Julia. "I will do what I can with Sloane, but do not be disappointed if the man of your dreams turns out to be a nightmare. I tried to warn you that you can't fit a wolf into sheep's clothing and expect anything more than a woolly wolf."

Julia beamed as she grasped Tara's hand and pulled her along behind her. "Thank you. I appreciate your concern, but I can handle Sloane once you have cautioned him on the appropriate way to court a lady."

Tara rolled her eyes heavenward and grumbled to herself as Julia led her to the dining room. *She* would become the appetizer for the wolf, and by the time Julia got her hands on him, Sloane would not be so hungry for the main course. What was that adage about there was no greater love than sacrificing one's self for a friend? Tara heaved a despairing sigh, wondering if she were about to become a human sacrifice. She had waded in over her head when she consented to while away the hours with Sloane Prescott. That rugged cowboy would gobble her up if she didn't keep him at a safe distance. And Lord, there weren't enough miles, even in Texas, to keep them a safe distance apart. Sloane had warned her that they were playing with fire, and she had the apprehensive feeling that she would be roasting above it if she didn't watch her step.

After taking their evening meal, Tara wandered outside while Merrick and Julia made their arrangements for the upcoming ball. Tara welcomed the moments alone, the opportunity to sort through her muddled thoughts. Sloane Prescott still preyed heavily on her mind, and she was still searching for a way to exorcise him when she glimpsed the movement amid the trees. Her gaze narrowed as the apparition vanished in the shadows and then reappeared a good distance from where she had first spotted it. The starlight reflected the silver-white vision and a chill ran down Tara's spine, tapping at a dim memory of a night she would have preferred to forget. Again the haunting image darted across her line of vision, and then she found her footsteps leading her to the horse pen to retrieve a mount, her gaze glued to the incandescent figure that appeared to be floating among the sagebrush.

Hurriedly, Tara bridled a horse, wasting no time with a saddle in her haste to see with her own eyes what was causing the strange illusion that was playing tricks on her. As she reined the uneasy steed toward the clump of bushes, the specter disappeared momentarily and then emerged from the rocks ahead of her. Clamping a tight rein on her pounding heart, Tara told herself there were no such things as ghosts. And she would not rest that night until she had verified that fact.

She trotted her horse to the location where she could have sworn she had seen the apparition, only to hear the chirping of crickets invading the dark silence. Her keen gaze swept her surroundings, and then she slumped back to heave an exasperated sigh. There *had* been someone prowling the night, she assured herself.

A horrified gasp burst from Tara's lips as she glanced sideways to see the shapeless phantom flying through the air to land a stone's throw away from her. The sudden movement caused her mount to rear in fright, and Tara groaned as she slid from the horse's back and landed on the ground with a thud. She frantically scrambled to her feet to pursue her frightened steed, but she found her path blocked by the specter that floated silently toward her. Tara gulped over the lump of fear that had lodged in her throat and dismally reminded herself that her inquisitiveness had often led her into castastrophe. Blast it, why couldn't she have remained on the stoop instead of trotting off into the darkness? Because she had the curiosity of a cat, she reminded herself resentfully.

Tara courageously drew herself up in front of whoever or whatever it was that hovered before her. "Who are you?" she demanded to know, calling upon all the bravado she could muster. Her legs were wobbling like a newborn foal's as the apparition emerged from the shadows to glisten in the moonlight.

A low, eerie rumble of laughter rattled around in what Tara assumed to be his chest, if indeed a ghost had one. Stop this! Tara gruffly chided herself. There were no such things as wraiths roaming the earth . . . were there?

"Are you flesh or spirit?" she squeaked, taking a cautious step back for each movement that propelled the phantom toward her.

"*Algun diá se lo contaré,*" came the muffled reply from the distorted image of a head that sat upon the specter's shapeless body.

Tara peered into the dark, fathomless holes in the ghastly hood that resembled nothing she had ever seen, and then retreated another cowardly step. Surely this phantom could speak to her in her native tongue, for heaven's sake. Heaven? Tara choked down her heart, which had catapulted to her throat, and reminded herself that there were no hard and fast rules stating ghosts had to be heavenly. With that distressing realization, Tara took another backward step, wondering if what she *thought* she was seeing was the devil in disguise. Wasn't she in enough trouble, cavorting with ghosts, without finding a language barrier between them? How were they to communicate? Swallowing her apprehension, Tara blurted out another question, although she doubted she could translate the answer, if indeed the apparition offered one.

"What do you want with me?" Tara squeaked nervously as her wild eyes darted about her, searching for some means of escape in case this haunting bogey flew at her with some dastardly purpose.

"What is it you want with me, *noncherniego?*" the Night Rider questioned, his voice barely above a whisper.

"I wish to know your purpose," Tara said unevenly and then gulped when the glittering radiance of the phantom caught in the moonlight.

"I am here to repay a longstanding debt, inquisitive imp," the Night Rider informed her in that soft, hushed voice that set her nerves to tingling.

"One you feel Merrick owes you?" Tara was determined to get to the bottom of this if it was the last thing she ever did!

Stumbling on that thought, Tara swayed precariously, certain her stampeding heart was about to pop out of her chest. There was so much she wanted to do in her lifetime. What if this were the last night she ever witnessed? What if . . . God help her. She was shaking like a leaf in a windstorm, wondering if this elusive phantom was about to make a meal of her for interrogating him.

"If you wish to remain unharmed you will ask no questions and tell no one you have spoken to me," the Night Rider warned, his voice carrying a deadly chill that went right to the bone.

How could she, Tara asked herself, her wide eyes flooding over the silver-white image that seemed to rustle in the wind. Only a madwoman would admit to carrying on a conversation with a ghost!

"*Si va haciendo tarde.* Go now before someone misses you," he ordered.

"But you haven't told me why you are . . ."

Tara's voice trailed off as the specter waned, evaporating into the shadows, and then she pinched herself to ensure that she had not been haunted by another nightmare. With her ears pricked, she waited for some faint sound that might alert her to the fact that she was not alone, but the night was deathly quiet, and all she could hear was her heart pounding in her ears.

A perplexed frown captured Tara's features. Mulling over the incident that left her wondering if she *had* been conversing with the shadows, she spun around and stomped off in the direction from which she had come. Confound it, she was not giving up, she told herself firmly. There *had* been someone or something beneath the low-hanging cedar branches . . . hadn't there?

Tara was not abandoning her crusade until she knew

exactly what she had seen and heard. She couldn't possibly have been talking to herself . . . could she? Certainly not, Tara convinced herself. She might have been startled and confused, but surely she wasn't mad. Determined to get to the bottom of this hoax, Tara would not allow herself to be frightened off by what she thought she had seen and heard. No faceless image that leaped from the shadows, warned her away, and then melted into the darkness was going to keep her from learning the truth. She was going to trail after that phantom until she knew for certain whether it was flesh or spirit, or whether her malfunctioning brain had played tricks on her. Ghost indeed, she thought cynically. There had to be a logical explanation for what she'd seen . . . or *thought* she had seen.

A deep swirl of laughter bubbled from Sloane's chest after watching Tara stalk off in a huff. He had been prowling around the ranch, intending to add more fuel to the tales of ghost sightings, to cause more unrest among Merrick's superstitious ranch hands. The last person he had expected to see trailing after him was Tara. Damn, but she was a curious little imp. Like father, like daughter, Sloane surmised. Terrance had always been determined and relentless in his pursuit of the truth, and Tara had obviously inherited his thirst for obtaining facts.

On several occasions, the phantom of the canyon had very nearly scared the breeches off cowboys, but Tara had stood her ground instead of turning tail and running for her life. Although he and Tara had their conflicts, Sloane could not help but admire the young beauty's fortitude. She was indeed made of sturdy stuff.

A heavy sigh, muffled by the incandescent white hood, tumbled from Sloane's lips. The mere sight of Tara bathed in moonlight had triggered memories that Sloane was having great difficulty controlling. Damnation, was every encounter with that distracting minx to be a battle of self-conquest? How was he to look upon her without envisioning her as she had been that night in his cabin, her curvaceous body bared to his all-consuming gaze, her kisses burning brands on his mind?

Expelling a frustrated breath, Sloane ambled away, knowing he would be visited by his own private phantom with intriguing violet eyes if he dared to return to his cabin. How was he to sleep when Tara had shared his bed, had wrapped her silky arms about him and taken him halfway to heaven?

"Miss Winslow, is that you?"

Tara nearly jumped out of her skin when Cal Johnson's deep voice sliced the silence. Having taken a moment to collect her scattered composure, Tara had strolled toward the stock pens to ensure that her runaway mount had returned. "I was taking a walk," she explained, attempting to keep her voice from cracking nervously.

"At this late hour?" Cal swaggered toward her, his hawkish gaze circling her voluptuous figure and lighting upon the full swells of her breasts that were exposed above the scooped neck of her yellow gown.

The scant light from the window sprayed over Tara, and Cal felt the fierce urge to touch what his eyes devoured. Tara was all woman, every perfectly formed inch of her. She had been on Cal's mind since the moment he saw her parading about the ranch.

When Tara caught the lusty gleam in his eyes, she hurriedly brushed past the lanky cowboy to position herself in the shadows. "I enjoy the peacefulness of the evening," she insisted, hoping he would take the hint and make himself disappear. But, as she aimed herself toward the house, his callused hand snagged her arm, pulling her against him.

"There ain't no need to rush off, honey," he purred seductively. "I don't mind keepin' you company."

He smelled of sweat and whiskey as he breathed down her neck, and Tara was repulsed by his touch.

"Thank you, but no. It is late and Julia is expecting me back," Tara said firmly as she attempted to worm free of his viselike grip.

Cal's arms encircled her in a bear hug, and Tara's gasp of surprise died beneath his brutish kiss. Waves of repulsion flooded over her as his cruel mouth devoured hers. She twisted her head to avoid his nauseating kiss, shocked to find herself comparing Cal to Sloane and preferring Sloane's forceful but compelling embrace.

An enraged growl burst from Cal's lips as Tara writhed in his arms. He yanked on her hair, forcing her head back, leaving her no choice but to accept his hungry kiss or risk having her blond mane pulled out by the roots. Tara reached for the derringer that was stashed in her sash and jabbed it into his ribs, demanding his undivided attention, and Cal jerked away, his eyes wide in disbelief.

"Don't ever lay a hand on me again," Tara hissed venomously as she aimed the derringer at his heaving chest. "No one takes privileges with me unless I permit it."

Cal raised his arms in surrender as he stepped away, a taunting smile dangling from his thin lips. "Did you let Prescott have permission?"

He couldn't have known how close Tara came to blowing a hole in him for voicing that mocking remark. It was all Tara could do to prevent herself pulling the trigger. "There is nothing between us," she snapped back at him.

"No?" Cal's slurred voice held an undertone of laughter. "He told me to stay away from you. That sounds to me like a man who's put his brand on a woman. But it don't matter, I like what I . . ."

110

"I suggest you march yourself to the mess-house and find yourself a strong cup of coffee," Tara gritted out, her eyes blazing as she glowered at the drunken cowboy. "I want nothing to do with you or Sloane. The less I see of both of you, the better I will like it."

Silently fuming, Tara stalked toward the porch and then let herself into the house. Men, she muttered under her breath. The whole lot of them were a pain in the . . .

"Did you enjoy your evening stroll?" Julia questioned as she ambled out of the parlor to greet Tara.

Pasting on a smile, Tara nodded slightly and forced herself to sit still for another hour, listening to Julia describe the party she and her father were planning. When she finally retired for the night, she was a bundle of frazzled nerves. Her thoughts kept stumbling over the angry wraith of Merrick's long-dead brother, the strange apparition she had confronted in the shadows. Over and over again she told herself that the shapeless image shrouded in white was no more than a phantasm. The blow to the back of her head had caused memory lapses that came to haunt her occasionally. And yet . . . Tara conjured up the vision again. It had had a phosphorescent glow about it. That strange, unexplainable light that radiated from the specter disturbed her. A muddled frown carved deep lines in her exquisite features as she strolled over to the window to peer down on the grounds below, searching, waiting for the vision to reappear in the moonlit darkness. Her heart stopped when she thought she spied something skipping through the shadows, but as she moved closer to the window it disappeared from sight. Heaving an exasperated sigh, Tara spun away and flounced onto her bed, only to be tormented by a creaking sound that seemed to come from directly above her. Holding her breath, she waited an apprehensive moment until the eerie sound died in the silence.

She was only imagining she saw and heard someone,

111

Tara lectured herself, only half-believing. There were no spirits floating about the ranch house. And yet, she was prepared to swear she had visited a phantom in the moonlight. Confused, but determined to sleep, Tara squeezed her eyes shut. Finally, she drifted into dreams, but they seemed just as puzzling as reality. Somewhere in the night, Tara had the strange sensation that soft, cool lips were whispering over hers, while light, caressing fingertips skimmed her cheek like an evening breeze stirring against her face.

Sloane had found his restless footsteps leading him toward Tara's room, even when he knew he should return to his cabin. Before he realized where his footsteps had led him, he was over the windowsill and in her room. The sight of Tara's exquisite features glowing in the moonlight lured Sloane closer. Impulsively, he bent over the sleeping beauty and, taking a great risk, he peeled off his hood to press his lips to her sensuous mouth.

Perhaps the backward cowboy, Sloane Prescott, could not make a notable impression on Tara, but a mysterious phantom could, he mused before he lost himself to the soft, luring fragrance that clung to her. The Night Rider intrigued this inquistive nymph, rather than repulsing her as the illiterate, straightforward cowboy did. Sloane had been waltzing back and forth between two worlds, shrugging on a new personality when darkness shrouded the ranch. Both the Night Rider and Sloane Prescott were fascinated by this incorrigible beauty.

And neither of them should have been, Sloane preached to himself as he withdrew to place a bouquet of flowers upon her pillow. He was asking for trouble by allowing himself to be distracted. There was no room in his life for entanglements, especially not until he had settled his score with Merrick. He had allowed very few people to get close to him, and his compelling attraction to this sultry blonde had him teetering on an emotional tightrope, wanting to keep his distance, but unable to do so. Dammit, what was it about this vixen that drew him like a moth to a flame, knowing he would get his wings scorched if he wasn't careful?

A devilish smile rippled across Sloane's features as another thought hatched in his mind. Instead of drooling over this minx like a lovestruck schoolboy, he would taunt her. It had to be safer than allowing his lusty thoughts to run rampant, he suddenly decided. Besides, he needed to repay Tara for allowing him to believe she was ignorant of horses. And just why *had* she misled him? What had been her purpose? Sloane was unable to read the complicated workings of her mind, but he was certain that one mischievous prank deserved another. Grappling with that thought, he dragged the ghastly mask over his raven head and vanished into the shadows.

Another eerie sound, which reminded Tara of a congregation of banshees howling at the moon, interrupted her dreams. Tara blinked in the darkness, flinching when she found wild flowers lying beside her on the pillow. The petals were strewn about her as if they had been plucked and left to drift in the wind. Her wild eyes flew to the window and she swallowed with a gulp. Had she left it open? She could have sworn it had been closed when she wandered over to stare up at the stars.

A shiver ran down her spine and curled her toes. Instinctively, she drew the sheet up to her neck, wondering if something or someone was tarrying in the shadows. "This is ridiculous," Tara muttered aloud. She was alone in the room, and specters were only the products of one's overactive imagination. When she squirmed to find a more comfortable position, her gaze fell back to the wild flowers beside her. Her nostrils flared to the sweet scent of violets. Tara jerked back as if she had been stung, and then she groaned in torment. Was someone trying to drive her mad? Well, she would not

113

allow it. She would find an explanation for these strange occurrences before she left the Diamond R Ranch. There were those who swore that tormented souls roamed the earth, but Tara was not among them. No, there had to be a logical explanation, she mused as her lashes fluttered against her cheeks.

But when Tara awoke the following morning her heart flip-flopped in her chest. She glanced beside her to see not a single wild violet petal lying on her pillow. God, had she dreamed it all? Shakily, she climbed from bed and hurriedly dressed, eager to flee from the room before some other strange happening rattled her. Tara didn't dare tell anyone about her unsettling experiences for fear they would think she had toppled off the deep end. Had she? She would consider that possibility later, she told herself as she descended the stairs to join Merrick and Julia for breakfast.

But the thought kept cropping into her mind throughout the day, and she had difficulty casting it aside. She even found herself wishing Sloane had been at the ranch to preoccupy her troubled mind. He was a very distracting man, and although he tested her temper, he allowed her no time to dwell on any other thought.

When she returned to her room that evening, she cautiously poked her head inside and peered at the dancing shadows cast by the lantern. Breathing a thankful sigh that nothing was out of place and that her bed had not been infested with wild violets, she sank down on her pillows and prayed for sleep to come quickly. But the darkness was a swirling sea of visions that tormented her dreams, and she awoke with the same lingering sensation that someone had been watching her sleep and had reached out to touch her.

Chapter 7

When Tara seated herself at the supper table she offered Merrick a cheerful smile, but, as usual, it had little effect on him. It seemed to Tara that Merrick was plagued with a sour disposition. He rarely smiled and always kept to himself, barely acknowledging her presence. It set Tara to wondering if Merrick disliked her father so much that he naturally extended his animosity to her, or if he just didn't appreciate having her underfoot. While Julia chattered on about the preparations for the party, Merrick simply sat there, silently taking his meal.

"Damn!"

Tara jerked up her head to see Merrick vault from his chair and rush to the window, glaring angrily at the silver stallion and its rider racing along the caprock high above the ranch headquarters. When Tara hurried over to follow his gaze into the darkness, a small gasp bubbled from her lips. There in the pale moonlight, flying along the rim of the canyon, was the Night Rider, the specter she thought she had seen on two other occasions.

The shrill whinny of the horses in the corrals pricked the strained silence, and Merrick cursed when he saw his prize stallion leap the top rail of the fence and thunder off across the grounds, as if he were answering the call of the white stallion that spirited along the sandstone ledge.

115

Merrick stormed toward the door, his voice booming as he yelled to Sloane, who had not yet left for the evening. "Bring back that horse before he breaks his damned neck!"

Tara watched wide-eyed as Sloane hopped to his steed's back and galloped after the stallion in fast pursuit. She unwillingly admired Sloane's lithe movements. He was like a black panther springing to action, and she had no doubt that he would retrieve the flighty stallion. After visiting with several of the ranch hands, she had learned that they all admired Sloane's abilities. They all looked up to him, showing him more respect at times than even Merrick received when he voiced his brisk demands.

Julia intercepted Tara's stricken glance and then urged her back to the table to finish their meal. "Do you believe that there could be such a thing as a ghost?" she questioned quietly.

"Well, I . . ." Tara wasn't certain what she believed after her weird experiences over the previous few weeks.

"Each time this unexplainable vision appears on the rim of the canyon it spooks the livestock and the men. No one knows what to make of it. My father swears it is the spirit of his long-dead brother, Vernon, who returns to gather his share of the cattle and remuda of horses. We have lost several head of livestock over the past few years, and objects disappear and then return, but never do we find them in their original places."

"What sort of objects?" Tara questioned, her face peaked.

Julia indicated the portrait of Merrick and Vernon Russel that sat on the mantel above the fireplace. "One evening we heard strange noises in the house and came back downstairs to find the picture missing. And then two days later it was sitting in the middle of the dining room table. And then not long ago, Papa's pistol . . ." Her voice trailed off as Merrick strode back to the table.

116

Tara had the uneasy feeling that she had taken up residence in a haunted house. No wonder Merrick possessed such a sour disposition, she mused as she cast him a quick glance. One night he might wake to find his bed being hurled over the rim of the canyon with him in it. Indeed, Tara had run that fearful thought through her own mind after spending the night in a room where windows opened of their own accord and wild flowers sprouted on the pillows.

"I thought I had been visited by this so-called phantom," Tara murmured, and then paused hesitantly when Merrick's penetrating gaze drilled into her.

"Go on," he demanded gruffly.

Tara squirmed uneasily beneath his probing stare and cursed herself for mentioning the subject in the first place. "I had heard about the Night Rider of Palo Duro Canyon, and I had the strangest dream," she explained before she lifted her fork and nibbled on her meal, allowing herself time to collect her thoughts. A faint smile hovered on her lips as she shrugged. "But I attributed the episodes to my active imagination. No doubt, that is all it is. We are merely seeing something that is not truly there. I have heard of many cases in which townspeople swear they have seen strange visions and unidentifiable lights glowing in the darkness. Perhaps that is all it is, some natural phenomenon that we have yet to understand."

"I wouldn't be so certain," Merrick grunted as he parked himself in his chair. "There are several cowboys who claim to have had close encounters with the Night Rider. And Burns Dixon, the cook, swears it isn't a figment of the imagination. He believes in ghosts and has assured me on several occasions that my dead brother seeks retribution for what he lost when he passed on from this life."

Tara suddenly lost her appetite. The conversation was

unsettling, and Merrick continued to elaborate on several incidents that had cost him long hours of rounding up stampeding herds that were startled by abrupt sounds and the appearance of shapeless specters.

Now Tara wasn't certain what to believe. She knew she wanted to deny the visions and sounds she *thought* she had seen and heard, but it was difficult when her companions had accepted the strange happenings and openly attributed them to the phantom rider of Palo Duro.

When Sloane's baritone voice echoed outside the house, Tara jumped as if she had been stung. Composing herself, she followed Merrick and Julia outside to see Sloane sitting atop his gelding, leading the skittish stallion behind him.

"Vulcan cut up his leg," Sloane informed Merrick. "I'll doctor his wound before I leave for the night."

Tara would have been content to leave it at that, but Julia nudged her in the ribs. "Go with him," she insisted.

Sure, why not track a starving tiger or swim across an alligator-infested swamp, Tara thought dismally. That would be no more dangerous than traipsing after Sloane. Reluctantly, Tara ambled off the stoop and walked toward the pen to watch Sloane clean and bandage the gash on Vulcan's fetlock. She marveled at the way the flighty steed calmed when Sloane stroked his tense neck and softly reassured him.

Sloane flinched when he heard the rustling of skirts behind him and then glanced over his shoulder to see the shapely blonde in her pink taffeta gown, her bewitching face glowing in the moonlight. Lord, she was like an angel poised by the corral, so soft and desirable, and yet unapproachable.

"I thought I had seen the last of you," he murmured, careful not to raise his voice for fear of startling Vulcan. "Do you plan to race the stallion around headquarters after I patch him up? Usin' all the skills you pretended *not* to have?"

Tara winced at the undertone of mockery in his voice. "I owe you an apology," she grudgingly admitted. "I am quite capable of handling horses, and I needed no instruction."

"So I noticed," Sloane grunted caustically as he smoothed the poultice over Vulcan's tender fetlock.

"And I am sorry I left you to walk back to the ranch. I just lost my temper," she quietly confessed.

"All is forgiven," Sloane said absently as he focused his full attention on the horse's wound, coaxing Vulcan as he wrapped the bandage around his front leg. "Now, when am I to begin my dance lessons? You may be able to ride as well as I can, but I ain't particularly light on my feet when it comes to waltzes." His cobalt gaze anchored on Tara, lingering on the full swells of her breasts, just as surely as if he had reached out to caress her. "It seems we got off to a bad start, but we both have a great deal left to learn about each other."

Tara wasn't certain she wanted to learn more about Sloane Prescott. The man intimidated her, and he had the uncanny knack of causing her to lose her notorious Irish temper. Casting aside her straying thoughts, she steered the conversation to the incident that had sent Sloane in fast pursuit of the runaway stallion.

"Have you seen the Night Rider at close range?" she questioned point blank.

Sloane rose to full stature and eased the rope from Vulcan's neck before he ambled toward Tara. His gaze flooded over the trim-fitting pink gown that so temptingly displayed her tantalizing figure. He caught his breath as the moonlight spilled over her exquisite features, brushing over her inviting lips as he ached to do. She was a vision, one far more fascinating to him than the phantom rider she seemed determined to discuss. For

119

a long, fanciful moment Sloane allowed his lusty thoughts to run rampant before he finally corralled them.

"Once or twice," he belatedly replied as he braced his forearms on the top rail to devour the pert beauty on the opposite side of the fence with his eyes. "Have you, Tara? Or have you just been listenin' to Merrick rant and rave about the ghost that has appeared to haunt him?"

Tara wasn't sure she wanted the tables turned on her. She didn't want to discuss the strange happenings that haunted her, she preferred to listen to someone else's opinion. "I simply question the so-called phantom I saw tonight," she said evasively.

"You stand to see a great deal more of him if you stay here long," Sloane assured her as he smoothed an unruly strand of her silver-gold hair back into place.

The gesture surprised Tara. Sloane seemed strangely gentle, more so than she had anticipated. Perhaps her attempt to tame his forceful nature had mellowed him slightly. Maybe there was hope for him after all, she thought. Julia had her heart set on waltzing in Sloane's powerful arms, and it would be a shame to disappoint her.

When Sloane swung one long leg over the rail and then lowered himself directly in front of her, Tara tensed, her senses invaded by the manly scent of him, by the arousing way his thighs brushed against hers. Why did he have to have such a devastating effect on her? She wasn't certain she even liked the man, for heaven's sake!

Sloane studied her wary expression and then moved away, softly chuckling at her vivid reaction to him. Perhaps she found him offensive because he smelled of lathered horses and perspiration. No doubt, Tara was accustomed to perfumed dandies who had never worked a day in their lives.

Impulsively he let his hand fold around hers and he led her toward the back door of the mess-hall. "Let's go see if

120

the 'old lady' has any biscuits left over from supper. I had to miss my evenin' meal when I went ridin' off after Vulcan.''

Tara felt strangely content with her small hand buried in his. That was ridiculous, she told herself. Sloane was not the type of man who was capable of compassion or consolation. He was a callous, uncaring man, she reminded herself firmly. She had learned that much after her first encounter with him. He looked out after himself and expected others to do the same. He derived no sense of accomplishment in rescuing damsels from distress. He considered women to be a troublesome lot, a necessary evil that served only one purpose . . . Tara studied his broad, muscled back and then smiled secretively. She knew exactly what Sloane thought of women, what purpose they served for him. Although she condemned him for being a womanizer, she could not ignore the flame he kindled in her each time he touched her. He was indeed the devil's temptation. She knew exactly what kind of man he was, and yet she was still strangely drawn to him like a moth to the flame.

''Why can't you show up to eat with the rest of the men instead of lumberin' in here while I'm in the process of cleanin' the kitchen?'' Burns Dixon grunted sourly when Sloane appeared in the entrance. ''If you want somebody to prepare yer food when you finally come draggin' in at odd hours of the night, git yerself a wife.''

Sloane chortled at the cook's irascible disposition and then flashed him a grin. ''I was off chasin' ghosts again,'' he explained as he drew Tara around in front of him. ''Burns Dixon, this is Tara Winslow. She came all the way from St. Louie when word spread that the Diamond R boasted havin' the best cook this side of the Mississippi.''

The wiry-haired man grinned as his pale green eyes fastened on Tara's bewitching face. ''Chasin' ghosts, huh? Are you sure that's what you've been doin', Prescott?"

"The *lady* don't approve of anythin' else," Sloane assured him with a subtle wink. "So watch yer tongue, Burns. And for God's sake, don't offend her by suggestin' that she's got some interest in me. Tara has a fiery temper, and I've been scorched once too often by it already."

As Sloane strode toward the washroom, Tara sized up the plump, gray-haired man, who looked as if he had eaten a great deal of his own cooking. "It's a pleasure to meet you, Mr. Dixon," she said politely.

"What are you doin' hangin' 'round with a rakehell like Prescott?" Burns questioned point blank. "You look like too nice a lady to be seen with the likes of him."

Tara silently agreed, but she didn't divulge her real reason for associating with the rowdy cowboy. "Slim pickings, Mr. Dixon," she teased, her violet eyes flaring with mischief.

"I heard that," Sloane grumbled from the other room. "I thought you said it was my immaculate clothes and perfect manners that attracted you to me."

Burns snickered as he stabbed a leftover steak, dropped it on a plate, and then piled several biscuits around the edge of the tin platter. "I prefer to believe the lady, Prescott. You ain't got no manners to speak of."

Sloane's muscular form filled the doorway, his coal-black hair damp, his shirt gaping to reveal the dark matting on his chest. His grin stretched from ear to ear, and he looked so recklessly attractive that Tara could not help but gawk. Her curious eyes followed the crisp furring of hair that trickled down his lean belly and then disappeared beneath the band of his breeches. Sloane had stripped from his dusty chaps, exposing the bulging muscles of his thighs, and Tara's all-consuming gaze flickered over his virile torso. Lord, he was all man, every

122

hard, masculine inch of him!

"So Tara has informed me," Sloane remarked, and then raised an eyebrow when he glanced in her direction to see *her* undressing *him* with those intriguing lavender eyes. "But I think maybe *she's* forgotten that it ain't polite to stare."

Tara blushed seven shades of red when Sloane caught her studying him with something more than casual interest. She could have kicked herself for being so obvious. The last thing she needed was for Sloane to think she had some interest in him besides polishing his manners.

"Would you care to sample my cookin'?" Burns questioned as he set Sloane's plate at the table and gestured for Tara to take her seat.

She nodded agreeably and sank down in the chair Sloane pulled out for her. "You have taken a step in the right direction," she assured Sloane.

"I've got a few manners," he insisted as he folded his long, muscular body into the seat across from her. "I just don't usually have much call to use them."

Tara was surprised to find Burns's biscuits melting in her mouth. Obviously, he had mastered the culinary art, she decided as he pushed a slice of blueberry pie beneath her nose, tempting her past resistance. She had lost her appetite earlier that evening when the phantom had appeared, but now she found it had returned, thanks to Burns's delicious pastry.

After Sloane had finished his meal and properly raved about Burns's cooking, he shuffled Tara through the back door. "His name don't imply that he cremates his cookin', does it?" he chuckled.

"No, he seems to be an excellent cook," Tara concurred and then peered curiously at Sloane. "Why do you call Burns the 'old lady' behind his back but never to his face?"

123

"Because he'd poison my food," Sloane snickered as he led Tara around the corrals. "It's only a teasin'ly affectionate term the cowhands use, but nobody would dare to call him the 'old lady' while they was within earshot. Burns's temper is as fiery as yers. That's how he got his nickname, not from his cookin'.'"

Tara chose to ignore his jibe, certain it would instigate another argument. Sloane had the ability to irritate her, and Tara was trying very hard to be civil to him, for Julia's sake, of course.

"Burns seems to be a very likable sort. Has he always worked for Merrick or did he wander in, just like you did?" she inquired.

"He's been with Merrick since the beginnin'. I heard he was there the night Vernon Russel was killed, but he never talks about it to anyone. You might say Burns is another cornerstone of the Diamond R Ranch," Sloane explained blandly.

"Do you believe Merrick murdered his brother?" Tara questioned as they ambled back to the pen to check on Vulcan. She had interrogated Sloane on the matter once before and had come to a dead end, so to speak. And to her chagrin, Sloane tactfully avoided the probing inquiry again.

"I thought you was goin' to teach me to dance instead of firin' questions at me," he reminded her, flashing her one of those ornery grins that assured her that he would not be pressured into conversing on subjects he had no desire to discuss.

Heaving a defeated sigh, Tara decided to save her questions for Burns Dixon, since Sloane was as tight-lipped as a clam. "My pleasure, Mr. Prescott," she murmured with mock politeness. Curtseying gracefully, she offered Sloane her hand. "Shall I hum the appropriate rhythm for the waltz, or would you prefer that I count the steps?"

"We'll make our own music," Sloane drawled melodically. A grin of roguish anticipation grazed his lips as his hand molded itself to the shapely curve of her derriere.

Tara promptly resettled his wayward hand on her waist, leveling Sloane a condescending frown. "We will do this *my* way, or we will not do it at all," she told him curtly. "I will not have the stuffing squeezed out of me or fight for my virtue with the pretense of teaching you how to dance."

Sloane's sensuous lips turned down at the corners. "Is the only way to get along with you to let you have your way? Must you *always* have your way, woman?" he questioned in a pouting tone.

"Must you always have *yours?*" she parried.

"Obviously not," Sloane grunted disgustedly. "If I had my way we'd be doin' more than dancin'."

"That is all I'm offering." Tara laid a stiff arm against his broad shoulder to keep him a respectable distance away. "The basic step is quite simple," she explained matter-of-factly, trying to keep her heart from hammering against her ribs and alerting Sloane that his nearness had an unsettling effect on her.

"Let's hope so," Sloane murmured, pulling her closer, dissatisfied with having her so far away. "I never considered myself to be light of foot."

"I only ask that you tread lightly on mine," Tara teased as she pressed a determined hand to the hard wall of his chest, holding him at bay (or as far away as anyone could when approached by an overpowering cowboy who was too hard-headed to accept defeat). "Now step forward with your left foot . . . and then your right one moves . . . ouch!" Her pained squawk echoed in the darkness.

"S'cuse me," Sloane whispered, his warm breath caressing her cheek, causing her to forget the pain in her foot.

When his sinewy arm tightened about her, drawing her full length against his muscular body, her heart catapulted into her throat, nearly strangling her. The musky aroma and the titillating feel of his virile body swaying with hers were causing a riptide of sensations. Tara was having one hell of a time concentrating on dancing when she was engulfed in the unending circle of Sloane's arms.

"We had better begin again," she insisted all too breathlessly. Her lashes fluttered up to offer him an encouraging smile and her overworked heart missed several vital beats when her eyes locked with his. She couldn't have looked away if her life depended on it. There was a subtle message in his cobalt gaze, one Tara was afraid to interpret.

She held her breath as his raven head descended toward hers. His mouth took hers hostage, snatching her breath away and then generously giving it back, surprising her with his unusual display of tenderness. The fire of desire was still there, but he did not assault her with abrupt force. Tara feared she would melt all over him when his strong arms gathered her even closer. She could feel his heart thundering against her breasts, hear his ragged breath as his kiss deepened to explore the soft recesses of her mouth.

The world tilted sideways as his tongue mated with hers in a most seductive way. A tiny moan bubbled in her throat as his exploring hands rediscovered each curve and swell she possessed. His index finger traced the creamy swell of her breast and then intruded beneath the taffeta and lace to tease the dusky peak.

Sloane groaned in sweet torment as his lips skitted along the trim column of her throat and then mapped the soft curve of her shoulder. Tara swallowed air as his moist lips investigated the neckline of her gown, leaving her flesh tingling in response to his skillful touch.

"Sloane . . . no." Tara made a feeble attempt to protest as he drew the sleeve of her dress from her shoulder, exposing her breasts to his appreciative gaze.

The arousing feel of his lips whispering across her bare skin touched off a chain reaction of sensations, and Tara was vividly aware of the longing that unfurled in the pit of her stomach. She was drawn beneath his hypnotic spell, lured deeper into the tangled web of desire Sloane had woven about her.

What was the matter with her? She had never allowed a man to take such outrageous privileges. She had been tempted to blow Cal Johnson to smithereens when he had assaulted her, but when Sloane intimately caressed her, logic fled in the path of fire that his touch created, and every barrier of defense fell before he confronted it.

"I want you," he assured her hoarsely. "I've never wanted another woman the way I want you."

His hushed words brought Tara to her senses and she tore herself away, clutching to cover herself from his devouring gaze. How many times had he whispered that line to the woman he had captured in his arms? Tara hesitated to guess. Sloane probably had a harem of women waiting for him in every town, and he undoubtedly used that comment so often that it naturally tripped off his tongue. Next he would be insisting that he had fallen in love with her, she mused, and if a woman wasn't closely guarding her heart she might allow herself to believe it. But Tara was not so naive that she didn't realize a man's purpose when he was squeezing her in two and fantasizing about making love to her. She was not so vain as to think a man like Sloane could truly care for her. He was physically attracted to her, she was available, and that was all that mattered to him. After one tumble in the grass he would be on his merry way to carve another notch in his bedpost, and Tara had no doubt that Sloane's bedposts resembled intricately carved totem poles.

"I cannot allow it," Tara choked out, attempting to regain her flustered composure as she retreated against the shed. But Sloane crowded her like the cavalry pinning the enemy's back to the wall. "Please, Sloane, can't we just . . ."

"No," he rasped, cutting her off in midsentence, his dark blue eyes searing her with the heat of his desire. "I'll never be satisfied with a kiss or caress." He braced his arms on either side of her, allowing her no means of escape. "I want more from you, and I think you would be willin' if you would step down from . . ."

"Prescott, where the hell are you?" Burns Dixon called.

Sloane swore under his breath as he pushed away from the wall. "Damn, can't a man have a moment's privacy around here?" He swung around to see Burns lumbering toward him, causing him to scowl in annoyance. "What do you want?"

"Loren is lookin' for you," Burns informed him, snickering at Sloane, who looked like black thunder.

Grumbling at the untimely interruption, Sloane stalked off after Burns as he waddled back toward the bunkhouse. Tara half-collapsed against the shed and breathed a shuddering sigh as the two men disappeared from sight. She had only known Sloane a week, and already he was making outrageous demands on her. Sweet merciful heavens! What was she to do? She had never met anyone as persistent and forceful as Sloane, and she was at a loss as to how to handle him. Breathing hard in exasperation, Tara wobbled to the porch and smoothed her gown into place before entering the house. What she needed was a cold bath to cool the fires that had come dangerously close to blazing out of control. Tara wasted no time in filling a tub and soaking in it. And then a thoughtful frown knitted her brow as she remembered

128

seeing Julia lingering in the shadows with a man at the corner of the house just as she had stepped onto the porch. What the devil was going on around here, she asked herself. Something was *rotten* in *Texas*.

Glancing cautiously about him, Terrance Winslow made his way to the abandoned shack where the Night Rider had requested their rendezvous. Reasonably certain that he had escaped Clarendon unnoticed, Terrance cast one last fleeting glance over his shoulder and then pushed open the door to find the Night Rider sprawled in a chair with his feet propped up on the edge of the table.

"Hasn't anyone ever told you it isn't wise to keep the devil or a phantom waiting?" the Night Rider taunted as Terrance strode over to plop down in the seat across from him.

Terrance snorted at the Night Rider's meager attempt to humor him. There was a great deal on his mind, and nothing could amuse him until they had finished their conversation and his fears were put to rest.

"Have you seen my daughter since she arrived at the Diamond R?" he questioned, cutting to the heart of the matter.

The hooded figure nodded slightly and then straightened in his seat to prop his forearms on the edge of the table, his long shiny poncho spilling about him to disguise the size and shape of his body. "I have seen her on more occasions than I would have preferred," he grumbled sourly. "Your daughter has the curiosity of a cat. One night she was even foolish enough to straddle an unsaddled horse and come ghost hunting."

The faintest hint of a smile found the corners of Terrance's mouth. "I should have warned you about her. She is relentless when it comes to knowing exactly what is going on around her. I doubt you will be able to frighten her away," Terrance informed him.

"*Dar por cierto*," the Night Rider grunted. "It takes more than a word of warning to send her scampering like a frightened rabbit."

A proud smile pursed Terrance's lips as he peered over at the hooded face across from him. "She is a great deal like her father," he boasted. "I only hope her inquisitiveness doesn't hinder you. I think she would be of assistance to your cause, if you would take her into your confidence."

"I prefer to continue my crusade against Merrick without her help," the Night Rider insisted flatly. "I'm not sure I want to trust her with my carefully guarded secret." Cobalt-blue eyes drilled into Terrance. "Why did you allow her to come to the ranch in the first place if you knew she would hound me? I have enough difficulty playing this charade without your inquisitive daughter sniffing at my heels like a bloodhound."

Terrance's shoulder lifted in a noncommittal shrug. "Julia invited Tara to visit Palo Duro," he explained evasively. "Tara is a vivacious woman. She would soon tire of following me around the office. I don't want her to rush back to St. Louis after we have been separated these past three years. At least, while she is staying at the Diamond R I can visit her occasionally." A wry smile pursed his lips. "It also gives me a good excuse to invade Merrick's kingdom without causing suspicion."

Sloane let the matter drop to pursue the matter that was foremost on his mind. "What did the sheriff have to say about the bullet that killed Don Miguel?"

Terrance fished into his pocket to retrieve the bullet and then dropped it in the Night Rider's gloved hand, sighing heavily. "This one didn't match the one that took Don Miguel's life."

130

Sloane growled disgustedly. He had taken Merrick's pistol, certain it was the murder weapon. He should have known Merrick was too clever to leave evidence lying around his house. Or had Merrick hired someone to dispose of Don Miguel instead of seeing to the grizzly matter himself?

"I told you it wouldn't be easy to trap a weasel like Merrick. Even the locket didn't offer solid proof, as you had hoped. You will have to find another way to entrap him and force him to confess to his crimes."

"His financial investors are certain he is swindling them out of their profits, and I can't prove that either," Sloane grumbled irritably. "But Merrick must be stashing cattle somewhere and pocketing the cash when the beeves reach market. He has to be working with someone. But damned if I know who it might be."

Terrance eased back in his chair and heaved a perplexed sigh. "It certainly has me bumfuzzled. I have tried to find out everything I can about Merrick, but I can't figure what he's doing. My harassment only infuriates him, and I'm beginning to think it would have been wiser to pretend to befriend him."

The Night Rider nodded mutely and then climbed to his feet, his incandescent poncho swirling about him as he moved silently toward the door. There he paused to glance back at Terrance. "I would give most anything to know how Merrick has shuffled his ledgers to cover his conniving tactics. But surely he will expose himself during spring roundup. I intend to make careful inventory of his stock. He has to be moving cattle and hiding them until the majority of the herd is driven to Harrold. But no such arrangements could be made without assistance. Someone has to be selling Diamond R cattle under another brand."

"If we have the patience to wait a few more weeks,

perhaps you can uncover his ploy," Terrance encouraged him. "And I am itching to see the look on Russel's face when he realizes the Night Rider of Palo Duro has exposed him for what he is—a swindler and a murderer."

"You cannot be as anxious as I am," the Night Rider muttered, his quiet words seeping around the edge of the door as it silently closed behind him.

Chapter 8

Two more days of carefully avoiding Sloane had played havoc with Tara's sanity. She felt as if the world were crowding in on her. Each time she saw him at a distance she could feel his penetrating blue eyes drilling into her, watching her every move, silently calling to her. Tara was frankly bewildered by her reaction to a man she was trying very hard not to like. But when he touched her, she could feel her traitorous body yielding to his brazen touch, wanting more, aching for him in ways that startled her. It was as if she had been there before, enjoying his caresses as they explored her trembling flesh. But that was impossible, Tara kept reminding herself. She had never experienced those sensations before, certainly not with Joseph Rutherford. It was as if there were another woman imprisoned inside her, one who knew and understood the meaning of passion, the brand Sloane was offering.

Tara frowned at her straying thoughts, wishing she could sort out the muddled visions that flowed and then ebbed into the hidden corners of her mind. It was Sloane who aroused her, and to make matters worse, Julia constantly hovered around him, insisting that Tara also spend time alone with him to groom him for the upcoming ball. But Tara didn't dare allow the magnetic attraction between them get out of hand. Sloane stirred a flood of emotions in her, and Tara wasn't sure how much longer she could trust herself to pull away when her body had developed a mind of its own and hungered for the taste of his devouring kisses and familiar caresses.

Her eyes took on a faraway look as she peered out at the glorious sunset. Another thought kept nagging at her. She was intrigued by the Night Rider, the phantom whose soft, velvety voice sent eerie tingles down her spine. How could she be fascinated by an apparition that blossomed from the shadows, she berated herself. She didn't know for certain if that quiet, husky whisper that had tried to communicate with her in Spanish and then English was flesh or spirit, or if she had dreamed that same crazed dream.

Her lashes fluttered shut as she called upon that forbidden memory that frightened her and confused her, trying desperately to untangle the recollections. In her mind's eye she could see that hooded face glowing in the golden light while she was hanging in limbo. The images were cloudy and distorted, the voice soft and raspy, compelling and soothing. Tara squeezed her eyes shut and then heaved a sigh as the memory twisted and swirled about her. The phantom had been looming above her with a knife, prepared to carve her to pieces, and then his strength had swallowed her. It was as if some strange spell had been cast upon her, as if gentle hands were swimming over a sea of bare flesh, arousing her, exciting her in ways she had never experienced until Sloane had boldly set his hands upon her to cause the memories to intermingle with reality.

Tara stared out the window, watching the waning sunlight fade above the sandstone ridge of the canyon. She had always prided herself on having her feet planted solidly on the ground. She had never been a hopeless romantic with her head in the clouds, until she had been knocked unconscious and lost what little sense she had

been born with. Now she was imagining she had been
visited by a wraith shrouded in phosphorescent white
whose husky voice could catch and hold her spellbound.
She was being drawn to a rough-edged cowboy who was a
far cry from Prince Charming, and who, despite his long
list of peccadilloes, aroused her. There was something
strange and frightening about Sloane. It was like standing
too close to a volcano that was about to erupt. She could
feel the fire and see the flames of desire in his eyes when
he swept her up in his arms. He could infuriate her and
excite her, constantly tempting her to discard her better
judgment and yield to his overpowering force.

Each time he touched her she found herself wondering
what it would be like to sleep in his arms, and she had to
pinch herself to bring her back to her senses, reminding
herself that she should avoid him as if he had contracted
leprosy. Lord, Sloane was the apple of *Julia's* eye. Her
young friend planned and plotted to spend private
moments with him, savoring every minute and losing
herself in his laughing eyes.

Damn, this mental tug-of-war was tearing her to
pieces, bit by excruciating bit! She was attracted to that
roguishly handsome cowboy who was as tough as leather,
strong as a bull, and as irresistible as the warmth of
sunshine on a spring morning.

"What do you think of Palo Duro now that you have
lived within these pastel-colored walls?" Merrick questioned as he strode up behind Tara, startling her out of
her pensive contemplations.

Tara continued to peer into the spectacular sunset. A
rueful smile hovered on her lips as she glanced toward
the corral to see Julia perched on the fence while Sloane
coaxed Vulcan to accept the bridle and saddle. Her gaze
swung back to the towering walls. It was like being within
the spectrum of a rainbow as the soft blues, yellows, and
oranges glowed in the faint light.

"I have never seen anything so glorious," she admitted honestly. "Your ranch makes everything in St. Louis seem small and insignificant in comparison."

"It has taken blood, sweat, and endless toil to maintain the Diamond R Ranch," Merrick replied, his voice grating with a hint of bitterness.

"Do you ever regret laboring over it?" Tara turned to study Merrick's stern, commanding features. Even when he attempted to be pleasant to her, there was something distant and remote about him. She couldn't quite put her finger on it, but there was something subtly threatening about Merrick Russel.

"I do what I have to do to keep what is mine. Even my own brother tried to shatter the dream of making Palo Duro a rancher's paradise. What I struggled to make reality, Vernon would have allowed to slip through our fingers. And still he haunts me, even after all these years," he gritted out, his eyes flashing with something akin to hatred. As if he had caught himself putting the secret thought to tongue, Merrick stiffened, his expression becoming a carefully blank stare. "I suppose nothing worth having is obtained without sacrifice."

Tara frowned at Merrick's words. Had there truly been dissension between the two brothers? Had anyone ever bothered to listen to Merrick's rendition of what had happened those many years ago, or had they relied upon suspicion and rumor? Had they made Merrick out to be a villain when he was only a man with an obsessive dream? Was this phantom rider who tormented Merrick really a vindictive spirit that sought to torture him and make him pay for what he had created on the edge of civilization? Her experience with the Night Rider was something totally different from the picture Merrick painted of the ghastly vision that kept constant vigil over Palo Duro. The contradiction that clouded her mind was confusing.

And what about her father? Had Terrance Winslow

taken it upon himself to destroy Merrick with the power of the press, just because he had taken a disliking to a man who kept to himself and ruled his kingdom with an iron hand? Tara chided herself for mistrusting her father. Surely he had good reason for disliking Merrick. But why had Terrance avoided the subject when she brought it up? She knew her father as a daughter would know him, but did she truly understand the man, Terrance Winslow? My God, how could she be suspicious of her own father? And worse, how could she be suspicious of *anyone* when she hardly knew anyone in Texas well enough to form an opinion of them? They were all strangers, except Julia, who was flighty, fickle, and yet charming company. Tara couldn't very well pass sentence on anyone after her brief stay in Texas, she realized. She had never been narrowminded or opinionated and she was not about to start now.

Merrick laughed without humor and then took a sip of the coffee he held clamped in his right hand. Thoughtfully, he stared across the valley.

"And as if I am not forced to live with enough torment from a phantom that spooks my livestock, frightens my men while they stand watch over the herd, your father hounds me unmercifully. He behaves as if I am a blackhearted soul who has committed any number of unforgivable crimes." His breath came out in a rush and then he shot forth a glance, holding Tara captive. "Rumor has it that I murdered my own brother, but it's a lie. We had driven our herd of longhorns into the canyon, and Vernon was sorting through the calves when the Comancheros decided to steal a few beeves to feast upon. All the confusion started the stampede, and Vernon couldn't get out of the way. There was nothing I could do to save him. But those who envy my power and position claim I am a murdering tyrant."

"I'm sorry." Tara blinked misty violet eyes as he

137

painted the ghastly picture. Perhaps it was jealousy that incited the cruel rumors. His neighbors had made life hell for him. No wonder he possessed such a sour disposition.

"I wish your father was as compassionate and understanding." Merrick managed the semblance of a smile. "But he has his heart set on detesting me, blaming me for Don Miguel's death, when I was nowhere near the scene of the crime."

Tara bit her tongue before she confessed that she had been with Don Miguel that night. Her father had cautioned her to keep silent. Although she wasn't certain whom to believe, she decided discretion was advisable. It was best to remain neutral until one knew friend from foe. Whoever had murdered Don Miguel knew they had not been alone that night, and if she exposed her involvement, her life might be in more danger, even if she couldn't identify the assassin.

"Excuse me, Merrick," Tara murmured as she ambled across the parlor. "I think the long hours I have spent in the sun this afternoon have caught up with me. I would like to call it a night. Tell Julia I will see her in the morning."

Heaving a frustrated sigh, Tara stared at the confining walls of her room. In truth she wasn't fatigued, but rather as restless as a caged cat. She yearned for freedom to ride, to be alone with her confused thoughts. A wry smile pursed her lips as she watched darkness settle on the canyon. She would have the freedom she craved, she assured herself. She would sneak from the house and wander at will, away from Sloane Prescott and Merrick Russel.

Anticipation spurted through her as she stepped into her black riding skirt and black blouse, hoping no one would notice her if she blended in with the darkness. Cautiously she moved down the stairs, hearing Merrick and Julia's quiet murmurings in the parlor. Tara tiptoed through the hall and veered around the corner toward the back door near Merrick's downstairs bedroom. Once she had carefully closed the door behind her, she breathed a thankful sigh. She caught the scent of rain in the southwest breeze, but she didn't care if she were caught in a downpour. She longed for solitude, and besides, she would return long before the storm clouds rolled over Palo Duro.

Tara murmured a silent prayer of thanks when she crept to the horse pen to find Sloane had left for the night. The last person she wanted to see this evening was that distractingly handsome cowboy. She was in a wild, reckless mood and she didn't trust herself alone with Sloane. After leading Hazel from the corral, she retrieved a saddle and bridle from the tack room. She swung onto the mare's back and picked her way through the trees until she reached the path that led up to the towering caprock. The wind whistled around the ledge, sending an eerie chill down her spine, and she tensed when the mare pricked up her ears and quivered beneath her.

The sound of hooves thundering above her made her gasp, and she glanced up to see the silver-white stallion flying around the ledge a few hundred yards away from her. It wasn't the howling wind that sounded like a galloping stallion, Tara told herself. It wasn't the distant rumble of thunder that reminded her of a raspy voice that echoed in her mind. She was not seeing a phantom on horseback, she assured herself, only half-believing it. There was someone on the ledge above her, and she would not rest until she knew who it was!

While her heart played a frantic tune on her ribs, Tara nudged the uneasy mare up the winding path. She would follow the Night Rider until he evaporated into the darkness or showed himself to be mortal, she decided impulsively. After all, what else did she have to do besides chase ghosts?

Keeping a cautious distance, she watched the white stallion spirit along the rim of Palo Duro, directly above the headquarters of the Diamond R Ranch, and then swing south, clinging so dangerously close to the jaws of the canyon that Tara was certain only a phantom and his horse could keep such a reckless pace in the darkness without tumbling from the caprock and falling the twelve hundred feet to the jagged rocks that lined the floor of the canyon. The longer she watched the amazing feats of the shapeless specter and his winged stallion, the more confused she became. Tara was sure she would have fallen to her death if she had forced the mare into her swiftest gait and reined her so near the canyon rim. She could not fathom that even the most surefooted animal and experienced rider could accomplish what the phantom was doing and survive it!

Relentlessly she trailed behind the Night Rider, but at a safe distance from the canyon rim, her eyes fixed on the specter that raced the wind. But then he was gone, and Tara blinked bewilderedly as she reined Hazel to a halt. It was as if the winged stallion had sailed off the edge of the cliff. Squinting in the darkness, Tara urged the mare toward the clump of sagebrush ahead of her and spied a narrow path that wound into the canyon. Another rumble of thunder caught in the wind and echoed about her as she clamped her hand on the saddle horn and held on tightly as Hazel skidded down the loose dirt. Below her, partially concealed by the jagged ledge and thick cedars, Tara glimpsed the swirl of incandescent white, and her heart very nearly leaped from her chest and plunged off the cliff. Drawn by the mysterious vision, Tara forced Hazel to pick her way along the ragged boulders, descending deeper into the jaws of the canyon.

And then the vision disappeared completely, and even the jagged bolt of lightning that sizzled across the sky did not bring the specter from the whistling darkness. Had

140

her eyes truly played tricks on her, Tara asked herself as she twisted in the saddle to look behind her? Where the devil was that phantom?

Tara covered her mouth to muffle the frightened shriek when Hazel lost her footing and stumbled on the narrow ledge. When the steed had recovered her balance, Tara decided to dismount instead of risking the fall. Slowly, she wove her way deeper into the canyon, which was shrouded in darkness, pursuing a vision that she was beginning to wonder if she had seen at all. Had the Night Rider ridden into the sandstone walls? Tara gulped over the lump of fear that lodged in her throat, strangling her breath. Her lashes swept up to see that the looming clouds had finally swallowed up the moon and stars, leaving her no guiding light. Another crack of thunder rumbled along the stone ledges, and Tara nearly jumped out of her boots. The scream of terror that would have burst from her lips died in her throat when a gloved hand clamped over her mouth.

Her rigid body was pulled against the solid form of a man, not a ghost, Tara told herself. He was cloaked in white from head to toe, and Tara nearly died from fright when the taunting dreams that had been hounding her the past few weeks collided with reality. This was no supernatural phantom. It was a man dressed in a flowing white poncho and hood that disguised his identity. Ghosts didn't have bodies, did they? Had Vernon Russel been alive all these years, letting his brother think he was being haunted by a vindictive phantom?

"Keep quiet, *querida*," came the low raspy voice so close to her ear. "If you value your life, you will do exactly as I command."

Tara nodded her consent and then breathed a ragged breath when the Night Rider removed his gloved hand from her mouth. As if she were as light as a feather, the Night Rider scooped her up in his arms and strode back to

141

the cedar tree where the white stallion was tethered. The steed pranced uneasily beneath her as his master swung up behind her and then touched the reins. After snatching up Hazel's trailing reins, the rider urged his steed along the ledge.

Another clap of thunder rattled off the sandstone walls, coming at Tara from all directions, and she shivered uncontrollably, certain the same curiosity that had killed the cat was about to become the death of her as well. Blast it, why hadn't she minded her own business? She delighted in uncovering secrets, but she didn't relish the idea of burying herself in the process.

Her wild eyes searched the darkness, frantically trying to devise a method of escape. But she was trapped! If she threw herself off the prancing stallion she would break her foolish neck. Damnation, why couldn't she have been content to remain in her room, counting the flowers in the wallpaper? Why hadn't she ridden in the opposite direction when she spied the so-called phantom racing against the wind? Because Sloane Prescott had stripped her of what little sense she had! She might discover the truth about the Night Rider, but at what price . . . Tara swallowed hard and attempted to inhale a breath, but it was next to impossible when her heart had broken loose and was stampeding around her rib cage.

An unseen smile played on the Night Rider's lips as he held Tara's quaking body against his. The inquisitive little imp. He should have known she couldn't leave well enough alone. The cowhands had spent too many nights on the open range listening to coyotes howl and the wind whisper to risk chasing phantoms. Never once had he been followed, until this whirlwind of trouble blew into Palo Duro Canyon. If he frightened the life out of her by abducting her, it would serve her right.

When the white stallion set his feet on solid ground, the Night Rider swung from the saddle, clamped a vise grip on Tara's arm, and then led the steed to the cave that was carved in the side of the canyon.

"You have risked a great deal to learn the truth, *mi niña*," he murmured as he pulled the bridle from the stallion's head and then fastened the gate at the mouth of the secluded cave.

"Who are you?" Tara demanded to know, wondering where she had found the courage to pose the question when she was trembling as if she were straddling a fault line during an earthquake.

The Night Rider's husky chuckle caught in the wind and was whisked away as he propelled Tara toward the shack that was nestled beneath the cottonwood trees. "You will know soon enough. I only pray that the shock of seeing my ghastly face will not frighten the life out of you. The shock may be too great for one so delicate, señorita."

Tara choked on her breath as she peered up at the hooded face, seeing no more than the jagged holes where his eyes should have been. It was like peering into a bottomless pit, and Tara began imagining all sorts of horrible things. Had Vernon Russel's face been broken to bits during the stampede? Had he survived when Merrick and Burns had given him up for dead? Could he have scratched and clawed his way out of a shallow grave, and with the vengeance of Satan, returned to hound his brother for the rest of his days?

The impulse to flee was overwhelming, and Tara threw herself away from the phantom shrouded in glowing white, screaming bloody murder as she ran blindly ahead, uncaring where she was going as long as it was *away* from the distorted figure of a man who lurked beneath the concealing poncho and hood.

An enraged growl erupted from behind her, and Tara hit the ground as the phantom leaped at her. "You should have run the opposite direction the first time you saw me," he jeered as he rolled to his feet and yanked Tara up beside him. "You shall learn my secret, *querida*, but the price will be higher than you can imagine."

Tara had no difficulty imagining what price she would be forced to pay for her knowledge. No doubt she would die with the carefully guarded secret. Dead women could tell no tales, she reminded herself shakily as she was dragged along with the Night Rider's swift, impatient strides.

Dammit, why hadn't she stayed in St. Louis? Her mother would never forgive her for traipsing off across Texas and getting herself killed. If she lived through the ghastly nightmare she would change her ways, Tara instantly decided. From this day forward she would control her fiery temper, never allow a foul word to escape her lips, and behave like a veritable saint. Her eyes drifted heavenward, only to see lightning bolts popping like punishing whips. Tara had the unnerving feeling she wouldn't be able to talk her way out of this one. She was staring death in the face, and he was shrouded in white and possessed bottomless black pits where his eyes should have been!

Chapter 9

Tara's wide violet eyes circled the dark cabin as the Night Rider hustled her inside. A muddled frown captured her features when the cloaked figure lighted the lantern. There was something strangely familiar about her surroundings, as if she had visited this shack before. Her heart stopped when she peered over at the awesome form shrouded in white, seeing a thin mesh of black covering the ragged holes in his hood.

She *had* been here before, her mind screamed at her. It hadn't been a dream. This man, whoever he was, had tried to kill her, and then he had tried to . . . Tara's terrified thoughts swirled in chaotic disarray as she tried to sort through the incident that had remained a clouded mystery in her mind. His hands had been on her and his lips had played on hers! Sweet merciful heavens! What else had the Night Rider done to her while she was drifting in a mindless whirl? She shuddered, remembering the night she had discovered the wild violet lying on her pillow, only to wake the following morning to find the petals had vanished. The Night Rider had been prowling around her room, just as he had sneaked into the dark house to swipe Merrick's protraits and pistols.

Impulsively, Tara reached for the derringer she carried with her, and then, forgetting that she had intended to behave in a saintly manner, she cursed under her breath. The Night Rider reached beneath his poncho to retrieve her hand gun, holding it just out of her reach.

"Looking for this?" he questioned, his voice ringing with mocking amusement. "I took the liberty of removing it from your pocket when I felt it lying against my leg during our ride."

When he stepped from the shadows, allowing the lantern light to filter through the hazy veil that covered his eyes, Tara strangled on her breath. Her discerning gaze caught the hint of blue behind the dark mesh. Twinkling pools of cobalt flooded over her, and Tara half-collapsed in astonishment.

"Sloane?" Her trembling voice was no more than a whisper. But how could it be? She had seen him in the corral the night the Ghost Rider had appeared to send Vulcan leaping over the fence. "It can't be," she mused aloud, refusing to believe what she thought she had seen behind that crumpled hood. That wasn't Sloane's voice. The Night Rider's tone was like rich, black velvet, and the Sloane she knew could massacre the English language. This stranger had perfect command of both Spanish and English. Could Sloane have had a twin? she asked herself frantically. Those eyes! No one had eyes like his, eyes that leaped with living fire, ones so sparkling blue that a woman could drown in them.

A low chuckle erupted from his massive chest as he dragged the white hood from his raven head and watched Tara's lavender eyes grow round with shock and disbelief. Bowing overexaggeratedly, he swept his arm through the air and laid it over his heart. "At your service, señorita."

The lazy drawl had vanished, and for a long, breathless moment Tara could only stare at him. "But I saw you on the ranch when the phantom appeared. How could you have been two places at once?" she croaked and then peered bug-eyed at him. "Unless there *are* actually two of you?"

"I truly wish there were," he said with a forlorn sigh. "It would make this charade immensely easier to carry out. But being merely mortal, I find myself burning the candle at both ends to continue working during the day and prowling the night."

"But how . . ."

Sloane spun on his heels, strode over to the rug that lay before the hearth, and kicked it aside with the toe of his boot. Lifting a trap door, he retrieved a dummy dressed in an identical poncho and white leggings.

Tara's mouth gaped open wide enough for a covey of prairie chickens to nest, and she shook her head as if she still couldn't make any sense of it.

"I train horses, remember?" he prompted, flashing her a devilish grin. "It took me four months to teach the moon-eyed stallion to nudge open the gate with his nose and gallop along the caprock with *this* phantom on his back instead of me. Diablo runs the route and then returns to the cave, patiently waiting for me to arrive and unstrap his rider."

Tara would have wilted onto the floor if she hadn't braced her hands on the chair beside her. "But why? I don't understand your personal vendetta against Merrick. And why did my father lie to me? He must have known you were the one who delivered me to safety that night I murdered Don Miguel."

"You?" It was Sloane's turn to stare at her in disbelief.

Tears bled down her cheeks as the horrible memory loomed before her. "I may as well have," she choked. "Don Miguel warned me not to retrieve my derringer, but, like a fool, I fished it from my purse and his assassin reacted. It was my fault."

Sloane moved silently toward her, his eyes mellow with compassion. "You are not to blame," he murmured as he gently curled his finger beneath her chin and raised her misty eyes to his. "Don Miguel posed a threat to Merrick and he disposed of him. My appearance could have been just as much to blame for what happened."

"How can you be so certain it was Merrick who was behind the killing?" Tara questioned as she studied Sloane in an altogether different light, fascinated, and yet very unsure of a man she thought she knew, but obviously didn't know at all.

"There is much you don't understand," Sloane insisted as he scooped up the dummy and tossed it into the tunnel. "And yet you know too much." He turned back to her, his eyes falling to the full swells of her breasts that were exposed by the gaping neckline of her black blouse. "The question is . . . what am I to do with you?"

Tara wasn't certain she wanted to know the answer that was buzzing through his mind. He looked blatantly dangerous with that mischievous glint in his eyes. She had been frightened within an inch of her life and then very nearly shocked to death. She pivoted toward the door, hoping to escape before Sloane caught up with her. He lunged like a mountain lion, pinning her against the door before she could whip it open and flee into the darkness.

The feel of his virile body mashing into hers triggered memories that Tara was in no mood to face at the moment, memories that were riddled with confusion, that swirled around a rough-edged cowboy and a phantom who had the uncanny knack of disappearing into thin air when it suited his whim.

His strong hands fastened around her waist as he turned her to face his roguish grin. Deep blue eyes blazing with passion held her captive, and Tara trembled uncontrollably as his muscled thigh insinuated itself between her legs.

"I assured you that the price of learning my identity

would come high," he rasped, his voice bubbling with barely contained passion.

Sloane had never been able to put the memory of that first night out of his mind. Each time he looked at this violet-eyed beauty he could envision her lying on his bed, her ivory skin glowing in the lantern light. He could feel her soft lips surrendering to his kiss. He had become obsessed with her, forcing his attentions on her even when she shied away. But the fire was there each time he touched her, and it was like flying into a flame. Tara burned him alive with frustrated passion, and he longed to lose himself in her, as he very nearly had that first night. He had lived with the foretaste of heaven, craving more each time he took this silver-blond minx in his arms and forced her to surrender to a passion that was eating him alive.

And yet, Tara knew enough to be dangerous. As much as he desired her, he wasn't certain he could trust her.

"I want you," he breathed as his raven head moved deliberately toward hers. "But damned if I know what to do with you."

"Let me go!" Tara railed, frightened by the upheaval of emotions that were tearing at her sanity. His body pressed intimately to hers, kindling fires Tara knew could burn out of control. "Please . . . I won't betray your secret."

At the moment, his carefully guarded secret was not his foremost concern. He wanted this feisty minx and had since the moment he'd laid eyes on her. He knew Terrance Winslow would be livid with rage if he laid a hand on his precious daughter. But dammit, a man could only endure so much temptation, and Sloane had found his breaking point.

"What are you prepared to offer in exchange for your life?" he queried as he studied her with incredible hunger.

149

Tara met his probing stare, feeling her temper rolling at a slow boil. She knew full well what he insinuated. How could she surrender to this mysterious man when Julia wanted him? Wasn't it enough that his kisses and caresses made mincemeat of her emotions? Hadn't he humiliated her by allowing her to believe he was a backward cowboy who saw her as an available plaything? And she shuddered to think what had happened that night he had brought her here to his cabin. The lout! He had his nerve!

Her delicate chin lifted to a proud angle as she pressed her small, but determined, hands to his chest and shoved him away. "I am not about to compromise my virtue, if that is what is running through your sordid mind. However, I am prepared to offer you money. My grandfather is quite wealthy, and . . ."

Sloane scoffed at her attempt to bribe him with coins. There wasn't enough gold in the federal treasury to match what he craved. "Money doesn't interest me, *querida*," he assured her, his cobalt eyes pouring over her like hot liquid, scorching her. One tanned finger investigated the plunging neckline of her thin black blouse, which had come partially unbuttoned during their tussle. "It is you I want, and in my position, I do not need to compromise."

His warm breath whispered against her neck, and Tara felt as if a flock of birds was rioting in her stomach. He touched her and she turned to mush. Damnation, his amorous assaults always caused her defenses to fall like uprooted trees toppling in the path of a cyclone. As his wayward hand slid beneath her blouse to trace the full swell of her breast, Tara squealed and ducked beneath his arm, but Sloane clamped his fingers on the collar of her blouse. A shocked gasp burst from her when she found that, although she had escaped him, she had sacrificed her clothing, leaving her unclad body exposed

150

to his consuming gaze.

Sloane was all eyes as Tara dived onto his cot and hurriedly covered her bare breasts from his hawkish stare. Lord, she was a gorgeous goddess!

"Now you listen to me, Sloane Prescott," she gulped as he swaggered toward her, grinning in roguish anticipation. "I know you well enough to realize that you are not about to dispose of me just because I have uncovered your secret." God, she hoped she hadn't misjudged him. He was rough, tough, mysterious, but surely he was not capable of murder.

"*Mi vida*, I don't think you know me at all," he insisted as his warm gaze rested on her bare shoulders.

A terrifying image sizzled through her mind, of him hovering over her with knife in hand. "You would murder me?" came her half-strangled question, her eyes round as saucers.

"I can think of things far more enjoyable than marring this body."

When Sloane crouched above her, Tara yanked the sheet up under her chin and curled up in the corner of the cot, peering wide-eyed at him. He was stalking her like a jungle cat playing with its prey, and Tara had the uneasy feeling he was about to gobble her up. There was nowhere to run. If he was inclined to take her, then there would be little she could do to forestall this lithe mountain lion of a man.

Tossing aside her rambling thoughts, she focused her full attention on his handsome face, only to be drawn into the depths of those incredible blue eyes.

"I don't think I could ever please you," she chirped, and then flattened herself against the wall as he crouched above her. "I've never been with a man and I don't know how. . . ."

"Let me be the judge of how well you can please a man, *mi niña*," he murmured before his lips rolled over hers,

151

causing her resistance to droop another dangerous notch. "I will be only too happy to show you how it is between a man and a woman."

His warm breath feathered against her cheek as his adventurous hands pulled away the protective sheet to expose her creamy skin. His parted lips hovered over hers like a bee courting a flower, and then his questing tongue explored the velvety recesses of her mouth, drawing a response Tara was helpless to withhold. His musky fragrance warped her senses, and she closed her eyes and mind to all except the arousing feel and taste of this intriguing man who could easily bend her to his will.

Tara thought he had sprouted an extra pair of hands as his caresses wandered over her quaking body, igniting fires that left her blood simmering through her veins when she would have been content to allow it to flow in a cool, normal pace.

It had always been like this with Sloane, she thought as his hand cupped her breast, teasing the pink peak to tautness. Sloane fed her gnawing hunger for passion and then created monstrous new ones with his whispering kisses and tantalizing caresses. The last of her weakened defenses fell away as his moist lips tracked across her shoulder, his tongue flicking at the ripe bud of her breast, compelling her to follow the flames until they consumed her entire being. Nothing seemed to matter when he touched her so tenderly. Reason abandoned her and riptides of sensation channeled through her, leaving her yearning to appease a need she had never realized existed until she had experienced Sloane's fiery kisses and soul-shattering caresses.

"You feel as soft as a rose petal, and the feminine scent of you fogs my mind," he murmured as his lips trailed from the peak of her breast to recapture her sensuous lips. "I can't get enough of the taste of you."

A groan of unholy torment echoed in his throat as he

twisted her beneath him and then eased down beside her on the cot. His all-consuming gaze followed the path of his exploring hand as it slid over the slope of her shoulder, scaled the creamy mound of her breast, and then glided over her belly. For the moment he was content just to look upon her as he had that first night, to rediscover the feel of her satiny flesh beneath his caress, to seek out each sensitive point on her body. He wanted to learn this gorgeous nymph by touch, to make her first encounter with lovemaking an experience she would long remember.

His arousing explorations dragged a moan from her trembling lips as his hand tracked across her thigh, stroking her, fondling her. And then deft fingers worked the buttons on the waistband of her skirt, sliding it down her hips, leaving not one inch of her feminine body untouched by his tender hands and marveling gaze.

A becoming blush stained her cheeks as he devoured her with his eyes, but modesty soon gave way to the onrush of pleasure as his head moved back to hers to whisper words of how he enjoyed looking at her, touching her. With concentrated deliberation, his hands splayed across her trembling flesh, sketching intricate patterns on her belly, wandering to the inner softness of her thighs before receding to swirl around the rosy tip of each breast.

Tara sighed in pleasure as he worked his subtle magic on her flesh. Denying him would mean denying herself this sweet torment. Sensations of wild, indescribable rapture were blossoming somewhere deep within her, unfurling like the tender petals of a flower to feed upon the warmth of his intimate caresses.

Somehow she had known it would come to this, that she would surrender to this overpowering man. He made her want him as she had wanted no other man. Sloane was an enigma, a walking contradiction, and he totally fascinated her. She could no longer hide behind stubborn pride and pretend disinterest. She had been battling her attraction to him since the first day she arrived at the ranch, and there was no fight left within her.

Tara caught her breath as his probing fingers discovered her womanly softness, exciting her, driving her mad with a need that she was sure nothing could fulfill. She yearned to fully understand his brand of passion, to become his possession, if only for the night. Her body instinctively arched toward his exploring hands and lips, aching to satisfy this wild, tormenting craving that gnawed at every part of her being until she could think of nothing besides total surrender.

"Do you know how exquisitely beautiful you are, Tara?" His voice was ragged with barely contained desire and held a hint of awe as his wayward hand slid along her rib cage to settle on the shapely curve of her hip.

His marveling gaze flooded over her perfect body as the golden lantern light sprayed across her skin, making it glow like honey. He stilled the urge to ravish what his eyes beheld. She was a vision of incomparable loveliness, the specter who had long haunted *his* waking and sleeping. She was what dreams were made of, a seraph with such spellbinding beauty that it boggled his mind. As if his hand possessed a will of its own, it lifted to tug the pins from her hair, letting the silver-blond waterfall cascade over her bare shoulder to spill across his pillow. His index finger traced the delicate line of her jaw and then followed the silky strands of hair before wandering to the pink crest of her breast, loving the feminine feel of her beneath his hand.

Tara wasn't sure what demon possessed her, but she found herself aching to touch him as intimately as he was touching her, to feel his hard, bare contours beneath *her* exploring caresses. She resented the garments that concealed his virile form, and a deliciously wicked smile

154

rippled across her lips as she moved above him to peel off his poncho.

"I have no desire for my first encounter with passion to be with the mysterious phantom who haunts Palo Duro. Is it man or ghost who tempts me so?"

When she had shrugged away his shirt, her gaze fell to the broad expanse of his chest and the thick matting of hair that trickled down his lean belly. There was not an inch of flab on his powerful body, and Tara again compared him to a sleek, agile mountain lion.

Two eyebrows shot straight up as Sloane watched this seductive nymph glide her hands over his laboring chest to unfasten his breeches. A low rumble of laughter tumbled from his lips as he eyed the pert beauty who had set about to strip him naked.

"Feminine curiosity?" he mocked and then sucked in his breath as her adventurous hand slid beneath the band of his breeches and then pulled them from his hips.

Her delicate fingers hovered lightly over the taut tendons and hard muscles of his thighs. Tara studied him inquisitively as her caresses glided over his masculine contours, mapping his hair-roughened flesh until he groaned in torment.

"Do you know what you are doing to me?" he rasped as he attempted to hook his arm around her waist and drag her against him.

A playful giggle bubbled from her lips as she eluded him. "No, tell me, my intriguing phantom who abducts innocent women and drags them to his lair."

"You're slowly but surely driving me mad," he assured her huskily. "Come here. . . ."

But Tara had only begun her intimate explorations, and she reveled in the power she seemed to hold over him. Her innocent techniques were driving him to the brink of insanity. He was ablaze with a hunger only Tara could satisfy. He had promised himself that he would be

155

patient and gentle with her, but it was going to be next to impossible if she kept this up.

The amused smile that played on her lips vanished when her wandering hand brushed against his bold manhood. Wide violet eyes locked with cobalt-blue ones, and her cheeks flamed bright red. Sloane chuckled as he drew her down on top of him. It was obvious that she didn't know the first thing about men. He reached over to snuff the lantern, deciding she had seen quite enough of him for one night.

"You are much too daring for your own good," he said with a soft laugh as his hand absently strayed over the velvety curve of her hip. "I think perhaps it's time *you* follow *my* instruction."

Tara was having serious second thoughts about exchanging intimate secrets with Sloane. She had no idea what to expect. Her mother had never discussed the birds, bees, or men at any length. Tara was beginning to feel like a naive little fool. What had she gotten herself into? And why hadn't Sloane been embarrassed as she was? He seemed so casual about seeing her in the altogether, while she had blushed seven shades of red, and still was, even in the darkness.

"You seem so . . ." Tara struggled to formulate her thoughts, trying to find a way to approach such a delicate subject. "I didn't realize you were . . ."

Sloane chortled again as he combed his fingers through the strands of spun silver and gold. "Men and women are very different. Is this nothing at all like what you expected, *querida?*"

If she had known what to expect, she wouldn't have been so shocked, she reminded herself. "Sloane, I'm afraid you will be greatly disappointed in me," she murmured, her voice failing her as his hot kisses tumbled over her shoulder to sear the swell of her breast.

"Disappointed? No, I think not, *mi niña*. I will teach

156

you all you need to know of love, just as you have taught me to be gentle with the lady I hold in my arms."

His touch sent her apprehension scattering in all directions, and she was mesmerized when he raised his raven head. The flash of lightning reflected the blue flames in his eyes, and she knew she would follow wherever this intriguing phantom led.

"I have no desire to hurt or frighten you, Tara," he murmured, his body rousing as he rolled above her, cradling her soft feminine body in his powerful arms. "I only wish both of us to find pleasure tonight, the kind you have never known, something words can never touch. . . ."

His voice was so soft and reassuring that Tara could feel herself melting against him. His practiced hands stroked her quivering flesh like a gentle massage, leaving her soft and pliant in his arms. His kisses investigated every inch of her flesh, as if he had forgotten the feel of her ripe body beneath his hands. His long tanned fingers tracked across her silky curves, making her arch toward him in instinctive response. His titillating caresses traveled over her knee and leisurely trailed over her thighs, gently guiding her legs apart. And then, with heart-stopping tenderness, his hands flowed upward, tracing patterns on her breasts while his mouth gently savored hers.

Tara dug her nails into the hard muscles of his back as his skillful hands ventured along the same arousing path, leaving a trail of leaping flames in their wake.

Finally she could endure no more of this maddening torment. She wanted him totally, completely, ached to relinquish her soul to the man who had filled her senses with exquisite rapture.

"Sloane . . . please." Her breathless voice whispered across his shoulder and hungry kisses splayed across his chest.

He braced himself above her, staring down at her shadowed face, bewildered by the fire of desire that sparkled in her amethyst eyes. Compelled by the emotions that were mirrored in her expression Sloane settled himself between her thighs. A moan of pure pleasure echoed in his chest as he pressed intimately against her, losing himself in the sweet softness of her womanly body.

Tara clutched him closer, burying her head against his shoulder as the pleasure ebbed and a sharp pain shattered the dreamlike trance. When she tensed beneath him, Sloane withdrew, surprised by her fearful reaction. This was a new experience for him as well, and he found himself feeling inadequate in dealing with a woman who had never made the most intimate of journeys with a man.

A strange feeling engulfed him. It was an odd combination of sensations—passion, possessiveness, and an overwhelming need to be gentle and understanding. This was not some experienced woman who knew what to expect when she gave herself to a man. This was Tara, an innocent violet-eyed nymph who would never dare come near him again if he hurt her the one time he had pushed her past resistance.

With all the patience he could muster, Sloane moved carefully against her tender flesh, waiting breathlessly for her to relax beneath him. His hands slid beneath her hips, lifting her to him, guiding her, arousing her until she wanted him again, as badly as he ached for her.

The burning pain of innocence vanished as he taught her the true pleasures of lovemaking. Tara was caught up in the whirlwind of sensations that touched every nerve and muscle in her body. She was moving in gentle rhythm to a melody that strummed on her soul as their bodies forged and melted into one essence. She felt as if she were soaring toward the sun, consumed by such intense heat that she was sure she would never regain her singular identity.

Sloane thrust deeply within her, taking her further from reality, holding her suspended in the vortex of passion's storm, a storm that generated windswept fires which engulfed everything within their path. She couldn't think. She couldn't breathe. She could only cling to the one stable force in a world that was alive with wind and flames. And just when she was certain she would die in the quintessence of pleasure that sizzled through her, she was soaring higher than the towering clouds, drifting in a universe where time and space ceased to exist.

His heavy body shuddered against hers as they enjoyed passion's sweet release. His strength escaped him, thought eluded him, and he was numb to all except the wild, wondrous sensations that spilled through him. He had anticipated pleasure beyond description when he took Tara in his arms, but what he had discovered staggered the imagination. He had taken her virginity, but he had lost something of himself. She had requested gentleness and he had offered it, but not without forfeiting a part of his soul. Somehow, in that ecstatic moment that pursued and captured time, he had become *her* possession, a living, breathing part of her.

Sloane wondered at the feelings that nagged at him in the aftermath of love. In the past he had been anxious to slip from a woman's arms and continue on his way when his hunger had been appeased. He had expected to be satisfied with sending Tara, too, on her way once he had lived the end of the compelling dream that had tormented him since the night he had first kissed and caressed her. But his desire for her was like an eternal spring from which he had only temporarily quenched his thirst and had yet to drink his fill of passion's intoxicating brew.

"Sloane?" Tara stared up at the darkness, bewildered

by her reckless response and the strange tenderness Sloane had displayed. Was this the same rough, abrupt cowboy she had encountered on so many occasions? She thought she knew Sloane Prescott, but the man who had made wild sweet love to her had gentle qualities she had never expected. He had been a tender lover, his kisses warm and compelling, his touch like a butterfly skimming over her skin.

"Hum?" He raised his dark head and then dropped a fleeting kiss to lips that melted like summer rain beneath his.

"I cannot truly say I'm sorry I ended up in your bed," she confessed, her voice still raspy with the side effects of passion.

He chuckled quietly. How this curious imp amused and pleased him! "Neither am I, *querida,* and I wish I could keep you here with me for the remainder of the night." He sighed longingly as he memorized the shadowed face below his. "But it might draw suspicion to have you come trailing back to headquarters with me in the morning."

Tara heaved a disappointed sigh. The very last thing she wanted to do was ride back to the ranch. "I suppose you're right. I don't relish being accused of cavorting with a ghost. Someone might label me a witch."

"Ah, but you are," Sloane insisted as he flicked the end of her upturned nose and then rolled away to gather his strewn clothing. "Why else would I be so spellbound by the sight of you? Next time I hope I do not find it necessary to . . ."

"There cannot be a next time," she assured him as she sat up beside him and pressed her fingers to his lips to shush him.

"Why not?" Sloane demanded as he pried her hand from his mouth.

What an idiotic question, she thought huffily. "Do

you think just because I stumbled and fell into your bed that I will allow it to happen again? I don't even mean enough to you that you will offer me an explanation about why you are masquerading as Vernon Russel's ghost."

"I don't want you involved in this conflict," Sloane grumbled, soured by her insistence that this would be the first and last time they enjoyed passion's embrace. "The less you know the better. It is best to be ignorant of some matters, and this is one of them."

"My father is also involved, isn't he?" Tara fired the question at him. "He knows your identity, and he has kept the legend alive with his newspaper. I want to know why he is aiding you in this madness."

Sloane scowled in irritation. Tara was too quick-witted and curious to let the matter drop. Damn, why hadn't he simply frightened her away instead of bringing her to his cabin? Because he could not ignore the opportunity of being alone with her, he chided himself gruffly. And what price would he pay for this one night of pleasure, one that Tara insisted would never come again?

"*Se va haciendo tarde,*" he muttered as he tossed Tara her clothes and strode toward the door. "I'll fetch the horses while you dress."

When he closed the door behind him, Tara pounded her fist in the pillow, wishing she could take her frustrations out on the source of her problem—Sloane Prescott, or whoever he really was. He wanted her in his bed, but he didn't care enough about her to trust her with his secret. Well, what had she expected, she asked herself miserably. She was hallucinating if she thought she could change Sloane. He was as solid and immovable as the walls of Palo Duro Canyon. Confound it! Now what was she to do? She had surrendered to the very man Julia fancied herself in love with, and she would go stark raving mad if she didn't discover why Sloane was playing this dangerous charade. Why was her father involved? How could she keep silent and betray her friend's father? And how could she divulge Sloane's secret when Merrick would crucify him and her father as well?

Grappling with those disturbing thoughts, Tara shrugged on her clothes and strolled outside, wondering how she would endure the suspense. Sloane had only piqued her notorious curiosity, and it would hound every step she took until she knew the truth, all of it, from beginning to end. Damn, she would need a crowbar to pry the information out of this tight-lipped cowboy, and he was as determined not to budge as she was determined to discover the truth.

Chapter 10

A fine mist sprayed against her kiss-swollen lips as Tara ambled toward the dark silhouette of Sloane. She broke stride as she approached the looming figure and his magnificent silver stallion. When she stepped into the stirrup to climb onto Hazel's back, Sloane grasped her arm.

"No regrets? No fiery display of temper?" he questioned as he peered up into her exquisite face.

"My temper seems to have no effect on you, and yes, there are plenty of regrets," she told him stiffly as she wormed free.

Sloane swung into his saddle and then reined the stallion up the weaving path that led to the caprock. "Perhaps when I am certain I can trust you, I will explain myself. But for now, I feel it best to leave things as they are."

"You are insane!" Tara flung at his broad back. "All I have to do is march up to Merrick and spill the truth. He would have you dangling from the tallest tree in Texas."

Sloane twisted in the saddle to glance at Tara, knowing full well she was glaring daggers at him in the darkness. "But you won't breathe a word about this," he had the nerve to say. "Not unless you want to implicate yourself or allow the world to know we have slept together when we are practically strangers. You boast of being a lady, but I seriously doubt your aristocratic friends in St. Louis would approve of your submitting to a backward cowboy whom you have barely known a month."

Tara was hopping up and down with indignation. He could be cruel and cutting when the mood suited him. "Damn you. You can take something beautiful and twist it until there is nothing left of it."

"Was it beautiful?" he inquired in that infuriatingly lazy drawl.

If she could have gotten her hands on that maddening cowboy she would have pounded him flat and wedged him in the cracks of the sandstone walls. "It was to me," she burst out without thinking. "But obviously you are so accustomed to this sort of rendezvous that it means little or nothing to you."

"I didn't say that," Sloane chuckled, amused by her fiery display of temper. He knew it would come eventually. It always did.

"You may as well have," Tara pouted, clinging to Hazel's neck as they wound around another narrow ledge that was slick with rain.

"Tonight will long linger in memory, and, despite your protest, this will not be the last time for us," Sloane calmly assured her, his voice drifting down from the plateau above her. "No matter whose side you choose to take, it doesn't change the way things are between you and me. Remember that, *mi alma*. There will be other nights, and next time you will come willingly to me."

"When hell freezes over!" Tara snapped at him. The nerve of that man! She was itching to snatch up a pick and shovel and chip away his monumental arrogance.

"We shall see about that," Sloane snorted. Damn, this lively tigress was the stubbornest woman he had ever met. She would admit to finding pleasure in his arms in one breath and then deny him his rights the next. He had been the first, and there was magic in their embrace. If

164

that little firebrand couldn't see that, she was as farsighted as a mole! "When another man tries to take you in his arms, it will be my face you see, my kiss that lingers on your lips."

If Tara could have pried loose a boulder she would have hurled it at him. "You are incredibly arrogant. When Cal Johnson kissed me, I can assure you I was not having visions of being held in your arms." She threw the rejoinder at him instead of a boulder, and it proved to be just as effective.

Sloane's eyes turned a mutinous shade of blue. He had warned Cal to keep his distance, but obviously the man had a short memory, either that or he was a fool. "Stay away from him, Tara. Cal Johnson is poison."

"I doubt that I will be forced to deal with him again," she said. "I threatened to blow him to bits if he came near me."

A wry smile hovered on Sloane's lips as Diablo scaled the crumbling wall and trotted along the rim of the canyon. Tara was spouting insults at him, but she had shown a preference, whether or not she wanted to admit it. Gloating over that fact, Sloane rode toward head-quarters.

Tara pouted all the way back to the house, muttering under her breath, wondering why she was being polite when she should have been shouting disrespectful epithets at the mule-headed man who rode beside her. Where did he get off issuing threats? Where did he find the unmitigated gall to suggest that she would come traipsing through the sagebrush to search him out in the stillness of the night? From now on she would keep her distance from Sloane. She had played with fire, and now that she had been scorched she would be more cautious. He was only using her to ease his male needs and she damned well knew it. Tara could remain indifferent and aloof toward him. After all, she had managed to do just that for the past few weeks.

She would hand Sloane over to Julia, and she would be well rid of that infuriating, mysterious man. And the moment she set foot in Clarendon, she would pry the truth from her father, she promised herself. Something was brewing, and she was itching to know what it was.

After Sloane tethered the horses, he led Tara to the back of the house and then gestured toward the tall cottonwood tree he had often scaled when seeking entrance. Tara didn't bat an eye at climbing up the tree and creeping across the roof to reach her room. As she pulled the back hem of her skirt between her legs and tucked it in the waist band, Sloane strode up behind her and pulled her into his arms.

"You can protest to your heart's content, little she-cat, but I think you are in love with me, whether you realize it yet or not. You would never have given yourself to me so freely tonight if I meant nothing to you. You are not that kind of woman, Tara."

"Oh?" Tara lifted a perfectly arched brow. "Just how many kinds of women are there?" she scoffed caustically.

"At least a dozen," he insisted with a rakish grin. "And I have seen my fair share, but you, *mi vida,* are in a class all by yourself."

The man continued to flabbergast her, and she fully intended to tell him what she thought of him and his comparisons when his mouth descended on hers, devouring her with a kiss that stole the protest from her lips and fed the flames of desire, flames Tara could have sworn had burned themselves out. But they blazed anew when her body came in close contact with the powerful contours of his. She knew him by touch, and they had shared the most intimate of secrets. He knew things about her that she hadn't known about herself until she had surrendered to passion.

166

And that was all it had been, Tara reminded herself. She could detach herself from her emotions, just as easily as Sloane could. It was over and done, just as soon as he released her from his arousing embrace and she corraled her stampeding heart. Dammit, why did he have to affect her so? She had been very comfortable hating him, and now he had turned her world wrong side out. If this be love, she wanted no part of it. She didn't dare fall in love with this daredevil. He would get himself killed, and she would be chained to the forbidden memories of a man who had touched each and every one of her emotions. How could she exist without him when every thought, every pleasure she had experienced was entangled with his dancing blue eyes, his raven hair, and the rakish smile that tore at her heart?

When he finally broke the fiery kiss, Tara teetered and then braced her hands against the tree trunk. She flung him a frozen glare, complete with icicles, and then reached up to grasp the limb above her. "I cannot and will not fall in love with you, Sloane Prescott," she vowed as she hooked her leg around the branch and twisted to sit on her perch, staring down her nose at the arrogant man who was snickering at her acrobatic maneuvers. "As a matter of fact, I am engaged to Joseph Rutherford, a prominent banker in St. Louis."

Suddenly Sloane wasn't laughing. He was glowering at the golden-haired sparrow who chirped haughtily at him. "You won't be marrying Joey what's-his-name," he told her flatly. "I doubt that St. Louis dandy could handle you. What you need is a man who won't allow you to walk all over him."

Tara would have cheerfully leaped from the limb and left her footprints on his back, but this was not the time or the place to go another round. The last thing she needed was to be caught with Sloane in the middle of

167

the night.

"And you think *you* are man enough, I suppose," she scoffed as she balanced on the branch and reached up to clutch a higher limb.

"I didn't say I was interested in marrying you," he tossed back at her as he followed her flight onto a towering branch.

"Thank God for small favors." Tara's sarcastic voice dripped from the twigs.

Sloane chuckled all the way back to his steed. Tara Winslow was an intriguing combination of fire and ice. She could stir the flames of passion with her innocent caresses, but she was also capable of freezing him in his tracks with her frosty glares. That lively nymph had taken hold of his heart, and he wasn't certain what caused this strange sensation that was eating at him. He had never been plagued with jealousy before. What did he care if that bundle of trouble spirited off to St. Louis to wed a well-to-do banker? He was physically attracted to this fiery beauty, but his fascination would fade in time, he told himself confidently. It was just that her presence upset his scheme and that he had been distracted, he rationalized. This odd emotional upheaval he was experiencing would pass when he focused on the more important matters at hand.

Clinging to that thought, Sloane made his way back to his cabin, only to be bombarded by memories. Like an alluring phantom of the night, Tara's exquisite face materialized from the darkness, her soft lips whispering over his, her violet eyes compelling him to her, forcing him to chase a dream that had become reality. And when he yielded to sleep, it wasn't Merrick Russel who invaded his fantasy. It was that feisty temptress with hair the color of sunbeams and moonlight and soft lips that tasted like cherry wine as they melted on his.

And while Sloane was wrestling with his memories, Tara was pacing the floor, grappling with Sloane's remark. Why *had* she yielded to him? Was it simply because he had made her a slave to passion and she could not be content until she knew exactly where his arousing kisses and caresses could lead? That had to be the reason, Tara told herself. He had satisfied her curiosity, and now that she knew the ways of love, she would forget the night ever existed. She would wrap the forbidden memory and tuck it away in the far corner of her mind.

A frustrated sigh escaped her lips when she found her pacing had taken her to the window. She was looking for that confounded Night Rider with the rich, silky voice who could weave dreams about her! Tara spun around and flounced back to bed, wishing she had never left her room in the first place. What had she accomplished? Nothing, she reminded herself drearily. She had been trapped in a secret that still made no sense, and she had found herself yielding to a man who had captured her in his arms and kissed her senseless. How could she face Julia? Tara had betrayed a friend!

Groaning miserably, Tara lay back on her pillow and squeezed her eyes shut, trying to forget. But he was there in the shadows, and she could smell the musky scent of him on her skin, taste the impatient kisses that had swept her up in a rapturous storm.

Stop this! Tara scolded herself as she squirmed to find a more comfortable position, turning her back on the bittersweet memories. She would never be lured back to his cabin beneath the rock ledges of the canyon. He had stripped her of all else, but she had her pride! She would not allow herself to fall in love with a phantom. And that was what he was, she reminded herself. He was the keeper of dreams, dreams that had collided with reality. But when the sun raised its weary head to greet the new day, she would close the door on the past and never think of Sloane, except as the slow, drawling cowboy. They had no place in each other's worlds, and if she had any sense she would never allow herself to forget that. That man could get her into trouble, and she seemed to stumble into her fair share of it anyway without any help from Sloane Prescott.

Chapter 11

"I cannot understand why you are making such a fuss," Julia sighed in exasperation. "What can it hurt for you to stand on the opposite side of the fence and casually chat with Sloane? You already have him tipping his hat to me when I approach. He even tarries long enough to converse with me instead of rushing off to train those four-legged nags."

Because I can't trust myself alone with him, Tara thought to herself and then forced a faint smile for Julia. "I think you should be satisfied with the improvements and stop expecting miracles," she argued. "Why don't you invite him to the party and stop dragging this out? He can fumble his way across the dance floor well enough to escort you. And besides, it is apparent that his dancing abilities are not what interest you most."

Julia grinned mischievously. "Am I so obvious in my intentions?"

Tara tossed her a withering glance as she followed Julia out the door. "Only a blind man couldn't see that you have been drooling when you look at him. Why Loren Marshall still follows you around like an obedient pup is beyond me. And I cannot fathom why you would choose Sloane over Loren."

"I am only trying to be very certain before I make a commitment," Julia defended herself. "Are you positive

171

you can be content living the rest of your life as Joseph Rutherford's wife?"

Tara fell silent as she fell into step. She could never marry Joseph, no matter how forceful her grandfather became. She was as restless and impulsive as her father, and Joseph was starched and stuffy. And when Joseph learned that he had taken another man's leavings he would be humiliated beyond belief. God, she could never marry anyone now, Tara thought despairingly. Sloane had spoiled any chance of that. No one in Ryan O'Donnovan's circle of friends would accept a tainted woman for a wife, no matter how large the dowry. She was destined to become a spinster.

"Good morning, Sloane," Julia called, dragging Tara from her pensive deliberations and leaving her staring into a pair of laughing blue eyes.

"Mornin', ma'am." Sloane fastened the check reins onto Vulcan's bridle and then ambled over to the fence, his keen gaze making a fast sweep of Julia's trim figure and then lingering overlong on Tara, making her fidget like a skittish colt. "Are you ladies goin' ridin' this mornin'?"

"I thought I would show Tara the scenery to the southwest. There are some spectacular rock formations there and I wouldn't want her to return to St. Louis without viewing them," Julia explained and then licked her bone-dry lips, working up the nerve to invite Sloane to the ball. "Sloane, I was wondering if you would . . ."

Tara rolled her eyes when Julia stumbled over her tongue.

"If I would what, ma'am?" Sloane cast her a curious glance and then frowned at Tara, who was behaving as if she would have preferred to be anywhere except within ten feet of him.

Julia inhaled a courageous breath and then blurted it out. "I would like for you to escort me to the ball Papa

172

is giving."

Sloane's face fell. *Julia?* He had thought all along that Tara was that certain young lady who would request his company. His blue eyes narrowed on Tara's carefully blank stare. That little minx. Had she coaxed Julia into inviting him to that confounded party just so she could continue avoiding him as if he were some detestable creature who had slithered out from under a rock? Well, two could play her game, he thought spitefully. Before the party was over, he would have that violet-eyed vixen wishing she hadn't traded partners!

"I'd be honored, ma'am," he murmured as he flashed Julia a smile that was glazed with such a thick coating of sugar that Tara was certain she would develop a toothache just witnessing the sticky-sweet scene.

"I don't know how Loren is goin' to take this, but I'm sure I'll be the most envied man at the ball." Sloane tipped his hat and swaggered away. "Now if you'll excuse me, I got some work to do, but it won't be half as enjoyable as whilin' away the hours with you, Julia."

Tara gnashed her teeth, wondering why she had been stung with jealousy. She wanted nothing more to do with Sloane Prescott. Well, she didn't, did she? Tara fired the question at herself again when the answer didn't readily pop into her head. Of course she didn't, she told herself firmly. Julia was welcome to him.

Sloane stopped suddenly and turned. "Do you want me to saddle the horses for you before I start workin' with Vulcan?" he questioned, as if it had just occurred to him that would have been the polite thing to do.

When Julia nodded agreeably, Sloane looped the stallion's reins over the railing and swung his leg over the fence. As he hopped to the ground, his virile body brushed against Tara's, her nostrils picking up the manly scent she had tried desperately to forget. The memory of their night together sliced like a sharp-edged knife, and

173

Tara detested herself for allowing that thought to creep from the shadowed corner of her mind. She didn't want to remember the scent and feel of him, or what it had been like between them.

With her confidence established, Julia curled her hand around Sloane's arm and bubbled with conversation as he strode across the grounds to retrieve the saddles.

Tara gathered her pride and presented Sloane with a cold shoulder when he tried to assist her into the saddle. His touch burned like wildfire, spreading through her like a sea of flames. What was the matter with her? Her well-meaning lectures had melted away each time their bodies made physical contact.

Gouging her boot heels into Hazel's flanks, Tara thundered off at a reckless pace. Sloane scowled at her breakneck speed. If she didn't watch where she was going, she and Hazel would wind up in broken heaps, he thought as she blazed by him.

Tara leaned against the mare's neck, urging her into her swiftest pace, veering away from Merrick, who was just riding back to headquarters. As Tara rounded a boulder to head for open range, the horse bolted sideways, startled by the rattlesnake that was coiled in the shade of the rocks. Tara's scream pierced the morning air, and Sloane felt his heart catapult to his throat as he watched her fly over the mare's head to land facedown on the ground.

"It's a rattler!" Julia shrieked, her gaze darting to her father, who had not made a move to assist Tara.

An agonized groan spilled from Tara's lips as she dragged herself up, dazed by the fall that had jarred every bone in her body. And then she froze when she heard the snake's deadly rattle. God, she detested snakes! The mere sight of them caused her to panic. Tara wasn't sure where she found the strength to move, but she was scrambling to her feet.

174

"Don't move!" Sloane yelled at her as he elbowed Julia out of his way and leaped to her horse's back.

But Tara heard nothing but the deadly hiss. Her bloodcurdling cry alarmed the rattler, and it retaliated in self-defense. Horror shot through her veins when she felt the snake's fangs on her leg. Nausea flooded over her as she inched away, certain the snake meant to come at her again. Her terrified gaze locked with a pair of beady black eyes and she stood paralyzed until Sloane yanked her up off the ground and carried her a safe distance away.

"You little fool," he growled as he set her to her feet to inspect the wound.

Tara clung to him like a choking vine, her body shuddering uncontrollably. The picture in her mind's eye came at her again and again. She knew if she lived through this ordeal she would never forget that horrible moment.

"Lie back and relax," Sloane ordered gruffly as he pried her arms from his shoulders and pulled the bandanna from his neck to use as a tourniquet. With no regard for her modesty, he shoved her skirt over her thighs and tightly wrapped the neckerchief just above her knee. His keen gaze swept the surroundings and he gestured to the left.

"Julia, fetch that twig. She'll need somethin' to bite into while I draw out the poison." Once Tara had the twig between her teeth, Sloane stared soberly at her. "No matter how much it hurts, don't move your leg."

Tara nodded mutely as Sloane reached into his pocket for his knife and then clamped his steady hand around her thigh before making two small crisscross incisions on the wound just below her knee. Tara watched wide-eyed as Sloane crouched over her, kneading the wound, sucking the poison. Her gaze flooded over the raven-haired man whose shirt strained against the hard muscles of his arms and chest as he attempted to save her from

175

painful death. She was mesmerized by the way the bright sunlight was absorbed in his coal-black hair, the way his chiseled features cut severe lines in his face as he concentrated on his task. Nothing rattled this mountain of a man. He was steady and confident in the face of calamity, well prepared to meet whatever disaster came his way. There seemed nothing Sloane Prescott couldn't or wouldn't do. The man was incredible. Tara was stung by another sensation that was even more painful than a snakebite. God help her. She *was* in love with Sloane!

She wilted back on the ground to breathe a disheartened sigh, unconcerned about her leg. After all, what good was a leg when she had lost her heart and soul to Sloane Prescott, the apple of Julia's eye.

"Tara?"

Her tangled lashes swept up, tears misting her eyes as his tanned face hovered over hers, his rugged features etched with concern. But no words formed on her lips. She could only stare helplessly at him, shocked by the realization that she had somehow managed to lose her heart to a man who cared nothing about her. Lord, have mercy on her soul, if there was anything left of it when Sloane finished tearing it to pieces.

"Tara . . . are you all right?" Sloane's worried frown sliced into his bronzed face. Why was she looking at him like that? She must be in shock, he decided as he scooped her up in his arms and set her across the saddle. "Julia, ride back to the house and fetch some hot water and bandages. I'll bring her along at a slower pace."

His accusing glaze slid to Merrick, who had not lifted a hand to deter the snake or help Tara escape. Fear had never paralyzed Merrick before, and it set Sloane to wondering if he had purposely allowed Tara to suffer. Perhaps he intended to . . .

"Sloane . . . I . . ." Tara's voice crumbled when she met his probing stare. She couldn't speak what was in her heart. She could only peer up at him, wondering what she was to do now that she had stumbled on this depressing realization.

"I'll take care of you," Sloane whispered as his lips brushed over her perspiring brow and then he released a heavy sigh. "God, you scared ten years off my life."

"And since you live so dangerously, you have none to spare," she murmured back to him, strangely content to nestle in his arms.

One dark brow arched acutely as he drew back to look into her amethyst eyes fringed with long, thick lashes. He was amazed to find her curled up in his arms like a contented kitten. He usually had to fight his way through several barriers of defense to get this tigress in his arms. But at the moment she was making no protest about their close physical contact. It was only because she had been frightened half to death, he speculated. If Tara had been in full command of her senses, she would have insisted on walking back to the house rather than ride in his arms.

When Sloane pulled her from the saddle and carried her upstairs, Tara laid her head against his sturdy shoulder. The feel of his strong, capable arms about her chased away all her fears. Nothing could harm her when she was in Sloane's embrace.

After Sloane eased her into the bed and shuffled Julia and Merrick out of the room, he drew her skirt up around her hips to check the wound and then carefully plucked the stickers from her leg.

"Would you mind telling me what that little tantrum was all about?" he questioned and then tossed her a wry smile. "Were you a mite jealous, minx? Why did you con Julia into inviting me to the ball? Have you been having haunting regrets about the night we shared?"

Tara's mouth dropped open and suddenly she was back to hating him again. Damn that man! He had her tripping over an emotional tightrope, adoring him one minute and detesting him the next.

"I had no intention of asking you to accompany me to that blasted ball. It was *Julia* who insisted that I groom you for your social debut so she could waltz in your arms. The certain young lady I referred to was Julia, certainly not me! I wouldn't invite you to my funeral, Sloane Prescott," she snapped furiously.

So they were back to pistols at twenty paces, Sloane mused as he watched the sparks fly in her lavender eyes. "I suppose you intend to tell me that you *allowed* me to make love to you, just in preparation for wooing the wealthy rancher's daughter," Sloane snorted derisively. "My, what personal sacrifices you have made for a friend. The admirable martyr." His husky voice dripped with sarcasm. "Good God, I don't know which of us played the other for the biggest fool."

Tara was itching to climb out of bed, seek out the rattlesnake, and stash it under Sloane's pillow. That lout! Why couldn't he let the memory of their night together die a peaceful death? Because he delighted in tormenting her, she thought acrimoniously. Sloane Prescott stayed up nights devising new ways to torment her and haunt Merrick. The man was a painful thorn in her side, and she wished he would extract it along with the stickers he was digging out of her bruised and battered leg.

"You were merely available to satisfy my curiosity about passion," she flung at him, childish vindictiveness spurring her remark. She wanted to strike out and slash a gash in his pride, a hole the exact size of the one he had sliced across her heart. "We both know I have an overabundance of curiosity, and since you possess an oversupply of lust, we both appeased our needs. You may have been the first, but you won't be the last man with whom I share a bed."

Sloane ground his teeth and scowled at her cutting remark. Showing not one ounce of tenderness, he yanked another thorn from her hip. "Do you intend to try out every cot in the bunk house during your stay at the Diamond R Ranch?" he questioned, a distinctly unpleasant edge on his voice.

"I may do just that." Her bruised chin tilted a notch higher. "I would expect *any* of the hired men could satisfy me as well as you did. Regardless of your high opinion of yourself, you are only a man. I can be as indiscriminate as you can!"

Sloane could cheerfully have shaken the stuffing out of her, and he most certainly would have if she hadn't been snakebit. His mouth narrowed in a grim line. Bracing his powerful arms on either side of her shoulders, he loomed over her, his swarthy face only inches from hers.

"No other man will please you, minx. Each kiss and caress would only serve to remind you of the night *we* made wild, sweet love in the darkness while the rain trickled from the roof of *my* cabin and thunder rumbled above us, blocking out the rest of the world. We were alone, hungering to touch and kiss, to give ourselves to each other." His moist lips feathered over hers while his hand slid over the slope of her shoulder to fold around her breast. "We made our own kind of music that night, *querida*. It was satisfying and unique, and all your denials cannot change that. Why won't you admit it?"

His skillful kiss and caress turned her into liquid desire. Tara was most grateful to hear the voices in the hall. The interruption allowed her to bypass his question and regather her crumbled composure.

When the door swung open, surprise flashed across Tara's face. There, looking angry and concerned all in the same moment, stood her father.

Terrance had arrived only minutes after Sloane had carried Tara up to her room. When he learned Tara had met with an accident, he had found considerable difficulty controlling his temper. Although he was tempted to accuse Merrick of neglect, he was more apprehensive about Tara's welfare than interested in his vendetta against Merrick Russel. God, if something happened to Tara, Terrance could never forgive himself. And neither would Libby, he thought sickly. If she didn't despise him now, she would when she learned of Tara's misfortune.

"Will she be all right?" Terrance questioned worriedly, his gaze anchored on Tara's flaming-red face, unaware that it was Sloane who had her burning, with the fever of unappeased desire.

"I think I was able to extract the poison before it spread," Sloane assured him in his lazy Texas drawl as he dipped the cloth in hot water and laid it over the wound. "She will need to stay in bed for several days to ensure the poison hasn't spread into her blood."

"Thank you for caring for our guest," Merrick remarked and then strode over to inspect the scratches on Tara's leg. "I wouldn't want anything to happen to Tara. I have become very fond of her."

Sloane's expression was unreadable, Terrance's was blatantly cynical, and Merrick's was sickeningly sincere. Tara glanced at all three men and frowned pensively. Damn, she wasn't certain which one of them was trustworthy. Her father had not been totally honest with her, and both Sloane and Merrick were plagued with peccadilloes. One day the three of them would manage to destroy each other because of something that did or didn't happen those many years ago. If Sloane and Terrance continued to torment Merrick they might become reckless and Merrick would learn the truth about the phantom rider and his accomplice. Tara wasn't certain she wanted to be in the same state when these men clashed. Sloane was as stubborn as Merrick. In fact, they . . . Tara stumbled on the thought that darted across

180

her mind. No, that was a ridiculous notion, she chided herself. Surely that wasn't the reason Sloane seemed to have a personal vendetta against the powerful, influential Merrick Russel. But just the same, Tara decided to do some investigating on her own. She had the feeling there were skeletons dangling in both men's closets and that the closets were sorely in need of airing. And perhaps Terrance would answer a few of her questions, now that she knew who the Night Rider really was, she thought hopefully.

When Sloane ordered everyone out of the room for the second time, Tara stared at her horse doctor with narrowed eyes. "I intend to find out what your grievance is with Merrick," she assured him firmly. "Will you tell me, or must I dig for the truth? I am not above making my father betray his confidence. I have every right to know what is going on around here, and why."

"Leave it alone, Tara," Sloane ordered sternly and then wound the fresh bandage around her leg. "The knowledge will only force you into a precarious situation. You know too much already."

A startled gasp burst from her lips when Sloane reached up to unbutton her pale blue blouse and draw it from her shoulders. "What in heaven's name do you think you're doing?" she hissed as she slapped at the long lean fingers that were now working the stays on her skirt.

"Making my patient comfortable." His eyes danced with deviltry. "It isn't the first time, you know. When I found you on the road and took you to my cabin, I discovered a very shapely lady with ivory skin that felt like velvet beneath my hands."

Tara gasped and then blushed beet-red as his hand slid beneath her buttocks to shift the skirt out from under her, exposing her to his bold gaze. "I can undress myself. You have incredible nerve!"

"And you have an incredibly beautiful body," he

181

affirmed as his eyes devoured every inch of her curvaceous form. "It seems such a shame to conceal it." Nimble fingers flew across the tiny buttons on the front of her lacy chemise and he chortled seductively when her breasts came dangerously close to spilling from the gaping bodice of her undergarment. "Doctoring such a gorgeous creature brings out the beast in me."

Tara scrambled under the sheet and yanked it up to her neck as she flashed him a condemning frown. "Leave me be. We have already seen too much of each other, and I do not appreciate your gawking. Go fiddle with your horses and let me recover from my snakebite. It is less painful than having your hands on me."

Sloane took advantage of having Tara pinned in bed. An ornery smile spread across his lips as his raven head moved deliberately toward hers. Impulsively, he reached out to smooth the wild mass of spun silver and gold away from her exquisite face. "I think you like having me touch you. And you will recuperate much faster with my tender, loving care, *mi niña*," he whispered against her flushed cheek. "I will be only too happy to accommodate you."

"I would rather . . ."

His mouth took possession of hers, savoring, devouring, spreading unwanted tingles of delight up and down her spine. The sheet served as only meager protection as his roaming hands traversed her abdomen and then circled her breast. A soft moan bubbled in her chest as his caress wandered over her hip to her thigh. Tara knew how hot the fires could burn when his hands began to work their provocative magic. He could transform her into a smoldering mass of desire with his skillful touch. She resented her strong reaction to Sloane. Loving him made her too vulnerable to his kisses and caresses, and it was easier to despise and mistrust him than to surrender to a man whose heart was carved from solid rock. She meant nothing to him, she reminded herself, fighting to keep her traitorous body from responding to his arousing caresses. He would tear her into a thousand miserable pieces if she allowed her heart to rule her head. Sloane Prescott didn't know the meaning of love. He was too preoccupied with some long-harbored bitterness to see that love was staring him in the face. He saw her as a challenge, and if she surrendered to her emotions she would become another link in his chain of broken hearts.

She could never confess to love him, not unless he showed some sign that he cared for her, truly cared for her, she told herself determinedly. And if he gave no indication of softening, she would collect the fragile pieces of her heart and take the train back to St. Louis. He would never know he had taken a firm hold on her soul or that she had left part of herself in that small, secluded cabin in Palo Duro Canyon.

Sloane willed himself to drag his lips away from the softness of hers. His breath was ragged as he withdrew and stood up beside the bed. "No more daredevil rides," he ordered as his longing gaze focused on her kiss-swollen lips. "A woman with your feisty temperament seems out of place when she is confined to bed." A sly smile dangled from one corner of his mouth as he gave the remark further consideration. "But I wouldn't complain if you were convalescing in my bed. A restless spirit might not be so apt to haunt the night if his troubled soul had such a shapely distraction awaiting him."

Tara flung him a withering glance and then pointed a dainty finger toward the door. "Will you please leave me in peace. I am sick to death of your suggestive remarks. I told you there can be no repeat performance of that disastrous night."

"You are a very stubborn lady, *querida,*" he chuckled. "And *your* sophisticated manners seem to be lacking. You could very well have been sick to death if I had not come to your rescue this morning. I didn't expect you to shower me with gratitude, but a simple thank-you would have been nice, even if you can barely abide the sight of me."

The fire dwindled in Tara's eyes. If he only knew the truth, she mused despairingly. "I truly appreciate what you did for me," she assured him in a soft, appreciative tone, startling him with her quicksilver change in mood. "I owe you my life, and I am indebted to you."

A quiet smile grazed his lips as he strolled across the room and leaned against the door. "You owe me nothing, Tara. I know you don't understand me, but hear this and believe it." His deep blue eyes held her level gaze. "I have never meant to hurt you, nor do I ever intend to. You and I share more than one secret, but what is between Merrick and me is something I cannot confide. I have committed myself to my obligation, and it is a promise I must keep. I don't want you caught in the middle of this, and I would never forgive myself if something happened to you."

As the door closed behind him, Tara stared thoughtfully at her lingering mental image of him. He was right. She didn't understand the workings of his complicated mind, but that didn't stop her from loving him, even though this one-sided affair had no future.

Tara heaved a heavy-hearted sigh and then willed herself to sleep and dream . . . a dream she was certain would never become reality. Oh, why did she have to want what she knew she couldn't have? She could have Joseph Rutherford and all that his money could buy, but she would have exchanged him and all his gold for that raven-haired devil with the dancing blue eyes.

When Terrance had Merrick alone, he dropped all pretense of politeness.

184

"I sent my daughter to your ranch in good faith. When I come to visit I find she has been snakebit. What other catastrophe has befallen her while she has been under your irresponsible care?" His accusing tone had a grating edge that instantly put Merrick on the defensive.

"You are blaming *me* because a rattlesnake made Tara its meal?" he snorted caustically. "Do you honestly believe I planted that snake and then sent Tara riding into its path? Really, Terrance, you have stretched your active imagination until it snapped." Merrick snatched up the newspaper and shook it in Terrance's reddened face. "You know you are groping for accusations, just as you concocted these lies you printed about me in the newspaper. I am tired of your innuendoes. I offer to entertain your daughter, and this is how you repay me."

"Repay?" Terrance pounced on his choice of words. "Do you expect favors for allowing Tara to visit Julia? Is that what motivates all your actions?"

"I do *not* expect to have my name constantly slaughtered in print!" Merrick burst out, fighting to contain his temper. "You have no right to link my name in your stories about Don Miguel's untimely death."

"There are rumors buzzing about Clarendon, speculating on the reason Don Miguel died. I am only printing the story to ensure the sheriff does not forget that the murder is still unsolved." An intimidating grin rippled across Terrance's lips. "You wouldn't, by chance, be paying the good sheriff to have a memory lapse, would you?"

Merrick looked like a volcano preparing to erupt. "If you would concentrate on *finding* the assailant instead of pointing an accusing finger at an innocent man and damaging his good name, perhaps you could obtain results," he snorted disdainfully.

"Perhaps, if you would agree to answer a few of my questions instead of claiming that you have a perfect

185

alibi, I would," Terrance threw back. "I find it very odd that you are never *alone* when catastrophe befalls one of the good citizens of Texas." A mocking smile surfaced on Terrance's lips. "I don't suppose you had heard that someone broke into my newspaper office and damaged the type shortly after my last article, concerning Don Miguel's death, appeared in the paper."

Merrick managed to regain control of his temper and countered with his own taunting smile. "No, I hadn't heard about your misfortune. I'm sure you were distressed by the inconvenience. I hope that doesn't mean your paper will be delayed. That would indeed be a pity."

"Your sympathy is touching," Terrance smirked sarcastically. "And now, if you will excuse me, I think I will check in on my daughter. After all, she is the reason I rode out here."

"Is she?" Merrick scoffed, plopping down behind his desk. "I rather thought you came out to needle me, since it has become your favorite pastime these past years. Nothing would make you happier than to see my cattle empire crumble down around me. But it won't, Winslow. I won't be intimidated by a snoopy reporter who has made our medium of information a gossip column. . . ."

Terrance paused by the door and turned to meet Merrick's insolent smile. "The truth will out, Russel. It often takes time and perseverance, but a ransacked office will not deter me from uncovering the facts."

When Terrance eased open the door to Tara's room, he cast aside his feud with Merrick. A tender smile grazed his lips. Quietly he walked over to ease down on the edge of the bed. Tara's lashes fluttered up and she reached out to give her father's hand a loving squeeze.

"This is not how I intended to greet you when you traveled to the ranch to visit me."

His shoulder lifted and dropped in a careless shrug.

186

"I'm only sorry that you met with trouble. I would take you back to Clarendon with me if I thought you could endure the ride."

"Aren't you staying?" Tara's voice registered disappointment. There was so much she wanted to ask her father, so much she didn't understand, things he knew, if only he would tell her.

"I'm afraid I can't. Vandals broke into the newspaper office to destroy the type and, it will take a great deal of time to reorganize what is left of it," he explained.

Tara's jaw sagged on its hinges. "But why would anyone want to . . ."

Terrance pressed his index finger to her lips to shush her. "There is no need to fret. I will be able to repair the damage. You just rest. I will stop back by to see you before I return to Clarendon."

Nodding in compliance, Tara discarded her questions. She would press the matter of Sloane's vendetta against Merrick and Terrance's speculations about who had ransacked the newspaper office when her father paid a return visit.

Terrance smiled fondly, watching Tara's long lashes flutter against her pale cheeks. She would be in competent hands, he assured himself. Sloane harbored deep resentments, but Tara had touched the tender side of his emotions. Terrance had seen the concerned expression on Sloane's face while he fussed over Tara, tending her wound.

Another thought skipped across his mind and he frowned pensively. Had Merrick sabotaged the newspaper office to retaliate against the article about the unsolved murder? Terrance wouldn't have put it past Merrick. Maybe the cattle baron had destroyed the type to ensure that Terrance spent the next few weeks in the office instead of snooping around the ranch. That underhanded scoundrel, Terrance thought acrimoniously. Merrick was capable of murder, and he wouldn't bat an eye at ransacking a man's office to distract him. Clinging to that suspicious thought, Terrance unfolded himself from the edge of the bed and returned downstairs to harass Merrick any way he could. And by the time Terrance bid him adieu, Merrick was so furious with the jibes and offhanded insults that he had very nearly reduced himself into a pile of smoldering ashes.

Chapter 12

After being left in solitary confinement for more than a day, Tara was ready to climb the walls without a ladder. Her rambling thoughts were playing havoc with her sanity and she was determined to find some answers for the myriad of questions that were whirling through her mind.

When Julia brought up the supper tray, Tara subtly steered her into a brief explanation of her childhood. It seemed Julia had no recognition of her mother, who had died of pneumonia during one harsh winter when Julia was only two years old. Tara could not help but wonder if there had been no other women in Merrick's life. It had been sixteen years since his wife's death.

A thoughtful frown creased Tara's brow as she eased back on the pillow and peered at the comely strawberry blonde. "Doesn't your father ever get lonely for a woman's companionship? Has there been no one else in his life all these years?"

Julia sighed heavily. "There has been no one for many years. I faintly remember once when a woman came to visit Papa. I was still very small, but I remember thinking how very beautiful she was, that I would have liked to have her for a mother."

"Did your father show an interest in her?" Tara pried.

Julia's shoulder lifted and then dropped. "I think he

cared a great deal about her. But she only stayed a few days and before she left she and Papa had a terrible argument. Before I could say good-bye, Carmelle was gone, and I have never seen her since. Papa refuses to speak of her, and to this day I don't know why they quarreled. My father is a very private man, and sometimes I feel as if I don't know him at all. He shuts me out of his world at times."

"And there has been no one else . . . ever?" Tara queried, frowning pensively at her newfound knowledge.

Julia gave her reddish-blond head a negative shake. "There have been one or two who have come and gone, but Papa has never been serious about anyone." Her brow arched curiously. "What brought on this rash of questions?"

Tara shrugged evasively. "I have nothing else to do but wonder about you and your father while I am confined to bed." A sheepish smile slid across her lips. "And as you well know, I have alway been a curious soul."

"Curious about everyone, except Sloane," Julia contended. "You don't seem to want anything to do with him, even when he saved you from disaster. If it had not been for him, you could have been in serious trouble."

Perhaps he had done her a disfavor, Tara mused begrudgingly. If he had allowed the poison to run its course, she wouldn't be battling this maddening emotional tug-of-war. Tara could feel depression closing in on her. Maybe a warm, relaxing bath would cure her blue mood, she thought hopefully.

When Julia had removed the tray and ordered the servants to fill the tub, Tara tossed back the sheet and tested her tender leg, relieved that it was on the mend.

A contented sigh escaped her lips as she sank down in the warm water. She would have preferred to glide across the river below the waterfall that lay northeast of

Diamond R headquarters, but under the circumstances she decided it was best to stay where she was. The last time she had impulsively fled from the house she had wound up in . . . Tara compressed her lips, trying to halt the thought. That night never existed. It was like a dream, and she would think of it as such.

Tara lifted a handful of perfumed bubbles and then let them scatter like splinters of a forbidden dream. Damn, why had that impossible man taken up permanent residence in her mind? Wasn't her life in enough turmoil without dwelling on Sloane and his mysterious antics?

When her lashes swept up, Tara gasped in surprise, finding she had a captive audience. "What are you doing in here?" she croaked.

Sloane moved silently away from the drapes and emerged from the shadows. For several minutes he had stood watching the bewitching mermaid with the silver-blond hair piled recklessly on top of her head exposing her swanlike neck and the delicate curve of her jaw. Her ivory skin glowed in the golden light, and Sloane was stung by the compelling need to caress what his eyes brazenly touched. Just watching her sylphlike movements was enough to send his blood pressure soaring.

"I came to check on my patient," he murmured, his probing gaze burning away the clinging bubbles that covered her bare flesh.

Tara glanced toward the door, certain someone would blunder down the hall and overhear them. Someone like Julia. It would crush her to learn that Sloane had seen her wearing less than a bathtub of bubbles. "Don't you know what you are risking by coming here, especially by means of the window?"

A provocative smile hovered on his full lips as he swaggered toward her, sending Tara diving deeper into the tub. "Don't you know what I might miss if I came in the usual way?" His eyes dipped to the rosy peaks of her

191

breasts that no amount of water could conceal. "I consider *seeing* you worth any risk," he assured her, his voice raspy with desire as he knelt beside her.

The heat of his gaze was so intense that Tara feared her bubble bath would become a cloud of steam, fully exposing her to those ravenous blue eyes. "Sloane, this has to stop. It must be obvious to you that Julia fancies herself in love with you. You are putting me between a rock and a hard spot," Tara squeaked as his index finger glided across her cheek and then ventured into the water, sliding languidly against her silky skin.

"That is not where I want you," he murmured huskily as his penetrating eyes focused on her heart-shaped lips.

Tara resettled his wayward hand on the rim of the tub. "Just exactly what is it you want from me?" she demanded and then shrank away when he moved closer. She was afraid he would touch her again and her defenses would dissolve.

"I thought I had made that clear, *mi niña*. I want you any way I can get you. . . ."

He moved closer, filling the room, the world. He smelled of the whole outdoors, and her senses were consumed by the overwhelming fragrance. When his mouth slanted across hers in a kiss that was slow, sweet, and achingly tender, Tara was lured closer to the flame that had begun to burn between them. His tongue traced the curve of her lips and then probed deeper, his kiss stealing her breath and then offering it back in a most arousing way. Sensations as wild and free as the wind whispered across her skin and sang in her soul as his hand cruised over her bent leg to map the generous curve of her hips. And then his warm, moist lips abandoned hers, spilling over the velvety terrain of her shoulder to tease each pink bud that grew taut beneath his thorough, tantalizing attention. His breath was hot against her quivering flesh as he murmured words of need, words expressing a craving that merely touching her left unfulfilled.

A feeling of exquisite helplessness flooded over her as his bold caresses tracked across the sensitive flesh of her thighs. Passion raged like a roaring tempest swirling through her veins, channeling into each nerve and muscle until he had made his will her own. Her body moved instinctively toward his seeking hand, reveling in the rapturous pleasures of his ardent fondling. Tara could not contain the tormented moan that tumbled from her lips as his practiced hands roamed over her supple body like a harpist stroking the strings, composing a soft, compelling melody that played in her soul.

The last of her resistance eroded away when a tidal wave of pleasure splashed over her, lifting her onto ecstasy's bubbly crest and then towing her downward, only to be picked up and carried higher and higher. . . .

The aching throb of desire left reason drowning in a whirlpool, one with such forceful, overpowering currents that Tara knew all was lost long before she was dragged into the churning depths.

"Lord, how I love touching you," Sloane moaned as his lips caressed one ripe bud and then the other. His left hand glided over her trim waist and then curled around the soft swell of her breast. "But it will never be enough, not after that night I cradled you in my arms. Don't deny me, Tara. I need you. *Ven acá.* . . ."

Tara could not have denied him anything he asked of her. She wanted him, ached to touch him as intimately as he had touched her. She yearned to set her hands upon his hair-roughened flesh, to run her fingers through the dark furring of hair on his muscled chest, to press her lips to his lips and feel him surrender to her adoring caresses.

As he lifted her from the tub and carried her to bed, Tara held his hungry gaze, memorizing each and every rugged feature, tracing the stern, commanding line of his

193

jaw, smoothing away the frustrated tension of wanting her so desperately.

His grasp on her velvety skin eased, allowing her to slip to the floor. Her body sang when it made intimate contact with his hard contours. She ached to arouse him until he was oblivious to all except the splendorous sensations that would build into a wild crescendo. Her inquiring hands slid beneath his faded brown shirt to mark the location of each rib and lean muscle. Her fingertips skimmed his chest and then her lips followed in their wake, gently forcing his shirt aside so her kisses and caresses could roam unhindered. With deliberate patience, Tara tasted his skin, her hands weaving over his heaving chest to settle on the band of his breeches.

A moan of sweet torment bubbled in his throat as her tantalizing caresses trailed daringly lower. Sloane wasn't certain how she had divested him of every article of clothing or when they had come to lie naked on the bed, nor did he care. His mind reeled as Tara crouched above him. Her golden hair tumbled about them like a silken cape. The tips of her breasts brushed wantonly against his thudding heart. He was on fire, and this seductive tigress was the flame of his desire. Her butterfly kisses and caresses were driving him mad.

"Do I please you?" she questioned huskily. Her exploring hands glided over his muscled thigh to trace the firm contour of his hips and then descended to retrace the same sweet, tormenting path.

"Too much," Sloane breathed hoarsely.

Never had he allowed a woman to take the initiative, to discover each sensitive point of his body. But he granted Tara every privilege. She had learned to bring his passions to a fervent pitch with her gentle touch. His senses were alive with the alluring scent of her. Even when he closed his eyes he could see this lovely seraph hovering over him, granting him a glimpse of heaven.

Erotic sensations unfurled, one upon the other, until raw instinct took a firm hold on him. Sloane twisted away to appease the craving she had instilled in him. He longed to become a part of her, to forfeit his soul for that one splendorous moment that transcended reality.

Tara caught her breath when Sloane lifted himself above her. His eyes were blazing with passion. His powerful body rippled as his muscles flexed and he braced himself above her. His hips guided her thighs apart and his head bent to hers, his mouth taking hers in impatient urgency. Tara arched to meet his hard thrust, consumed by her own compelling need.

It was a wild coming together. They clung to each other in reckless abandon as the sensations of ultimate pleasure engulfed them. Tara was living and dying in the same breathless moment. She had surrendered her body and soul, experiencing feelings that transcended all she had ever known.

His hard male body surged toward hers, seeking infinite depths of intimacy, and then she felt the world split asunder. She was soaring somewhere beyond reality, suspended in time and space as the fervent splendors of lovemaking came at her from all directions. Indescribable sensations spilled over her, to be followed by yet another soul-shattering wave of feelings that made her shudder uncontrollably.

Sloane crushed her to him, his body blending into the soft curves of hers, their hearts beating in thunderous rhythm. The wild rapture left him senseless, and he held her to him as his body trembled and quaked with the aftereffects of exquisite passion.

It was a long moment before Tara felt the dark sensations ebb and she drifted back to reality. She had never experienced emotions that could take such fierce control of her, and she was certain no other moment could compare to the quintessence of rapture she had discovered in his powerful arms. It was like reaching up to touch heaven, knowing she would be allowed just one glimpse of paradise in her lifetime. No other night could hold such wild splendor, she told herself, and she would cherish this memory always, even when it would have been wiser to let it flit away.

"Surely it cannot always be like this," she mused aloud.

Sloane's soft laughter made her realize she had spoken aloud. "Shall we find out for certain? I was wondering the same thing."

Tara's inhibitions had abandoned her long ago, and she could not pretend to oppose the idea. Indeed, it had an arousing appeal to it. She looped her arms around his granite shoulders and flung him an agreeable smile.

"I cannot seem to resist the temptation, dark phantom," she teased as she raised parted lips to him.

Sloane raised an eyebrow as he peered down at the impish grin that curved the corners of her mouth upward and made her eyes glisten like priceless amethysts. "Do you think you are up to experimenting after your bout with the rattler? I wouldn't think of overtiring you when you are on the mend."

"Snake?" she purred seductively. "I cannot honestly remember anything before this night."

An amused smile tracked across his lips as he gazed down at the waterfall of blond hair that sprayed across the pillow. Somehow he had managed to free the provocative temptress whom Tara had so long concealed behind her pride and stubbornness. He had never known a woman as bewitching and unpredictable as this lovely nymph. She could make him bubble with laughter with her playful antics, stoke the fires of his temper with her biting remarks, and still leave him smoldering with passion, even when he swore the blaze had completely consumed him. Tara was the picture of feminine beauty

196

and grace, and yet she could become a wildcat when she felt threatened. She gave a new and intriguing meaning to the word "woman," and he found himself hungering to explore the realm of her complicated personality, to share her innermost thoughts.

"Tara . . ." The sound of her name on his lips rippled with emotion. "There is so much I want to . . ."

"Tara?" Her name echoed in the room, but this time the questioning voice came from the hall. "Is there anything I can get for you before I retire for the night?" Julia inquired.

Horror flashed in Tara's eyes as the doorknob turned and Julia started into the room. But like the phantom he portrayed, Sloane vanished from beside her, leaving her feeling cold and alone when she had been warm and content the previous moment.

"I'm fine, really," Tara insisted as she settled the sheet about her and attempted to sound casual, even while her heart was galloping around her rib cage like a runaway stallion.

"Not even a warm cup of tea?" Julia tempted her.

"No, thank . . ." Tara's stampeding heart stopped when her eyes fell to the boot that lay at the end of the bed and she died a thousand times, certain Julia would notice it. With trembling hands she reached over to snuff the lantern. "Thank you for checking on me. Good night. . . ."

Tara held her breath as Julia murmured a quiet goodnight and then closed the door behind her. Lord, they had come dangerously close to being discovered, and Tara wasn't certain how she would have explained her way out of such an embarrassing predicament.

A startled gasp clambered around in her throat as she glanced sideways to see Sloane's dark hand rising from the bed. "We were very nearly caught," she whispered as he eased down beside her.

The incident hadn't rattled Sloane in the least. But why should it? Tara asked herself. The man had been leaping in and out of the shadows for so long that narrow escapes never disturbed him.

"You really should go," Tara insisted as he leaned over her, his mouth fluttering lazily over her lips.

"I truly should," Sloane agreed as his languid kiss spilled over her cheek to trace the trim column of her throat and his hand slid beneath the sheet to make arousing contact with bare flesh. When his mouth trailed back to hers like a bee hovering on a flower and her soft lips melted against his, he knew a team of wild horses couldn't drag him away. "But I have always been a stickler for finishing what I have begun. And we *have* only begun. . . ."

Tara felt herself surrendering to the flood of sensations that washed over her. He could make her forget everything that had any resemblance to reality. Her body moved instinctively against his hard contours, aching to become one with him, to rediscover the heights and depths of intimacy, to recreate the moment that had been like a fantastic dream. Each kiss and caress fed the gnawing hunger, and Tara couldn't seem to get enough of him. She was addicted to the drugging taste of him, the manly scent that warped her senses.

Sloane's body caught fire and burned as her shapely hips insinuated themselves against his, her full breasts boring into his chest. She had taught him things about passion with her innocent techniques, things he never believed possible with one so inexperienced in the ways of love. And each time he set his hands on her velvety skin, it was a unique encounter. Each response was warmer and wilder than the time before, and Sloane marveled at the passionate woman who seemed to come alive in his arms. Her reactions to his intimate caresses gave him a feeling of power over her, something force could never accomplish with this free-spirited nymph.

He was oblivious to all except this obsessive need for her, as if he had only sampled passion's bubbling spring and had instantly become addicted. Their fierce need for each other could be appeased for a time, and each time Sloane roused, knowing he should leave the magic circle of her arms, he could not tear himself away.

Throughout that splendorous night, he kept awakening to place one last kiss to her sweet lips, but each kiss served to create a wild new beginning to another passionate encounter. Before dawn's first light, Sloane finally forced himself to move away, finding it practically impossible.

As he silently gathered his clothing and shrugged it on, his gaze strayed back to the bed and he was spellbound by the scant moonlight that caught in her hair and sprinkled across her cheek. One small, delicate hand lay on the empty pillow where she had cradled his head, and Sloane forced himself not to return to the cozy warmth. The sheet was recklessly draped over her hips, leaving her breasts and one shapely leg exposed to his devouring gaze.

Questioning his willpower, Sloane took another hesitant step toward the window and paused to stare at her one last time before he fled. He yearned to spend one uninterrupted night in her arms. He wondered if she would look even more enticing when sunbeams filtered into the room to skip across her alabaster skin. Sloane shook his head to banish the whimsical thought. He had already dared too much with Terrance Winslow's daughter. It seemed he had forsaken every ounce of common sense where Tara was concerned. Lord, what spell had that enticing witch cast upon him?

Scowling to himself, Sloane slipped through the window, made his way down the tree that served as a ladder, and then crept to the bunkhouse to catch a few hours of sleep before the sun cast its golden halo on the horizon.

Sloane eased down on the cot next to Burns Dixon and quietly expelled the breath he had been holding since he had sneaked from the house. He had risked a great deal to spend the night in Tara's arms, and it would surely cost him his strength. Sloane seriously doubted that he would be able to manage his duties throughout the day without his eyes slamming shut. Lord, he was exhausted.

Burns reared his unruly red head and flung a grin across the narrow distance that separated him from the dark silhouette stretched out on the cot. "It's a little late to be out roamin' around, even for you, Prescott," he taunted.

Sloane propped up on one elbow and glared at the beaming smile that could have led a lost traveler through a raging blizzard. "I had a few matters to attend," he said evasively.

Burns scoffed at the bald-faced lie. "You ain't foolin' me a bit. You've been with that Winslow girl, and you ain't been worth shootin' since she landed on Merrick's doorstep. It's a wonder to me them broncs ain't throwed you, the way you've been gawkin' at her."

"Don't preach," Sloane scowled as he pulled the quilt over his shoulder and turned his back on Burns.

"Somebody's got to." Burns flounced back on his pillow. "I swear you've lost what little sense you was born with, which, by the way, wasn't much to boast about. Yer gonna git yerself into a lot of trouble chasin' after that woman. She ain't like the ones in Tascosa who can be bought with a drink and a smile."

"Will you go to sleep," Sloane hissed, trying to keep his voice low and having one hell of a time refraining from bellowing at the meddling cook. "Damn, you're becoming more like a nagging wife every day."

Burns puffed up like an indignant toad. "Mind yer

200

tongue, you bowlegged, good-for-nothin' cowboy, or you'll find ants crawlin' in yer bed, if you ever stay in it long enough to feel the sting."

"At least you haven't threatened to poison my stew," Sloane grunted sarcastically.

"I was gittin' to that," Burns snorted.

Sloane heaved an agitated sigh. Burns was as good as gold, but he had become as protective as a mother hen. He was always fussing over Sloane, cautioning him when he attempted some daredevil feat that Burns swore would be the last foolish stunt he ever pulled.

"Tara is like no one I've ever met," Sloane admitted when he heard Burns fluttering around like a hen situating herself on her nest.

"I ain't arguin' with that, but you better watch yer step," Burns warned. "Yer gonna find yerself wadin' in so deep you can't swim out. And you don't even know whose side she's on, for God's sake!"

Sloane didn't argue the point. After all, Burns was right. Tara knew just enough to cause him trouble. Perhaps he should keep his distance and allow the flames to cool. They had already blazed hotter than a thousand suns, and Sloane could find himself cremated if he wasn't careful. Tara was virtually unpredictable and . . . the thought froze in his mind. Was she waiting to catch him unaware and then inform Merrick of his scheme? She had been very determined to learn why he had a personal vendetta against Merrick.

No, Sloane told himself. He couldn't have misjudged that feisty minx, and yet . . . Sloane grumbled sourly. Was his strange attraction to that silver-blond vixen with the violet eyes distorting his logic? Was he seeing only what he wanted to see in her, something that wasn't really there? If Terrance thought he could trust his daughter, he would have told her the whole of it, even when Sloane insisted that she remain in the dark. And

201

just why had Tara arrived in Texas at the beginning of the summer, instead of in the fall when his dealings with Merrick would have been concluded? Suddenly Sloane didn't know whom he could trust.

He had made a tragic mistake by involving Don Miguel. Burns and Terrance could face a similar disaster if they weren't careful. And who really had sent for Tara? Could it have been Merrick? A muddled frown plowed his brow, remembering the remark Merrick had made about becoming fond of Tara. Was he planning to use her to get back at Terrance?

Grappling with those disturbing thoughts, Sloane tried to sleep, but it was impossible. He was plagued with doubts he didn't want to believe, but was forced to consider for survival's sake. Things were not always as they appeared—he himself was a living example of that. Good God, *was* he wading in over his head, as Burns suggested? Sloane had the sinking feeling he was treading quicksand. The more people who knew his purpose and his second identity, the greater the risks. He could well be cutting his own throat, and if he didn't keep his wits about him, he would be a dead man.

Chapter 13

During Tara's convalescence she had taken careful
note of Merrick's activities, eavesdropping on conversa-
tions between the boss of the Diamond R Ranch and his
hired men and those of several neighboring ranchers who
had visited the house. Tara wasn't certain if any of the
information she had overheard was pertinent, but the
bits and pieces of knowledge she had pried from Julia and
Merrick began to disturb her. She still wasn't sure why
and how Sloane fit into the scheme of things, but the
fragments of information were playing havoc with her
inquisitive nature and she had begun to piece them
together in some sort of logical order.

The first time she had ventured from the house, she
had wandered to the stock pens to see Sloane tending one
of the geldings that had torn a ligament in his leg. Sloane
had barely acknowledged her presence and had begun to
play up to Julia, who was walking on air more often than
not.

Tara was bitterly disappointed when she realized that
Sloane had quickly tired of her, just when she had fallen
in love with him. Courageously, she picked up the
shattered splinters of her heart and glued them back
together with what was left of her pride. She would be
damned if she allowed Sloane to know how deeply she
was hurting. It was obvious that she had served her

purpose for him. Now that she had become his conquest, he had turned his charismatic charm on Julia. No doubt, he had decided to use another method of revenge against Merrick—the seduction of his daughter.

"It seems we have both lost our fascination," Loren muttered sourly as he ambled up behind Tara as she watched Sloane and Julia stroll around behind the tack room.

Tara pivoted to see Loren's heart in his eyes. "You really do love her, don't you?" she said sympathetically.

Loren nodded his chestnut-brown head and heaved a heavy sigh. "Not that it matters any more. Julia seems to have forgotten that I exist. I suppose she is still too young to give up her childhood dreams."

"Perhaps it's time we remind her that you are alive and well and hiding right under her nose." Tara grinned mischievously. "Have you a date for the party?"

"I'm not going," Loren grumbled, his expression sour enough to curdle milk. "It would tear me apart to see Julia drooling all over Sloane, especially when I can't fault him. Julia has been following him around until he has finally quit running from her."

Tara curled her hand around Loren's arm and tossed him a wry smile. "Sulking will not solve your problem," she insisted as they disappeared behind their own concealing shed, just as Julia and Sloane reappeared. "What you need is someone to help you make our fickle friend jealous."

Loren's answering grin was as wide as the rim of Palo Duro Canyon when he met the lavender twinkle in Tara's eyes. "But I won't be pretending to enjoy myself at the party," he assured her, taking careful note of the bewitching young woman who had the other hired hands bumping into fences when she sauntered past them.

"And if Julia doesn't open her eyes to see what she is missing, she doesn't deserve a man like you," Tara insisted saucily.

When her radiant smile cut becoming dimples in her cheeks, Loren melted like snow thawing on a campfire. Escorting this lovely lass to the ball could well be the distraction he needed. For more than three years he had thought the world revolved around the comely strawberry blonde. But perhaps he had been a mite too hasty with love, he thought to himself. And what was good for the gander might be even better for the goose. If Julia could cavort with Sloane Prescott, he could certainly enjoy this dazzling young beauty's companionship.

Impulsively, Loren's head moved toward hers, cautiously testing her reaction to his embrace. Their lips met in a light kiss, one that might have deepened into intimacy if Sloane and Julia hadn't caught them in the clinch.

"Loren Marshall, of all the . . ." Julia's mouth fell open. If she had been wearing false teeth they would have fallen to the ground to snap at the toes of her boots.

Tara peered around Loren's broad shoulders to see Sloane glaring murderously at her. It did her heart good to know his male pride had suffered a nasty gash. If he thought she would decompose just because he had turned his attention on Julia, he had made a gross error in judgment. She was not some simpering twit who fell to pieces when the man she had fallen in love with found his eyes straying to seek out another conquest.

"I can't wait until the party," Tara cooed, sending Loren a conspiratory wink and then coyly batting her eyes at him.

Loren pulled Tara against him. "I will be counting the hours in the days," he rasped. With a captive audience, he planted a very passionate kiss to Tara's responsive lips. When he withdrew from what looked to be the most romantic of encounters, he strutted off like a proud peacock. "Lovely day, isn't it?" He touched the brim of

205

his hat as he swaggered past Julia, who would have collapsed in shock if she hadn't been hanging on Sloane's brawny arm.

Two pair of narrowed eyes followed Loren back to his chores before swinging around to riddle Tara's mock-innocent expression. Julia opened her mouth to fling a harsh remark, thought better of it, and then stalked off to give Loren the tongue-lashing she thought he deserved.

"Since when have you taken to public displays of affection?" Sloane gritted out. He was bewildered by the sting of irritation that attacked him like a swarm of disturbed hornets.

Her shoulder lifted in a reckless shrug, sending the fringe of her red bolero dangling about her. "Since I have found it to be a pleasurable pastime," she replied breezily.

When she sailed past Sloane, his hand snaked out to haul her back beside him, holding her in his bone-crushing embrace. "For a woman who is supposedly engaged, you are certainly making the most of your last months of freedom," he grunted sarcastically.

Tara made no attempt to resist their close physical contact. He was actually jealous, and that delighted her. Now that the boot was on the other foot, Sloane was feeling the pinch, and it served the rascal right, she thought spitefully.

"You have no reason to criticize me when I have only adopted your philosophy," she told him blandly, pleased with herself for sounding so cool and indifferent when her heart was hammering in response to the feel of his hard body molded to hers.

"My philosophy?" Sloane hooted. "I don't go around kissing every man I meet, but you damned sure do."

Tara giggled at the thought and then took their argument right into the middle of enemy camp. "I am only making comparisons, as you do, with every woman who crosses your line of vision. And I have found that Loren Marshall has possibilities," she informed him, her violet eyes flaring with mischief when she felt him tense in agitation. "Perhaps you could learn a few pointers from Loren."

"I have managed thirty-two years on my own," he growled as he bent her backwards, literally sweeping her off her feet. "And I have heard no complaints . . . until you came along."

"Unhand me, you big . . ."

His greedy mouth took firm possession of hers, his teeth grinding against her lips, forcing them apart to admit the entrance of his probing tongue, taking from her without the thought of returning pleasure. But what had begun as a forceful, overpowering kiss became a passionate embrace, even when it had been Sloane's intent to exert his superior strength over this infuriating gamin. The memories of the passion-filled night he had spent in her arms leaped from the corners of his mind, hurling him back in time. He could feel his body melting into the soft, shapely contours of Tara's, succumbing to a power more potent than force. Before he realized it, his hands were drifting down her spine to press her hips suggestively to his. He had intended to shake the stuffing out of this blond-haired hellion for allowing Loren to kiss her, but now he was squeezing the stuffing out of her, as if he could not get close enough, as if he would not be content until his male body had taken intimate possession of hers.

Tara felt herself surrender, inch by agonizing inch, and despair crowded in on her. His flaming kiss only served to ensure that Loren's embrace could not hold a candle to Sloane's. When he touched her, the world faded into oblivion and she went up in smoke. And where there was smoke there was fire, fire so devastating that Tara knew if she lived to be one hundred she would never forget the way this rough, rawhide man aroused her.

When Sloane finally came up for air, Tara pushed him away, struggled to rewind her unraveled composure, and then flung him an icy glare to cool the lust that had sparked between them. "Thank you for reminding me of the difference between being mauled and embraced," she sniped as she readjusted the clothing Sloane had twisted about her. "You still have a lot to learn about courting women. I only hope Julia can be patient with you. Personally, I find it something akin to steer wrestling, and I pity the poor calves that have their necks wrenched when you throw them to the ground."

"Damn you," Sloane growled, his blue eyes blazing like torches.

"Damn *you* to hell and back," Tara threw at him, fighting to keep a straight face when she could have easily burst out laughing. Sloane's composure had cracked, and he looked as if he would reduce himself to a pile of smoldering cinders if he didn't get a grip on himself, and quickly. How she loved taunting him. He had used that technique on her since the day they'd met, and she was delighted to see that she had managed to creep beneath his leathery hide. So he was human, she mused as she pivoted away and strutted out of the shed. That was an interesting bit of knowledge. For the past few days Tara had thought for certain that Sloane Prescott had been carved from rock.

As Tara disappeared around the corner, Sloane seethed. Damn that gorgeous, tormenting vixen! She had forced him to battle his way through a barrage of defenses before she melted in his embrace. Now, like a bolt of lightning in a cloudless sky, she was accepting Loren's kisses and claiming to prefer them to his. What the hell was he anyway, her guinea pig? Sloane asked himself sourly. Well she could ridicule him until she was blue in the face, but she could never deny that flames exploded when they kissed and touched. There had been something magic between them, and it was far from over, he promised himself. Even Loren Marshall wasn't tough enough to control that free-spirited wildcat. She would be leading him around on a leash, and Loren would find himself another conquered heart laying around that silver-blond she-cat's neck, along with her other trophies. The Diamond R foreman didn't know how to handle a woman like Tara, Sloane grumbled as he stomped back to the corral. She was like a flighty colt that required a firm hand and a strong will to control her, unless a man wanted to risk having his heart trampled. Sloane gritted his teeth as he yanked up the stallion's reins and led him around the pen. The thought of Loren touching Tara kept him fuming for the remainder of the afternoon. That violet-eyed chit made him burn with a kind of fever that couldn't be measured in degrees, and Sloane cursed, knowing Tara was both the cause and cure of his ailment. She was like a poison in his blood, and he wondered bitterly how long it would take before the mere thought of her no longer touched off myriad emotions churning inside him.

Biting back a smile, Tara glanced over at Julia who had been sulking most of the afternoon. "Don't you think you are taking this a bit too hard for a young lady who insists that one should sample several fish in the sea before she settles for one worthy catch?" she teased lightly.

Julia's bottom lip jutted out in an exaggerated pout. "Loren said he was in love with me, but he certainly has a strange way of showing it."

"What did you expect him to do, follow you indefinitely?" Tara inquired and then bit into a lemon tart.

"Well, he could have given me some time and space without turning his attention on you, not that I can blame him for that," Julia grumbled begrudgingly and then focused her full attention on her lovely friend. "Did he . . . I mean . . . did you . . ." She stumbled and faltered, attempting to regroup her thoughts.

"Do I think there could ever be anything between us?" Tara questioned for her, since Julia seemed to have difficulty embarking upon the subject.

Julia tossed her a grateful smile. "I couldn't help but wonder if Loren affects you the same way he affects me. I can't think when he kisses me, but when I stop to consider if it is love that causes the upheaval of emotions, I cannot say for certain." She breathed an exasperated sigh and then collapsed against the back of the sofa. "Papa has given me no guidance, and I'm not certain what I'm feeling."

"Sometimes a woman must simply trust her instincts," Tara told her solemnly. "Loren's kiss assured *me* that *we* will never be more than friends. I enjoy his company, but if you decide that what you feel for him is love, I will not complicate matters."

"Do you truly think you are in love with Joseph Rutherford? You didn't seem overly fond of him when I visited you in St. Louis."

Tara stared at the folds in her skirt and then lifted a faint smile as she glanced sideways at Julia. "No, I don't love Joseph, but that is of little consequence to my grandfather. He seems to be more concerned with seeing me properly married than happy."

"You mean he intends to force you into an unwanted wedding?" Julia gasped in dismay. Lord, she thought she had problems, but they were insignificant compared to the possibility of wedding a man she could never love.

An impish grin pursed Tara's lips as she gathered her feet beneath her and set the cup of tea aside. "If I am unable to talk my grandfather out of this absurdity, and if I am forced to leave dear Joseph standing alone at the altar, may I take refuge here?"

Julia grinned and gave her strawberry-blond head an affirmative shake. "You will always be welcome here, even if you are running from an unwanted marriage. And Tara?"

Tara glanced back at Julia as she ambled toward the door. "Yes?"

"Thank you for making me see that I feel something very special for Loren."

"Have you decided to allow him to escort you to the party?"

A wry smile pursed Julia's lips. "No. I still haven't decided which man stirs me most, Sloane or Loren."

Tara rolled her eyes toward the ceiling. "Fickle woman," she mocked before veering around the corner and stepping onto the stoop to gaze across headquarters.

A thoughtful frown knitted Tara's brow as her eyes settled on the mess-house. Since this seemed to be a day for stirring up trouble, Tara decided to seek out Burns Dixon. She was still looking for answers to the questions that plagued her inquisitive mind, and she would have bet her right arm that man knew everything that went on around the Diamond R Ranch.

Inhaling a courageous breath, Tara pushed open the back door of the mess-house and peered inside to see Burns poised on a chair with a bushel basket of potatoes situated between his legs. Pasting on a cordial smile, Tara strolled over beside him and parked herself in the chair, took up a spare knife, and carved the skin off a potato.

"I never thought I'd see the day a person resorted to cleanin' potatoes for sport," Burns snickered as he cocked a bushy brow and winked at the comely lass who had volunteered to help him with his mundane task. "You ain't bored, are you, lass?"

"No, mostly curious." Tara focused her attention on the potato, but she cast Burns a quick glance to catch his reaction to her intentional baiting.

The plump old cook shifted uneasily in his chair. "Curious about what? Didn't nobody tell you I keep to myself and steer clear of gossip? If yer lookin' for some kind of answers, yer barkin' up the wrong tree. I don't know nothin' about nobody else's business but my own."

"I think you do," Tara said simply and then caught his shifting gaze, holding him hostage. "I know just enough about our mutual friend to be a threat to him. And you are going to tell me why he maintains this double identity."

"I don't know nothin'." Burns buttoned his lips and thrust out a stubborn chin. "I've been doin' my job 'round here for thirty years without causin' no trouble, and I ain't goin' to spoil my record."

"Who was Carmelle?" Tara questioned point blank.

Burns yelped when his knife slipped and he cut a chunk out of his own hide. "How'd you find out about her?" he chirped like a disturbed meadowlark.

"Sloane mentioned her," Tara lied through her teeth, hoping to entrap Burns, who was becoming more rattled by the second.

"That fool! I told him not to. . . ." Burns bit his lip and swallowed the last half of his sentence as he glared holes in Tara's wry smile.

"You know exactly what her relationship was with Merrick, don't you, Burns?" Tara pressed. "You have been with Merrick far too long not to know why Sloane bears a grudge. And you are helping Sloane with his charade. The night you interrupted us, you said Loren was looking for Sloane, but he wasn't. I saw him with Julia when I returned to the house. Did you have some tidbit of information to pass on to Sloane?"

Burns muttered under his breath. This little chit was

too clever and observant for her own good. He had sought out Sloane to inform him that Terrance Winslow would be meeting him at the abandoned shack between Clarendon and the ranch, but Tara had caught him in his lie.

"Who was Carmelle? Why did she come to see Merrick? Was she Sloane's mother? Is he the illegitimate son Merrick Russel refused to acknowledge when Carmelle and Merrick had their fiery argument those many years ago?"

Burns's face whitewashed and he tugged at the bandanna to relieve the pressure around his neck. "I can't tell you nothin'," he squeaked. "And you've been jumpin' to a lot of conclusions. Your pa . . ." He scowled, disgusted with himself for allowing his tongue to outdistance his brain. Lordy, this quick-witted nymph was groping to untangle the facts, and Burns feared Sloane would be frying alive if he didn't tell her the whole truth before she managed to twist it into another nightmare! Great balls of fire, this scheme was going to blow up in Sloane's face, just as sure as the sky was blue.

"I got other chores to do," Burns muttered as he bolted from his chair and waddled out the back door as fast as his stubby legs would carry him.

Tara tossed the knife and potato back in the basket and heaved a frustrated sigh. She had thought she could pry information out of Sloane's confidant, but the cook was as tight-lipped as Sloane. Had she guessed correctly about the mysterious woman who had walked in and out of Merrick's life those many years ago? And if it were true, Julia could never have Sloane, even if she did fall in love with him. Lord, what a tangled mess, she thought, disheartened.

Had Sloane's mother asked him to destroy Merrick, since he would not acknowledge a child born out of wedlock? Tara threw up her hands in a gesture of futility.

Maybe she had allowed her imagination to run rampant, fitting bits and pieces of information together that didn't really match at all. Maybe she was making a simple matter far too complicated, but dammit, no one would enlighten her and she detested being left in the dark! What the devil was Sloane up to, and why? Those two questions were driving her mad.

The sound of the door crashing against the wall jarred Tara from her troubled deliberations. Tara glanced up to see Sloane's ominous frame filling the entrance. He looked like black thunder, his rugged features dark and foreboding, his cobalt-blue eyes matching diamonds in hardness. He was fuming like a volcano that was about to erupt. If looks could kill, Tara would have been roasting on coals, waiting to be served as the main course for lunch. When he stormed toward her, Tara instinctively shrank away, certain he meant to strike her with the fists of steel that were clenched at his sides.

"What the hell do you want from me?" he hissed venomously, his glare slicing her to shreds. "I told you not to stick your nose in places it didn't belong, but you never give up, do you?" His lean fingers bit into her arm, cutting off the circulation as he slammed her back against the wall.

Tara's seething irritation bolstered her courage. Sloane might have been as tough as leather and as fierce as an injured lion, but he wasn't going to make her cower. She was a strong, willful woman, and he was not going to push her around. She had every right to know what her father was involved in, and she wasn't going to quit firing questions at Burns or anyone else until she knew the truth. "I will not drop the matter, so it is useless to threaten me," she assured him curtly as she tilted a belligerent chin and met his fuming scowl. "You should know by now that I have no intention of exposing you to Merrick. If I wanted to see you hanged I would already

214

have told him who was haunting his ranch. I am only searching for the truth. We all have our vices, and mine happens to be curiosity. I demand to know what is going on around here."

The rigid muscles of his jaw relaxed slightly, but his fierce grip didn't. Sloane was still mad as hell after witnessing her rendezvous with Loren and then watching Burns hop up and down raving about how Tara had stormed the kitchen to give him the third degree.

"Why should I trust you? How do I know it wasn't Merrick who sent for you to use you against your own father, a man who abandoned you three years ago, a man who still has a great weakness for his precious daughter? Merrick wants to destroy Terrance, just as he disposed of Don Miguel. Will you be a party to that? Are you that vindictive?"

Tara's mouth dropped open and her eyes bulged. How dare he even suggest she had come to Texas to punish her father for abandoning her? That was the most idiotic conclusion she had ever heard. "My father wrote to me and sent the money for my visit. I had only met Merrick briefly when he came to retrieve Julia in St. Louis. Talk about jumping to ludicrous conclusions!" Tara sniffed sarcastically. "Don't you think I could have recognized my father's handwriting? It was *not* Merrick who sent for me, you ignoramus. It was my father!"

"My conclusions are no more ridiculous than your thinking *Merrick* was *my* father!" Sloane howled and threw up his hands. "*¡Que ideas tan descabelladas tienes!* Good God, woman, you have twisted the truth so far out of proportion that I almost didn't recognize it myself!"

Tara slumped back against the wall after Sloane slashed a mile-wide gash in her calculated speculations. Her attempt to fit the pieces of the puzzle together had been all for naught. She was no closer to the truth than she had been the first time she laid eyes on this mysterious cowboy, and it infuriated her that she didn't know a blessed thing about what was going on.

"You really should stick with something you are more familiar with," Sloane smirked, the faintest hint of amusement replacing the cold, deadly gleam that had flashed in his eyes a few minutes earlier. "A private detective, you are not."

"And just what is that supposed to mean?" Tara demanded.

"It is easier to show you than tell you," he murmured as he pulled her against him.

His arms were like iron bands, forging her flesh to his as his mouth came crushing down on hers. He smelled of horses and perspiration, but the rugged scent of him still aroused her. There was no hope for it. She was all too familiar with Sloane's brand of passion. She could claim she found it distasteful, but when he touched her, she melted all over him like a witless fool. He set fires in her blood as no other man had been able to do. Whether he was forceful or gentle, Tara responded to him, despising her weakness for this callous man, but wildly responding just the same.

His hands roamed at random, mapping the shapely contours of her body, leaving fires smoldering in their wake. His kiss deepened in devouring impatience, stripping the breath from her lungs. She was drowning in the taste and feel of him, and she was no longer certain she wanted to be rescued. He could make her will his own, and she would have sacrificed her last breath if he commanded it.

His huge body shuddered as he straightened and then bent his right arm against the wall to hold her captive. "Leave well enough alone, inquisitive imp," Sloane ordered, his voice heavily disturbed with desire. "You are tying me in knots, and I will be forced to deal severely with you if you keep pressing me."

With that, he pushed away and stalked toward the door, refusing to allow her not one meager shred of information. Tara came apart at the seams. Impulsively, she grabbed the discarded knife, wheeled around, and hurled it toward the door. His eyes rounded with astonishment as he jerked away from the quivering blade that lodged in the door casing only a few inches from his right ear.

If Tara hadn't been so furious she would have burst out laughing at the frozen expression on his paling features.

"You could have killed me," Sloane croaked like a sick bullfrog that had very nearly keeled off the side of his lily pad.

"If that had been my intention, I would have," Tara assured him tartly and then snatched up the second knife, sending it sailing through the air to notch only an inch above the first. "Don't think your threats affect me, Sloane. We may share a mutual dislike for each other, but I demand your respect. I have come to expect no more from a man like you, but I will accept nothing less. Do I make myself clear?" Tara's sharp glare pinned him against the wall. "I have every right to know what is going on around here, because I am in the very middle of what could become a fiery feud. I should like to know where to take cover when all hell breaks loose. I witnessed a murder, and I don't even know who my enemy is or why Don Miguel's life was sacrificed. Don't you think I would like to know if my name will be added to the obituaries? I don't know which direction to turn. Dammit, can't you understand that?"

Sloane's stunned gaze drifted from the two knives that were embedded in the door to Tara's flaming red face. Christ, he had a tigress by the tail. And what was a man to do when he found himself on the receiving end of an attack by a feisty little hellcat as adept with weapons as he was? He should toss her into a nest of rattlesnakes, he thought vindictively. That was the only varmint that seemed to frighten this violet-eyed firebrand.

Scowling at his futile scare tactics, Sloane whipped open the door and then slammed it shut behind him, his words rushing at her in the draft of wind. "I will tell you when I'm damned good and ready, and I'm not ready yet! Dammit, leave it be!"

Tara yanked the frying pan from the stove and heaved it at the closed door. She heard Burns yelping as he tried to enter his own kitchen and found himself assaulted by his own skillet. His eyes bulged from their sockets when he spied his paring knives in the door and his frying pan lying upside down on the floor.

"It's a wonder to me that Sloane walked out of here alive!" he squeaked, eyeing the blazing-eyed minx with the utmost caution.

"It's a wonder to me why I allowed it," Tara muttered as she sailed out the door and stalked back to the house.

That man was positively infuriating, Tara grumbled as she paced the confines of her room. What had she done to deserve Sloane's mistrust? *He* was the one who was behaving suspiciously, she reminded herself huffily. All she had attempted to do was sort out the facts, as any good news reporter's daughter would do. Damn that man! He was giving her fits!

Chapter 14

After Tara's unproductive confrontation with Sloane, she decided it would be best to return to Clarendon to visit her father. She hoped her separation from Sloane would cool her irritation with him and his obvious annoyance with her. When she explained her intentions, Julia offered to travel with her, insisting it would be the perfect opportunity to purchase a gown for the party.

When the twosome arrived in Clarendon, Julia aimed herself toward the boutique and Tara headed straight for her father's office. She had expected to find the room still in shambles, and she was surprised to see that Terrance had put the office back in working order.

As Tara swept through the front door, Terrance glanced up, gracing his daughter with a welcoming smile. "What are you doing back in Clarendon? Aren't you going to that elaborate ball Merrick is throwing?"

Tara set her purse aside and nodded affirmatively. "I am, but I thought it high time I came back to visit you. After all, you are the reason I came to Texas in the first place."

Terrance smiled at that. "It is a relief to know that even if I am out of sight, I am not out of mind," he chuckled lightly.

Tara sorely wished absence would ease her agitation with Sloane, but that had not been the case. Even while

Julia rattled on about the upcoming party during their ride, Tara's thoughts kept drifting back to that taciturn cowboy who would reveal nothing about himself. Casting Sloane's disturbing memory aside, Tara pasted on a smile and accepted her father's kiss.

"Are you coming to the ranch for Merrick's grand ball?"

Giving his head a negative shake, Terrance eased down into his chair. "I have just finished repairing the type. If I take time to travel to the ranch, my newspaper won't be printed on time. I'm afraid my work comes first."

Ambling up to the desk, Tara studied the article that lay on the top of the stack of papers. Abruptly, she commented, "I know who the Night Rider is."

Terrance leaned back in his chair, a wry smile pursing his lips. "And your ulterior motive for returning to Clarendon was to interrogate your poor father," he speculated.

Easing her hip onto the edge of the desk, Tara picked up the article pertaining to Don Miguel's unsolved murder that subtly pointed an accusing finger at Merrick Russel. "It would be extremely helpful for my understanding of what is transpiring around me if I knew what truly motivated the phantom of Palo Duro."

"Just what has our mysterious specter told you?" Terrance questioned quietly, his eyes intently focused on his daughter.

"Nothing to clear up my confusion," Tara blurted out in exasperation. "I tried to fit the pieces of the puzzle together. When I confronted Sloane with my speculations he vehemently assured me that I had grossly misread the facts. But that mulish man refused to enlighten me." Her violet eyes fell to her father. "Won't you tell me why Sloane is so determined to destroy Merrick—and why you have sided with him?"

Terrance heaved a heavy sigh. "I'm afraid I cannot."

"But why?" Tara vaulted to her feet, pacing back and forth in front of her father's desk. "No one seems to remember that I was there the night Don Miguel was murdered and that I could expose the Night Rider for who he really is . . . if only I knew who he really is. Confound it! I detest being left in the dark. And you have been just as secretive as Sloane." Tara stopped her pacing to cast Terrance the evil eye. "Just what is your connection with Sloane? Why are you aiding him in his attempt to name Merrick as a murderer? Do you believe Merrick guilty of the crimes Sloane holds against him?"

Terrance had been afraid it would come to this. Tara was inquisitive by nature. She had always been, even as a child. If she didn't understand, she pursued the matter until someone finally explained it to her complete satisfaction. Now Terrance found himself in an uncomfortable situation. He had promised Sloane the secret would never pass his lips. Although Terrance thought Tara could have been an asset to Sloane in uncovering facts during her stay at the Diamond R Ranch, Sloane was not prepared to take her into his confidence. And yet, the mysterious phantom had exposed his true identity to Tara, leaving her more frustrated and confused than she had been in the beginning. Why had Sloane done that?

"Well?" Tara's impatient voice filtered into Terrance's contemplations. "Do you intend to be as closemouthed as Sloane?"

"Unfortunately, it is not my place to divulge that information." Terrance expelled his breath and then shrugged helplessly. "I promised Sloane I would aid him by keeping the legend alive with my newspaper. When he brought you to me, injured and unconscious, he asked that I tell you no more than necessary, hoping your ignorance of the events surrounding Don Miguel's death would keep you safe."

"And you do not even trust your own daughter with

the truth?" It was an underhanded question and Tara knew it. But her curiosity was eating her alive.

A wry smile rippled across Terrance's lips. "Do you intend to shame me into divulging the facts? Would you have me betray Sloane's confidence when he considers me a friend and confidant?"

Dammit, Tara hated to admit that her father was right. Terrance had been sworn to secrecy, and whatever the two of them had been planning had begun long before she set foot in Texas to wedge her nose in places it probably didn't belong.

"No, I suppose not," Tara muttered grudgingly.

"Why have you taken this sudden interest in Sloane Prescott?" Terrance questioned point blank.

"Outlaws and phantoms intrigue me," she countered with an evasive shrug.

"That is your *only* reason for wanting to know what makes Sloane tick?" Terrance prodded, arching a graying brow. "He wouldn't happen to be accompanying you to Russel's party, would he?"

"No, I value my feet far too much for that," she sniffed. "I don't relish having that clumsy cowboy waltz all over them. Loren Marshall is escorting me to the ball."

Disappointment claimed Terrance's features. He had hoped Tara's fascination with Sloane would lead to an emotional involvement, an attachment that would make Tara see that she would never be satisfied wedding Rutherford and setting up housekeeping in St. Louis. Sloane would have been a far better match for a free-spirited woman like Tara. If he hadn't thought so he wouldn't have requested that Tara come to Clarendon before Ryan roped her into a marriage that bore the O'Donnovan stamp of approval.

Perhaps his meddling had been a waste of time, Terrance thought, disheartened. But at least with Tara in

Texas he had the opportunity to see her occasionally. If his attempt at playing matchmaker failed. . . .

"Tara, wait until you see the gown I bought for the party!" Julia burst into the newspaper office in her traditional manner, bubbling with enthusiasm.

Reluctantly, Tara turned her attention to the strawberry blonde. She had hoped to gain some insight into the workings of Sloane's mind after speaking privately with her father. She should have known Terrance's loyalty would not allow him to betray a confidence, not even to his own daughter. So where did that leave her? She was still floundering in a sea of swirling facts that had no logical order.

Ah, well, what had she expected when she began tampering with phantoms, she reminded herself sullenly. Sloane had said he would enlighten her when he was ready. If only she could live so long! By the time that suspicious, mistrusting cowboy got around to explaining his motives, she would probably be old and moldy.

Giving Sloane up as a lost cause, Tara focused her attention on Julia, determined not to have the day spoiled by dwelling on a man she couldn't change.

Tiptoeing quietly toward the back door, Terrance glanced back over his shoulder to make sure that Tara and Julia hadn't heard him making his late-night departure. When he had eased the door shut behind him, Terrance let out the breath he had been holding. After leading his mount away from the sleeping settlement of Clarendon, he made his way to the shack to await the Night Rider's appearance.

When Sloane stalked into the room, sounding more like a herd of stampeding buffalo than a floating phantom, Terrance chuckled.

"How do you hope to convince anyone you are spirit

223

rather than flesh when you make such disruptive entrances?"

Sloane was in no mood to be taunted. Tara's last attempt to pry information from him and Burns had soured his disposition. When he learned that Tara had returned to Clarendon, he feared Terrance would tell her what she wanted to know. The man worshipped his daughter, Sloane reminded himself, glaring at Terrance through the crumpled white hood.

"By the time that . . ." Sloane bit his lip, deciding it would be best not to slander Tara's name in front of her father, ". . . that daughter of yours finishes digging around for information, the entire county will know whose face is camouflaged behind this white hood." He grumbled, plopping down in his chair, "I suppose she appealed to your strong sense of fatherhood and you told her everything."

Terrance puffed up, his chin jutting out in self-defense. "I gave you my word that your secret was safe with me," he hurled at the sulking phantom. "But I must admit it seems inconceivable to me that you have exposed yourself to Tara without explaining what the devil is going on and why."

Sloane winced at Terrance's choice of words. If Tara had told her father they had become as close as two people could get, Sloane could expect more than a verbal lynching. Dammit, he had not been able to help himself. That comely blonde had him behaving strangely, even for a phantom!

"She wouldn't leave me alone," Sloane explained gruffly. "When I was prowling the canyon she followed me. She had become so persistent that I feared she would learn my identity sooner or later." Sloane's breath came out in a rush. "I finally threw up my hands and revealed myself, but I sorely regret it. Now she is hounding me to explain why I'm haunting Merrick and I'm not at all

224

certain I should trust her with the information."
Dragging the ghastly hood from his tousled hair, Sloane
peered solemnly at Terrance. "Did you send for Tara, or
was it Julia and Merrick's invitation that brought her to
Texas?"

"I did," Terrance replied, eyeing Sloane, puzzled.
"Whatever gave you the idea Merrick sent for her?"

His broad shoulders lifted and dropped in a shrug.
"You never mentioned that she was coming to spend the
summer. How was I to know what ill-fated wind blew that
inquisitive imp onto my doorstep?"

Terrance leaned forward, propping his forearms on the
table that separated them. "I don't think my daughter
feels any particular allegiance to Merrick. She only wants
the truth. If you would only take her into your
confidence, she could . . ."

Sloane cut him off with a sour scowl. "What purpose
would that accomplish? She could only get herself into
trouble. Is that what you want? Isn't Tara flirting with
danger just being at the ranch?"

"Obviously, she has no recollection of the man who
murdered Don Miguel. If she did, she would have told
me," Terrance pointed out. "But Tara has free run of
headquarters. She knows when Merrick comes and goes
and with whom. She has access to rooms where you have
never gained entrance, except when you prowl the
darkness. My God, man, think what you might possibly
have to gain if Tara was working with you instead of
against you. You trust me. Why won't you trust my own
flesh and blood?" Pushing back in his chair, Terrance
sadly shook his head. "Assistance is staring you in the
face and you refuse to accept it. Tara may be many
things, but she is not a fool. She could have exposed you
to Merrick after she learned your identity. But did she?"
Terrance didn't give Sloane the opportunity to slide a
word in edgewise. "Hell no, she didn't. Tara is fascinated

225

by your charade. If you confessed your reasons for believing Merrick was a party to crime, she might be willing to uncover information that could link Merrick to the accusations we have against him."

Sloane pulled the hood over his head and rose to full stature. "I'll give the matter some consideration," was all he mumbled as his swift strides took him to the door.

"Give it a great deal of consideration," Terrance insisted, standing up to follow the Night Rider. "I may have been away from my daughter for the past three years, but I know her well. She is not flighty and irresponsible."

Sloane digested the conversation as he spirited off into the night. How much longer could he restrain Tara when she was obsessed with learning the truth? She already had Burns in a tailspin and now Terrance was taking her side, speaking in her defense. Urging Diablo toward the rim of Palo Duro, the Night Rider raced along the jagged caprock, haunted by his own tormenting thoughts. What the hell *was* he going to do about that inquisitive minx? Grappling with that disturbing question, Sloane flew along the precipices that jutted out over the valley. He could not help but wonder if his double life would ever be the same now that Tara Private Investigator Winslow had made the Night Rider her crusade.

Chapter 15

After returning from her journey to Clarendon, Tara began to prepare for the ball the Russels were giving that night at headquarters. She peered at her reflection in the mirror, reasonably satisfied with the image that stared back at her. She fully intended to enjoy herself during the party. Loren was pleasurable company and Tara was comfortable with him. Although they could never be more than friends, Tara wanted to make Loren appear somewhat of a prince in Julia's straying eyes.

It would never work between Sloane and Julia, not when Merrick finally learned who had been hounding him. If Julia did fall in love with that hard-hearted devil Sloane Prescott, she would be miserable. There would be constant conflict between Julia's lover and her father. No, it was best that Julia marry Loren, Tara convinced herself as she smoothed an unruly strand of golden hair back in place. Julia deserved happiness, and Tara doubted her friend could find it with Sloane, just as she was every kind of fool for falling in love with him herself.

God, what a mess she had made of things, she thought with a heavy sigh. It was unforgivable to feel some deep emotion for the very man her hostess had her heart set on. Tara rolled her eyes toward the ceiling, half-hoping the answer to her troubled questions would be printed on it. But her luck had run amuck when she met Sloane

Prescott, and she seriously doubted there were simple answers where that mysterious man was concerned.

Pasting on a polite smile, Tara picked up the front of her lavender silk gown to start down the steps to meet the guests, but she very nearly tripped over her own feet when her gaze slid to the bottom of the stairs. There before her stood Sloane, dressed in black breeches that clung to his well-muscled thighs like tight-fitting gloves. His black coat accented the broad expanse of his chest and his white shirt complimented his bronzed features, features that were curved in a wry smile as he lifted one dark brow and boldly assessed Tara. His dark blue eyes ran the full length of her, swimming over her curvaceous body like an arousing caress, and Tara was certain her pounding heart would pop from her chest and tumble down the stairs to fall at his feet.

Lord, he *did* look like Prince Charming, not some backward cowboy who was out of his element at a grand ball. His raven hair glistened in the lantern light, and the wild nobility that was stamped on his rugged features gave him a recklessly handsome appearance. Obviously, she wasn't the only one who thought so, Tara mused as she dragged her admiring gaze from Sloane and allowed her attention to circle the crowded entryway. Every woman from eighteen to eighty was gawking at him, especially Julia, who was proudly standing at his side.

But Sloane's all-consuming gaze flooded over the stunning nymph who stood at the head of the stairs like a regal queen entering court. She had that air of poise and grace about her that had always fascinated him. His eyes traced every exquisite detail of her form-fitting lavender gown, knowing full well what lay beneath the soft, seductive folds of silk. The ripe swells of her breasts rose above the décolleté of white lace. It was with concentrated effort that he shifted his attention to her trim waist and the swirling skirt that camouflaged the shapely contours of her hips. Making a slow, meticulous ascent, Sloane worked his way back to Tara's oval face to admire her delicate features and the sophisticated curls that dangled about her temples and forehead.

Their eyes met for a split second, and Tara gulped nervously. How could she gracefully descend the stairs without falling pell-mell down the winding steps to land at Sloane's feet? His gaze was so intense that it rattled her. They had parted on such a sour note that she expected him to be glaring daggers at her. But the message she deciphered in those piercing blue eyes did not translate as anger. Indeed, she had wasted her time dressing for the evening. Sloane had stripped her naked with his penetrating gaze, reminding her they shared the most intimate of secrets.

With an effort of will, Tara unglued her eyes from his piercing stare and sought out her date. She was determined to put the handsome rake out of her mind, at least for the evening. When she spied Loren leaning against the door of the study, she breathed a constricted sigh of relief. His eyes were warm and complimentary as she floated down the steps to curl her hand around his arm. Only now did she feel safe. Seeing Sloane standing at the foot of the steps devouring her had made mincemeat of her emotions. But the man was not going to dampen her spirits. She was going to make Julia realize that Loren was more than man enough to satisfy any woman.

"You are breathtaking," Loren murmured as his lips brushed across her forehead. "I will be the envy of every man here."

A becoming smile blossomed on her lips as she met Loren's gentle eyes. "Flattery will get you everywhere, despite what you might have heard to the contrary," she teased him saucily. "And may I bring it to your attention that a certain young lady seems to be fascinated with *my* escort." Her twinkling violet eyes indicated Julia, who was openly admiring Loren's fashionable garments, which Tara was certain must have cost him two weeks' wages.

"I'm surprised she managed to pry her eyes off Prescott long enough to notice there was another man in the house," Loren smirked, leaning close as if he were whispering sweet nothings in Tara's ear.

Tara reached up to pat his clean-shaven cheek, giving the impression that she was flirting outrageously with her escort. "I hope both of them have a perfectly miserable evening at our expense. I intend to have the time of my life."

Loren chuckled at the lively glint in those captivating amethyst eyes. "Katy, bar the door. I have the feeling the sophisticated young lady from St. Louis is about to give Texas a night to remember."

Indeed, she was in a most mischievous mood, feeling reckless and uninhibited. Each time a servant passed her, a glass of champagne seemed to find its way into her hand. When she wasn't sipping the bubbly brew, which left her feeling giddy and light-headed, she was being passed from one man to another. After two hours of being whirled and twirled around the ballroom, Tara found a secluded corner and stood in it, hoping to catch her breath and curb her dizziness.

"You have enchanted Merrick's guests, *duquesa*," Sloane whispered against her flushed cheek, causing her to spill the drink she had just brought to her lips. An amused grin dangled on one side of his mouth as he retrieved his handkerchief from his vest pocket and lightly brushed it over her creamy breasts to wipe away the droplets of champagne. "Wouldn't they be surprised to learn that such a dainty nymph cannot only glare daggers but hurl them with amazing accuracy when she loses her temper."

Tara recovered her composure, her temper mellowed by her overindulgence in champagne. A mocking smile touched her heart-shaped lips as she met his dancing blue eyes. "And wouldn't it be a pity if Merrick's guests learned that the *gentleman* who looks so dashing in black can be equally awesome in ghostly white."

Sloane caught her free hand, pretending to draw it to his lips for a gentlemanly kiss, and Tara tried not to grimace when the bones of her fingers cracked beneath the tremendous pressure.

"Mind your loose tongue, my lovely minx," Sloane gritted through his tight smile.

"It is difficult, kind sir," Tara purred, her lips dripping with sticky-sweet sarcasm. "It seems to have a *mind* of its own."

"It would give me immense pleasure to bob it for you," Sloane offered. His smile was polite, but his words were laced with venom.

"Here? In front of Merrick's guests?" Tara questioned in mock horror. "What a daring man you are to issue threats with all these witnesses present."

"What I wouldn't give for ten minutes alone with you," he seethed.

Tara reached up to smooth away his harsh frown. Amusement flickered in her eyes as she watched his carefully controlled composure come unwound like a ball of twine on a downhill roll. "Temper, temper, Prince Charming," she purred with mock sweetness. "Or I shall be tempted to give you a potion and turn you back into a toad."

"Vicious witch," Sloane flung at her.

His insult slid off like water trickling off a duck's back. Tara had had just enough to drink to make her reckless. She was delighting in sparring with the handsome rake. "Why don't you run along and practice your social graces on the harem that has been swarming around you

231

this evening?"

"Sloane?" Julia called to her escort, gesturing for him to join her. "The orchestra is playing one of my favorite songs. I should hate to sit this one out."

"Try not to waltz all over Julia's feet," Tara cooed before taking another sip of champagne. Her gaze fell to the floor and then lifted to meet Sloane's faintly annoyed expression. "Shall I label your freshly polished boots so you can determine your left foot from the right one?"

Tara had murmured the gibe so sweetly while she batted her big violet eyes that Sloane grinned in spite of himself. Even while Tara was under the influence of champagne, taunting wit didn't fail her. When confronting this frustrating minx, Sloane was constantly tossed back and forth between the impulse to fly at her in a fit of temper or for an altogether different reason. And he never knew to which side of that fine line he would fall until the moment was upon him. To be totally honest with himself, Sloane had to admit that he never knew how to handle Tara. And usually he did so quite poorly. She was not easily maneuvered. But then, neither was he. Holding true to form, Sloane gave what he got—a pride-pricking taunt.

"I truly doubt that Julia will find complaint with my dancing," he insisted, bowing elegantly before her and then gracefully backing away. "And when a woman behaves as if she adores a man, he finds a certain fondness for her swelling in his heart."

Shrugging nonchalantly at his attempt to intimidate her, Tara gestured toward her waiting friend. "Julia also has a soft spot for stray pups and mavericks. I'm sure one day she will outgrow it," she said breezily.

"My dear Miss Winslow, you wound this simple cowboy to the quick and crack the cockles of my heart," Sloane assured her, his mocking tone belying his words.

"Would that I could, Mr. Prescott," she countered as

she sailed past him. "But you have no quick beneath that leather hide, and I question the possibility that you possess a heart." Her full attention anchored on Loren. "Ah, there you are. I thought perhaps you had overlooked me in this sea of lovely Texas beauties."

"Impossible," Loren murmured, loud enough for Julia to overhear him. His arm curled around Tara's waist, propelling her toward the dance floor. "You are like the evening star that outshines all the rest. I was hardly aware there was another woman in the room."

Julia's fuming glare burned holes in Loren's broad back, and Sloane gritted his teeth as he guided Julia across the room. As if he had been born dancing, Sloane whirled Julia across the floor, attempting to put a greater distance between him and the infuriating blonde who had Merrick's guests whispering and smiling as she floated past them.

The effects of the liquor had Tara dancing on air, and when her mind began spinning like a runaway carousel, she slipped from her partner's arms, pleading the need for fresh air. She wove her way through the crowd and curled her arm around the supporting beam of the porch. She inhaled a deep breath and listened to the lighthearted melody that wafted its way through the open window.

"You certainly seem to be enjoying yourself," came the husky baritone voice from behind her.

Tara's numbed gaze slid over her shoulder to see Sloane clinging to the shadows, but she had difficulty focusing on his dark face. "Why shouldn't I?" she slurred out. "I have a pleasant escort."

"Who happens to be holding Julia at the moment, as if he means to squeeze her in two," Sloane smirked as he ambled up behind Tara.

Her shoulder lifted and drooped as she clung to the post for support. Lord, she was beginning to see two of everything! "Must I remind you that I am engaged to

233

another man? If you are attempting to make me jealous by tattling on Julia and Loren, your ploy failed." Tara hiccupped and then covered her mouth. "S'cuse me."

A low chuckle rumbled in his massive chest as he hooked his arm around Tara, pulling her back against him. "It seems the *lady* has forgotten herself this evening. I was unaware you had such a penchant for liquor."

Her penchant for Sloane was more the source of her distress, Tara mused. The feel of his virile frame pressed to hers unchained memories that she was desperately trying to imprison in the dark corner of her heart.

"Unhand me," she demanded sluggishly. "I have been squeezed and cuddled enough for one night." Tara tried to skew her face up in a condescending frown, but the liquor had numbed her facial features and the frown dangled from one side of her mouth.

Sloane burst out laughing at the intoxicated beauty as he cupped her chin in his hand, tilting her head back against his shoulder. "The lady protests too much, I think. I am not one of your many admirers," he reminded her, his voice low with caressing huskiness. "We share far too many intimate secrets to pretend indifference." His wayward hand slid over her breasts, making Tara flinch uncontrollably. "I can feel your heart racing beneath my touch." He twisted her in his arms, forcing her to meet his penetrating gaze, a gaze that could see right through her and pluck out her most private thoughts. "We may always be at odds, but each time I dare to touch you, I remember . . . and I want you again . . . and I think you want me, Tara."

His lips whispered over hers as he molded her soft feminine curves to his hard contours. Gone was the forceful assault he had employed the previous day. There was nothing but compelling gentleness, a quality rarely seen in this lion of a man. Tara berated herself for wilting

234

against him, but there was no defense left. Each and every one of them had crumbled so often that it would take an entire army to rebuild them.

His mouth opened on hers, drinking fully of her response, which Tara no longer attempted to restrain. A tiny moan spilled from his lips as his practiced hands rediscovered the sensitive points of her body, tracing each curve and swell until her fogged mind was clouded with a haze of pleasurable sensations. She was vaguely aware that her arms had slid over his shoulders and that she had drawn him ever closer. And then, when she would have tossed her pride aside and yielded to the turmoil of emotions that boiled within her, Sloane set her from him to flash her a victorious smile, one that had Tara itching to rearrange a few of his handsome features.

"I believe I've made my point, ma'am," he drawled lazily. "You may have a fiance and a ballroom full of willing beaux, but there is still magic between us when I take you in my arms."

Tears of humiliation scalded her eyes. Oh, how she detested that arrogant monster! He delighted in toying with her and then strutting away like a conquering warrior. She *had* to forget him if she hoped to salvage her sanity. He was trampling all over her heart, and if she didn't guard it carefully there would be nothing left to stitch back together. The impulse to flee overwhelmed her, and she flew off the porch, anxious to be swallowed up by the darkness.

"Tara, come back here!" Sloane called after her, but Tara paid him no heed.

After confiscating one of the carriages, Tara popped the whip over the horse's rump, aiming him toward the river, to the quiet sanctuary that had lured her the first day she had arrived in Palo Duro Canyon. When the sound of bubbling water reached her ears, Tara peered across the moonlit stream to see the sparkling waterfall spilling over the rocks like entangled threads of silver. Her footsteps took her to the riverbank, and she impulsively shed her gown, hoping to rid her senses of the champagne that garbled her thoughts.

Like a swan that had long been denied a swim, Tara glided across the water and then sighed contentedly as a feeling of tranquility rippled through her body. Here she could drift forever, with nothing and no one to disturb her. She could be alone with her thoughts, and she reveled in the exhilarating sensations that breathed new life into her deflated spirits.

Chapter 16

An appreciative smile skimmed across Sloane's lips as he braced himself against a tree and watched the enchanting mermaid disrobe. She was like a goddess hovering close to the earth, compelling him to follow wherever she led him. And Sloane could no more have allowed this bewitching minx to spirit off into the night than he could have swung his lariat and lassoed a star. Each time she flitted away he pursued her. When other women had come to him, willingly and occasionally uninvited, Tara had not. Perhaps if she had chased him, he would have lost interest in this impetuous vixen, he mused as his eyes flowed over every inch of her exquisite body. But Tara was like an unattainable dream, and *he* was the one chasing rainbows, wondering whimsically what it would be like to have this seraph creeping into his cabin from the shadows to sleep in his arms. But Tara had never come to him, and, berating his lack of willpower, he had gone to her.

Like a bee in its lifelong pursuit of nectar, he followed where Tara's footsteps led, knowing he could be stung, but unable to resist the temptation of being alone with her. A strange warmth flowed through his veins as she dived into the water and then stretched out to glide through a river of glistening silver. As she spun around and arched upward, the cloak of water fell away from the taut peaks of her breasts, and Sloane's heart flip-flopped in his chest. His temperature rose a quick ten degrees as she frolicked in the river. His footsteps took him to the water's edge and he silently stripped from his clothes and piled them beside Tara's. Like a man in a trance, he moved toward the bewitching mermaid who seemed just beyond his reach.

Sloane wasn't certain if he had walked on the water or merely waded into it, but suddenly he found himself closing the distance between them, aching to touch what his eyes had so boldly caressed.

Tara felt his presence behind her and glanced over her shoulder to see the dark silhouette gliding toward her. The instinct to flee gripped her. She was too vulnerable where Sloane was concerned, and she could no longer trust herself alone with him, especially not now, not here. It was as if they were the only man and woman on earth, swimming in a river of moonbeams.

"Go away," Tara commanded as she swam toward the opposite shore. "I came here to be alone, and you are intruding."

His hand folded around her leg, towing her back to him. "Only a fool would turn his back when he finds a siren beside a waterfall." His voice was husky with passion and his cobalt eyes flickered with a need Tara had often seen in them. "You are too tempting, *ninfa marina*, and I have become addicted to the sweet taste of you."

Tara could no more have escaped the possessive circle of his arms than she could have flown to the moon. She knew there was no future in loving Sloane, but it didn't stop her from wanting him. He created a need in her, and she ached to satisfy the emptiness of longing. She could feel the heat of his body fusing to hers as his ever-tightening embrace crushed her breasts to his rock-hard

238

chest. His thick raven hair glistened with water droplets, as if chips of diamonds had been sprinkled about him. His rugged features were alive with desire, a longing that seemed to touch every handsome line that was carved in his face. He was like a powerful panther stalking his prey, and she was helpless against him. She loved this swarthy, virile man of mystery. He had become her sun and moon, and there seemed to be no light in the world until he graced her with a smile.

"I want you," he growled with hungry impatience. "And I would move heaven and earth to have you."

His descending mouth rolled over hers in hot, demanding pressure, and Tara was bombarded by the aura of primitive maleness that radiated from him. The sensual possession of his hands and lips blotted out every thought as the exciting sensations of desire sizzled through her body to singe the very core of her being. Tara heard her own surrendering moan whispering in the wind as his adventurous hand folded around her breast. The pink peak tautened against his caressing fingertips, creating a need that defied reason. She craved the feel of his skillful hands mastering her quivering flesh, weaving a spell of enchanting black magic. She longed to lose herself in the musky fragrance that clung to him, slowly entangling her senses. She yearned for that ecstatic moment when she would soar beyond the horizon.

"God, Tara, I can never seem to get enough of you," Sloane groaned in torment as her hands splayed across his back, her nails digging into his hard muscles.

"Nor I of you," she whispered as her seeking caresses curled around his ribs to fan across the lean muscles of his belly.

A steady flame burned within him as her moist lips hovered on each male nipple and her roaming hands sought out each sensitive point on his body, leaving a path of white-hot flames blazing in the wake of her touch. And just when Sloane felt the maddening need to crush her to him and claim her as his possession, Tara arched backwards and glided from his arms, taunting him with that delicious body of hers. Sloane swam deliberately toward her, but Tara dived into the dark depths and Sloane grumbled when he found himself holding nothing more than an armful of water.

His keen eyes searched the water's surface, and he caught his breath when he spied Tara bobbing in the frothy bubbles at the base of the waterfall. Strands of spun silver and gold cascaded about her, and he could see her violet eyes sparkling in the moonlight. Liquid silver silhouetted her curvaceous body as she stood upon the boulder in front of the waterfall and then gracefully dived into the shimmering whirlpool.

Sloane was burning alive, even while he was standing neck-deep in the river. The picture she presented was like some wild, fantastic dream, and he was totally absorbed in it. The gushing water tumbled from the rock ledge above her, drowning out the furious beat of his heart as Tara weaved around the narrow path to perch on yet another boulder. Sloane was all eyes as Tara spread her arms like a dove taking to her wings, arcing through the air and then disappearing into the base of the waterfall. Her graceful movements captivated him. Her tantalizing body aroused him to the limits of his sanity. He wanted her as he had wanted no other woman before her. She had taunted him until he was no more than a flaming mass of unappeased passion.

When he started toward her, Tara slipped from the water and climbed upward to greet the spraying mist of the waterfall. And then, as if she had been no more than a figment of his imagination, she disappeared into the sparkling cascade like an angel vanishing before his wide, disbelieving eyes.

Sloane frowned bemusedly, his ears pricked to the murmuring sounds of the river that reminded him of whispering voices. His eyes narrowed on the silver waterfall. He waited an impatient moment for his elusive seraph to reappear, but she never returned.

His long, steady strokes took him to the bubbling whirlpool and he pulled himself from the water to retrace her path along the stairsteps of rocks that wound into the falls. The spilling stream of water was like a curtain camouflaging a shallow cave behind it, and Sloane blinked bewilderedly. The vision behind the sheer curtain of water sent his heart somersaulting around his chest, and he was sure the thundering palpitations would be the death of him before he could seek the end to this delightful fantasy.

Tara sat perched on a smooth boulder, her blond hair falling about her in reckless disarray, her knees drawn up to barely conceal her full breasts, her silky arms curled around her bent legs. Her alabaster skin glistened with sparkling dewdrops, and the inviting smile that brushed her heart-shaped lips lured him closer.

"Had I known of this secluded paradise beneath the waterfall I would have brought you here the first night I found you," Sloane rasped. "You belong here, *ninfa bella*."

Tara was just as enchanted by the sight of him. His raven hair lay carelessly across his forehead, and the chiseled lines of his face had softened. His eyes mellowed like the sky at sunset, and she could see a wild, alluring horizon in his gaze. She boldly admired his striking physique and she sighed longingly, content just to gaze upon this lithe, powerful man. He was all male, every muscular inch of him, from the top of his dark head to the tip of his toes. Her marveling gaze traced his granite shoulders, his massive chest, and then fluttered across his narrow waist to the hard contours of his hips and

241

thighs. Tara hungered to run her hands over his hair-roughened body, to rediscover the feel of his masculine flesh beneath her caress.

And then her all-consuming gaze retraced its languid path, only to be held hostage by a pair of blue eyes that burned with a living fire. She caught her breath as he eased one hip on the rock ledge and slid a sinewy arm around her waist. Her hand made contact with the solid wall of his chest, feeling his heart racing at the same erratic pace that claimed her own. Her moist lashes fluttered up to view the flash of recklessness in his smile, and she fell in love with him all over again.

His fingers tunneled through her hair, twisting the damp strands around his hand like a rope, tilting her head back to grant him free access to the swanlike column of her throat. His warm lips whispered across her skin, tracing a light path from the sensitive point beneath her ear to the tip of her collarbone. With deliberate dedication to every inch of her silky flesh, Sloane's butterfly kisses skied over the slope of her shoulder to capture the swell of each breast. His touch was like warm sunshine as his wandering hand glided upward to circle one dusky peak and then the other.

Tara moaned softly as his mouth suckled at each ripe bud and his hands began to move in leisurely exploration, offering unbelievable gentleness. She mentally retracted her spiteful remarks about his rough handling. His caresses were like a light breeze stirring on her skin. His ragged breath skimmed her flesh, sending a fleet of goose pimples cruising across her trembling skin, diverging, spreading until the sensation left not one inch of her untouched. His fingertips spread across her belly and then slid over the shapely curve of her hip. Tara closed her eyes as his questing hand gently guided her legs apart. A coil of wild, unreasonable longing unfurled somewhere deep inside her as his knowing fingers further aroused her. She clutched him closer, cradling his head against her breast, reveling in the exquisite sensations that flooded over her like the tumbling waterfall that concealed them from reality.

She was drifting with the forceful currents of passion as his tongue thrust inside her lips to explore the hidden recesses of her mouth, stealing her breath, leaving her suspended. Not once, but over and over again his titillating caresses swam over a sea of bare flesh, his hands stroking the smooth planes of her body, investigating the supple curves that seemed to melt beneath his touch.

He was driving her to abandon, and she could not grasp the thoughts that skipped across her mind before they escaped her forever. The only thought that came at her and remained to take command of her mind was that she needed him more than life itself. He was her reason for being. His kisses offered to feed a growing hunger and his caresses promised forthcoming pleasure that compared to no other feeling in the realm of reality.

"Sloane . . ." His name tumbled from her lips as she delved her fingers into his hair and drew his handsome face to hers. She needed no other words to express the engulfing emotion that sang in her soul. His name was synonymous with love.

His hands folded over her hips, lifting her to him as his hard, eager body answered the aching need of hers. He came to her with desperate urgency, as if holding himself from her those past few minutes had cost him his tenderness. He caught her cry with his mouth, and his arms were like chains, imprisoning her to him as he strained against her womanly flesh.

He groaned in the sweet satisfaction of their union, driving into her, thrusting against her, seized by primeval needs that sent logic fleeing from passion's blazing path. All thought dissolved as he was swept up in the tempest like a windblown leaf flung high into the air. He could not escape the raging gale that encompassed him, nor did he attempt to. He was a part of her, his heart rumbling like thunder, his body tensing as if it had been charged by bolts of lightning. Every nerve and muscle was alive with unrestrained passion, passion that pleased and tormented him. The intimacy of their lovemaking was wild and sweet, and Sloane wasn't certain if he could survive rapture's devastating storm.

And then he was consumed by the soul-shattering sensations that converged upon him, his body shuddering in release, his strength spilling like a river flowing ever so slowly toward the sea. He was basking in the warmth of a pastel-colored rainbow, granted the priceless treasure that lay at the rainbow's end. He couldn't move. He could only cling to Tara, enjoying the rapturous splendor of a universe that transcended time and space. He was dimly aware of Tara's fingertips gliding up and down his spine and her soft breath against his shoulder. Although the fine mist of the waterfall drifted over them, cooling the flames of passion, nothing dampened the contentment that filled him. He wondered if anything could ever extinguish these compelling fires Tara had always been able to set within him. It was like an eternal torch, kept alive by an occasional kiss and caress and then fed by the wild intensity of their lovemaking.

When he finally found the strength to move, he glanced around and then chuckled quietly. They lay together on a bed of rock smoothed by the eroding forces of the water, but never softened. No doubt this tempting mermaid would be marred by bruises after he had been so forceful with her, he mused as he dropped a fleeting kiss to her lips and then scooped her up in his arms.

Tara had suffered the same paralyzing effects from their tryst of love, and it wasn't until Sloane pulled her to him that she realized what he was about. A shriek burst from her lips as he walked through the waterfall and plunged into the whirlpool with her chained in his arms. Tara gulped for breath as a wave of water splashed over her and she was dragged beneath the depths.

His hearty chuckle rang in her ears as he hooked his arm about her and glided toward shore. Tara felt her spirits sink to rock bottom as Sloane led her to the bank. Never once had he said he loved her, even in the heat of passion. Their enchanting rendezvous had not stirred an emotion deeper than lust in him. But Sloane was as hard as bedrock, and she reminded herself that it would take a chisel to carve her way into his heart.

Silently Tara climbed into her clothes and then turned back toward the carriage, but Sloane's long fingers closed around her arm to detain her. His free hand curled beneath her chin, forcing her to meet his probing gaze.

"Tara, one day when I am no longer. . . ." His voice trailed off and he jerked up his head, his ears pricked to the muffled sounds in the distance.

Leading Tara along behind him, he followed the quiet voices to their source and crouched in the brush.

"We can make the switch after the roundup," one man insisted. "It will be a simple matter to add the beeves to your herd before we reach the pens in Harrold."

"Are you sure you want to risk it this year, with Winslow sniffing at your heels each time you move? This won't be as easy as before, and my men are about half-spooked by the sighting of the ghost who trails the Diamond R herd." The second voice sounded hesitant.

Tara blinked, certain she was about to sneeze and spoil Sloane's chances of eavesdropping. She frantically tugged on his arm and then buried her face in his jacket, muffling her sneeze as best she could. The stirring in the brush caught both men's attention, and Sloane scowled when he heard the crackling of twigs and the annoying sound of silence.

"Damn," Sloane muttered as he dragged Tara back to the carriage. "You picked one helluva bad time to catch cold!"

"I couldn't help it," she defended herself tersely. "You didn't have to haul me along with you."

Sloane hoisted her onto the seat and then stalked back to tie his mount behind the carriage. "I'm not certain if my purpose would best be served by having you with me or against me," he grumbled sourly. "I swear you are the biggest bundle of trouble I've ever stumbled over."

"And if you hadn't followed me out here, Peeping Tom, you wouldn't have overheard a single word of that conversation, although I cannot imagine what interest you would have in it," she sniffed as she crossed her arms under her breasts and moved as far away as the carriage seat would allow when he clambered in beside her.

"And if I had remained at the party instead of ensuring that you did not meet with disaster, I might have known who had sneaked away from the crowd for a private conversation," Sloane parried, his voice slicing like a knife.

Tara was itching to slap him silly, for any number of reasons, and so she did. Sloane squawked in surprise when he felt the sting of her hand on his cheek. "What the hell was that for?"

"For making me so damned furious that I cannot control myself," she spouted.

Sloane clamped his hand over her mouth. "¡Chiton! I don't relish the thought of being discovered just now."

Tara pried his fingers from her face and glared holes in his expensive garments. "Why, because you don't want to be seen with me when you are supposed to be courting Julia?" she hissed.

"Because I don't want whoever that was to know we were here," he snapped back at her and then urged the

246

horse toward the nouse. "Naive little imp, can't you see Julia can't match you in anything she does? If I had wanted to get to Merrick through Julia I would have used that ploy long ago. But I happen to have a few scruples."

His remark silenced Tara. She stared bewilderedly at him. Was he implying that he did care for her, in his own unconventional way? Tara breathed a hope that one day Sloane would come to trust her enough to take her into his confidence. Perhaps he did enjoy her company, as well as the fiery passion they shared. Perhaps he . . .

"I want you to inform Merrick and Julia that you are going to Clarendon to visit your father," Sloane said out of the blue. "I want you out from under Merrick's nose for a few days."

And out from under Sloane's feet, Tara thought, disheartened, her lifted spirits crashing down like an avalanche. Just when she thought Sloane might have found a soft spot for her he wanted to send her away. Oh, what was the use? She couldn't win Sloane's love, not in two weeks or twenty years. She might as well attempt to hitch herself to a passing cloud. It would prove no more successful than waiting for this rugged, singleminded man to forget his purpose and notice she had fallen in love with him. Obviously, he had taken what he wanted from her, and now that he had conquered her, he had become bored with her.

"I will be all too happy to visit my father," Tara assured him, tilting a proud chin. "And now that I have had my fling in Texas, I might even decide to catch the first train to St. Louis."

Sloane's face fell, his eyes cold and unreadable as he narrowed them on the silver-blond minx who could enflame his passions one minute and stoke the fires of his temper the next instant. It took a great deal of self-control to choke back the sarcastic rejoinder and issue another order, but Sloane managed to hold his tongue. Damn her stubborn hide! What they had shared was no fling, and he resented being referred to as such.

"Take the back door to your room. I'll make the proper excuses for you. And be prepared to leave early in the morning," he ground out as he focused on the light that sprayed from the windows of Merrick's mansion.

"The sooner the better," Tara muttered.

"You stole the words right off the tip of my tongue," Sloane snorted derisively.

When the carriage halted by the back door, Tara lifted her skirts and hopped to the ground, grumbling derogatory epithets appended to Sloane's name with each step she took. Damnation, how could such a splendorous evening turn sour so quickly? That man was driving her mad and she should thank her lucky stars they would soon be miles apart. Another dose of Sloane Prescott could prove fatal. If she had any sense, she would refuse the next of Julia's invitations and remain in Clarendon with her father for the duration of the summer and avoid Sloane as if he were a carrier of bubonic plague!

Clinging to that thought, Tara flounced onto the bed and cursed the lingering image of Sloane walking through the waterfall, his magnificent body outlined by a curtain of glistening silver, his eyes flaming with a fire that had eventually consumed her.

Stop this! Tara scolded herself. She never wanted to see Sloane again. She had shamelessly offered herself and her love, and he was such a lusty dragon that he had never even noticed. A runaway tear slid down her cheek and she brushed it away with the back of her hand. Love was hell, pure and simple. Maybe it would be easier to marry Joseph than to endure a one-sided love that was tearing her to pieces, bit by excruciating bit. She had been happier before she left St. Louis, and she hadn't realized it until now. God, what a fool she had been! Who had the nerve to say it was better to have loved and lost than never to have loved at all? That was the most ridiculous rationalization she had ever heard! There were some things in this world that one was better off not experiencing, and loving a heartless vagabond like Sloane Prescott was at the top of the list.

Tara muffled another sniff as she pulled the quilt over her shoulder and stared at the darkness. From now on she would regard Sloane in the same perspective as the grippe. She had had him, she had endured her affliction, and now she would recover. Time and distance would mend her broken heart, and she would return to St. Louis to become Joseph's wife . . . a miserable groan tumbled loose when she landed on that depressing thought. Even if Joseph would have her, she couldn't marry him now. She would compare him to Sloane each time he touched her, and she would die a thousand deaths if that ruggedly handsome cowboy's face materialized before her eyes. She would become a spinster, she decided. There would be no more men in her life. She would simply learn to live without them. The whole lot of them were exasperating and she wanted nothing to do with any of them. Why, if the man of her childhood dreams, the dashing knight on his white charger, came galloping toward her this very minute she would tell him to take his gallantry and stuff it in his armor and leave her be. She was a strong, independent woman, and she needed no one to lean on. A rueful smile played across her lips, remembering what her father had said to her. *Some things are just not meant to be.* She and Sloane were like two leaves caught up in a whirlwind, flung together for that brief moment, and then split apart to flutter off in their own directions. Her ill-fated love had caused her grief, but she was determined not to allow it to destroy her. She would laugh and smile again when the memories faded, when she was far away from everything that reminded her of that blue-eyed devil.

Breathing a hope that tomorrow would be a brighter day, Tara surrendered to sleep, to a darkness void of troubled dreams. . . .

Chapter 17

Much to Tara's chagrin, the day dawned dreary and gray. Even the sun refused to show its face and bring one bright spot into Tara's world. Well, what had she expected, Tara asked herself as she gathered her luggage and started down the steps. Life seemed to be an uphill struggle, and she would simply have to make her own happiness.

As she turned the corner to step into Merrick's study, she froze in her tracks. The greeting smile she had pasted on her lips evaporated the moment her gaze landed on the man who slouched back in the chair across the desk from Merrick.

Thrusting out her chin, Tara looked past Sloane and focused her full attention on Merrick's weather-beaten features. "I would like to spend a few days in Clarendon with my father," she announced stiffly. "I was wondering if I might impose on you to lend me a mount for my journey."

Merrick's gaze wandered over Tara's rigid stance and he managed the semblance of a smile. "Whatever you wish, my dear." His eyes slid to Sloane momentarily before resettling on Tara. "I could have Sloane accompany you, since he is taking some horses to Tascosa."

Tara groaned inwardly at that possibility. It was like

sending a fox to guard the geese. The last person she had expected to see on the first day of her new life was Sloane, and the thought of sharing his company after she had decided to forget he ever existed made her cringe.

Merrick glanced back at Sloane. "You don't mind detouring to escort our lovely guest to her father, do you?"

Sloane's shoulder lifted lackadaisically. "I s'pose I could manage to veer toward Clarendon," he said, his tone less than enthusiastic.

Tara gnashed her teeth, annoyed with his begrudging remark. Obviously, he was wishing he had already taken the horses and galloped away. Mustering a civil smile, she peered at Merrick. "I have already said my good-byes to Julia, and I want to thank you for your hospitality. You have a splendid ranch, and I shall fondly remember my visit to Palo Duro Canyon."

"You don't plan to return?" Merrick arched a graying brow, and Tara could have sworn he was disappointed. "Julia would love to have you come back to us. She has enjoyed your company."

"Well . . . a . . . I . . ." Tara stammered, fumbling for an excuse to avoid the Diamond R Ranch and Sloane in particular.

"We will be beginning our spring roundup next week. I think you would find it a fascinating experience," Merrick baited her.

Her gaze darted to Sloane who was regarding Merrick as curiously as she was. My, but Merrick had turned over a new leaf. Tara was sure Merrick had resented Julia's invitation in the beginning, and now he behaved as if he were eager for her to return. And just why was that, Tara asked herself suspiciously. What did Merrick want from her?

"Perhaps when Sloane returns from Tascosa he could stop by Clarendon to escort you back for another visit,"

Merrick suggested.

"Perhaps . . ." she murmured evasively.

"At least consider it," he encouraged her as he rose from his chair and strolled over to usher Tara into the entryway. "I want your father to know how much we delight in your company."

So that was it, Tara mused as she was propelled down the steps. Merrick was trying to buy her father by allowing her the luxury of his spacious mansion. Well, it would take more than bribery to sway Terrance Winslow, Tara thought to herself.

After Sloane had strapped her belongings behind the saddle, he swept Tara up to her perch on Hazel's back and then gathered the string of horses Merrick intended to sell in Tascosa. When they had ridden a quarter of a mile from headquarters, Sloane twisted around in the saddle to see Tara glaring mutinously at him.

"Do you plan to pout the entire way?" he smirked.

"I do not need you to escort me," Tara insisted tartly. "I am quite capable of managing on my own. Indeed, I would prefer solitude."

"I heard no complaints last night while we were swimming naked in the river," he mocked, his eyes raking her shapely body as if she were sitting in the saddle as underdressed as Lady Godiva.

Tara blushed up to the roots of her hair. "I would prefer to forget last night. I had entirely too much champagne and I was not in full command of my senses. If I had been, I assure you I would not have behaved so shamelessly."

Sloane reined his horse to a halt, waiting for Tara to catch up with him. "What does it take to melt your heart of ice? I swear you deny me even a smidgeon of satisfaction. You are the most obstinate woman I have ever met!"

"*My* heart of ice!" Tara echoed incredulously. "*I* am

obstinate?" She pointed an accusing finger at him. "*You* are the one who is impossible. You treat me as if I were your private whore, and you have the gall to criticize *my* behavior?"

His bronzed features melted into a sly smile as he winked at her. "I've heard it said a woman is always temperamental when she is falling in love. I suppose that explains your behavior," he diagnosed. "You are fighting the strong attraction between us, and you are very annoyed with yourself for being vulnerable to a man who has fallen short of your expectations," he had the nerve to say.

Tara split apart at the seams. His magnificent arrogance incensed her, and the fact that he was right made her even more furious. The fool, if he knew anything about love he would have realized that she would have traded all the money in the world to spend the rest of her life with him. What did he think she was anyway, some spoiled, vain princess who would not fall in love with a man until he produced proof of his financial worth? Well, of course, he did, Tara reminded herself. She had thrown Joseph Rutherford and his wealth in Sloane's face for self-defense.

"I think you are experiencing delusions," Tara sniffed and turned up her dainty nose. She would be damned if she admitted she was in love with Sloane. After all, he could have cared less. He was only taunting her. "If I loved you, I wouldn't care if you were a prince or pauper. I am not fortune hunting. My grandfather happens to be a very wealthy man, and when I wed I shall be accompanied by a sizable dowry."

"In that case, will you marry me?" Sloane's grin was as wide as the Prairie Dog Fork of the Red River that wove through the canyon.

"Not in a million years," Tara lied through her teeth. Indeed, she wouldn't have hesitated for a moment if she knew he cared about her.

One dark brow lifted as he flashed her a teasing smile. "Not even if I offered to explain why I garb myself in incandescent white and prowl the darkness like a restless spirit?"

Tara eyed him warily. Had he decided to take her into his confidence or was he merely taunting her as he had done so often in the past? "The simple satisfaction of understanding your odd behavior would be more than enough compensation," she said finally. "You, Mr. Prescott, are the epitome of everything I would not want in the man I marry."

Sloane's deep blue eyes danced with amusement as he leaned over to flick the end of her upturned nose. "Oh, how you warm my heart with your generous compliments," he chortled sarcastically.

Tara slapped his lingering hand away from her face and gave him a cold shoulder dripping with icicles. "You cannot know how anxious I will be for you to deposit me on my father's doorstep," Tara muttered, her patience at the end of its rope. Sloane was a constant source of irritation, always turning her wrong side out. She longed to throw up her hands and be done with him, even if he breezed away with her heart. "It seems you and I are more compatible when we never see each other."

"Be that as it may. I have no intention of detouring to Clarendon. You are coming to Tascosa with me," he informed her flatly and then squirmed to find a more comfortable position in the saddle.

Tara stared at him bug-eyed and then jumped as if she had been stung when a loud rumble of thunder rolled across the gloomy gray sky. "I thought you were eager to be rid of me. You said as much last night," she replied and then cast the threatening sky another cautious glance. She did not relish the idea of weathering another storm with Sloane. The last had cost her dearly.

255

Sloane followed her gaze, surveying the rolling black clouds, and then he veered west to cross the river before it swelled with rain. "I said nothing of the sort," he countered. "Why the hell do you think I wanted you to be prepared to leave at the same hour of the day that I was to set out for Tascosa? I was eager to be alone with you." He tossed her a sober glance and then focused on the river ahead of them. "We have a great many things to discuss, and I do not wish to be overheard." He eased back in the saddle and tied the lead rope for the eight horses on the pommel. "You were correct in your assumption that Carmelle was my mother, but Merrick is *not* my father. Vernon was."

Tara edged Hazel closer, hanging on his every word. She had waited an eternity to learn what motivated Sloane, a man who behaved like a backward cowboy during the day and haunted the canyon like a foreboding spirit during the night. Whatever the price she was expected to pay for this knowledge would be well worth it, she assured herself.

"When Vernon and Merrick Russel came to Palo Duro over thirty years ago to establish their ranch, there was dissension between them. Vernon intended gradually to build up the herd from the prize stock they had raised near Palo Pinto, but Merrick had dreams of expanding within a year by allowing investors to finance the vast operation. They quarreled over the arrangement, but Merrick had taken it upon himself to contact a wealthy Scottish merchant who was looking for opportunities to make another fortune in cattle." Sloane's eyes turned to icy blue chips as he stared up at the heavy black clouds that were hanging over them. "Burns Dixon worked for the Russel brothers, and he was there the night they had their last heated argument, the night my father was supposedly killed by a stampede."

Tara eyed him sympathetically, knowing he had grown

up without a father, undoubtedly hating the man he deemed responsible.

"Vernon had decided to split the herd and move north, since they could not come to terms, but Merrick could not allow that, not without forfeiting the contact with his financial investors, who had stipulated that he offer at least a thousand head of cattle as his part of the bargain."

As Sloane unfolded the web of the past, the pieces of the puzzle began to come together in Tara's mind. "And you think Merrick started the stampede to kill his own brother so he could gain control of the herd," Tara guessed.

"I would stake my life on it," Sloane growled as he reined his steed to a halt on the bank of the river to allow the horses to drink before they crossed. "It seems too convenient that Merrick sent Burns back to the mission at Valquez to fetch my mother, who intended to join Vernon when he had settled. He and my father were left alone, and we have only Merrick's word that Vernon started the stampede by trying to split the herd. After the supposed accident, Merrick pinned the herd in the canyon and returned a few days later with the news of Vernon's death. But my mother was already suspicious of him because she had received a letter from Vernon, confiding that he and Merrick were very much at odds." Sloane sighed bitterly and then cast Tara a fleeting glance. "Carmelle and Vernon were to be wed at the mission after the ranch was established, but there was no wedding, and Merrick denied me the right to know my father." Sloane halted his explanation when a flash of lightning slashed across the sky. "Circle behind the remuda and help me herd them through the river. If they are frightened by the storm we could lose a few of them."

Tara trotted Hazel back to urge the skittish colts into the river as Sloane gouged his mount in the flanks, sending his splashing through the stream leading the hesitant string of horses behind him.

"Damn," Sloane scowled as raindrops pelleted about them, startling the colts, sending them swimming off in all directions. Tara glanced up to see the horses circling in chaotic disorder, tensing at the sound of their shrill whinnies as they fought to escape each other's thrashing hooves. The powerful force of the contrary horses tugging on Sloane's lead rope caused his mount to flounder, and Tara watched in horror as steed and rider were towed backward into the path of flailing hooves. Frantically she tugged on the floating rope beside her, guiding the string of horses away from Sloane who had disappeared beneath the surface. Her heart hammered wildly against her ribs as she led the horses to the bank and then dashed back into the river to retrieve Sloane.

When she reached him, a gasp of alarm spilled from her lips. A bloody gash slashed across his forehead where a powerful hoof had collided with the side of his face. Tara hooked one arm around his neck and grasped the saddle horn of Sloane's steed as the wild-eyed gelding swam toward shore.

An agonized moan escaped her when the horse's hind leg slammed into her hip, but she didn't dare release her grasp on the saddle for fear of drowning in the river, which had already begun to rage, fed by heavy rains to the north.

When Tara found solid footing, she dragged Sloane to shore, intent on inspecting his wound, but he flung her hand away and glanced dazedly about him.

"Tie up the horses before they kill each other," he ordered and then collapsed back on the ground.

Tara moved mechanically toward the flighty colts, limping on her injured leg. Once she had secured both ends of the lead rope to the cedar trees, she hurried back to Sloane who had managed to crawl on all fours.

"There is a cave on the rock ledge," he informed her,

gesturing toward the sandstone wall of the canyon. "We better wait out the storm. I'm seeing two of everything at the moment."

Tara wrapped a supporting arm around his waist and grimaced as a sharp pain shot down her thigh. Following Sloane's directions, she steered him along the slick mud path. A startled squawk burst from her when his floundering footsteps slid sideways, entangling her feet. Helplessly, Tara tumbled in the mud, grunting uncomfortably as Sloane fell off balance and sprawled on top of her.

As she twisted beneath him a low, groggy chuckle tumbled from his ashen lips. "This is not the time or place to attempt to seduce me," he rasped as he eased beside her. "I am not a well man."

Tara flung him a withering glance and then got up and pulled Sloane up beside her and continued toward shelter. "I swear, you would be making jokes even when you were lying on your death bed," she admonished him.

"Another of my annoying traits," Sloane sighed as he squinted in the pounding rain to see the blurred cave entrance.

When they finally reached the lair, which overlooked the river, Sloane collapsed. It had taken every ounce of strength to make the climb, and his head was hammering in throbbing rhythm with his heart.

The faintest hint of a smile brushed across his pale lips as he peered up at the bedraggled beauty who eyed him with concern. Her blond hair was caked with mud and her oval face was smeared and bruised. Her gown was dripping wet, clinging to her shapely curves like an extra set of skin. As she reached down to rip the hem of her petticoat for a makeshift bandage, Sloane eased back against the rock wall and sighed contentedly. Her gentle hands smoothed the tousled raven hair away from his forehead to tend the wound.

259

"It is most fortunate for me that I brought you along. You saved my life," he murmured as he feasted on the hazy image that hovered over him.

"Now we are even. You saved me from a rattler," she said absently as she cleaned the gash and then ripped off another layer of her petticoat to dress the wound.

When she had bandaged his head, Tara sank back to inspect her own injury. As she drew her blue skirt up above her thigh, Sloane growled disgustedly at the discolored knot that marred her shapely hip.

"Was that caused by my rough handling last night?" He cursed himself for being so inconsiderate. He had feared their tête-à-tête on a bed of rock would leave her with bruises, but he had never expected anything like this!

Tara blushed profusely at the reminder of the previous night. "It was a painful gift, probably from the same frightened colt that scrambled your brain," she informed him as she yanked her skirt down around her ankles.

"Thank God I didn't do that. You would never have forgiven me. It's enough that you believe me to be some lusting beast with a dragon's appetite," Sloane snorted and then frowned when Tara grinned impishly. "What the hell are you smiling about?"

"I find it amusing that I referred to you as just that last night when I returned to my room," she confessed.

Her smile was contagious, and despite the sharp pain on the side of his head, his lips curved into a grin. "I cannot help what I am, but you are to blame for bringing out the beast in me."

Had she known that, she would have equipped herself with a chair and a whip before she confronted this sleek black panther. It was as she had feared. She brought out the worst in Sloane. He had been polite and courteous to Julia, treating her with the utmost respect. But he had declared open season on blondes with violet eyes, she speculated.

"I have done nothing to warrant that accusation," Tara insisted as she rubbed the mud from her cheeks and then braided her wild hair. "As a matter of fact, I have tried very hard to avoid you, but you are a very persistent man."

"Because I have been unable to get you out of my blood," he grunted and then grabbed his throbbing head, cursing himself for raising his voice above a whisper. It rattled through his sensitive skull like a booming bass drum. "What a tangled mess I've made of things. I should have taken you back to Terrance without explaining my purpose."

When another peal of thunder rang through the cave and the wind whipped around the corner, dousing them with cold, driving rain, Sloane hooked his arm around Tara and scooted into a secluded niche.

"But, Sloane, I . . ." Tara stopped herself in the nick of time. The feel of his sinewy arms about her brought back the bittersweet memory of the previous night, and she shoved it aside before it entrapped her. "You said Vernon and your mother were to be wed when he returned for her," she prompted, steering him back to the previous subject.

Sloane slid his arm around her shoulder and followed her gaze, watching torrents of rain sail past the cave entrance. "I'm sure you're wondering why the bastard son of a man he never even met has such determined purpose," Sloane predicted and then sighed heavily. "Although it seems my father and mother were caught up in the heat of passion and an endearing love, they were never granted the opportunity to repeat the vows. But I am still my father's son, and my mother begged me to avenge the tragic injustice before she died two years ago. I gave her my word that Merrick would pay for destroying her happiness and humiliating her by forcing her to bear

261

a child without the man who dearly loved her."

A muddled frown plowed Tara's brow as she peered over at Sloane. No wonder Sloane had kept his distance from Julia. They were first cousins. But how had he come by the name of Prescott? "Why didn't Carmelle give you the name of Russel? Is Prescott an alias?"

"My mother gave me her name and kept my father's memory alive, as well as her fierce hatred for Merrick." His somber gaze swung to Tara, watching the rash of questions flicker in her violet eyes. "We lived with my grandfather on his ranch near Palo Pinto. Don Miguel Chavez was my grandfather, and it is the name Chavez that I claim, though I chose Prescott to avoid suspicion when I came to Merrick's ranch."

While Sloane unfolded the story of the past, Tara sat silently, wondering if Carmelle had purposely instilled this bitter hatred in her son and why she yearned to seek her revenge long after her death. But Tara reminded herself that she was hearing a slanted story, handed down to the second generation, and that she might never understand Carmelle's true motivation for forcing Sloane to carry on her vendetta against Merrick Russel.

"If it is revenge you want, why haven't you confronted Merrick face to face?" she asked him.

"Merrick would only proclaim his innocence, as he has the past thirty years," Sloane insisted, an undertone of bitterness finding its way into his voice. "It has taken me more than a year to piece the evidence together, and still I am relying partly on speculation. But I have yet another reason for being here, and why I must be secretive in my investigation. The Diamond R Ranch, a once thriving operation, has shown very little profit to its investors, and I was hired to check into the ranch operations without formally confronting its boss. Merrick has managed to sell part of his cattle crop and pocket the profit without sharing it with his investors, two of whom are closely related to you and one who very well could be if you offer him your hand in marriage." A wry smile pursed his lips as the color seeped from Tara's cheeks and her jaw gaped. "I should think you would be interested in getting to the bottom of Merrick's swindling tactics, since your livelihood also depends on it. I assume you recall the names Terrance Winslow, Ryan O'Donnovan, and Joseph Rutherford." He chuckled at the stunned expression plastered on Tara's peaked features.

"You are the man Grandfather met in Dallas last year?" she croaked in disbelief.

He nodded affirmatively. "Ryan hired me to investigate the Diamond R Ranch for the Cattle Investment Corporation of St. Louis, a division of your grandfather's speculative enterprises. That is why Terrance has taken a particular interest in harassing Merrick every way he can. Terrance knows Merrick is shuffling money under the table, and nothing would please him more than to expose Russel and have someone else step in to manage the Diamond R Ranch."

"And who would be more capable than the private investigator who had a rightful claim to the ranch and who managed to reveal Merrick's underhanded dealings?" Tara arched a delicate brow and surveyed the ruggedly handsome cowboy who had more ties to the Diamond R Ranch than a saddle had cinches. "No doubt, your revenge would taste twice as sweet if you had stripped Merrick of his wealth, just as he supposedly deprived Vernon of life and happiness. What a devastating blow Merrick will receive when he learns your identity, along with all else," she surmised.

Sloane was like a carefully calculating machine, Tara mused as her narrowed gaze flooded over his muscular profile. He planned to come at Merrick from all directions, subtly working his way closer until he finally sprung his trap. It seemed Sloane Prescott was far more than the ill-mannered cowboy he portrayed by day. Who would suspect him? Certainly not Merrick. He didn't seem to have a clue.

"But why do you think Merrick is responsible for Don Miguel's death?" Tara inquired. "He was a gentle man who was opposed to violence. Surely Merrick did not see him as a threat to his existence after he has lived with the rumors all these years. What proof could Don Miguel have presented to undermine Merrick?"

"Don Miguel would never have harmed a living soul," Sloane agreed, his eyes darkening as he looked back through the window of time, fondly remembering the man of Spanish descent, the man who had taken him into his home and raised him to be proud of his heritage. "But his mere appearance and his association with your father disturbed Merrick. No doubt his guilt caused him to view Don Miguel as a threat." Sloane sighed heavily as he absently brushed his hand over Tara's shoulder. "For almost two years I wrestled with my mother's dying words, words I could not quite understand until I had spoken with Burns and pried bits and pieces of information from him. When I finally realized what she meant, I asked Don Miguel to return to the mission at Valquez. My mother had begged me to expose Merrick for what he was, a murderer and a swindler. She said the proof lay in the locket of Valquez, which she had stashed for safekeeping after she escaped from Merrick. Don Miguel searched the abandoned mission, and although Merrick could not have known where he had gone, he was awaiting his return, waiting to dispose of Don Miguel before he stirred up trouble. The locket was an engagement present from Vernon to my mother, and when he died, she buried *it* instead of the memories. Those she kept alive every day of her life."

"Do you think Merrick has possession of this locket, the one you sent your grandfather to retrieve?" Tara queried, her violet eyes so full of lively curiosity that Sloane could not help but chuckle.

He extracted the heart-shaped gold locket from his shirt pocket and dangled it in front of Tara. "I found this in the bodice of your gown when I took you to my cabin to tend your wounds. Don Miguel must have managed to plant it on you before he died."

Tara took the locket from his hand and opened it, finding a small excerpt from a letter that was brittle with age.

We will inevitably clash, Carmelle. I cannot even trust my own brother and I fear I will be forced to dissolve our partnership. His greed has poisoned him and I no longer feel I know him. . . .

Her sooty lashes swept up, her eyes anchored on Sloane's face. His jaw was clenched, his eyes like hard blue chips.

"Do you suppose Carmelle came to Merrick's ranch to confront him with the truth? Do you suppose that is why they argued before she left his house and never returned?" she asked softly.

Sloane let his breath out in a rush. "I wish I knew what transpired the day Carmelle traveled from my grandfather's ranch to confront Merrick. I can only guess she tried, in her own way, to force Merrick to admit the truth that continued to torment her. But now the only person who knows what was said is Merrick himself. He has harbored so many secrets all these years that I cannot expect to gain the truth from him, unless he is so fiercely shocked that he reacts instinctively."

"A shock as staggering as learning that you are his nephew and that you have exposed him to his investors, shattering his precious dream?" Tara speculated.

She didn't like the sound of Sloane's insinuation. He

265

was implying that once Merrick had been exposed to his investors and stood to lose his ranch he would do something desperate. Tara didn't doubt for a moment that Merrick Russel could be ruthless if he were backed into a corner. She had never seen him lose his temper, but she expected that once he did, he would be as ominous as the devil himself. The mere thought of having Sloane in Merrick's path when his dream was crumbling about him made Tara shudder uncontrollably.

"Are you cold, little nymph?" Sloane murmured as his arm tightened about her.

"No, only apprehensive," she admitted. "If you and Merrick clash, he will be furious, and you could well be another of his victims."

Sloane drew back, a taunting smile gliding across his sensuous lips. "Would you truly care if something happened to me?"

Tara bristled indignantly. "Of course, I care," she insisted hotly. "Do you see me as such a frightful witch that I would find spiteful pleasure in watching you die?"

His shoulder lifted in a casual shrug as he flashed her another teasing smile. "I have never been certain what runs through your complicated mind. At times, I have been on the receiving end of your murderous glares. If looks could kill, you would have saved Merrick the trouble."

"Well, I am not that cold-hearted," Tara protested as she flung his arm from her shoulder and scooted a few feet away. "We have had our differences, but that does not mean I want to be rid of you."

"Oh?" One dark brow raised suggestively. "Then what is it you would like to do with me, *chiquita?* Tell me what you are thinking."

Tara crossed her arms under her breasts and leveled him a go-to-hell look that would have had him roasting over the eternal fires in a matter of minutes.

A low rumble erupted from Sloane's chest. "Don't bother. I believe I can read your mind." He leaned toward her, his index finger bringing her chin down a notch as he offered her a repentant smile. "Forgive me for teasing you so unmercifully, but I adore seeing that fire in your eyes." His expression sobered as his hand fell away and he turned to stare out at the rain. "I need your help, Tara. Merrick seems to want you on his ranch, perhaps as a buffer between him and your father. There is much you can learn within the confines of his home, things that could help me determine what Merrick intends to do about shuffling his cattle and depriving his investors to further profits."

"You want me to discover who Merrick has employed to aid him in his underhanded dealings?" A mischievous grin blossomed on her bewitching features. "I already know the answer to that. What else would you like to know?"

Sloane's jaw sagged from its hinges. "If you knew who was talking with Merrick last night, why didn't you tell me?"

"You didn't ask me," Tara countered with a saucy smile. "And besides, I wasn't quite certain I trusted you. I was waiting for you to explain why you have been hounding Merrick."

A slow, wide grin worked its way across his swarthy features as he reassessed the bedraggled beauty with the wild blond hair and mystifying lavender eyes. "Had I known you were so adept at digging up bits and pieces of vital information, I would have taken you into my confidence long ago." With rakish anticipation he moved toward her, backing her against the rock wall. "I offer a kiss in exchange for the man's name. . . ."

His lips were dangerously close, his smile inviting, but Tara was in a playful mood and she could not be bought for little or nothing. "A gentlemanly kiss? One that speaks of courtesy and respect?"

His cobalt-blue eyes slid over the full swells of her breasts and the trim curve of her hips. "I had in mind something a bit more tantalizing than the mere meeting of lips," he rasped, his gaze refocusing on her heart-shaped mouth with deliberate concentration.

"Very well." Tara sat rigidly before him. "Let us see what you have to offer, and I will decide if it is a fair exchange for my information."

Sloane was pleasantly surprised by her remark. This minx never ceased to amaze him. At times she was so evasive it drove him mad with frustration, and then occasionally she could be so agreeable that it drove him crazy with desire. And this was one of those times when he felt the gnawing hunger that chased all other thoughts from his head. Merrick Russel's conspirator was the furthest thing from his mind.

One sinewy arm curled about her, taking her with him to the rock floor. His dark head descended toward hers. "If this kiss doesn't suit you, tell me, *por favor*," he murmured, his voice ragged with anticipated passion. "I wouldn't want you to feel cheated. . . ."

Sensuous lips rolled over hers as his straying hand crept across the soft cotton gown, his palms molding themselves to her generous curves, leaving a fire smoldering in their path. His questing tongue traced her lips and then intruded to explore the hidden recesses of her mouth, their breath merging as one.

A moan of pleasure bubbled in her throat as his virile body pressed closer and his kiss deepened to savor her response. Her arms slid over his shoulders, drawing him ever closer, aware of nothing but the musky scent of him, the feel of his lips taking firm possession of hers. Her body arched to meet his wandering hands, aroused and excited, craving the wild splendor she always found when he took her in his arms and sent her soaring beyond the stars.

Sloane dragged his lips from hers to stare down into her exquisite features, watching her violet eyes ripple with unmistakable desire, an expression that mirrored his own emotions.

"Was the kiss fair compensation?" he queried hoarsely.

A thoughtful frown knitted her brow and then she shrugged nonchalantly. "I suppose that will suffice . . . although I have experienced far better," she taunted mischievously.

One bushy brow arched acutely. "And whom may I ask was the donor of a kiss that puts my offering to shame?" Tara reached up to trace the chiseled lines of his face and then trailed her finger over his pouting lips. "You don't know him, but I can assure you no man can equal his ability to stir a woman, so you need not be insulted."

She had piqued his curiosity and he was now itching to know what type of man interested this free-spirited vixen. "Then I envy his abilities," he murmured as his mouth grazed hers. "Who is this charming rogue?"

"The phantom spirit of Palo Duro," Tara whispered back to him, knowing she was a fool for allowing him a fragment of her carefully guarded secret. But she was unable to deny him the satisfaction of learning that she hungered for those fiery, devouring kisses with which he had seduced her the night she had followed him along the canyon rim and discovered his true identity.

A rakish grin dangled from one corner of his lips as his hand slid around the trim column of her neck, tilting her head back to his. "Is it his mysteriousness that arouses you, *querida?*"

"Partially," she confessed in a throaty voice. "But it is his masterful embrace that moves me and tears sane thought from my mind." Her violet eyes compelled him closer. "Come, let me show you how he entrances a woman with his spell and makes her surrender without relying on force."

A groan of torment rattled in his chest as her soft body melted against his and her sensuous lips opened on his. Her fingers tunneled through his hair, holding her to him until he ached to shed the confining garments that separated them and lose himself in the feel of her feminine curves. Another moan died beneath her seductive kiss as her adventurous hand dipped beneath the band of his breeches, intimately touching him, arousing him to the limits of sanity. She had become a skillful lover, one who no longer needed instruction. Tara could send his heart racing at such a breathless pace that Sloane wondered he could survive the maddening pleasure.

Her wandering hands glided across his hips and then swirled around his thigh, causing a quick intake of breath when she brazenly caressed him. Her exploring touch receded to begin the same arousing path again, and Sloane was consumed by a need that burned him alive. Impatiently he twisted away to press her beneath him, hungry to appease a craving that only the softness of her womanly body could fulfill. She was his addiction, and he had no intention of denying his compelling attraction to her. It was as if he fed on passion's flame, and although he knew how hot the fire could burn, he welcomed the engulfing blaze.

As the heat of desire consumed him, he found himself wrapped in a web of black magic. He was a pawn moving upon command. He was this spell-casting witch's possession. No matter how forceful or gentle he was with Tara, he could never claim her wild heart. It was as if she held it just out of his reach, like an unattainable star that outshone all the rest, an elusive dream that only allowed him a glimpse of heaven. He wanted to touch all of her, to make her his, body and soul. But not once had she spoken

270

of love, and he could no more pry such a declaration from her lips than a spider could fling out its web and seine the twinkling stars from the black velvet sea.

And just why was he so obsessed with winning her love, he asked himself as her supple body moved in hypnotic rhythm with his. Why couldn't he walk away and allow this violet-eyed vixen to return to the security of the world from which she had come? Because he could not remember feeling so young and alive before Tara had swept into his life like a devastating whirlwind. Because she had touched each and every emotion and he had given so much of himself each time he made wild sweet love to her that he had become half a man, one who could never be content with admiring her from afar, not after all they had shared.

Tara sighed in abandon as his hard thrusts drove into her, lifting her, sending her spiraling like an eagle climbing higher and higher. Rapturous sensations converged upon her, leaving her dizzy and breathless, and she clung to the one stable force in a careening universe. His lovemaking blanked out all memory, and when Tara closed her eyes she could see nothing but Sloane's bronzed face before her, remember nothing but the sweet, tormenting feelings that flooded over her as his body surged into hers, filling her with indescribable pleasure.

And when the shuddering climax came, she cried out to him and clung to him for what seemed eternity while the ecstatic sensations spilled through her, channeling outward to engulf every part of her being. She was floating on a sea of bliss, content to drift forever in the protective circle of his arms. When he shifted beside her, pulling her against the hard wall of his chest, Tara breathed a ragged sigh, knowing she could never make the most intimate of journeys with any other man. He had stirred her. He had taught her the true meaning of passion. No other man could erase the memories of his lovemaking.

"John Everett Simpson," Tara whispered against his cheek.

Sloane's soft chortle echoed in the cave as he propped up on an elbow and peered down into her flawless face. "Must I make love to you again to pry any other information about Simpson from you?" The suggestion had an appealing ring to it. Sloane would not have hesitated to employ such pleasurable tactics.

Tara giggled playfully as she rearranged the disheveled hair across his forehead and smoothed the bandage back in place. "I'm beginning to wonder if there isn't anything you wouldn't do to acquire information."

His roguish grin exposed even white teeth and his gaze dipped to the rosy peaks of her breasts before his lips grazed the ripe buds. "I have no aversion to mixing business and pleasure," he whispered against her quivering skin. "Shall I force you to tell me everything I want to know?"

There was no hope for it. When Sloane touched her, all was lost. And if they tarried much longer, they would never arrive in Tascosa. Attempting to gather her crumbling resistance, Tara inched away to fasten her blouse and rearrange her skirt. "That isn't necessary," she said in a half-strangled voice that still quavered with the aftereffects of passion. "I will tell you all I know. Simpson has come to visit Merrick on several occasions to discuss driving their herds to Harrold before the other ranchers take to the trail and deplete the supply of grass. I can only assume that if a switch is to be made, it will come soon after roundup."

Sloane frowned thoughtfully. "I thought perhaps Merrick was cutting out a few beeves from the herd and allowing them to wander in the thick mesquite and chaparral while he sent his hired hands on the trail. But you could be right. He could be mixing his stock with Simpson's smaller herd and then taking the profit once they have sold the beeves in Harrold." He unfolded himself and rose to full stature, pulling Tara up with him. "I think perhaps it is safe to travel, and we are miles behind where we should be by nightfall."

Tara followed silently behind Sloane as he inched his way down the ledge to mount his steed. A feeling of contentment washed over her as she stared at his broad back. He had finally confided in her, assuring her that she was worthy of his trust. Now if he would only see her as . . . Tara shut out the whimsical thought. Sloane had only one thing on his mind—dealing with Merrick. And she would help him expose Merrick for what he was.

A troubled frown settled on Tara's smudged features. What would become of Julia? She would be an innocent victim. She had no knowledge of her father's treachery. She had been pampered and spoiled by Merrick's ill-gotten gains, and when Merrick's world crumbled, so would Julia's. She would make certain Julia did not become a vagabond because of these two warring men, Tara promised herself. She would ensure that Sloane gave his cousin first consideration. He couldn't drive her from her home; he could not be that cruel. Could he? she silently asked herself. Had bitterness and desire for revenge poisoned him against anyone who bore the name of Russel? Tara prayed that he wouldn't hurt Julia. She faced enough heartache without Sloane adding insult to injury.

Chapter 18

The sprawling plains of West Texas reached toward each horizon. After two days at a fast pace, they spied the town on the north bank of the Canadian River just before dusk. Tara was apprehensive about crossing the boggy waters after their catastrophe the first day. But to her relief the colts proceeded across the river channel without mishap.

After they reached the settlement and delivered the livestock, Tara's eager gaze searched this outpost on the edge of civilization, anxious to find an accommodating hotel. Never again would she overlook the luxury of soaking in a warm bath.

Tara's anticipation was shattered when Sloane requested only a single room for the night. When she vehemently objected, Sloane clamped his hand over her mouth and forced a polite smile for the bewildered owner.

"She is a rather shy bride," Sloane explained as he wrestled with Tara and then subtly winked at the proprietor. "It is to be our first night together."

When Sloane had propelled her up the steps and locked the door behind them, Tara twisted from his arms to glare murderously at him.

"What in the name of heaven did you think you were doing?" she railed, her breasts heaving with every

274

frustrated breath she took. "I told you at the onset of this trip I would not be your whore, even if I have consented to help you. I demand my own room!"

Sloane listened to her rant and rave with amused patience as he shed his shirt and waited for the innkeeper to fill the bath he had requested. He had managed to keep his distance from Tara for two nights, allowing her to heal from her bumps and bruises, but forty-eight hours was his limit. He wanted Tara and he meant to have her. In the past they had made love in the most impractical places, and he damned well intended to enjoy the luxury of a double bed. He could see little reason for her to pretend modesty. There was nothing they didn't know about each other, and the morning they had spent in the cave, waiting out the storm, had assured him that Tara felt more for him than she would admit. But she had a stubborn streak as wide as Texas and it was apparent that they would continue to clash, no matter what they had shared in the secluded cave.

"We will be sharing the same bed, so you may as well warm to the idea," he told her flatly. "In fact, before the night is out . . ."

His voice trailed off when a knock at the door interrupted him. He grasped the latch, swung the door open wide, and then winced uncomfortably when the young woman carrying a bucket in either hand graced him with a welcoming smile.

Tara's eyes narrowed as the voluptuous brunette raked Sloane's bare chest with open admiration, and she would have bet her grandfather's fortune the girl had seen him in less than his breeches, judging by the way she was drooling over him.

"Sloane . . . I wondered when you would return. I have never forgotten the night . . ." Angela swallowed the remainder of her sentence when she caught sight of Tara out of the corner of her eyes. "Forgive me, *por favor*,

I did not realize you already had a guest for the evening."

"I am not his guest," Tara insisted, all too sweetly. "I am Mr. Prescott's new wife."

If Sloane intended to use his fabrication to his advantage, she could damned well employ the same tactics. The lout! No doubt Tascosa was swarming with women Sloane had taken to his bed. She spitefully hoped the comely señorita would pass the news along the grapevine that Sloane was married, so his harem would avoid him when next he showed his handsome face in town. That was what he deserved, Tara thought acrimoniously. She cringed to imagine how many women had wound up in his arms, sharing a night of passion with him. Damn him! And damn her for being such a fool. How could she ever hope that Sloane would feel something special for her when women chased after him like kittens on the trail of fresh milk? He could pick and choose his lovers, never sleeping with the same one in the same month!

His twinkling blue eyes circled to Tara, who was silently seething. It seemed the little wildcat wanted nothing more to do with him, but she wanted to ensure that no other woman would have him either.

"Sloane, is this true?" Big brown eyes remorsefully flooded over Sloane's powerful physique. "You are married?"

"I'm afraid I am, *mi niña*. My wandering days are over," Sloane chuckled and then cocked an eyebrow when he noticed the smug expression that was plastered on Tara's face. "The lady and I are very much in love."

Tara nearly choked on his words. She wondered how Sloane had allowed the lie to tumble so easily from his lips without strangling on it. Sloane in love with her? His wandering days were over? That would occur immediately after the Sahara desert froze over!

Angela poured the water into the tub and turned to

offer Tara a meager smile. "My congratulations, señorita. You are a very lucky woman to have such a man."

"I am aware of that," Tara acknowledged, her honey-coated smile implying that she was hopelessly infatuated with the big brute.

When the door eased shut behind Angela, Tara flounced over to test the water, hastily stripped, and then sank into the tub before Sloane could step into it. His devouring gaze traced each delicious detail of her curvaceous figure, feeling the quick rise of desire as his eyes wandered unhindered over her silky skin. If Tara had intended to taunt him with that tantalizing body of hers, she had done a most thorough job of it, he thought to himself. He was well warmed and ready to appease a need he had held in check for the past two days.

One perfectly arched brow raised when she noticed the bulge in his breeches, knowing full well that her state of undress had a dramatic effect on this surly cowboy with the voracious appetite. No doubt the entire female population of Tascosa could not appease this lusty beast, and she was not so vain as to think it would have mattered if it were she or Angela soaking in his tub. Either of them would do, she thought bitterly. But Sloane had taken advantage of her affection for him on so many occasions that she decided he deserved to become uncomfortable with his lust. Let him soak in a cold tub when she had finished with her bath, she thought spitefully. Perhaps that would cool his ardor.

"The soap please." One dainty finger indicated the bar of soap that waited on the commode.

Sloane studied her with piercing scrutiny. So this was to be his torture, he realized. Having and having not, he muttered under his breath as he groped for the soap without ungluing his gaze from Tara's bewitching figure. He swallowed a room full of air when one slim leg emerged from the water and Tara lathered her calf and thigh, her hands gliding over her smooth skin, reminding Sloane that the privilege he had once been granted was now off limits. When she proceeded to give the same languid attention to the other leg, Sloane groaned in torment. Lord, he would have given almost anything to become a bar of soap!

Suddenly, he froze in astonishment. It had finally happened, he bellowed to himself. Tara had driven him over the brink of sanity. What man in his right mind would wish to reduce himself to soap bubbles, just to be near this violet-eyed vixen? Only a love-starved imbecile, he thought disgustedly. Well, there was more than one woman in Tascosa, he reminded himself, and he could name any number who would be willing to accommodate him. Let that ornery witch stew in her kettle. He would march off to find a woman who would not have to be coaxed into his arms. Two could play this chit's game, and if she wanted her private room, she could damned well have it!

Whirling around, Sloane snatched up his discarded shirt and strode toward the door, refusing to cast the appetizing minx another glance for fear he would rip off his clothes and join her in the tub. He would not give her the satisfaction of winning this round!

"Where are you going?" Tara tried desperately to keep disappointment from seeping into her voice. Did he no longer find her desirable? Did he intend to seek out Angela and inform her that he really did not have a wife? Damn, the first time she had purposely attempted to seduce him, he turned and walked away. Tara's heart fell down around her knees. She had wanted some meager commitment of affection, but she received not a smidgeon. She meant no more to Sloane than she had the first time they'd met. He had only taken her into his confidence because he needed her help to get at Merrick. She was his pawn and that was all she would ever be.

"I thought you intended to bathe." Tara studied his broad back, praying he would turn and she would see a spark of love flickering in his eyes. Damnation, at this point she would even have settled for fervent desire—anything to keep him from seeking out another woman!

"I will be in the saloon, quenching my thirst," he grumbled without daring to look back at the stunning silver-blonde whose enchanting image had already materialized on the wooden door.

"Do you intend to quench your thirst for whiskey or women?" she questioned, a distinctly unpleasant edge on her voice.

"Perhaps a little of both, since you have made it clear that you prefer privacy to my brand of passion. I'll be back later to fetch you for dinner. Don't leave without me. Tascosa is a rough town, and I don't want you wandering the streets alone. Enjoy your bath, *duquesa*," he grumbled, the words whipping around the door as it slammed shut behind him.

Tara hurled the soap at his lingering image and then cursed his name, finding that tactic far more satisfying than counting to ten when she had lost her temper. Don't leave without him? Tara silently smoldered at his brisk order. She had confronted her fair share of unsavory characters, Sloane included, and she could damned well handle any man who thought to give her trouble. Blast it, she wasn't going to sit here twiddling her thumbs, staring at these four blank walls until the cavorting rake returned to their room!

After thoroughly drying herself, Tara drew out her best gown and smoothed out the wrinkles. If Sloane thought she would follow his orders, he had made a gross error in judgment. No man was going to order her around—and certainly not Sloane. The man was positively infuriating, and she was too rebellious to allow him to think he could waltz into another woman's arms

279

while she patiently sat and waited for his return.

Tara fluffed out her lavender gown and then checked her appearance in the mirror. Pasting on a cheerful smile, she descended the stairs and stepped onto the street. As she ambled past the saloon, her heart came to a screeching halt. There, in the midst of the crowd, sat Sloane, with a calico queen draped on each arm. They were slobbering all over him, whispering in his ears, running their fingers through his thick wavy hair, making all sorts of suggestive movements as they drew his arms closer about them. Tara's eyes flickered with disgust, certain that if Sloane had as many arms as an octopus, there would have been a woman in each one of them. Damn him! Didn't he have one shred of decency? Obviously not, her mind screamed. If he did, it had been squashed flat when those bar flies planted themselves on his lap.

Her eyes blazed like torches as she spun away from the lively piano music and disheartening sight of Sloane and his armload of painted women. Damn him to hell and back! She'd thought he cared a little about her, but it was now apparent to Tara that he didn't care enough. The insult stung like salt on an open wound. He preferred to lounge in the saloon with any number of available women than to spend another hour with her.

Who was she kidding, she asked herself miserably as she marched back down the street to the restaurant, intent on feeding her frustration. Now that Sloane was back in Tascosa, he didn't need her to satisfy his lust. Oh, what a fool she had been to live on the hope that time would soften that rock-hard cowboy. Sloane would never see her as that special woman in his life, the one he couldn't live without. But then, Sloane was like a tumbleweed, a man without roots. He was content to go where the wind took him, taking pleasure where he found it, with *any* woman. He was too cynical to allow love to burrow into his heart, and it was high time Tara accepted that fact. There was nothing for her to do but gather her crumbled pride and return to Clarendon, she decided. She would busy herself in the newspaper office and then return to St. Louis, where she should have stayed in the first place. With that thought she entered the restaurant and sat down at the closest available table.

"Miss, would you mind some company?" came a hushed voice from so close beside her that Tara nearly dropped the silverware she had been examining absently.

She glanced up to see a blond-haired man who was hovering over her. Offering him an agreeable smile, she gestured toward the empty chair. She welcomed conversation, anything to take her mind off the ruggedly handsome cowboy whose memory was tying her in knots.

"You must be new in town," the man surmised, and then let his pale green eyes drift where they would, lingering on the scoop neck of her lavender gown. "I would have remembered seeing such a lovely sight, Miss . . ." He paused, waiting for Tara to supply her name.

"Winslow," she informed him. "I have just arrived this evening, Mr. . . ." She used his tactic to discover his name.

"Yates. Stephen Yates." He eased back in his chair to survey the pert beauty. "Will you be staying in Tascosa long?"

Tara gave her blond head a negative shake and then feasted on the steak that was set before her while Stephen related the history of Tascosa and insisted that she should delay her journey to view all the interesting landmarks there.

When she finished her meal, Stephen offered to show her around town and Tara eagerly accepted the invitation. It sounded far more appealing than pacing the confines of her room, waiting for Sloane to drag himself back to the hotel like a wayward tomcat who had been on the prowl.

Stephen unfolded a spellbinding tale of how Tascosa had become the occasional resting place of Billy the Kid and his notorious outlaws. He explained that the town had once been the campsite of *ciboleros,* Mexican buffalo hunters who met to barter with the Indians, exchanging contraband goods, white captives stolen from Texas settlements, and beeves. Later Tascosa became the wild trail town for ranchers driving their cattle herds to Dodge City.

Tara was not the least bit surprised to learn the town boasted such a colorful history, since it was still full of numerous gambling rooms, saloons, and dance halls. And, no doubt, Sloane would have gallivanted his way through most of them before he returned to see if she had died of starvation or drowned in the tub during his lengthy absence. The inconsiderate cad. He didn't give a fig about what had become of her.

As they strolled in the moonlight, a startled gasp attempted to force itself from Tara's lips when she found Stephen's mouth taking rough possession of hers. She had been too immersed in thought to realize that Stephen had veered them into an alley.

"Sir, you are much too presumptuous!" Tara sputtered as she pressed small, determined hands to his chest, shoving him a respectable distance away. "If I desired to be kissed, I would have informed you!"

Stephen chuckled at the violet sparks that were snapping in her eyes. "Come now, Miss Winslow. Any woman who wanders about Texas without an escort has probably picked up her fair share of male companions along the way. There is no need to pretend coyness. I think we have the same thing on our minds, don't we?" Stephen captured her in his arms, chaining her to him. "You are quite a temptation, my dear. But you are well

282

aware of that, aren't you?" His head moved deliberately toward hers to breathe down her neck, "Name your price, love. I will be only too happy to pay it."

Tara would have cheerfully punched him in the mouth if it hadn't fastened over hers. Never in her life had she met such a miserable excuse for a gentleman. Stephen was dressed fit to kill in his gray jacket and trousers, and he was making a feast of her! Even Sloane, with all his peccadilloes, had never really mauled her, certainly not like this! She squirmed to escape his suffocating embrace, repulsed by his devouring kiss. Furiously, she raised her knee, catching him in the groin, evoking a pained grunt from her overzealous companion.

While Stephen was doubled over, protecting the sensitive part of his anatomy from another blow that might render him useless to any woman, Tara fished into her purse to retrieve her derringer and then pointed it between his wide, disbelieving eyes.

"Either you are hard of hearing or you are a blundering idiot," she hissed venomously. "No man takes liberties with me, Mr. Yates. Do I make myself clear?"

Stephen unfolded himself and lifted his arms high in the air as if he had been held up by a marauding band of outlaws. "Calm yourself, honey," he cooed. "I didn't mean any harm. Perhaps I had the wrong impression. I certainly didn't mean to offend you. . . ."

Like a rattlesnake coiled to spring, Stephen leaped at Tara in the wake of his apology. Her surprised yelp pierced the air as his hand shot toward the derringer, knocking her sideways as he made a grab for her pistol, intent on taking up where he had left off.

Too late Tara realized Stephen Yates had been insincere. He didn't care what kind of woman she was. The man intended to have her, right in the alleyway!

"You bastard," Tara spat at him as he straddled her

belly, his knees pinning her arms to her sides.

"You'll change your opinion of me shortly," he assured her as he tossed the derringer aside and set his hands upon her, leaving Tara no doubt of his intent.

Her scream of alarm died beneath his ravishing kiss. Tara cursed her foolishness. She had left her room to spite Sloane, but she was about to pay for her defiance. Stephen Yates meant to rape her, and the terror that rose with that thought was as blinding as staring into the summer sun.

Maria Orñate peeled off her blouse and then glanced back at the strikingly attractive cowboy who was sprawled on her bed, puffing on a cigar and sipping brandy from the bottle he held in the crook of his arm. A disappointed frown creased her brow as she ambled up in front of him in her skimpy chemise. She could have sworn a man with Sloane's usual appetite for passion would have sat up and taken note, but to her dismay, Maria realized she could have been standing there as naked as a jay bird and he would have overlooked her.

"He! Hombre. No seas tan exigente! Ven acá," she purred once she had his attention.

Sloane climbed from the depths of his pensive musings and rose to stand beside the comely Mexican maid, determined to banish that blond-haired minx with the stunning amethyst eyes from his mind. Tara had driven him to this, he reminded himself sourly. She deserved to sit and stew while he sampled Maria's charms, a woman who knew how to please a man, a woman who knew there were no strings attached to their night of passion.

His hands drifted over her soft shoulder, and Sloane closed his eyes to accept her eager kiss, one that promised fiery passion until he wanted no more of it. As her lips opened beneath his, the scent of her seemed unfamiliar and the feel of her skin beneath his caresses was all wrong. And then, like a phantom of the night, a vision rose before him, one with dancing violet eyes and hair of spun silver and gold, one with lips as soft as rose petals and skin as delectable as honey.

His eyes flew open to see the dark face below his, and, scowling, Sloane lowered his head once again, determined to chase away the tormenting vision. But Tara came like a genie rising from a lantern, wedging herself between him and this scantily dressed woman who offered to help him forget his troubled thoughts. Damnation! Wouldn't that lavender-eyed she-cat ever allow him to forget her?

"Something is terribly wrong," Maria murmured as she leaned back to appraise the dark frown that was stamped on Sloane's rugged face.

His arms dropped heavily at his sides and he cursed himself for kissing Tara when it was Maria who had been in his embrace. It would serve no purpose to pretend to find pleasure with Maria when it was Tara he craved. Confound it! That blond-haired hellion seemed to have taken up permanent residence in his mind, and it was virtually impossible to rout her.

"Se va haciendo tarde," Sloane grumbled as he stalked over to retrieve his hat and douse his cigar in the bottle of whiskey. "I am sorry. Another time perhaps." He tossed her a coin and then aimed himself toward the door, but Maria's mocking tone halted him in his tracks.

"Is it what the señorita Angela says—that you have married?" Maria shrugged on her blouse and looked at him with amusement. *"¡Dios mío!* I never thought I would live to see the day Sloane Prescott was hobbled by a woman."

Grinding his teeth to prevent taking his frustration out on Maria, Sloane yanked open the door and stormed out, anxious to direct his irritation on the source of his troubles. Like cavalry answering a bugle's signal to charge, Sloane marched down the street and stomped to his room.

As the door crashed against the wall, his furious gaze circled the empty room and he cursed viciously. Where the hell was that little termagant? Had she flitted off into the night after he had told her to stay put? Frantically, he searched the room for a note, hoping the little fool had thought to inform him of her whereabouts, but she had left without a word.

God, he could have been lying in Maria's arms. But no, he wasn't allowed the smallest amount of pleasure. He was destined to spend his time tearing Tascosa apart to find that rebellious minx who had an uncanny knack of getting herself into trouble.

Chapter 19

Another wave of nausea flooded over Tara as Stephen's rough caresses roamed across her breasts and he fumbled to draw her gown up to her thighs, impatiently attempting to appease his need to bury himself in this feisty wildcat who refused to succumb to him.

"Let me go!" Tara screamed at him when he finally lifted his head to oversee the chore of ridding Tara of the confining dress.

His hand fastened over her mouth to silence any further protest as he scooted off beside her to pull her skirt up to her waist. Tara writhed for freedom, but it seemed Stephen had sprouted an extra pair of hands and no matter which way she moved he was there to snare her.

And then, like a shot in the dark, a man lunged from the shadows, knocking Stephen to the ground as if he had been trampled by a herd of stampeding horses. Tara scrambled to her feet and watched in delight as she recognized Sloane towering over Stephen, pounding some manners into the brutish oaf. Stephen yelped and squawked as Sloane's fists came at him from out of nowhere, dazing him so thoroughly that Stephen was no longer certain which way was up until Sloane grabbed a fistful of his shirt and hoisted him to his feet.

When Sloane shoved Stephen away he stumbled to maintain his balance and then braced his arm against the wall, following the alley in his escape from the vicious tiger who had sprung at him.

Tara offered Sloane a grateful smile and was about to voice her appreciation for being rescued from the hands of disaster, but all thought evaporated when she saw his murderous, glowering expression. If looks could kill, Tara would have been standing before a firing squad, riddled with bullets. His eyes were hotter than blue blazes and his shadowed features were like the smoldering molten rock of a volcano that was about to erupt. She had seen him angry before, but never like this! He was breathing the fire of dragons, and Tara shook in her shoes, praying he wasn't entertaining the idea of beating her to a pulp as well.

Sloane clamped his fingers into the tender flesh of her arm, drawing a pained shriek as he roughly dragged her along behind him. He was so furious with this feisty hellcat that it was all he could do to keep from shaking the stuffing out of her after her idiotic prank. Indeed, he had promised himself that he would do just that after turning Tascosa upside down trying to locate her. Sloane had imagined all sorts of catastrophes converging on this attractive bundle of trouble. Tascosa was noted for being a wild, lawless town, bulging with ruffians who wouldn't bat an eye at carting off an unescorted female and having their way with her. He had envisioned finding her mutilated body lying in the dirt, her life spilling from her. God, he had endured nine kinds of hell before he had heard her frightened voice wafting its way toward him from the dark alley.

"Give me back my arm!" Tara demanded, her voice crackling with irritation as she attempted to worm free from the crushing pressure of his fingers. She had been pushed and shoved enough for one night, and she wanted no more of Sloane's rough handling.

"You are coming with me," Sloane ground out as he towed her down the street, forcing her to run to keep up with his impatient strides or be dragged along in the dirt.

"What the devil is the matter with you?" Tara questioned as he hustled her along behind him.

"It would take the remainder of the evening to explain," he growled back at her. "And I can't spare the time." He veered around the corner, aiming himself in the opposite direction from their hotel.

"Where are we going?" Tara insisted in knowing.

"The very place I should have taken you the first night I found you," Sloane snapped as he halted in front of a quaint cottage that seemed a peaceful retreat until Sloane's impatient knock shook the structure's rafters.

When the door swung open, Sloane barged inside and hooked his arm around Tara's waist to ensure she didn't break and run. "I want you to marry us," Sloane demanded of the clergyman.

"What?" Tara croaked in disbelief.

"Don't you dare protest this wedding," Sloane challenged as his hard blue eyes riveted over Tara's stunned features. "I am in no mood for argument. You have already scared the hell out of me!" His gaze swung to the preacher whose mouth dropped open at Sloane's harsh remark. "Excuse me," Sloane murmured, his voice too brittle with anger to sound remotely apologetic.

"I couldn't have scared the hell out of you entirely," Tara muttered as she tried to twist from his muscular arms and then gave up her futile attempt to glare daggers at him. "You are still behaving like the very devil."

"If I am it's because you have provoked me," Sloane snapped accusingly. "You had no business leaving your room, for the very reason that found you face to face with disaster. *Valgame Dios, Eso me desespera!*" His voice thundered about the room and the preacher shrank away

289

as if he expected to be struck by a bolt of lightning after all the cursing that was going on in his home.

"I happen to be an engaged woman!" Tara flared, her glare hot enough to singe a normal man, but it had no effect on Sloane.

"One who will shortly be married," Sloane amended as he gestured for the preacher to begin the ceremony.

"I have a say in this matter," Tara spouted when the apprehensive preacher stepped in front of them.

"You will have the opportunity to speak your piece," Sloane gruffly assured her. "And until that time, be still. I only intend to wed once and I will not have the ceremony drowned out by your loud protests."

"This is preposterous. I . . ."

Sloane clamped his hand over her mouth and nodded for the clergyman to proceed. When the time came for Tara to speak her piece, Sloane removed his hand and then squeezed her ribs, forcing her to affirm the pledge or chance having her insides scrambled.

Deciding it best not to argue with a maniac, Tara begrudgingly muttered the words. Angrily, she flashed Sloane a glare that should have reduced him to a pile of dusty ashes, but Sloane was as hard and impregnable as the Rock of Gibraltar, and he showed no signs of melting.

A meek smile surfaced on the minister's lips, his questioning gaze focused on the obstinate cowboy. "Do you have a ring to give to the bride? It is customary to . . ."

The reminder had Sloane scowling under his breath. He hadn't bothered with that minor detail when his foremost concern was rounding up this runaway minx and keeping her out of trouble.

"I'll be right back," Sloane threw over his shoulder as his swift strides took him toward the door. His penetrating gaze drilled into the preacher. "And if you let her sneak away before I return, I'll . . ."

Tara's shocked gasp interrupted Sloane's harsh warning. "Don't you dare threaten a man of the cloth," she reprimanded him. "If your soul hasn't already been condemned to the eternal inferno, it surely will be if you begin issuing threats to one of the Lord's shepherds!"

"Then my soul's fate rests upon *your* shoulders," Sloane countered with a wry smile. "If you abandon me in the middle of our wedding, you will be the reason this wayward lamb has been lost from the flock."

Lamb? Tara sniffed acrimoniously at the thought of *Lamb* Prescott. He had undoubtedly strayed so far from the straight and narrow path that he could never find his way back. Impatiently, she tapped her foot, itching to make her escape but apprehensive about what Sloane might do if he returned to find her gone, especially while he was having a crazed fit. She shuddered to think what he might do to the gentle clergyman, who could only turn the other cheek twice!

When Sloane barged into the room after an absence of less than five minutes, Tara's mouth dropped open in surprise. Beaming, Sloane unfolded his hand, revealing a gold wedding band. Tara found herself wondering who the maniac had had to kill to acquire it so quickly. And before she could bite back the question, it flew from her lips.

"Where did you find a ring at this late hour? Surely, the proprietor of the . . ."

"Don't ask." Sloane cut her off in midsentence, closed the distance between them, and slipped the slightly oversized ring on her finger.

When the whirlwind wedding was concluded Sloane marched his new bride back to the hotel. Although Tara was breathless after being dragged along at such a swift pace, she gathered enough air to sputter out her question.

"Would you mind telling me whom you robbed, killed,

or both to acquire this ring?" she demanded to know.

Without breaking stride, Sloane replied, "I told you not to ask."

"I will not stop hounding you until you satisfy my curiosity," Tara assured him tartly.

Heaving an agitated sigh, Sloane veered around the corner and then flung Tara a glance. "I passed a woman on the street and, seeing her wedding band, I offered her twenty dollars for it. Being the sentimental sort, she refused."

Tara groaned miserably. "Don't tell me you held her at gun point and ordered her to take your money in exchange for the ring."

"Very well, I won't."

"You didn't!" Tara croaked in disbelief.

"I was desperate," Sloane defended himself gruffly.

"You are utterly mad," she sniffed distastefully.

"If I am, I have you to thank for it," he countered before whisking her into the hotel. After Sloane herded Tara into their room, he gave her a forceful shove, sending her sprawling. "And if you ever pull another hair-brained stunt like that again, I will take you over my knee and give you the paddling your father has obviously neglected." Sloane stormed toward her, pulling up short when Tara snatched the derringer from her pocket and pointed it at his heaving chest.

"And if you dare lay a hand on me again I will blow it off the end of your arm!" she fumed.

She was not about to let this rough-edged brute who had steam rolling from his collar bully her. She had been dealt quite enough misery from those of the male persuasion that evening, and she would take no more of it, especially from Sloane.

His irritation dwindled to mild amusement as he peered at her flushed face. Lord, she was beautiful when she was seething with rage. Her eyes glowed like wild violets fluttering in the wind. Her blond hair dangled about her in disarray and her torn gown left just enough to the imagination to allow it to run rampant.

"Since we both seem prone to violence, I suggest a truce," he said in a calmer tone. "It would seem a pity for one of us to be widowed on the very eve of our wedding." Carefully, he stretched out his arm, urging Tara to hand over her pistol before one of them was blown to smithereens. "If you promise never to go waltzing around Tascosa without a suitable escort, I will promise never to force you into another marriage."

Tara tossed him a withering glance, annoyed with his feeble attempt to humor her. "You realize, of course, that this little temper tantrum of yours has evolved into catastrophe. Now we will be forced to adjourn to the courthouse in the morning and have this ridiculous marriage annulled."

"*No del todo,*" he snorted, his reckless smile vanishing as he pinned Tara back against the wall with his piercing glare. "*Con la cuchara que, elijas, on esa comerias.*"

"Would you mind translating that," Tara requested. "I do wish you would stick to English. I have enough difficulty following your distorted logic as it is." Sarcasm dripped from her lips as she eyed the towering mass of brawn and muscle that hovered before her.

"Give me the pistol and I will translate for those of us who are not fluent in more than one language, *amanta.*"

Tara wasn't certain if his last word was an endearment or a curse, but if his scornful tone was any indication, her ears probably should have been burning. Reluctantly, she set the derringer aside, refusing to allow it to fall into Sloane's hands. She could think of nothing more humiliating than being killed with her own weapon, and as crazed as Sloane was, she wouldn't have been surprised if the maniac turned it on her. He must have been out of his mind to force her to wed him. What purpose could that possibly serve?

Once she was unarmed, Sloane moved toward her like an invading army, bracing his arms on either side of her, refusing to allow her to escape him. "I said, you have made your bed and now you will sleep in it," he translated and then leaned dangerously close, forcing Tara to lie flat on her back or be squashed by his heavy weight. "You may not approve of being my wife, but you are my wife, just the same. And if I give you the order to stay put, you damned well better obey it."

Tara flinched and pushed back as far as the bed would allow when his cobalt eyes bored into hers. "Why should I take orders from a lunatic who garbs himself in a white poncho and long-handled underwear and romps around in the dark on his silver-white charger?" she smirked caustically. "You really should get yourself in hand, Sloane. You have portrayed so many different personalities that you scarcely know who you are, phantom, bumpkin, or husband." Tara eyed him curiously. "Which one are you?"

"Who are *you?*" he parried as he eased down on the edge of the bed as if he belonged there, despite Tara's attempt to shove him a safe distance away. "The lady or the tigress? Beneath that prim and proper countenance lies a she-cat who can come at me with claws bared. Or are you the passionate vixen I found in the secluded cave behind the waterfall and in the abandoned lair carved in the rock walls of Palo Duro?"

Tara was allowed no time to reply. His full lips fitted themselves to hers, stealing her breath, erasing the memory of Stephen Yates's repulsive kiss, leaving her drowning in sensations she would have preferred not to feel at all. But the deep-seated feelings rose like cream on fresh milk when he touched her in his unique way.

There was no hope for it. Her love for him forced her to unconditional surrender. She could never muster the

294

will to deny him.

"You are the cause of my madness," Sloane whispered against her skin. "I was out of my mind when I returned to find you gone."

"I'm surprised you even noticed with all those calico queens draped on your shoulders," Tara said bitterly.

Sloane drew back to flash her a roguish grin. "Did jealousy drive you away?" His low chortle murmured about her as his tanned finger traced the creamy texture of her cheeks. "*¡Que ideas tan descabelladas tienes!* I have already told you that no other woman stirs me the way you do. What must I do to make you understand that?"

Offer your love, she silently responded as his lips took hers captive in another breathless kiss. That was all she would have asked of him, if pride had not locked the words in her heart.

His impatient hands moved over the buttons of her torn gown and then peeled the chemisette from her satiny skin. Tara moaned softly as his caresses flooded over her bare flesh, setting fires that had been long left to burn. Two days of wanting kindled and burst into flames as he rained kisses across her silky shoulder. His tongue flicked at the rosy peaks of her breasts, sending another wave of white-hot fire boiling through her veins and erotic sensations spilling through her. He was drawing upon her strength, making his will her own, and Tara was caught up in the swirling rapture that cast her upon a sea of fiery desire.

Her dark lashes fluttered against her cheeks and she reveled in ecstasy as his practiced hands descended from the slope of her breast to splay over her velvety hips. Her thighs opened beneath the gentle pressure of his questing fingers and moist lips and she became vividly aware of the sweet aching torment of wanting him. His kisses scattered across her hips and abdomen, retracting their tantalizing path to swirl around each taut crest of her breast.

His hands and lips were everywhere, tasting, touching, caressing, stroking, feeding the flames of passion until Tara could remember nothing in the world except Sloane's magical presence. Her senses were filled with the salty taste of him, the masculine aroma that always clung to her long after he had made her his possession. His husky voice whispered words of want and need, assuring her of how much he loved touching her. All five senses were keenly aware of the man who hovered so close beside her, and the throb of wanting him banished all other thoughts from her tormented mind.

Wild splendor spilled through her like wine flowing over the rim of a crystal goblet, flooding and swelling until there was nothing left but an aching emptiness that only Sloane could appease. Her fingertips glided down the rippling muscles of his back and then curled around his hips to caress his bold manhood, urging him closer, unashamed of her need to touch him, to arouse him as fully as he had aroused her.

Sloane sucked in his breath as her wandering hands found each sensitive point and triggered wild, maddening sensations. The feel of her soft fingertips sprinkling across his hard flesh was like an exciting massage that released the fierce needs he had so carefully held in check. He could not hold himself from her, not when she coaxed him nearer with her delightful caresses. This gorgeous temptress knew how to set him ablaze with passion, to take up the initiative and lead him down such tantalizing avenues that he could never find his way back. He was like a creature of habit, following where she led, lost in the dark depths of desire that would soon part and send him soaring into the sun to be consumed by love's devastating blaze.

Her writhing body excited him and he craved to know her by far more than taste and touch. She fed his growing hunger, and then, like a spell-casting witch, she created monstrous needs that drove him far beyond distraction.

With a surrendering groan, he let his arms fasten tightly about her, lifting her hips to his, crushing her to him as if he would never be content until their bodies were fused as one living, breathing essence. With desperate urgency he thrust against her, caught up in the windswept waves that crashed over him. Somewhere deep inside him budding rapture unfurled and blossomed with sensations that no language could accurately translate. His body and soul were consumed by the feel and taste of the woman in his arms.

Sloane couldn't think. His mind fogged with intensifying passion that continued to build as he sought the ultimate depths of intimacy. The maddening sensations drove him to her, possessing her, claiming her as his own. Needs as ancient as time itself took command, and he glided with the rhythm of a melody that danced in his soul.

Tara gasped for breath as the dark world exploded about her. She was being flung to a distant corner of the universe and then held suspended in ecstasy, wondering deliriously if she could endure the magnificent pleasure that engulfed every part of her being.

Sloane shuddered against her, his body surging into hers as ardent passions claimed sweet release. Every ounce of strength escaped him as he relaxed against Tara's soft womanly body. The sensations were so devastating that Sloane did not dare move until his stampeding heart slowed its reckless pace and his hazy thoughts cleared. Each time he took Tara in his arms to soar to passion's lofty pinnacle, the feelings that converged on him transcended physical pleasure. They compared with nothing he had ever experienced, and each encounter with Tara further erased the dim memories of other women he had taken in his arms. And just when he thought he could soar no higher, he found himself swept up to yet another erotic plateau.

A thoughtful frown etched his dark brow as he rolled beside her to trace his finger over her kiss-swollen lips. His gaze settled on those captivating amethyst eyes fringed with long, thick lashes. Lord, what had he done, he asked himself in amazement. He had been out of his mind with worry and insanely furious with Tara for abandoning him, so much so that he had dragged her kicking and screaming into a marriage she didn't want. And Sloane wasn't certain he did, either. Damn, didn't he have enough on his mind without worrying over Tara? No doubt, she would have fared better in St. Louis with Joseph Rutherford, a man who could lay the world at her feet, a world to which she had grown accustomed. Why had he become so obsessed with this silver-blond minx? They were as different as night and day. Tara was the essence of poise and beauty, like a delicate rose, and he was a windblown tumbleweed who had always followed a wandering star.

Heaving a heavy sigh, Sloane eased away to gather his clothes. "I'm sending you back to St. Louis where you belong, where you will be safe," he suddenly decided.

He might as well have slapped her in the face. Tara felt the sting of his words, and it hurt to realize that even after the splendor of their lovemaking he could walk away, untouched by any emotion. Damn him! He was as hard as cedar, and sap surely flowed through his veins. He was tearing her to pieces, bit by agonizing bit. How could he force her into a wedding and then announce that he was sending her away?

"Why did you do it?" Tara demanded to know as she wrapped the sheet about her and sat up on the edge of the bed. "Marry me, I mean," she clarified.

His eyes flitted past hers and he refused to be captured in her probing gaze. He shrugged on his shirt and then reached for his boots. "We all have our moments of madness," he hedged. "But what's done is done, and I can't, in good conscience, keep you here. When Merrick learns of the wedding and my purpose on the Diamond R Ranch, he might use you to get at me. I won't risk your life, and I cannot forget my obligation. Besides, you don't belong here. We are from two completely different worlds. I can't fit into yours, and the West is no place for a woman like you."

That ignoramus! How could he be so blind, she thought furiously. Did he still see her as some whimpering soul who would wither and die on the Panhandle Plains? She was not some dainty flower who couldn't endure his rugged way of life. She had just made a three-day journey without perishing in the wilds. Did that count for nothing? Well, she was not going to be ordered back to Missouri, and that was the beginning and end of it. She was made of sturdy stuff—and he should know that by now!

Tara pressed her hands to his shoulders and then pushed with every ounce of strength she could muster, sending him sprawling on the floor. His wide eyes focused on her flushed face and the wild disarray of tangles that cascaded down her back.

"I am going nowhere, Sloane Prescott," she informed him in no uncertain terms. "Don't think you can give me your name like a brand on a calf and then cart me off to the train station!" Her voice rose steadily, until she was practically yelling in his shocked face. "I am *not* leaving Texas until I'm damned good and ready!"

Sloane was certain everyone else in the hotel knew her intentions, since she was bellowing at the top of her lungs. His eyes dipped to see the sheet drooping over her breasts, and when Tara realized where his attention had fallen, she pulled it closely about her and then flashed him another fiery glare.

"When I decide to return to St. Louis, it will be because *I* wish to go," she assured him huffily, tapping herself on the chest to emphasize her point. "I will not have some wooden-headed cowboy spouting orders at me. I have taken quite enough from you and I will tolerate no more. You may be my temporary husband, but you are not my lord and master. Lincoln freed the slaves long ago." One delicate arched brow tilted mockingly. "You do recall hearing of the war, don't you? It was in all the papers," she finished on a caustic note.

"You are my wife and you will go where I tell you," Sloane insisted firmly.

"I am your wife in name only," she corrected. "And you are not going to order me around!"

When Sloane tried to gather his feet beneath him to confront this raging witch from a more advantageous position, Tara rammed her bare foot in his belly, flattening him against the floor. Sloane's eyes rounded to survey the wildcat who was poised to pounce on him. Her bewitching beauty often deceived him, and Sloane had to remind himself that Tara could become a stalking tigress when he stoked the fires of her temper.

"Tara, be reasonable. I am only thinking of your . . ."

"Yourself," Tara hastily interjected. "Don't play the gallant gentleman, Sloane. It doesn't suit you. Stick to something you are more familiar with, like unpolished manners and lack of consideration." She glared at him with scornful mockery and then gave him another shove for good measure before she pivoted on her heels and stalked over to yank up her strewn clothing. "I can endure the hardships of Texas just as well as you can. I could have sliced you into bite-sized pieces in Burns's kitchen if I had had a mind to do so. And I can handle a pistol if necessary. How do you think I managed to travel from Missouri to Texas without mishap? And who pulled *you* from the river and ferried the colts across while you were floundering like a drowning swimmer?"

"But who saved *you* from an assassin and who kept you from dying of a rattlesnake bite when you went thundering off at a breakneck pace and landed in a heap on the ground?" he shot back as he rolled to his feet and stomped after her.

"You did," she acknowledged as she poked her arms in the sleeve of her blouse and then hurriedly fastened it. "But you are not forcing me into a ridiculous marriage and then shuffling me out from underfoot." Her snapping violet eyes lifted to meet his icy blue ones. Damn, how she detested looking up to this giant of a man. If wishing would make it so, she would have been ten feet tall so *she* could have stared down her nose at *him*. "I will not let you off so easily. I want more from you than your name. . . ."

"What do you intend to do? Extract a pound of flesh from my hide?" he snorted derisively.

A deliciously mischievous smile caught the corners of her mouth curving them upward, and her gaze ran the full length of his powerful physique. "I have a signed certificate that grants me certain rights to you, my dear husband," she reminded him as her adventurous hand mapped the muscular contours of his hips and deft fingers worked to free the breeches he had just fastened into place. "Shall I show you which rights I refuse to abandon for safety's sake?"

One heavy brow shot straight up. "Brazen hussy," he growled, aroused by the feel of her hands tracing intricate patterns on his bare chest.

"Rough-edged cowboy," she flung at him. "You promised to love and honor your cherished wife and already you have fallen short. . . ."

Her lips parted in invitation as her head moved deliberately toward his, her hair hovering about her like a cape of warm sunshine, her eyes sparkling like priceless gems. Sloane could no more have refused the invitation than he could have flown to the moon. Her sweet mouth hovered on his and then her darting tongue intruded to deepen a kiss that had every indication of fueling the flame that Sloane could have sworn had burned itself out. Using the skillful techniques he had employed to send her sailing to rapture's paradise, Tara brought his passions to a fervent pitch. Her nails raked over his hard flesh like a tigress devouring her feast. She left not one inch of his masculine flesh untouched by her taunting kisses and caresses, driving him steadily toward abandon, forcing him to cast logic aside and surrender to the emotions that had tugged at his soul since the first moment he had taken this curvaceous beauty in his arms.

"Tell me you truly wish to send me away," Tara whispered as she drew him to the bed and then crouched above him. "Assure me that you prefer to spend your nights alone instead of making wild, sweet love beneath the waterfall or in a secluded cave. Each time you touch me you whisper that you want me. Do you want *me*, or are those empty confessions that you offer to every woman you take in your arms?"

Sloane groaned in agonizing torment as she boldly touched him, wantonly molding herself to him, her soft breasts boring into his laboring chest. "No, I don't want you with me," he insisted, his voice ragged with desire, belying his words.

"Don't you?" Tara smiled wickedly as her knee slid between the muscular columns of his long legs. "I think you protest too much. Do you wish me to rise and walk away?" Her hand made subtle contact with the lean brawn of his body as she melted against the hard contours of his hips. "Do you not find the same pleasure I enjoy when we are in the tight circle of each other's arms?"

Let him deny what he had told her from the first day he had kissed and caressed her, she mused as her hands

302

continued to seek out each sensitive point on his virile body. Let him disclaim the magic of their lovemaking. He had woven a web of passion about them, and no matter what their differences, they had become addicted to each other. Sloane might not love her, but she was no longer naive and she knew the power she had over him when she intimately touched him. This was Sloane's only weakness, and she would play upon it if it would keep her in Texas, knowing that living without him would be worse than roasting over the fires of hell.

Sloane cursed himself a thousand times as his arms involuntarily slid around her waist, clutching her closer. As much as he longed to have her safely tucked away from impending danger, he could not think of spending his nights alone, not when he had faced the realization that no other woman could satisfy him as Tara did. Each time he made love to this enchanting, violet-eyed seraph, he had surrendered a part of himself. He had taken the time to ensure that she enjoyed the splendor of passion and she knew how to please him.

"You win," Sloane breathed hoarsely as he cupped her oval face in his hands and brought her sensuous lips to his. "I'm afraid to keep you with me, but I know I'll go crazy if I send you away."

Tara's heart swelled with happiness as they set out on passion's journey. He didn't love her, but he needed her in his own way. She would prove to him that life without her would be meaningless, she promised herself. It was all she could hope for, but it would be enough; it had to be better than facing a sunrise without him.

As the heat of desire sent her sky-rocketing like a shooting star that blazed across the heavens, Tara reveled in rapture. In her way she had tamed this lion of a man, and she longed to remain in his sinewy arms. Whatever trials he faced would be hers as well. She loved him enough to remain by his side, praying that one day he would realize that she truly meant something to him.

She clung fiercely to him as his hard kiss stole her last breath. She was drifting in time and space, consumed by the soul-shattering sensations that defied description. They were one, their bodies moving together, sharing ecstasy's embrace. And then, the dam of wild sensations burst like the sea of twinkling stars pouring from the sky, and she sighed in contentment as she nestled against Sloane's sturdy chest.

Sloane pried one heavily-lidded eye open to peer at her exquisite face. A rakish smile dangled on one corner of his mouth as his hand slid around her neck, feeling the rapid pulsations beneath his fingertips. "You are a very persuasive lady," he rasped, his voice ragged with the aftereffects of passion. "I have been living with the misconception that force could master most anything. But, I swear, woman, I am powerless to resist your spell." His cobalt eyes glistened as his absent caress wandered over her shapely hips and then settled on her trim waist. "You have often berated me for not behaving like a gentleman, but neither are you a lady. A proper lady would never shove her husband to the floor and then demand her wifely rights, challenging him when he might have denied her."

Tara tossed her head back, sending a waterfall of silver-gold spilling over his arm. "Prim and proper has never really appealed to me," she confessed with an impish grin. "My grandfather says my free spirit and stubbornness have depleted most of his patience. I will always be who I am, no matter what orders you or he try to impose upon me."

"But who taught you to handle a gun and a knife so expertly?" Sloane queried curiously.

"Grandfather," Tara informed him, and then chortled when Sloane frowned bemusedly. "Ryan O'Donnovan also wanted a grandson, and since I was the only child he decided to pass on his abilities with weapons to me, should I find the need to employ them when reasoning failed."

"Is Ryan as mule-headed as Terrance claims?" He had only met the man once before beginning his investigation, and it had been a brief discussion, but Sloane knew Terrance was not particularly fond of his father-in-law.

"He and my father both have stubborn streaks. They did not see eye to eye on several issues, and my father refused to be dominated. My mother had spent her life obeying Grandfather and it caused tension in their marriage. She was not strong-willed enough to disobey Grandfather, and she let my father leave without her."

Sloane nodded thoughtfully. Although Terrance had raved about his lovely daughter, he had never divulged much more about his past life, and Sloane had never been one to pry into anyone's affairs. He had always wondered what had become of Tara's mother, but he had never bothered to ask and he imagined Terrance preferred to forget.

His expression became pensively sober as he studied Tara's lovely face. "Have you had any recollection of the man who killed Don Miguel?" he asked suddenly.

Her eyes dropped like a kite without wind to sustain it. She didn't want to remember that horrible night, and since she had learned that Sloane was Don Miguel's grandson, she had dreaded the inevitable question. Even knowing that it would come, Tara was not prepared to open that painful memory. Breathing a deep breath, she peered back through the window of time, grasping at bits and pieces of thoughts, conjuring up the incident on the road, hearing the pistol shots echoing in her tormented mind.

Finally, her lashes swept up to meet his probing gaze and she sighed heavily. "How does one describe a whispering voice and a faceless image?" Her lashes fluttered up as she forced a regretful smile. "I'm sorry, Sloane. It is still a hazy memory that seems just beyond my reach."

"Perhaps in time the mystery will unfold and you can view it in a clearer perspective," he said deflatedly as he leaned out to snuff the lantern. "Maybe the roundup will offer a few answers that have eluded me and I can obtain information that will also serve in solving the question of my grandfather's death."

"Perhaps between the two of us, we can . . ."

Sloane slanted her a disapproving glance. "I agreed to let you stay in Texas, against my better judgment, but don't think I will allow you to follow the roundup. I don't relish the thought of having you trampled by a herd of wild longhorns," he said gruffly.

"Will you stop hovering over me like a mother hen? I am not a child," she protested as she flounced to her side of the bed and drew the sheet around her.

"I am vividly aware of that fact," he growled seductively as his wandering hand slid beneath the sheet to draw her shapely body against his. "I would never have taken a child bride." His lips feathered against hers as he pressed her to her back. "But not a word about our marriage to anyone." His husky voice was riddled with an undertone of caution. "It must be kept confidential until my dealings with Merrick are resolved."

"And do you still intend to court Julia?" Tara queried and then winced at the thought of betraying her friend.

A wry smile caught one corner of his mouth as his warm breath whispered across her cheek. "Will I find you and Loren kissing each time I happen to pass one of the sheds?"

"Not unless I find myself deprived of affection," Tara purred as she stretched like a feline beneath his arousing caresses. "But I must warn you. I have developed a craving for passion somewhere along the way."

306

"Insatiable witch," he chided playfully as his roaming hand glided over the slope of her breasts to caress the taut peak. "A woman like you could make a *ghost* of a man of me with your relentless demands."

"I cannot *phantom* that," Tara giggled as she cuddled against his warm strength.

Sloane could not suppress the grin that found its way to his lips. Tara was like a breath of spring, giving life that special sparkle he had learned to live without until they had crossed paths. Everything had been neatly stashed in its place before Tara happened along to distract him. And distract him she had! Sloane couldn't think one thought without Tara's lovely image rising like a genie to preoccupy him.

And when her lips melted beneath his, quenching his thirst like summer rain, Sloane forgot everything that had any resemblance to reality. He was lost to the feminine scent that wrapped itself around his senses, the feel of her velvety skin beneath his caress, and the taste of kisses that had long lingered on his lips.

Chapter 20

Darkness had settled over the canyon by the time Sloane and Tara returned to the Diamond R Ranch. After Sloane had tended their weary mounts, he aimed Tara toward the house. Before they reached the stoop, he veered left, drawing her into the shrubbery.

Taking her hand, Sloane slipped the wedding ring from her finger. It was not the one he had originally acquired for her, but its humble replacement. Tara had insisted that he return the gold ring to its rightful owner. Conceding that he had behaved badly, Sloane located the woman he had encountered on the street, offered back the ring, and apologized for the incident. Once he had explained his dilemma, the woman had readily forgiven him. Sloane had purchased a simple band before leaving Tascosa, but now he took it back.

Tara glanced up at him, a muddled frown etching her brow. Her breath lodged in her throat when the moonlight caught his angular features, emphasizing the striking contours of his face. A warm tingle ran through her as he curled his index finger beneath her chin, tilting her face to his.

"The ring wasn't much to begin with, but wearing it might draw suspicion," he said, tucking it in his pocket with his free hand. "I expect you to behave as if nothing unusual has happened between us. As far as Merrick and

Julia are concerned, you have been in Clarendon with your father. If you learn anything you think might . . ." His hushed voice died in the darkness when the door creaked open and Merrick emerged from the house.

Tara muttered under her breath, resenting the interruption. She had anticipated one last kiss before they parted company, and Merrick had spoiled any chance of that.

Sloane clutched her arm and propelled her toward the house. "I'm sorry it took me so long to return for you, ma'am," he apologized in his lazy drawl. "I'm sure the boss expected me back long before this, but I had trouble with the horses when we crossed . . ." Sloane glanced up as if he had been startled by Merrick's appearance. "Good evenin', Merrick."

"Sloane." Merrick nodded soberly and then anchored his gaze on Tara, who was studying him all too closely. "I see you decided to return," he observed, still watching her like a hawk.

Tara managed a polite smile as Sloane herded her up the steps. "Yes, I hope you don't mind."

"Not at all." Merrick took her satchel and ambled toward the door. "I'm sure Julia will be delighted to have you back." As he ambled into the entryway he gestured for Sloane to wait for him in the study, and then he called to Julia who came bounding down the steps to greet her.

"Did you enjoy spending some time with your father?" Julia questioned and then leaned close as her gaze strayed back to the tall, ruggedly handsome cowboy who strode into Merrick's study. "I envy the time you spent with Sloane. Did he mention the party or say anything about me?"

Tara wasn't certain what to say. The truth would have broken Julia's heart. Sloane was Julia's first cousin and nothing could ever come of their relationship. "I thought you and Loren were back on friendly terms after the party." Tara steered off-course hoping to bypass a bald-faced lie.

"We are," Julia assured her with a sly smile. "But I cannot truthfully say I am not attracted to Sloane."

"You are much too fickle," Tara scolded as she unfolded her wrinkled gowns and stashed them in the closet. "Loren loves you, and I think he has been very patient with you. But if you push him too far, you might lose him."

The expression on Julia's face revealed her surprise at being lectured. "I am only trying to be very sure of my feelings," she defended herself. "I have no intention of marrying a man and then later realizing it was little more than fascination. I think I am being very practical."

Tara heaved a frustrated sigh. Julia did have a point. Caution was better than being corralled into a marriage with a man who wasn't at all sure why he had forced her to it in the first place. Now Tara was the one with a husband who was undoubtedly having serious second thoughts about their whirlwind wedding. Sloane had remained distant during their return trip from Tascosa, and Tara was certain he regretted his rashness. At least Julia wasn't snared in a trap from which there was no escape. Her only fault was that her straying eyes had landed on a man she could never have. But Tara could not reveal the truth to her without exposing Sloane. Damn, what a ticklish situation. She should never have pried open the window and fled from her grandfather's mansion. Now she was up to her neck in trouble, and when Ryan learned that she had married Sloane instead of the wealthy gentleman he had selected for her, he would be spitting fire.

"Forgive me for preaching," Tara apologized with a weary sigh. "Traveling always puts me out of sorts."

Julia blossomed into a forgiving smile. "I understand, and I realize that it puts you on edge when you are forced to tolerate Sloane's company."

If she only knew, Tara thought to herself. Julia would be beside herself if she were aware of what had transpired in Tascosa.

"But I must confess, I cannot fathom why you have your heart set on disliking Sloane. What is there not to like?" Julia wanted to know.

"We all have our different tastes in men," Tara replied, wishing they were discussing the weather, politics, anything but Sloane! "I just don't happen to think the man suits you."

"I still haven't decided whether he does or not," Julia sighed, her creamy features puckering into a thoughtful frown. "It is just that Sloane is like some wild, untamed creature, and that fascinates me."

"Then may I suggest that you round up a panther cub and make it your pet," Tara mocked lightly. "You can marry Loren and still satisfy your craving for wild things."

Julia flung Tara a withering glance. "I think your exhaustion has dulled your usually sharp wit," she admonished.

"I'm sure it has," Tara agreed. "Perhaps I can be my charming self after a decent night's sleep." When Julia eyed her bemusedly, Tara tacked on, "Papa's accommodations cannot compare to the luxuries of your home." Good grief, she had very nearly stuck her foot in her mouth! She reminded herself to be more careful in the future.

Julia accepted her explanation and then took her leave, imprisoning Tara with her depressing thoughts. Damn, she would have to guard against allowing her tongue to outdistance her brain or it could send her flying out of the frying pan into the fire. How had Sloane managed to play his charade for almost a year, she wondered. He must have had an abundance of self-control on that

311

count. Which was probably the reason he had lost his head and hastily married her, she then surmised. Sloane had carefully guarded his step when Merrick was underfoot, and his constant tension had relaxed when he fled the Diamond R Ranch. He, quite simply, had cracked, Tara decided. But Sloane would have recovered by the time the sun climbed into the sky the following day. He would forget that the night in Tascosa ever existed and would again be intent on his purpose, never giving her a second thought.

Despairing over the fact that everything in her life was in a state of chaos and she was unable to share her frustrations with anyone, Tara plopped down in bed and stared up into the darkness. As soon as Sloane had his evidence that Merrick was swindling his investors and had confronted him about his involvement in Vernon's death, she would be shipped back to St. Louis. But how was she to forget the feel of his sinewy arms pulling her against his hard chest? How could she bury the memory of devouring kisses that made her eager to relinquish her last breath for the wild pleasure that burned like a fire in her blood? Damnation, loving Sloane caused emotional turmoil, and Tara wondered how many years would pass before she could think of him without feeling the stab of longing in her heart. Perhaps one and twenty, she thought dismally. God, it would take another lifetime to forget the man who had touched every part of her being.

Grappling with those depressing thoughts, Tara squeezed her eyes shut and prayed for sleep. Thankfully, it came the moment before she was tempted to rise and walk off her frustration. She knew where her footsteps would lead her. Sloane had much on his mind, and the last thing he wanted or needed now that he was back at the ranch was for his unwanted wife to appear on his doorstep.

*   *   *

312

Wearily, the cloaked phantom aimed himself for the south range. He had an important mission to accomplish this night. Not only would he give Merrick's ranch hands something to feed their nightmares, but he would distract himself from his own tormenting specter. Sloane had spent the past few days quizzing himself about his actions in Tascosa. He had allowed his temper to get the best of him and had reacted impulsively. My God, he had actually forced Terrance Winslow's daughter into wedlock! The thought made the phantom groan miserably.

But dammit, that lovely nymph had *forced* him to do something rash after gallivanting about the streets of Tascosa, he rationalized. Sloane had been unaccustomed to having to battle to keep his wits about him, until Tara came into his life like a misdirected whirlwind. Now he had lost what little sense he had been born with. What was Terrance going to say when he discovered the Night Rider was his son-in-law? Sloane wasn't certain he wanted to speculate on the answer to that unsettling question.

What had he accomplished by taking Tara as his wife? He had given her his name, but he had offered her nothing else. Lord, he had even sworn her to secrecy, as if their marriage was something to be ashamed of. Ashamed? The Night Rider scoffed at the thought. How could a man be ashamed to call that feisty minx his wife? She was what dreams were made of—and yet it had to be a private dream. Sloane could not risk anyone's knowing that there was something going on between him and Tara until he had settled his differences with Merrick. But there was definitely something going on between them, Sloane reminded himself. When he came within ten feet of that free-spirited vixen, the sparks flew.

Turning his thoughts to his purpose, Sloane wove his way through the clump of cedars that lined the edge of the valley. Focusing on the cattle herd and its posted

313

lookouts, he nudged Diablo. The white stallion reared in the air, his powerful hooves slashing through the darkness. His shrill whinny pierced the evening air, bringing the other horses and riders to immediate attention.

And then, like a shooting star blazing across the heavens, the phantom and his silver steed flew through the cedars and chaparral, fading in and out of the moonlight. The shapeless specter floated above the glowing steed, his incandescent cloak billowing about him, his ghastly face appearing to be no more than a silver ball sitting atop his barely discernible shoulders.

Jonas and Harley, two of the Diamond R's night herders, nearly jumped out of their skin when they heard the thundering of hooves echoing in the canyon. A wailing voice intermingled with the white stallion's shrill whinny, and Jonas glanced quickly about him, searching for a safe place to hide.

"This is the last time I'm standin' watch in Palo Duro," he croaked. His face turned a peaked shade of white as the phantom became one of the swaying shadows and the hoofbeats died in the eerie silence.

Harley swallowed with a nervous gulp, forcing his stampeding heart back to its normal resting place. His gaze sketched the now quiet valley and then his eyes bulged from their sockets. "Oh Lordy, would you look yonder. The phantom gobbled up the boss's lead steer! I swear Old Ben was standin' there a minute ago. Now he ain't nowhere to be seen."

A hauntingly quiet voice whispered so close behind them that both men came apart at the seams. Jonas didn't wait around to learn the source of the eerie sounds. He bounded into the saddle and raced back toward headquarters at breakneck speed. Harley was only a horse's length behind his companion and he was cursing a blue streak. The phantom had scared twenty years off his life, and he wasn't risking what time he had left for all the beeves in Texas!

A wry smile spread beneath the crumpled hood as the Night Rider led the longhorn steer through the sagebrush. He had paid several late-night visits to Jonas and Harley the past few weeks. Tonight had been their undoing. The phantom doubted the night herders would be back. They seemed certain, beyond all shadow of a doubt, that there was no such thing as a friendly ghost, and they had no intention of standing watch with a phantom.

The amusement died in Sloane's blue eyes as his rambling thoughts settled again on Tara. He had attempted to keep his distance from her, proving to himself he was man enough to win the battle of self-conquest. But the nights he had spent beside her without quenching his thirst for her had begun to take their toll. God, would he outlive this insatiable craving for that spirited sprite?

Grappling with that disturbing thought, the Night Rider reined his steed toward the secluded cabin, wondering if he would have to tie himself in bed to prevent himself from sneaking into her room at headquarters. *This has to stop,* Sloane lectured himself. They would soon be involved in roundup, and he had to remain cool and aloof where Tara was concerned. And just how the hell was he supposed to do that when the memory of the passion they had shared bubbled just beneath the surface, aching for release.

There was only one possible cure for the fever that claimed him, Sloane diagnosed. Determined to cool the heat of lust, the Night Rider swung from his steed and submerged himself in the river. God, how many cold baths could a man take before he shriveled up like a prune, Sloane asked himself miserably as he waded to shore and then glared at Diablo. He could have sworn the damned horse was laughing at him.

"You *could* be replaced by a surefooted mule," Sloane muttered disgustedly.

Diablo threw his head and then snorted as the phantom swung onto his back, and Sloane cursed himself for trying to carry on a conversation with a horse. Lord, if he didn't get himself in hand, and quickly, he would never solve the mystery surrounding the Diamond R Ranch. This maddening conflict between him and Tara would have to be resolved *after* he tended to Merrick, Sloane told himself firmly. He had waited more than a year to uncover Merrick's underhanded dealings, and he could not allow his affair with Tara to garble his thoughts. Clinging to that thought, Sloane returned to his cabin, forcing himself to sleep when his restless soul yearned to wing toward Tara's room to satisfy a longing that even a cold bath couldn't cure.

When Julia invited Tara to accompany her outside the following morning, Tara declined. She feared Julia's stroll would lead her to Sloane. She had made up her mind to do what she could to aid Sloane, but she knew the less association she had with him, the better.

The hushed voices in the study caught Tara's attention when Julia ambled out the front door. Tara plastered herself against the wall and pricked her ears, hanging on Merrick's every word.

"If all goes well, I should meet you on Mesquite Mesa by midnight on Friday. Make sure you keep your beeves a few miles east of mine," Merrick ordered. "I've got enough trouble without someone noticing my brand in your herd until we can change the brands. Terrance Winslow is giving me fits. Did you see his editorial about the Chavez murder?" Merrick scowled disgustedly. "He suggested Texas law could be bought and sold when a

316

murderer was allowed to roam free as a bird in Palo Duro. I swear he would see me hanged without the slightest evidence. The man has his sights set on me."

"I thought the fact that you have been playing host to his daughter would sway him," John Simpson commented. "But I should have known nothing would deter Terrance when he is certain you were involved."

So Merrick *had* given her room and board in hopes of softening her father's harsh attitude toward him, Tara mused.

"I still think you are taking a great risk by allowing the girl to remain under your roof," Simpson went on to say. "What if she learns what is going on and runs back to inform her father?"

"I have my reasons for wanting her here," Merrick assured him gruffly.

"Well, if I were you, I would send her packing before she inadvertently learns something that might incriminate you," Simpson advised. "Terrance is itching to have you replaced, and if you are found guilty of wrongdoing, you could damned well lose the Diamond R."

"I won't let that happen." Merrick's voice was dangerously calm. "I've made too many sacrifices to keep it. Nothing has ever stood in the way of what I've wanted. If a man looks long and hard enough, he can always find a means to the end he desires."

Tara inched down the hall, feeling she had just begun to know the real Merrick Russel, a man who could have taken the life of his own brother to protect his dream, a man who would not bat an eye at cheating his investors to expand his profits and increase his personal land holdings.

"What are you doing in here?" Merrick's sharp inquiry made Tara wince uncomfortably. "I thought you were going riding with Julia."

Sorting through her most charming smiles, Tara

317

selected one of highest quality. "I had intended to, but the journey on horseback from Clarendon was more than enough to satisfy me," she explained, trying desperately to keep nervousness from creeping into her voice. "I was more inclined to seat myself on something more comfortable than a saddle this morning."

Merrick's probing gaze held her captive for what seemed eternity before he released her and then exchanged glances with Simpson. "Thank you for dropping by, John. I will see to the matter before the day is out."

Simpson nodded mutely and then disappeared through the door, leaving Tara to confront Merrick, who was watching her every move.

"If you will excuse me, I think I will go for a walk," Tara murmured as she brushed past Merrick, but he manacled her hand, bringing her around to face him.

Tara swore he was looking right through her and could read the thoughts that were printed on her mind. Then he graced her with the semblance of a smile, making her all the more apprehensive.

"You seem leery of me, my dear. Why is that?" Merrick questioned in the same dangerous tone that he had employed earlier.

"You are a very difficult man to get to know," Tara said, striving for a sincere tone. "I am never quite certain if you approve of my presence in your home."

"Why shouldn't I?" Merrick studied her like a panther poised to pounce on his prey.

"Why indeed?" Tara stared at the lean fingers that were clamped around her wrist and then flashed him a sticky-sweet smile. "It must be that I am a mite too sensitive," she dismissed, and then waited for Merrick to unchain her from his grasp.

Once he did, Tara sailed out the door, feeling his piercing glare pelleting her departing back. She expelled the breath she had been holding since Merrick had stepped from the study to see her tarrying in the hall.

She had to inform Sloane of the appointed time of Merrick's rendezvous with Simpson. He would be anxious to make plans to catch Merrick and expose him for what he was. Tara stopped short. How was she to approach Sloane when everyone at the ranch believed they wanted nothing more to do with each other? She couldn't just march up and blurt out the information. Heaving an exasperated sigh, Tara wheeled around, only to find Merrick studying her with a sinister smile.

"Is something wrong, Tara?" Merrick peered around the supporting beam of the porch like a snake winding its body around a tree limb, and even as she made the comparison she shuddered, repulsed. She detested those slithering creatures and she was beginning to think Merrick was a member of that beady-eyed species.

"What could possibly be wrong?" Tara countered, masking her uneasiness behind a carefully blank stare. "I am only having difficulty deciding which direction to take. No matter which way I gaze, Palo Duro is spectacular."

"That it is," Merrick concurred, his gaze narrowing in on her. "That is one of the reasons I am so determined to keep it."

"Then why did you sell forty acres to your horse trainer?" Tara questioned curiously.

"Occasionally a man has to compromise," he told her flatly. "I wanted Sloane and his reputation branded with the Diamond R, and the only way I could get him was to sell him a section of my land. Those were his terms, and I wanted him badly enough to agree." His gray eyes anchored on Tara, making her feel very uncomfortable. "When I no longer consider him useful I will find a way to convince him to sell the land back to me. As I told you, I am a methodical, calculating man, and what is mine will

319

never escape me."

His words hung in the air like a threat, and Tara pivoted away before she was sliced to shreds by his piercing scrutiny. If he realized she knew far more about him and his fraudulent dealings, her life was in danger. It was all Tara could do to keep from breaking into a run, but she managed to restrain herself until she turned the corner of the ranch house.

"Merrick?" Loren Marshall bit back a scowl, his disposition having soured a moment earlier when he had seen Sloane and Julia sneak off to the tack room together. He tried to focus his full attention on the man who was still staring pensively after Tara, but it was damned difficult when Loren was seeing red. Julia was flirting outrageously with Sloane, and Loren had impulsively considered quitting his job and galloping off into the sunset, putting as much distance as possible between him and that fickle young woman he had had the misfortune of falling in love with. Finally, Loren assembled his composure and blurted out the message he brought to the ranch boss. "I'm afraid I am the bearer of bad news. Old Ben has wandered off. I have had several of the men out searching for him, but he hasn't turned up yet."

Merrick growled in disgust. His dependable lead steer was a necessity for a smooth-running trail drive to Harrold. Old Ben had guided several herds of cattle to the railroad pens in Harrold over the years. Driving half-wild longhorns across unfamiliar country was extremely difficult without a lead steer that knew exactly where he was going and where to find water during the journey.

"It was the work of my haunting phantom, I suppose," Merrick gritted out. "We spend half our time relocating lost animals and herding them back to headquarters. Damn, that disembodied soul doesn't intend to leave me in peace, not for one day."

"Some of the men swore they were visited by the Night

320

Rider last night while they stood watch on the south range. Two of them quit. Jonas and Harley said they weren't standing guard with a ghost, not for any amount of pay. They swear the phantom warned them to leave the canyon before he took his vengeance out on them." Loren scoffed and then let his gaze stray back to the tack room, wondering what the devil Julia and Sloane were doing. No doubt they were engaged in something far more interesting than conversation. "Jonas and Harley were superstitious, but now they swear they saw the phantom hovering in a cedar tree and heard him chanting a death song. They took their gear and thundered off at first light."

It seemed his well-laid plans were beginning to crumble right under his nose, and Merrick seethed at the thought of losing his lead steer and two good hands before roundup.

"You better find Old Ben by nightfall," Merrick demanded gruffly, his eyes blazing as he glared at his foreman.

"But, Merrick, I have already . . ."

"Just find him!" Merrick ordered sharply. "Send Sloane out after him. He seems to have a sixth sense when it comes to contrary animals."

That idea appealed to Loren. But then, anything that kept Julia from trailing after Sloane delighted Loren. When he strode back to the corral, he flashed Julia a condescending frown. She was all but throwing herself at Sloane, and Loren was itching to take her over his knee and paddle her backside for behaving like a lovestruck schoolgirl.

"Sloane!"

Loren's biting voice jarred Julia from her romantic notions and she glanced back to see Loren glaring daggers at her.

"Somethin' wrong?" Sloane questioned lackadaisically, his cobalt eyes dancing with amusement as he watched Loren and Julia fling each other challenging glares.

"Old Ben has vanished into thin air, and Merrick thinks you can sort needles out of haystacks. He wants you to search the canyon to see if you can locate the lead steer."

Sloane nodded agreeably and then ambled over to saddle a mount, a gelding he had just broken to ride, but one that could use more experience with a cowboy on his back before he could be considered dependable. His discerning gaze swept the canyon and he nudged the skittish steed to the east, the direction he had seen Tara taking when she set out to explore the rock precipices of Palo Duro.

A wry smile pursed his lips when he peered up at the ledge above him, finding Tara staring out across the valley like a posted lookout.

"How is the view from your throne, *reina?*" he taunted with a chuckle.

Her eyes fell fifty feet to the ruggedly handsome cowboy who was dressed in a faded shirt and breeches, a leather vest and chaps. Tara's heart fell with her gaze, captivated by the potential strength and bold masculinity that seemed to radiate from his powerful physique. Sloane was all man, every hard, brawny inch of him. His Stetson was pulled down to shade his laughing blue eyes and angular features, and he looked as big as Texas, even from where she stood.

"I must speak with you," Tara insisted, tossing aside her arousing thoughts.

She wheeled away from the edge of the overhanging cliff and hurriedly made her way down the winding path between the boulders. Sloane's all-consuming gaze mapped each exquisite detail of her delicious figure as she descended toward him. She moved like a doe, picking her way through the rough terrain. The sunlight kissed her flawless features and her shiny gold hair sparkled as sunbeams sprinkled through it. The thin white blouse seemed transparent in the morning light, and his eyes caressed the full swells of the breasts that lay so temptingly beneath the gossamer fabric.

Sloane shook his head to reroute his derailed thoughts. He had promised himself that Tara would no longer distract him until he had dealt severely with Merrick. He was determined that no one knew there was anything going on between him and Tara. But there *was* something going on, Sloane reminded himself as desire trickled through his veins. He could feel that gnawing need in the pit of his belly each time he allowed his eyes to roam over her curvaceous body. And then he would remember the intimate moments they had shared, the feel of her velvety flesh beneath his exploring hands, the taste of cherry wine in her intoxicating kisses. . . .

"I overheard Simpson talking to Merrick this morning," Tara breathlessly blurted out, jolting Sloane from his arousing fantasy. "They intend to make the switch on Friday night on Mesquite Mesa."

The faintest hint of a smile dangled from one corner of his sensuous mouth as he leaned out to hook his arm around Tara's waist, hoisting her up in front of him. "You are full of pertinent information, *querida*," he murmured as his lips brushed lightly over hers. "What else did Simpson have to say?"

Tara didn't bother to mention that Simpson had suggested Merrick oust her from his house or that she had a strange premonition about Merrick, something that had crept from the corner of her mind the night they returned from Tascosa when she saw him lingering in the darkness. No doubt, Sloane would ship her back to St. Louis on the first train if he knew the tension had begun to mount between her and Merrick. There was something

323

in the way Merrick kept staring at her that worried her, and Tara had the uneasy feeling that their civilized warfare was beginning to disintegrate. Before long she and Merrick were going to clash. Although Tara didn't anticipate a confrontation, she knew it would come. She could feel the apprehension mounting each time she came within ten feet of Merrick and endured his piercing scrutiny. And she had begun to guess the cause of his guarded animosity after the subtle remark he had made that morning.

"That was all I was able to learn," Tara insisted and then eyed him curiously. "Why aren't you at the corral? Have you taken the remainder of the day off?"

Sloane pressed his knees against the dappled gray gelding beneath him. "No, Merrick sent me out to find his lead steer. Old Ben seems to have suddenly disappeared, and the day before the roundup. What an untimely inconvenience for the boss of the Diamond R," he chuckled spitefully.

Tara regarded him suspiciously. "It is rather ironic. You wouldn't happen to know the whereabouts of this indispensable steer, would you?" she questioned, certain she knew the answer. Sloane had that ornery look about him, one that spelled trouble for Merrick.

"He and Diablo are penned in the cave, and that is where Ben will remain until Merrick has been exposed for the deceitful bastard he is."

The harshness in his voice was like an icy wind whipping through the canyon, and Tara shuddered uncontrollably. Sloane had lived and breathed for the moment he would avenge his father's death and make good the vow he had offered his mother. But after her conversation with Merrick, Tara was troubled, and she intended to handle the boss of the Diamond R in *her* own way, one she was certain Sloane would vehemently protest if he knew what was buzzing through her mind.

"May I see your mother's locket?" she requested as she twisted in the saddle to face Sloane.

He frowned bemusedly, studying her thoughtfully for a long moment. "What do you want with it?" he demanded.

Her shoulder lifted in a leisurely shrug, her emotions masked behind a carefully guarded stare. "Nothing really. I only thought perhaps I should take it for safe keeping. If it should be lost during the roundup, you would have no evidence that Merrick and Vernon were having difficulties before Vernon's death. Without it there is only Burns's word against Merrick's. And I wouldn't be surprised if Merrick has kept Burns with him all these years just to ensure that Burns keeps that information to himself. Merrick seems to have bought Burns's silence and that closemouthed cook is not one to stir trouble. I am plagued by this odd sensation that Burns is protecting someone besides you, but for the life of me, I have been unable to understand why he continues to straddle the fence."

A troubled frown plowed Sloane's brow. He too had wondered why Burns had been content to sit back and allow the world to go by without taking an active part in his attempt to expose Merrick. Tara had put his very thoughts into words, and it left him doubting Burns's loyalty. It seemed obvious the cook had none. He had looked out for himself and had never risked becoming involved in Sloane's vendetta.

Sloane reached into his vest pocket and then stared at the gold locket as he brushed his thumb over the intricate carving. His calculating gaze anchored on Tara's all too innocent expression.

"You aren't planning to confront Merrick with this." His tone suggested a command, not a question.

"Of course not," Tara hastily assured him, and then flashed him a fleeting smile. "I would hate to see this keepsake destroyed should it happen to slip from your pocket while you are thundering across the valley in reckless pursuit of a contrary steer."

Cobalt blue eyes scrutinized her for another long moment before he dropped the locket in her hand. "Just don't try anything daring and reckless," he warned.

"Me?" Tara looked so sweet and innocent that it was almost sacrilege to challenge the angelic expression that was plastered on her face, but it didn't stop Sloane from doubting her intentions.

"You." He slanted her a reproachful glare, his brow forming a long line over his probing blue eyes. "You have a few reckless tendencies, Mrs. Prescott. Need I list them for your recollection?"

Tara squirmed beneath his intense stare. "I better return to the house before someone comes looking for me and finds us together."

When she tried to slide to the ground, Sloane tightened his grasp on her waist, but within a split second his restraining touch became a wandering caress.

"I missed you last night," he murmured as his lips investigated the swanlike column of her neck, causing a cavalry of goose bumps to march across her skin.

Why had he said that? Tara asked herself. He had behaved as if he couldn't wait to deposit her at headquarters and he had been so distant and remote during their return trip from Tascosa that Tara had begun to wonder if she knew him at all. He must be having another bout with the lusty beast within him, she decided. It wasn't her company that appealed to him, only a feminine body to warm his bed. And any feminine body would do, she thought resentfully. He had nestled her in his arms when they stopped for the night, but not once had he attempted to make love to her. Tara would have welcomed him with open arms, but she had not attempted to seduce him as she had in Tascosa. She had made a fool of herself once too often, and she had been determined to let Sloane make the first move toward her if he still desired her. But he hadn't, and that had nearly broken her already crumbling heart.

"Strange, I would not have thought it," Tara sniffed sarcastically as she squirmed for freedom. "You seemed to want nothing to do with me during our return trip."

Arms like steel bands chained her to the muscled wall of his chest, and his warm breath trailed along her shoulder, leaving Tara feeling as if a collection of butterflies had been freed in her stomach. Her wounded heart was limping around her rib cage like a crippled race horse, and she feared tears of humiliation would come boiling down her cheeks if she yielded to the touch of the only man who could make her weak and vulnerable. Dammit, she was trying to ignore the sensations that swarmed her senses and accelerated her pulse, but Sloane was hell bent on tormenting her fragile emotions.

"I had a great deal on my mind," he defended himself as his moist lips skimmed her cheek and nibbled at the corner of her quivering mouth. "But I have seen to the matters that distracted me and now . . ."

"Don't!" Tara tried to push his adventurous hands away before they slid beneath her blouse, but Sloane was not to be denied. His hand folded over her breast, his fingers teasing the ripe bud to tautness.

"We are man and wife," Sloane reminded her hoarsely. "I have every right to. . . ."

"No, you don't," Tara snapped tersely as she slapped away his brazen caress and hastily buttoned her blouse. "You didn't truly want this marriage. It came in a moment of madness. You want no one to know of the ceremony, and we do not live as man and wife. All you seek is the appeasement of your male needs, nothing more. You have stripped me of all else, but I refuse to relinquish my dignity!"

327

Sloane swore under his breath and then cursed at Tara. "Dammit, woman, what do you expect of me?" he ground out. "You know I have a job to do and that one false move could destroy months of preparation. How the devil am I to explain marrying you or carting you off to my cabin when everyone on the ranch thinks we have had a spat and that we want nothing more to do with each other? And *that* is your fault." His gaze was cold and accusing as he peered into her flushed face. "The last thing I wanted to do was pretend I had an interest in Julia, but the two of you plotted to groom me like a knight preparing to court a princess, one I had no interest in to begin with, for reasons that should be obvious to you."

"Well, if you had behaved as if you liked me, even a little, Julia would have backed away," Tara blurted out, wondering why she was being so blunt. But, blast it, there came a time when a woman had to lay her feelings out in the open, whether they would be trampled or cherished. Either Sloane cared enough about her to admit it or she would have this marriage annulled the moment she returned to Clarendon. She would not go through the paces of living, wondering if she had a snowball's chance in hell of winning his rock-hard heart. Tara had to know where she stood before she went stark raving mad! "You take privileges I have granted no other man. You sweep me into a marriage without giving one sound reason for wedding me, and then behave as if I don't exist all the way back from Tascosa. Then you stroll off with Julia each time she summons you. And now here you are, insisting you have missed me. How, I cannot imagine!" Tara wagged a dainty finger in his amused face, her temper rising steadily until she was all but screaming at the exasperating cowboy. "I am not some worn pair of chaps you shrug off and on when the mood suits you. We will either have a normal marriage or we will have it annulled, posthaste. Do you understand me, Sloane? I will not be used and taken for granted, not by you or any other man!"

"Damn, but you are one pushy lady," he chortled as he shoved her from the saddle. "Your Joseph Rutherford should thank his lucky stars he was spared this marriage. He would have found himself strapped to a very demanding wife."

A shriek bubbled from her lips when she landed on the hem of her skirt and fell facedown in the grass. Tara had been on the verge of losing her temper, but this was the last straw! Hot sparks flickered in her eyes as she scrambled to her feet and glowered at Sloane and his mocking grin.

"I wouldn't have made such harsh demands on him," she assured him tartly. "Joseph is a gentleman, and that is something you can never begin to understand. *He* happens to love me!" she sniped.

"Then your heralded cavalier has *one* fault," Sloane scoffed. "Turning you loose with that information is disastrous. He may love you, but you don't love him and you never will. He isn't man enough!"

If Tara could have gotten her hands on that infuriating cowboy she would have shaken him until his teeth rattled. "His love is beginning to sound more appealing with each day I tolerate you," she hurled at him, vindictiveness spurring her barbed remark.

"And what makes you think *I* don't love you?" Sloane smirked, flashing her that taunting grin that could make her come apart at the seams.

Lord, let me count the ways, Tara muttered under her breath. "It would take the remainder of the day to list the reasons a man like you would never fall in love with anything but his horse!" she hurled at him.

"I do not have some perverted penchant for nags," Sloane snorted indignantly. "Except perhaps the one I married in a moment of madness. She deliberately

329

harasses me until I . . . whoa!"

Tara was so annoyed at his remark that she had kicked his steed in the rump, startling Sloane and his flighty horse. The gelding reared and then bolted forward, attempting to unseat his rider. Tara watched in smug satisfaction as the dappled gray snorted and bucked as if he had been struck by a lightning bolt. As the horse twisted and kicked, Tara smiled in delight, watching Sloane teeter precariously on his perch, his head snapping back as the gelding reared and then vaulted through the air as if he had sprouted wings. When Sloane lost his grasp and sailed over the gelding's head like a speeding cannonball Tara laughed spitefully. Sloane deserved to be dethroned. His fall was broken by a mesquite bush, and Tara decided the aggravating varmint made an appropriate decoration hanging in the tree.

Muttering several epithets along with her name, Sloane untangled his bruised limbs from those of the prickly bush and then picked splinters from his hide. "I hope you're proud of yourself, termagant," he growled. "It took me a month to convince that skittish colt it is impolite to throw his rider. You have managed to destroy thirty days of dedicated training."

Tara shrugged off his attempt to scold her and flashed him an impish smile. He had made her appear the clumsy fool once too often, and she had finally managed to give him a dose of his own medicine. It did her heart good to see a man who usually had every situation well in hand plucking stickers from his backside. Each time she caught herself thinking Sloane Prescott was invincible, she would call this incident to mind. It would be easier to confront him, knowing he put his breeches and chaps on the same way every other man did and that he had had his pride and dignity bruised at least once.

"Indeed, I am very proud of myself," she assured him saucily. "I have spent the past month thinking you were

330

half-man, half-spirit. But it is a relief to realize you are quite human and that you dig thorns from your hide on occasion."

"And you are the one thorn that no knife can touch," Sloane assured her, flashing her a black look. "I swear you delight in causing me distress."

"I am only trying to acquire your attention," she threw back at him as she tilted a proud chin. "From now on, you will approach me with the proper respect or you will not approach me at all. I will not be dictated to and I will not be used as your plaything. I will not be your wife in any sense of the word until you have made some commitment to this mock marriage."

"You have made no pledge to me," Sloane countered. "You might as well have said you approved of my body and very little else!"

"I didn't think you cared what I thought about you as long as I appreciated your prowess in bed." Tara wrapped the words around her tongue and flung them at him like an arrow hissing toward its intended target. "You have never shown any interest in my mind. Why should I be impressed with yours?"

She wasn't certain why she was itching for a trenchant argument, but she was, one with mud-slinging, railing voices, and even a few flying fists. She was letting off steam and it did wonders for her pent-up frustrations. A good heated debate was exhilarating, and she hadn't enjoyed a shouting match since she and her grandfather had clashed on the subject of her marriage to Joseph Rutherford.

"Why have you selected this particular moment to pick me clean like a vulture devouring his midday feast?" Sloane snorted derisively.

"Because it damned well needs to be done, and now seemed the perfect opportunity to point out your peccadilloes," Tara shot back at him, ribbing him and loving every moment of it.

"And what about you, little miss high and mighty?" Sloane tossed the last sticker aside and stalked toward her, leveling her a scornful glare. "I hope to God you don't think you're perfect. Your tongue is so sharp you have sliced my pride to pieces with it. If you recall, I was minding my own business when you took it upon yourself to make me Julia's Prince Charming, and all you accomplished was throwing us together and leaving Loren dangling on Julia's leash." He scooped up a handful of dirt, squeezed it in his fist, and then tossed it at Tara's feet. "This is no fairy tale, little princess. This is Texas, a place where rattlesnakes nest under rocks and tarantulas the size of my hand prowl the darkness. This range land is a frontier where men are men, and they have no inclination to put on airs for every prim debutante who waltzes into Texas."

"I am not some fairy queen who expects to hold court wherever she goes." Tara puffed up indignantly and then pointed an accusing finger at Sloane's broad chest. "You have been behaving like a barbarian who stalks up and drags a woman off by the hair of her head. Like it or not, there is such a thing as civilization in Texas, and it wouldn't hurt you to conform to it. Women have feelings, you know, and I expect you to consider mine. If you don't want me near you unless it is to satisfy your lust, then admit it and consent to an annulment. If I cannot have a true marriage I don't want one at all!" she informed him huffily.

"Hypocrite. You had planned to settle for Rutherford, and I know you don't love him. If you did you would never have surrendered to me," he had the gall to say. "And I'm not sure you know what love is in the first place!"

Tara's face reddened with rage. "You idiotic fool, did it ever occur to you that I was being forced to wed

Rutherford, or that I might have found myself in . . ."

Tara could have cut out her tongue with a dull knife for coming so precariously close to blurting out her confession. Damn, she had intended to take that secret to her grave, and it had very nearly popped out of her mouth before she could bite it back. Furiously, she stomped her foot and then spun around to make a beeline for headquarters, but Sloane snagged her as she buzzed by, madder than a disturbed hornet.

"What did you intend to say?" he demanded to know, his cobalt eyes probing into hers, searching for an honest answer.

"You make me so blasted angry I don't know what I'm saying," she hedged, prying her gaze from his to focus on some distant point. "I only know I can't survive like this. I am married to a man who barely knows I exist, one who comes to me in lust and nothing else. I can't be content to live like this and I . . ."

Tara felt tears welling up in the back of her eyes. She would never forgive herself if she allowed Sloane to see her cry. He didn't understand weakness and he wouldn't tolerate it from her. Mountains of immovable rock like Sloane Prescott didn't crack under pressure, and he had no compassion for those who did not possess his inner strength. Tara had always considered herself to be reasonably strong and independent, despite her mother's coddling, but she ran a distant second to Sloane.

No wonder he had remained a bachelor for so many years, she thought bitterly. If he was looking for a woman to match his dominating personality, he would never find one on this planet. No wonder he had taken to thundering off with the phantoms of the night. Since Sloane could find no mortal woman to satisfy him, he was forced to cavort with spirits.

Before the tears boiled down her cheeks, Tara flung herself away and ran blindly in the direction of the ranch house.

"Tara, come back here!" Sloane called after her, but she didn't break stride or look back.

Heaving a breathless sigh, Tara wiped away the tears with the back of her hand and trudged up the steps to confront the second-to-last man she preferred to see in her state of frenzy.

Cold gray eyes flooded over her tear-stained face, and then Merrick broke into a jeering smile, assuring Tara that he wore that particular expression better than any she had seen plastered on his face. "Has something upset you, Tara? You haven't had another encounter with a rattler, I hope."

Tara swore Merrick would have been delighted to hear she had fallen headlong into a den of vipers, judging by his smirk. It took every ounce of self-restraint she could muster not to smear that intimidating expression all over his weather-beaten features. Without uttering a word, she clenched her fists in the folds of her skirt and stomped up the steps.

"Tara, what on earth happened to you?" Julia surveyed the dirt and grass stains on Tara's clothes and then focused on her grimy features and puffy eyes. "Are you all right?"

"I'm fine," Tara gritted out. "Or at least I would be, if Sloane Prescott would drop off the edge of the earth. I swear that man brings out every fault I admit to having and a few I never knew were in me."

"What has he done now?"

Julia's patronizing tone incensed Tara. Her mood was as sour as a lemon, thanks to Sloane. In Julia's eyes, that confounded cowboy was very nearly perfect, except for his unpolished manners, and if she had known he was nothing like the image he projected in her presence she would be swooning over him more often than she did now.

"That man has insulted me for the last time," Tara muttered as she stormed toward her room. "If you have any sense at all, you will marry Loren Marshall tonight and save yourself the misery of chasing the wrong man."

Julia shook her head in disbelief as Tara slammed her bedroom door. She would have to speak with Sloane and beg him not to antagonize Tara, she decided. It would never do for them to be at each other's throats. Strange, Julia mused as she ambled back outside. Sloane had the opposite effect on her. He had been reasonably polite and never argumentative in her presence. Indeed, she would have preferred that Tara had not taught him to be quite so perfect a gentleman to her. She was still waiting for their first kiss, and she was beginning to wonder if it would ever come.

Chapter 21

As the summer sun climbed toward its perch, Tara
crawled from bed and attempted to bolster her sagging
spirits. The temptation to ride back to Clarendon was
great, but she simply couldn't go, not until she knew the
result of Sloane's confrontation with Merrick.

When she had dressed in her riding habit, prepared to
accompany the ranch hands on their roundup, Tara sank
down on the edge of the bed and toyed with the gold
locket Sloane had given her for safekeeping. She brushed
her fingers over the heart-shaped pendant and then
opened it to study the photograph of the young man and
woman whose love had ended in tragedy. A concerned
frown etched her brow when she noticed one corner of
the picture had been peeled away, as if it had been
removed from its frame and then haphazardly pushed
back in place. Attempting to straighten the photo, Tara
slid her fingernail beneath the picture to reset it, but it
popped loose and fluttered to the floor.

As she leaned over to retrieve the picture she choked
on her breath, stunned by the message that was scrawled
on the back of the portrait.

"Oh, my God!" Tara's mind reeled as she stared at the
inscription. The truth of the locket ran deeper than the
fragment of the letter Sloane had discovered inside it.
"Oh, Burns, why are you doing this to him?" she

groaned. "You and Carmelle have been so unfair."

"We are ready to leave, Tara," Julia called from the hall.

Tara frantically situated the photograph in its frame and replaced the excerpt from the letter. "I'll be right down."

What an ironic twist of fate, Tara mused as she picked up her satchel and tucked the locket inside it. Should she show Sloane the real proof of the locket of Valquez, the proof Sloane had overlooked in his quest to gain evidence against Merrick? But it was not Merrick who should have been condemned for deceit. Burns and Carmelle were using Sloane as their pawn, and they had purposely lied to him for their own devious reasons, reasons Tara could not quite comprehend.

Grappling with the tormenting thoughts, Tara descended the stairs to find Sloane draped over the balustrade in his usual careless manner. A wary frown captured her brow as he tossed her a smile and then politely removed his dusty hat.

"Julia informed me that I've upset you, ma'am," he drawled and then glanced sideways at Julia before resettling his amused gaze on the shapely blonde, who was garbed in a brown skirt and matching vest that clung to her breasts and accented her trim waist. "I didn't mean to be rude to you yesterday." His tone implied that he couldn't have cared less if he had caused her distress, and Tara gripped the banister, wishing she could clamp a stranglehold on his thick neck. "I just seem to have the uncanny knack for upsettin' you, ma'am."

If they had been without an audience, Tara would have leaped on him and punched him in his insolent grin, but they did and she couldn't, much to her chagrin.

"Sloane has promised me that he will be on his best behavior during the roundup," Julia chimed in.

"But unfortunately, his best behavior is less than

acceptable," Tara sniffed and then stared down her nose at him. The cad. He was silently laughing at her and they both knew it. Her careless slip of tongue the previous day was mortifying, and Tara could barely look him in the eye without blushing profusely.

"I ain't had proper schoolin' like you, ma'am," Sloane defended himself, pasting on such a humble expression that Tara swore it would slide off his arrogant face.

"Haven't you?" She lifted a challenging brow, quietly shoving the words at him as she breezed past him and sailed out the door.

Tara aimed herself toward Hazel and promptly tied her gear in place. When she had swung into the saddle she glanced over to see Merrick stomping around the corral, muttering about how he was to conduct a roundup without his reliable lead steer. Obviously, Sloane had wandered around like the children of Israel searching the wilderness for the promised land and then returned without Old Ben. Let Merrick stew, Tara thought spitefully. He wouldn't need Old Ben, because he wouldn't be trailing the herd to Harrold anyway. Merrick would find himself without a herd or a ranch before the week was out.

Her eyes unwillingly strayed to Sloane as his long, confident strides carried him to the dappled gray that had given him fits the previous day. Oh, why did she have to find Sloane so appealing. Why couldn't she forget what they had shared? Surely she was being punished for her less than ladylike behavior, Tara speculated. That must have been it. She was to do penance for disobeying her grandfather's wishes.

"I love the excitement of the roundup," Julia sighed as she reined her mare up beside Tara's. "I think you will find this to be a thrilling experience."

"I'm sure I will," Tara said absently, her attention still focused on Sloane's broad back and the hard muscles of

338

his thighs as they molded themselves to the prancing gelding beneath him. There was not one flaw in his masculine physique to criticize, but Tara sorely wished there had been. She wanted to dwell on his defects in her attempt to deny her physical attraction and love. But it seemed she was as big a fool as Julia. Sloane was everything a woman would want in a man, and yet he was everything Tara couldn't handle—relentless, persevering, domineering, decisive . . . the list was so extensive that it staggered the mind. Tara had never been able to manipulate him or exert control over him, and she doubted she ever would, even if her last name was the same as his.

By late afternoon Tara was indeed caught up in the excitement of the roundup. Twenty cowhands diligently worked to dig a three-foot circular trench in the ground and stake out a sprawling corral. Strong poles were placed on end, forming a sturdy makeshift pen that would hold the wiry longhorns that had very little association with humans and preferred it that way.

Since Old Ben was not available to lure the wild steers into the central corral, Merrick led a decoy herd through the mesquite and chaparral, enticing the cattle that had been left to roam the range to follow them back to the pen. The procedure took the remainder of the day, and Merrick was still grumbling about having to repeat the tactic the following day in order to locate the missing beeves.

Tara's mouth dropped open when she heard Sloane's rich baritone voice drifting across the valley as he soothed the fidgety cattle that had been locked in the pen. Among his other rare talents he could sing like a skylark, she thought resentfully. Was there anything that man couldn't do, she wondered as she slumped back against

339

her mare and listened to his lullaby. He couldn't fall in love, she mused as her gaze lingered on his bulky silhouette. He was a cynical man, one full of suspicions, a loner like a wild maverick stallion that kept watch over his herd of mares, but always at a respectable distance.

As the sun drooped lower in the Texas sky, shielded by the sheer walls of Palo Duro Canyon, Tara wandered over to the chuckwagon. Burns had unfolded the portable table that was attached to the back of the stout wood-and-canvas wagon. He was in the process of unloading boxes of tin dishes, frying pans, and a Dutch oven when Tara strolled up beside him. She looked down to see the cowhide sling beneath the bed of the wagon. It bulged with bedrolls, rain slickers, kindling for the campfire, and an assortment of spades and axes that had been used to erect the corral. It amazed her that all the necessities for living and eating could be stashed in one wagon, but Burns had everything imaginable sitting in, dangling from, or tied under his chuck wagon.

"Did you come to help or give me the third degree?" Burns questioned as Tara reached over to pull several coffee pots from a wooden crate.

Her shoulder lifted lackadaisically as she set the pots aside. "A little of both," she answered honestly and then flashed him a sly smile. "But I promise not to use you for my target should I decide to sharpen my skills in hurling a knife."

"That's a relief," Burns snickered. "I don't relish the idea of bein' carved up and tossed in the stew." He dumped the ingredients for sourdough biscuits into a large tin bowl and then gestured his bushy head toward the cowboy who was circling the pen to calm the uneasy cows and calves. "I see you and Sloane still ain't on the best of terms. The two of you ain't said a word to each other since we left headquarters."

Tara's gaze followed Burns's, lingering on Sloane as he

walked his steed around the perimeter of the corral. "There is very little left for us to say to each other. I don't understand him, but at least now I know what makes him tick." Her penetrating amethyst eyes circled back to Burns, carefully watching his reaction. "As a matter of fact, you and I know more about Sloane than he knows about himself. I'm curious to know why you are denying him the right to know his own father. Why have you and Carmelle kept his parentage a secret? You baffle me, Burns. I knew you had a fond attachment for Sloane, but I never dreamed it was because you were . . ."

"I don't know what yer talkin' about, Miss Winslow." Burns cut her off in midsentence and the color seeped from his ruddy features, assuring Tara she had hit a sensitive nerve.

Tara took up the wooden spoon to stir the pot of beans that simmered over the fire. "You know very well what I'm talking about. But why have you hidden the truth from Sloane? I grew suspicious of you the day you dashed out of the kitchen to fetch Sloane when I confronted you with my questions. You were trying to distract me by calling Sloane to your rescue. You were trying to protect yourself and Carmelle. What do you think to gain by allowing Sloane to live with the lie? What kind of man allows another to do his dirty work for him? Did you and Carmelle plot this deceit those long years ago and then patiently wait for Sloane to become a man hard and tough enough to deal with Merrick Russel in the manner that would satisfy you and Carmelle? I always wondered why you stayed on at this ranch, and it is finally coming clear. You knew Carmelle would one day send Sloane to you, didn't you?"

Burns kneaded the biscuit dough more vigorously than necessary, refusing to meet Tara's probing gaze, refusing to admit that she had somehow stumbled onto the truth. "You got too much imagination, woman. I told you

341

before that I mind my own business and I don't make trouble for nobody."

"You will be making more trouble by keeping silent," Tara argued. "You know Sloane intends to show no mercy to Merrick, and you have purposely misled him."

"Merrick deserves to get what he's been givin' all these years." Burns gnashed his teeth and then flashed Tara a reproachful glare. "You wasn't there, girl. You don't understand, and you don't know everythin' that happened or why. I've waited a score of years for Sloane to come here to right the wrong. I made a vow to Carmelle, just like Sloane did, and I ain't gonna break it. I would've given her the world and all the happiness to be found in it if it would've been within my power. But nothin' worked out the way we planned, and Merrick is to blame. Now it's Sloane's right to make Merrick pay for the injustice. Can't you understand that? It's what Carmelle wanted, and I won't deny her that peace. I promised her, and I ain't breakin' my word!"

"But I contend that Sloane should be fully armed with the truth," Tara countered, her violet eyes narrowing on Burns's stubborn frown. "But you don't plan to tell him, do you?"

"No, and you better not either," he growled as he wheeled to face Tara. "Sometimes the truth is better left dead and buried. What Sloane don't know could do him more harm than good right now."

Tara heaved an exasperated sigh. Debating with Burns was as difficult as talking to a stone wall. They were both unreceptive to change. It was obvious that Carmelle's influence on Burns reached far past the grave. He cared deeply for her and he would be damned if he allowed anything to sever the strong bond between them.

"Perhaps what you say is true," Tara conceded. "But it is not your place to . . ."

"And it ain't yers either," Burns threw back at her,

along with a challenging glare. "I've got more right to decide whether or not he should be told the truth than you do. Sloane has everythin' planned, right down to the smallest detail, and you ain't gonna botch it up, not after I've waited all these years to see Merrick get his just reward."

"Is the coffee ready?" Sloane's lazy inquiry brought quick death to the argument and he frowned curiously when he noticed the agitated expressions that were stamped on Burns's and Tara's faces. "I didn't interrupt anythin' important, did I?"

If only you knew, Tara muttered under her breath. Sloane was merely a puppet and Burns was holding the strings, telling Sloane only what he wanted him to know, using him to avenge a bitter memory from the past, something even Tara did not fully understand.

"It was nothin' but the usual kitchen chit chat," Burns grunted and then pointed a floured finger toward the campfire. "The greenberry coffee should be brewed by now. Pour the man a cup, Miss Winslow. I got four dozen biscuits to make."

Tara fished through a box to locate a tin cup and then grabbed the coffee pot without thinking. "Ouch! Damn!" She sucked in her breath as the pain seared her hand and then frantically flicked her wrist, as if she could fling away the burning sensation that had wrapped itself around her fingers.

"Yer a mite careless in the kitchen, ma'am," Sloane drawled as he grabbed her arm and doused her hand in a nearby bucket of water. "It leaves a man to wonder what kind of wife you'd make if you can't heat a simple pot of coffee without burnin' yer fingers right off yer hand."

Tara acquainted him with her look of disgust as he bent her over, forcing her to keep her hand in the bucket. "Your wit is only *half* what it should be, cowboy," she sniffed distastefully.

343

Sloane chuckled, undaunted by her jibe, and then extracted her hand from the bucket to inspect the burn. "And you seem accident prone. If I was you, I would pay more attention to what I was doin'."

Tara gritted her teeth when she caught sight of Merrick standing close enough to overhear their conversation. Then she muttered under her breath when he strutted over to offer her an unsympathetic glance.

"I tend to agree with Sloane," he chimed in. "You always seem to be in the wrong place at the wrong time."

The look in his steel-gray eyes disturbed Tara. She was stung by the premonition that Merrick's underlying meaning foretold impending doom, but she was determined not to allow Merrick to rattle her. She would need to be in full command of her wits during this roundup, she reminded herself.

"I've got some salve in my saddle bag," Sloane broke in before Merrick and Tara cut each other to pieces with their razor-sharp glares. "Let me bandage yer hand." Before Tara could accept or reject the offer, Sloane took her in tow, leading her toward the dappled gray he had tethered by a cedar tree. "What the hell was that all about? First I found you antagonizing Burns and then, if looks could kill, you and Merrick would have disposed of each other like two cowboys gunning each other down. What is going on between you and Merrick?"

"Neither of us has much use for the other," she shrugged. "I'm sure you can identify with that."

"*Al contrario, amanta,*" he murmured as he gently smoothed the poultice over her inflamed fingers. "I find you enchanting."

His seductive voice sent tingles ricocheting across each vertebra in her spine, and Tara tried to still the accelerated beat of her heart when his lean, hard body brushed intimately against hers. She knew he was only mocking her, armed with the knowledge she had let slip the previous day. Oh, how he must be gloating over that, she thought acrimoniously. Sloane was probably inwardly chuckling over the fact that the only two women in forty miles were infatuated with him.

"You find everything in skirts enchanting," Tara scoffed and then presented him with a cold shoulder, complete with icicles. "When I consider the source, I cannot accept your comment as a compliment, especially since you have undoubtedly used it a hundred times before."

Apparently Sloane was immune to frostbite, since he showed no ill effects from her frigid rejoinder. "I happen to be a man of discriminating taste," he insisted, soft laughter strumming in his voice. "And if it weren't for Merrick and Julia, I wouldn't be keeping my interest in you a secret." His eyes boldly flooded over her, not missing the smallest detail.

"Then there is more than one secret looming in this canyon," Tara blurted out and then thoughtfully chewed on her bottom lip as her gaze flitted back to the chuckwagon.

A dark frown clung to Sloane's brow. "What is that supposed to mean?"

Indecision carved lines on her exquisite features as her eyes darted back and forth between the two men at the chuckwagon and Sloane. Tara grappled with Burns's stern command to mind her own business and the truth, which was even more baffling than the lie.

"Tara, you are hiding something from me." Sloane curled his hand beneath her chin, forcing her to meet his penetrating gaze.

Thank God for small favors, Tara breathed as Julia approached them. She still thought Sloane should be informed of the missing link she had discovered in his past, but she wasn't certain she should be the one to explain. Burns was the only one who could relate the

345

truth, the only one who could give Sloane an accurate account of what had truly happened.

"Papa asked if you would lead the moonlight roundup." Julia's gaze ran the full length of Sloane's muscular physique, admiring him from all angles before she finally focused on his bronzed face.

Sloane nodded agreeably and then stepped into the stirrup to uncoil his lariat. His gaze pinned Tara to the tree, and for a moment she thought he meant to request something of her. But then he turned away, gouged his steed, and disappeared in a cloud of dust.

"Damn. . . ."

Merrick's gruff growl shattered Tara's lingering thought of Sloane, and she wheeled around to see the silver-white stallion thundering along the rim of the canyon with its phantom rider on its back. The steed moved at such a swift pace that it gave the illusion that it was flying in the wind. Tara found herself wondering how many months of preparation it had taken to train Diablo to make his reckless run on this route. And when had Sloane found time to sleep, for heaven's sake? He trained Merrick's prize stock during the day and worked with the moon-eyed stallion during the night. A pensive frown captured her features, remembering what Burns had said about Sloane planning his scheme. He hadn't overlooked even the minutest detail, down to having the Night Rider appear during the roundup, as if he were following Merrick like a constant, foreboding shadow.

The entire group of cowboys paused when they caught sight of the apparition that sailed along the precipices of the canyon. The stallion's coat glowed like silver in the moonlight, and even at a distance Tara could hear the murmurings of the ranch hands, complaining about having to ride herd with Russel's phantom.

When the stallion disappeared and the men stepped into their stirrups to follow Sloane, Tara turned questioning eyes to Julia. "What is a moonlight roundup? I thought your father did not intend to run down the rest of the herd until tomorrow."

"There will be another full-scale roundup in daylight," Julia explained. "But many of the wilder longhorns take to the brush thickets and arroyos to hide. They have to be roped and tied down for the night. Tomorrow the decoy herd will be driven through the area and the wild cows and calves will be released to join them. After they have been tied down for so many hours their legs will be too numb and stiff to charge at the cowhands. It is far easier to herd them into the pen with the others when they have lost the ability to maneuver nimbly." Julia arched a curious brow as her gaze followed the departing cowboys. "Have you ever seen Sloane handle a lariat?"

Tara gave her blond head a negative shake, but she was certain if Sloane were as adept with a rope as he was with a caress that even the wildest calf wouldn't stand a chance of escaping him.

"Then it is something you should see firsthand," Julia insisted. "Even if you cannot tolerate Sloane, you will at least be impressed with his abilities with horses and cattle. Papa says he has never seen a cowboy who can outguess a four-legged animal the way Sloane can. They seldom outwit him, even the most contrary ones."

Julia was making Sloane a legend in his own time, but when Tara saw him in action, she tended to agree with her. The man's unique ability to remain on a horse that was sidestepping to prevent being gored by a protective mother cow left Tara wondering if he had tied himself to the saddle. How he managed to keep his seat and throw a loop over the longhorn's head without being flipped off the back of his steed was beyond her. He seemed to have as many lives as a cat, Tara decided. No matter which way Sloane was thrown, he always managed to land on his feet, no matter what catastrophe had befallen him, except the previous day when she had gouged his mount while he had one leg casually thrown over the saddle and was caught unaware. But now every keen sense he possessed was finely tuned and every muscle tensed. His jaw was set in grim determination as he leaped from his horse and hooked an arm around the bellowing cow's neck, twisting her head around until she relented and buckled to the ground. Before she could gather her senses and bolt to her feet, Sloane had whipped out a rope and bound her feet together. When the dust cleared, it was not the nine-hundred-pound cow who emerged the victor, but a two-hundred-pound mass of brawn and muscle who could even send a mountain lion cowering in his den.

No wonder she had such difficulty eluding Sloane, Tara mused as she watched Sloane vault into the saddle to pursue the half-crazed calf that was running circles around its hobbled mother. If he could toss a cow to her back and tie her in knots, how could Tara possibly hope to elude him? He was like an awesome centaur, half-horse, half-man, who wore jingling spurs and a daredevil smile.

Her jaw sagged on its hinges as she watched Sloane maneuver the bawling calf and leave him lying beside his mother, working tirelessly to gather eight head of contrary cattle in the span of a few short minutes.

After the ranch hands had gathered over a hundred head, they returned to the central camp to take their evening meal. Although Tara purposely avoided Sloane, she found him staring at her from a distance, watching her with that wry smile that made her want to dig a hole and climb into it. Concentrating on her meal, Tara tried to push all thoughts of him from her mind, but she jumped when she heard his soft voice behind her and very nearly spilled her plate of food in her lap.

"Do I disturb you, Tara?" he questioned, his eyes dancing in amusement as he watched Tara balance her plate in her shaky hands.

"Why don't you go pester Julia? She thrives on your company," Tara snapped brusquely.

The merriment evaporated from his expression, and as he towered over her, Tara found herself sitting in the shadow of a hard, massive mountain, one she could not possibly overcome.

"We have to talk . . . tonight . . . after everyone else is asleep. I'll be waiting at the river. Meet me there. . . ."

Without another word he pivoted away and ambled over to sink down beside Julia who was listening to the cowboys join in song. One of the men had retrieved his fiddle from the chuckwagon and had struck up a merry tune, accompanied by Burns's clanking pans as he washed the skillets and put them away.

Tara silently fumed as she listened to Sloane's rich voice rise from the chorus. Did he think he could march over and indicate the time and place for a rendezvous and she would come buzzing after him like a honeybee in search of nectar? Well, he could sit on the stream bank until he rotted!

Getting up, Tara flounced back to the chuckwagon with a half-empty plate and then aimed herself toward her tent. She heaved a frustrated sigh as she stretched out on her bedroll and watched the glow of the campfire through her canvas tent. Sloane's voice seemed to waft its way toward her, crumbling her defenses with its compelling melody.

Reality faded from her grasp as Sloane's haunting vision hovered over her, and she gave way to sleep, praying she wouldn't wake until the heat of the sun intruded upon her the following morning.

Chapter 22

A strange stillness settled over the grass-carpeted canyon as the full moonlight beamed down on the pastel-colored walls, giving them an incandescent appearance. The lowing of discontented cattle disturbed the serenity of the night, and Tara stirred, rousing to wakefulness, squinting at her surroundings to get her bearings.

Remembering that she was surrounded by cactus and cattle, Tara settled back on her lumpy bedroll. But try as she might to fall asleep, Sloane's hushed voice and compelling image came like a specter in the night to torment her. Just as Merrick was never allowed to forget what had transpired when his brother had threatened his dreams of grandeur, Tara was hounded by a love that granted her no peace, an affection she would have freely given if Sloane could have returned it.

As if called by some unseen force, Tara rose to her feet, knowing she would forever answer Sloane's summons. She crept from her tent and made her way toward the river. She could never keep her distance from Sloane. She was every kind of fool for going to him, but love had no common sense. She walked where angels feared to tread, chasing phantoms of the night, pursuing an impossible dream.

Sloane caught his breath when he saw the enchanting vision floating toward him. Tara's silver-blond hair lay recklessly about her, stirring as if some gentle hand lifted it and then allowed it to drift in the wind, fluttering about her like a shimmering cape. The white gossamer gown provided an enticing wrapper that glowed in the moonlight, displaying the high, thrusting peaks of her breasts and the shapely curve of her hips. She was like an angel hovering just above the ground, spellbinding him, leaving him to burn with unappeased desire.

His all-consuming gaze flowed from the top of her head, down her curvaceous contours, and then lifted to her exquisite face. He studied her as if she were a cherished portrait that had been stashed from sight for years on end. Tara could feel the intense heat of his eyes on her, just as surely as if he had reached out to touch her. Her assessment of Sloane was just as scrutinizing, and she could feel the warm glow of love coursing through her veins as she looked upon him. His tousled raven hair glistened with droplets of water, as if he had just emerged from bathing in the stream. His bare chest was lean and hard, his muscles rippling as he moved toward her with the silence of a stalking jungle cat. The faded blue breeches clung to his thighs and accented his tapered waist. Tara stood in awe, as if she were being approached by some magnificent creature, half-civilized, half-wild, bearing the stamp of nobility that made her heart flutter with a mixture of envy and pride. Tara was vividly aware that the reflexive tremors that flooded over her came from within, not from the gentle breeze that whispered over her skin.

"I hoped you would come, but I had almost given up on you," Sloane murmured as he closed the distance between them, watching her like a hawk, afraid that any abrupt movement would send this hesitant seraph to her wings to elude him.

The slow drawl in his resonant voice had vanished. Gone was that arrogant, mocking smile that often claimed his bronzed features. Tara was paralyzed, her senses filled with the arousing sight and fresh, clean scent of him. The manly aroma caught in the wind and curled about her like a transparent cocoon that blocked out all except the virile form of the man who towered before her.

His calloused hand glided over her bare arm, warming her with his tender touch. A gentle smile skimmed his lips as his gaze took in her flawless features and memorized them, his index finger following the delicate curve of her jaw to trace her cheekbone.

"Were you so ashamed of your feelings for me that you ran away yesterday and have continued to avoid me today?" he queried softly. "Is it so humiliating to admit that a woman like you might be attracted to a rough-edged cowboy?"

Tara was flustered by his point-blank questions and his tender touch. There was no taunting glint in those deep blue pools fringed with thick black lashes, but rather a mellow warmth that baffled her.

"I am not ashamed of my attraction to you, only hurt that you remain so remote and refuse to allow me into your private thoughts." Tara sighed tremulously as his roaming fingertips trickled over the column of her throat to trail along the rising swells of her breasts. "I know you have no time for involvements, that you live for one single purpose, but I cannot be content with an occasional night of love; I want to be a part of your life, sharing your hopes, your fears, and your dreams. But you are afraid of love," she insisted, fighting back the tears that swam in her eyes. "You see it as a weakness, and I . . ."

His full lips feathered over hers, silencing her with such a soft, alluring kiss that Tara couldn't remember what she had intended to say. Her body melted against his chest as his seeking tongue traced the curve of her mouth

352

and then probed deeper, savoring the taste of her. His lips were like velvet, caressing hers, and she reveled in their moist warmth. Streams of sweet torment pulsed through her as his sinewy arms enfolded her, holding her to him as if he never meant to let her go. A muffled groan caught in his throat as his mouth slanted over hers, stealing her breath away, leaving her prepared to surrender life itself to this potent mass of strength that engulfed her.

As rational judgment went down, her arms went up, her fingers combing through his crisp dark hair, pulling him closer until not even a particle of air could come between their bodies. Tara no longer cared that Sloane didn't love her. She yearned to give herself to this incredibly magnificent man, even if only for this one bright, shining moment. She longed to soar beyond the starlight, to feel the warmth of splendorous sensations that bordered on fantasy.

As his lips abandoned hers to seek out the sensitive point behind her ear, his roving hands spilled over her hips and then languidly glided across her ribs to brush the taut pink crests that ached for his touch. A tiny moan bubbled in her throat as he pushed the gown from her shoulders, and his kisses traced a path across her bare breasts, leaving a trail of fire blazing in the wake of his tantalizing explorations.

The gown fluttered to the ground, allowing him free access to every inch of her silky flesh. His mouth lingered on each roseate bud, suckling, arousing, stirring the hungry need that blossomed deep inside her, a need that unfurled and swelled with each kiss and caress, until passion's sweet magic had claimed her mind and body.

Like a light breeze lifting a feather and then carefully laying it to rest, Sloane took her down with him to the plush carpet of grass and stretched out beside her. His caresses became a stroking massage, dissolving the last of her tension, leaving her soft and pliant in his arms. His breath whispered across her flesh, assuring her of the pleasure he took in touching her.

It was easy to lose herself in the dreams he was weaving about her. Sloane could chase away her fears and reservations, along with every sane thought. She was drifting aimlessly, responding to the wild, uncontrollable feelings that rose and then spilled over her. Long, lean fingers glided over her abdomen to rediscover the trim curve of her waist and hips before ebbing like an arousing tide rolling over her body to begin the same sweet process again. He found each sensitive point, evoking new responses. Senses that had been forcefully suppressed came to the surface, and Tara sighed in rapturous delight, her body arching to meet his wandering hands, hands that were never still for a moment, gentle hands that created fierce desire and left her craving the moment of wild abandon.

"Te Quiero," he whispered huskily as his kisses and caresses worshipped her ripe young body.

Tara did not bother to ask him to translate, since she was incapable of thought in any language. The pleasure he offered engulfed all else, and Tara was drowning in it.

Again his hands mapped each enticing curve and swell, his lips traveling over her satiny skin, tasting her, savoring her, adoring her. Gentle pressure guided her thighs apart, his knowing fingers probing, arousing a need that spread through her like wildfire. Tara could barely draw a breath. Her heart was pounding so furiously that she swore it could never beat normally again. She was being consumed by maddening sensations. He was driving her to the edge and then plummeting her downward to be swallowed by the swirling currents of passion.

As his skillful caresses splayed across her thigh to trace intricate patterns on her belly, Tara cried out to him, pleading with him to cease the torment of having him so close and yet so far away. But Sloane was entranced by the beautiful nymph in his arms. He was like a man deprived of pleasure, one who had not been allowed to touch or taste, one who had merely survived in a vacuum of emptiness. The feel of her curvaceous body beneath his caress brought satisfaction. Her eager response thrilled him.

Tara's slim hands trailed down his spine and then slid along the band of his breeches, touching him familiarly, urging him closer. And like a moth flying into the flame, he moved against her upon command. His mouth returned to hers, twisting, slanting, devouring. His body possessed a will of its own, impatient to mold itself to the feminine softness of hers.

Her sooty lashes swept up as he braced himself above her. She could see the hunger in his eyes, eyes the color of sunset, glistening with fires to match the ones that leaped through her blood.

They had clashed like two warring armies more often than not, but neither of them could deny the spark of passion that ignited when they kissed and touched. She could never hope to tame him, but she craved him. The feminine softness of her flesh melted against the masculine hardness of his body as his muscled hips settled intimately against hers.

"God, how I want you," he whispered hoarsely before his mouth descended on hers and the bold manliness of him appeased the empty need, one that the merging of bodies and souls could satisfy when passion was embroidered with love.

And then he was a flame within her, the vital, life-giving essense of every sensation she had ever experienced. His powerful body surged into hers as his kiss deepened, taking her with that fierce, ardent hunger that was a part of the wild, reckless man she had come to love. He wanted to drive her to abandon, just as she had sent him skyrocketing into a universe of ineffable pleasure.

Tara answered his hard, driving thrusts, craving the depths of intimacy, relinquishing every part of her being to the rough-edged man with flaming blue eyes and raven hair who had captured her heart. Rapturous sensations flooded over them as they explored the remote corners of the universe. And then, as if rapture's dream had exploded about them, Tara felt herself being flung in a thousand directions at once. The dark world burst into a spectrum of magnificent colors, a shade for each tantalizing sensation she experienced when she was held in Sloane's possessive arms. Like an ever-changing kaleidoscope she found those enticing emotions swirling about her, converging back upon her, engulfing her, not once but again and again. It was inconceivable to touch the quintessence of pleasure and survive it, Tara thought deliriously. And the moment Tara was certain she had breathed her last breath, the entwining rainbow faded into a black horizon and she was spiraling downward, drifting past each rapturous plateau that had led her to passion's highest crest. For a moment Tara couldn't seem to move, as if her spent body needed adequate time to readjust after its incredible flight through time and space.

A low, raspy chuckle rumbled in Sloane's chest as he studied the stunned expression that claimed her bewitching features. "Passion like ours transcends all physical limitations, doesn't it, Tara?"

Her violet eyes fell that last million miles to settle on the darkly handsome face that hovered only a few inches from hers. How could he have plucked her very thoughts from her mind? Had he felt it too?

Sloane dropped a fleeting kiss to her heart-shaped lips and then brushed the unruly strands of hair away from her exquisite face. "I was skeptical of the emotions that touched me the first night I found you. There was something strangely compelling about your beauty, that naive innocence of your kiss, one I doubt you remember giving. You created a longing, stirring sensations that had lain dead and buried for so many years that I wasn't sure I even recognized them. Each time Julia threw us together, I found myself drawn farther into the flame, knowing it would consume me, but unable to keep my distance from you. Within the circle of your arms I have found something far more satisfying than destroying the man who destroyed my mother's world and left me drifting in search of happiness, something that always seemed to linger on the far horizon." His chiseled features softened in an expression she had never noticed on them before. "I should have forced you to return to St. Louis where you belonged, but I couldn't deny myself the one pleasure that has eluded me in all my years of fruitless searching."

Tara stared up at him, hearing his softly spoken words, but hardly daring to believe what she thought he was attempting to say in his roundabout way.

"You have taunted and tormented me, and with good cause, I suppose," Sloane admitted as he rolled away to retrieve his breeches. "But I was torn between this fierce dedication to a cause and my insatiable need for you." A rakish smile brimmed on his lips as he tossed Tara her gown. "You have gone to my head like an intoxicating wine, not to mention the effect you have had on the rest of my anatomy."

Tara blushed as she pulled the gown over her head and drew her blond hair over her shoulder. "It seems only fair that I have distracted you, since you have turned my world upside down and I have had difficulty distinguishing which way is up."

"It's this way," Sloane laughed softly as he grasped her hand and pulled her up beside him. His other hand cupped her buttocks, pressing her hips intimately to his while the other slid behind her neck, tilting her face to his impulsive kiss. "There is much I want to say, but we have tarried too long already. Someone might find you gone, and an explanation might be difficult to come by."

"This is the witching hour," she teased, content to remain in the circle of his arms. Her fingertips trickled through the dark matting of hair on his chest, feeling his heart leap in response to her teasing touch. "There are only ghosts and banshees about this time of night."

His dark brow climbed higher as he surveyed the suggestive flicker in her amethyst eyes. "Lord, woman, how can a man function if he's . . ."

A shocked gasp shattered the spell, splitting them apart. Sloane wheeled around, shielding Tara from the intruder. He scowled disgustedly when he saw Julia staring at them in shock and disbelief. The horrified expression on her face nearly broke Tara's heart, and she groaned miserably as Julia staggered as if she had had the props knocked out from under her.

"You could barely tolerate the sight of him?" Julia choked out. "You wanted to avoid him?" She laughed bitterly. "And I believed you had no interest in Sloane. All the while you have been sneaking around behind my back."

When Julia pivoted on her heels and stalked away, Tara dashed after her. "Julia, at least allow me to explain. I never meant to . . ."

Julia tore her arm from Tara's grasp and glared furiously at her so-called friend. "I suppose you intend to put the blame on me because I forced you on him," she muttered bitterly.

Heaving a frustrated sigh, Tara looked Julia straight in the eye, watching the tears stream down her flushed cheeks. "I know you are hurt and angry and you feel I have betrayed you. But you must believe I did not want this to happen."

358

"But you still allowed it," Julia pointed out in a brittle tone. She muffled a sniff and then peered up to see Sloane ambling toward them, his mouth set in a grim line. When she tried to dart away the second time, it was Sloane who manacled her wrist, refusing to let her flee with the broken pieces of her pride.

"Go back to your tent, Tara," he ordered, flinging her a stern glance. "I want to speak to Julia alone."

Tara hesitated a moment, thoughtfully glancing back and forth between Sloane and Julia, and then nodded in compliance. "Forgive me, Julia. I should never have come to Texas. I have brought you nothing but heartache and humiliation." A rueful smile found its way to her lips as her gaze swung to Sloane for a split-second and then resettled on Julia's frustrated expression. "I will make no attempt to see him again, and I will return to St. Louis where I belong as soon as the roundup is over."

When Tara disappeared into the shadows, Sloane focused his full attention on the teary-eyed young woman who looked helplessly at him. "I have been flattered by your attentions," Sloane assured her softly as he brushed his thumb over her cheek, rerouting the stream of tears. "But I think you've been toyin' with fascination and, forgive me for bein' so blunt, you *were* the one who threw Tara at me. You have no right to be angry with her. It was as she said, Tara didn't want nothin' to do with me. She would have backed gracefully away from me in the beginnin', and she has promised you that she won't see me again, in hopes of mendin' yer friendship." Sloane curled his finger beneath her chin, forcing her to meet his somber gaze. "The very last thing Tara wanted to do was hurt you."

Julia bit her trembling lips, anger and humiliation still nipping at her pride. What did she expect him to say, that he was in love with her, that he had only been using Tara to satisfy his needs? Silly little fool, Julia berated herself.

She had been behaving as if the entire world revolved about her, as if she could have everything she wanted and that wishing for it could make it hers.

"Loren loves you the way a man should love a woman. He's been patient with you, lettin' you decide if he's the right man for you, even when he's known for a long time that you were the only woman for him. He loves you enough to allow you that freedom of choice, even if it means losin' you. And Tara is prepared to make the same sacrifice in the name of friendship." His hand fell away from her face as he broke into a quiet smile. "You and I have known each other for almost a year. If there was somethin' magic between us, it would have grown into somethin' special without usin' Tara as yer go-between."

Julia's head dropped to study the grass beneath her feet, feeling all the more the fool, but still plagued by the sting of humiliation. She was behaving like a spoiled child and she knew it, but finding Tara in Sloane's arms had been a crushing blow, one to which she needed time to adjust.

"Next time you see Loren, take a close look at him. I think it's time you came to grips with yer emotions. Ask yerself if you will be content to spend the rest of yer life without him. And then ask yerself if losin' a friend who truly cares abut you is worth the pain yer puttin' Tara through." His lean fingers folded around Julia's shoulders as he heaved a heavy sigh. "It could never have worked between us, Julia, and not just because I find myself attracted to Tara. We can never be more than friends, and you must accept that."

As he turned and walked away, the dam of tears burst and Julia sobbed, mortified, angry, humiliated by the startling turn of events. God, how could she have been so blind as not to notice what had been going on? What an imbecile she had been, prancing around like a fairy princess who had her pick of the handsome knights in her father's kingdom. What childish dreams! But knowing that she had behaved abominably toward Loren and Tara didn't stop the hurting.

Muffling a sniff, Julia trudged back to her tent to grapple with Sloane's words, realizing, at last, that Tara had been the one who had suffered at her expense. Sloane had said he had been attracted to Tara, but not once had he admitted to love her. And now Tara was the one who would pay for Julia's foolishness. She had thrown Tara at Sloane, a man obviously incapable of love, a man who took what he wanted from women and then cast them aside when he became bored with them. How could she have fancied herself in love with such a cold, callous man? He was the one who should take a good long look at Tara, she thought bitterly. She was everything a man could want—beautiful, witty, graceful. But Sloane had more compassion for four-legged animals than he had for women, and Tara would return to St. Louis to wed a man she didn't love. God, what a tangled mess she had woven when she had tried to use Tara to tame Sloane Prescott. She should have her father fire him and send him packing, she thought spitefully. Then she sighed. Merrick would never dismiss Sloane. He had helped her father build a name that was known all over Texas. His prize horses brought high prices after Sloane had broken and trained them. Sloane was the main reason for Merrick's success with horses, and he wouldn't give Sloane up to any other rancher on the North American continent. She would have to find her own way to have her revenge on Sloane, she decided as she settled herself on her bedroll. Somehow, she would see that he paid for using Tara like a plaything, she vowed as she willed her eyes to close.

Tara attempted sleep, but it was next to impossible

361

after her confrontation with Julia. After pulling on her clothes, she went back outside, intending to speak with Julia, if she would allow it. But the soft whinny of a horse in the distance caught her attention and Tara's inquisitiveness urged her to seek out the source of the sound. She made her way along the rock ledge that overlooked a small ravine on the other side of the bluff. She crouched down to watch three riders releasing the calves Sloane and the other cowboys had worked so hard to subdue.

As the moonlight spilled into the canyon, Tara was struck by the appearance of one of the riders, an image that had haunted her dreams, hovering just beyond the hazy image that she wasn't certain she wanted to see clearly. The way the man carried himself in the saddle brought back the painful reminder of that terrifying night. And like a frightening ghost leaping out at her, recognition sprung to mind. At last she knew who had cut down an innocent man.

With grim determination, Tara forced the dreadful thought aside. It was imperative that she inform Sloane that Merrick's calves were being prepared for relocation in the Simpson herd. As she watched the wobbly-legged cows and calves being herded through the valley she could well imagine what excuse Merrick would give when his ranch hands reported the strays were missing. No doubt, he would blame the Night Rider. Merrick twisted everything to his advantage, she thought bitterly. Even Sloane's method of torment had become a means for Merrick to acquire what he wanted—a cattle and horse empire to surpass all others.

After watching the men drive the numb-legged calves farther from the main camp and stash them in a secluded corral that was backed against the sheer walls of the canyon, she silently picked her way down the precipice and then crept over beside Sloane, who was tucked inside his bedroll, sleeping like a baby. Tara was certain exhaustion must have caught up with him. He had lived on so few hours' sleep that once he laid his head against his saddle he was oblivious to the world.

When she nudged him he came awake with a start, his fist doubled as if he meant to knock her silly before he realized who had roused him. The tension drained when his eyes met Tara's alarmed ones, and he offered her a smile.

"You are lucky, lady," he chuckled softly, careful not to rouse the other men. "I almost planted my fist in your face when I would have preferred to plant a kiss." A bemused frown creased his brow as his gaze dropped to study her clothes. "Why are you dressed in the middle of the night? I thought you had gone to bed."

"I couldn't sleep," she whispered back to him and then glanced about, hoping they would not be overheard. "I heard something and I went to investigate. Merrick has freed the strays and moved them to the box canyon south of here." Tara paused a moment, trying to decide to disclose the secret Burns had been keeping from him and the identity of the man who had murdered Sloane's grandfather. "There is something else. . . ."

The cowboy who slept beside Sloane groaned and then stirred slightly. Scowling at the interruption, Sloane gestured for Tara to return to her tent. Carefully, she inched away, annoyed that she had been unable to finish what she had intended to say now that she had worked up the nerve to confront Sloane with the truth. Tomorrow she would tell him, she promised herself as she shed her garments and drew the gown over her head.

As her lashes fluttered shut, Sloane's image rose before her and her thoughts lingered on the words he had spoken before Julia had interrupted them. It was a cruel twist of fate that Sloane had finally begun to care for her in his own way and then to have Julia discover that they had become lovers. Perhaps his affection for her would never blossom into love, but he did care about her, Tara assured herself, and then sighed heavily. But it didn't matter now. She had promised Julia that she would never allow Sloane to come between them. She was curious to know what Sloane had said to Julia and how she had responded, but she wondered if she would ever learn what had transpired between them. Time was short and much was at stake. Her personal feelings would not stand in the way, she reminded herself. All hell was about to break loose, and her differences with Julia would have to wait until after the inevitable clash. Perhaps in time Julia would forgive her for betraying her. Tara scoffed at that remote possibility. When Julia found her world crumbling about her she would be far more bitter than she was now. She might never forgive Sloane or Tara for destroying her life. Tara had to make certain that once this ordeal was over Sloane would provide for Julia. She would have nothing and no one when Merrick was stripped of his wealth.

Chapter 23

The ranch hands had already begun to rope and brand the herd they had penned in the corral when Tara managed to crawl from her pallet. The morning sun had been on duty more than two hours before she had raised her weary head. When she stepped outside her tent, Julia's eyes darted to her momentarily and then she glanced away, focusing her attention on Loren and Sloane, who were moving through the fidgety herd, roping and throwing calves for branding.

As Tara's gaze swept the camp her eyes landed on Merrick and Cal Johnson, and she was unable to suppress the glare when she focused on them. Cal had carried a grudge since the night Tara had warded off his amorous advances with her derringer, and he was now ogling her with spiteful disgust, while Merrick's gray eyes bored into her, studying her all to closely.

Tara would have sprinted to the chuckwagon to nibble on what was left over from breakfast, anything to avoid Merrick, but he cut her off before she could cross the camp.

A menacing smile hovered on his lips as his shadow fell over her, and Tara instinctively backed away, feeling all the more threatened by his presence. "You seem a bit uneasy this morning," Merrick observed. "Is something wrong, my dear?"

Everything was wrong! Tara felt as if she were standing on a keg of gunpowder. She knew what Merrick was planning and she also knew who had killed Don Miguel. Tara had the sinking feeling that Merrick knew it, too, and it was difficult to act nonchalant when Merrick's cold gray eyes were boring into her.

"Excuse me," Tara tried to veer around him, avoiding him and his pointed question. "This fresh air seems to have stimulated my appetite and I would like to . . ."

His lean fingers bit into her arm as she brushed past Merrick, who refused to allow her to pass. "Why were you staring at Cal with that stricken look on your face?" he questioned gruffly, dropping all pretense of pleasantry. "Or was it me who caused that expression, Tara?"

His eyes were riveted on her and Tara winced in response to the flash of devilishness in his gaze. "I think you must have misinterpreted me," she said as she pried his fingers from her arm and then rubbed her numb flesh to revive the circulation. "I was only squinting in the sunlight."

Before Merrick could capture her again, Tara backed away, her gaze darting to Cal, who was grinning at her like a starved shark. Tara had the uneasy feeling she was treading thin ice. God, she would be relieved when Friday night had come and gone . . . if she lived to see it. She could swear Cal and Merrick had some surprises in store for her, and she detested surprises.

As Tara moved toward the chuckwagon, Merrick's low voice halted her in her tracks. "Don't cross me, Tara. You know more than you will admit, but don't think you can deliver the information to your father. If you breathe a word there will be no place on this earth you can hide from me." His eyes were like hard splinters of steel, and Tara knew the real Merrick Russel had begun to creep to the surface. He was as deadly as a coiled rattlesnake, and the hiss in his voice assured her that he would not think twice about striking at her.

"The phantom who haunts your canyon will see to it that you will receive retribution for your sins," Tara shot back at him. "You may find some sordid way to dispose of me, but I swear I will also come back to torment you. A devil like you may enjoy an occasional victory, but you will never truly win."

His mouth twisted in a sneer, and Tara was certain he would have delighted in clamping his hands around her neck and choking the life from her if they had been alone.

Since she had already dangerously flirted with disaster, Tara wheeled toward the chuckwagon and attempted to still the wild beating of her heart. Merrick considered her a threat, and she feared if she didn't keep her wits about her she would never live to divulge the information about Don Miguel's murder to Sloane.

It was with great relief that Tara watched Merrick and Cal step into the stirrups and ride from camp. Merrick rattled her, and when he focused those unnerving gray eyes on her she started shaking like a leaf tossed about in a thunderstorm. Heaving a determined sigh, she nibbled on her biscuit and climbed up on a boulder to watch Sloane and Loren sear the Diamond R brand on the cattle.

Within a few minutes Tara was engrossed in the procedure and marveling at Sloane's agility and quickness. He moved like a mountain lion springing into action. His muscles bulged as he wrestled calves four times his weight, forcing them to submit to his wishes.

The sound of thundering hooves caught her attention and she glanced back over her shoulder to see the partial herd of strays that had been left for the night stampeding toward her. The wild-eyed cattle charged into camp, their pounding hooves lifting the dust until it formed an ominous cloud that rose above the valley. Panic paralyzed her as the runaway herd converged on her.

Tara heard Sloane's booming voice, but his words didn't seep into her stunned mind. She was staring death in the face, and there was nowhere to run except straight up the walls of the canyon. As the thundering herd swarmed her she dived behind her rock perch and folded herself into a tight ball, clinging to the boulder, holding her breath as the fog of dust rolled over her.

The entire canyon rumbled as the cows galloped over and around her. The sound of revolvers firing in the air intermingled with the warning bellows of the cattle, but the herd did not change course. They ran blindly ahead, circling the canyon walls until there was no place left to run.

It seemed an eternity as she waited for the end to come—either to her life or to the stampede. Tara groaned in agony as flying hooves rammed against her back and ribs. There was no air left to breathe, and she coughed on the dust, feeling catastrophe crowding in on her. Merrick had seen to it that she would not live to tell who had murdered Don Miguel. He had planned this so-called accident, just as he had plotted his own brother's murder.

And then suddenly Tara found herself jerked to her feet and cradled in Sloane's trembling arms. Gasping to inhale a breath that wasn't heavy with dust, she stared up to see Sloane's cobalt-blue eyes racing over her to ensure that she was still in one piece.

"Are you hurt?" he questioned raggedly, his heart slamming against his ribs, forcing out his breath in uneven spurts. God, he had felt as if he were moving in slow motion as he had attempted to reach Tara.

"I'm alive," she choked out as he set her to her feet to test her wobbly legs. "But oddly enough, I feel as if I have been run over by a stampeding herd. . . ." Her voice trailed off as she glanced over Sloane's shoulder to see Merrick circling back toward them after he had ensured that the cowboys had managed to box the cattle in a narrow neck of the canyon.

"These strays are still barely manageable, even after being staked out for the night," Merrick said when he reached them. "I hope you weren't hurt, Tara," he added, in a tone that implied that he couldn't have cared less if she had perished during the ordeal.

Sloane's eyes narrowed on Merrick, conscious of his unsympathetic tone, and then his astute gaze shifted to the herd of cows without their calves. "Where are the rest of the strays we hobbled for the night?" he questioned, knowing the answer.

Merrick's shoulder lifted and then dropped. "There must have been a hundred lariats lying in the grass. The calves have vanished without a trace."

"The phantom rider again?" Sloane grunted, his voice dripping with sarcasm.

"What other explanation is there?" Merrick sighed. "Old Ben vanished into thin air, and now I've lost my calves. I would send a search party out for them, but we have a schedule to keep. We still have to gather the stock from the south range, brand them, and move the herd to the trail before the other ranchers use up the grass. I can't very well risk having my beeves drop weight and starve on the way to Harrold. My investors expect me to provide a profit, no matter what catastrophe befalls me."

"Of course," Sloane snorted as he guided Tara back to her tent. When they were out of earshot, he focused his full attention on Tara's peaked face. "I think you had better return to headquarters. I don't trust Merrick, and I would bet that stampede was no accident. For some reason he is trying to dispose of you."

Tara would have bet Sloane was right. She knew too much, and nothing would please Merrick more than to have her perish, accidentally on purpose! But she was not leaving camp until Sloane had snared Merrick and exposed him for the dastardly bastard he was. She was not about to scurry back to headquarters like a frightened rabbit. What good would it do? Merrick would only send Cal after her, and she had the uneasy feeling Cal was every bit as ruthless as Merrick was.

"I am staying here," Tara insisted as she raised a bruised and stubborn chin.

"Dammit, woman, your life is in danger!" Sloane snorted. "This is no time for foolhearted bravery. You have been tripping on the borderline of calamity and he means to . . ." His voice evaporated when he heard footsteps approaching the tent.

"Tara?" Julia's wide, apprehensive eyes settled on Tara's disheveled clothes and whitewashed cheeks. "I thought I had seen the last of you. My God, that was close! It seems this roundup has been plagued with one mishap after another." Her condescending gaze darted to Sloane, who backed away to join the other cowboys who had been sent to retrieve the herd in the south pasture. "I swear the ghost that haunts my father means to dispose of all of us."

"Do you think it wise to blame every disaster on the appearance of an apparition?" Tara questioned.

Julia shrugged slightly. "My father says his brother tormented him all his life, and he is not at all surprised that his ghost refuses to leave Palo Duro until he has succeeded in taking my father to the spirit world. I have grown up hearing the legend and watching good cowboys pack up and leave because they claim the Night Rider has sailed past them while they stood watch, urging them to flee for their lives."

"But you don't believe your father could have committed the crime that is whispered about with the rumors?" Tara finally asked.

"He is my father," Julia murmured, refusing to meet Tara's probing gaze. "I do not pretend to understand his moods or the events of the past. But the fact remains that he is still my father, and he is the only family I have ever known."

Tara heaved a heavy sigh and then stared at the scuffed toes of her boots. "Julia, about last night. I . . ."

"I don't want to discuss it," Julia cut in. "We both made a tragic mistake, and I would prefer that you never mention Sloane's name around me again. He deserves no consideration and I want to forget I was ever foolish enough to think I was interested in him."

Sweet merciful heavens! What had Sloane said to her? Julia was behaving as if Sloane was the lowest form of life ever to slither across the earth. If she only knew her father was a member of that species, Tara thought to herself as Julia spun on her heels and stomped out of the tent.

Tara collapsed on her bedroll. Lord, what a harrowing day—and it had only begun.

It was night. Heaving a frustrated sigh, Tara plopped down on her pallet and stared at the canvas walls of her tent. She had hoped to spend a few private moments with Sloane, to arm him with the truth, facts that he wouldn't want to hear but that Tara was certain he needed to know. Unfortunately, Merrick had his men rounding up cattle and herding them into the central pen for branding long past daylight.

Finally, Tara had given up and assured herself that there was still time to seek out Sloane before Merrick made his connections with John Simpson the following night. Burns would be hopping mad when he learned Tara had revealed the true secret of the locket, but Sloane was living with a lie, she reminded herself.

Tara had just dozed off to sleep when she felt a presence beside her. A drowsy smile played on her lips as she stirred, certain Sloane had come to speak with her.

371

But her pleasure was transformed into panic when she recognized the threatening silhouette that loomed over her. Before she could voice a cry of alarm, Merrick's gloved hand clamped over her mouth and she found herself staring down the barrel of his pistol.

Like the unsuspecting cattle that had found themselves entangled in a lariat, Tara was bound and gagged before she could regather her composure.

Merrick's wicked chuckle settled about her like a cloud of impending doom. "We are going for a moonlight ride, Tara," he informed her harshly. "You and I need to see to some unfinished business, something I overlooked the night I found you and Don Miguel on the road. When you pulled that derringer on me I should have disposed of you as well. I thought I could sway you to my way of thinking, but you have become as big a pest as your snoopy father."

He roughly yanked her to her feet, peered outside to ensure no one was about, and then herded Tara toward the three horses Cal Johnson had saddled and kept waiting as Merrick had ordered.

Cal's hawkish gaze flooded over Tara's sheer gown and a sardonic grin rippled across his lips as Merrick shoved her toward him. A wave of repulsion splashed over Tara as Cal's calloused hand folded around her breast and he scooped her into his arms to toss her on the saddle. If Tara could have ripped off her gag she would have loudly cursed the low-minded varmint, but she was not to be granted even the smallest whim. God, if only she would wake to find the horsey smell that infiltrated her senses belonged to a nightmare! But she knew this was all too real. Merrick wanted to be rid of her, and she was helpless to protect herself from him.

"I've decided to meet Simpson tonight instead of tomorrow," Merrick told Cal and then gestured toward his hostile captive. "My meddling guest probably intended to set a trap for me when I made the cattle exchange, and I have no intention of driving the herd across the mesa, only to find Terrance and the sheriff awaiting me."

"Do you want me to get rid of her for you, Merrick?" Cal offered, his hungry eyes devouring her shapely figure. "I got a score to settle with this feisty little bitch, and I'd be all too happy to see to the matter for you when I've finished with her."

Merrick stared down his nose at the unkempt cowboy, who was sorely in need of a shave and haircut. No doubt, Cal would be so overcome with lust that he would insist upon having his way with this little termagant before he disposed of her. His dallying could mean her escape, and he couldn't risk that, Merrick reminded himself.

"I'll see to this grisly business," he insisted as he grabbed the reins to Tara's mount. "Get Jesse to help you bring the calves to the mesa."

As Merrick led Tara away, Cal grumbled under his breath. He would have much preferred to get his hands on that haughty chit. He hadn't forgotten the night she had made a fool of him. What she needed was a man who would put her in her proper place, and he was itching to be the one to subdue that blond-haired hellcat before he put her out of Merrick's misery.

When they had ridden a safe distance from camp, Merrick leaned out to pull the bandanna from Tara's mouth and then smirked when she glared mutinously at him. "It is a pity you were unable to inform your father that I was sending part of my herd with Simpson. Nothing would make him happier than to catch me redhanded, but I am far too clever for that, and Terrance knows it." His gray eyes fastened on her flaming violet ones, undaunted by the hatred he saw in them. "I knew you had overheard our conversation, and I knew I would eventually have to dispose of you."

373

"Just like you disposed of your own brother and Don Miguel," Tara gritted out, loathing the man more with each passing minute.

"There is no proof of that," Merrick reminded her with a mocking smile, one Tara would dearly have loved to slap off his face if her hands hadn't been tied. "And even if you lived to tell your father that you recognized me as Don Miguel's murderer, John Simpson and Cal Johnson are prepared to swear that I was with them that night. Who would believe you could have recognized a masked man in pitch darkness?"

"You can gloat all you wish," Tara hissed venomously. "But you won't escape penance, Merrick. Someday, somehow, the phantom of Palo Duro will lead you into a trap from which there will be no escape."

"Nothing and no one will stand in my way," Merrick growled at her. "I have always been able to take every twist of fate and use it to my advantage. I have no fear of the ghost that guards the canyon, even though I let it be known that I mourn my brother's disembodied spirit when it suits my purpose."

Tara fell silent, stung by the dismal realization that Merrick had not been caught in thirty years and that his past record gave him confidence. Now Sloane's plan to catch Merrick on the mesa had been spoiled. How could Sloane possibly know Merrick would ride tonight? A feeling of despair closed in on her. She might not live to see Merrick receive his just reward, but she vowed to return to haunt this miserable excuse for a man. If there were indeed such things as ghosts, she would be among them, she promised herself. And she would see to it that Merrick was hounded for the rest of his days.

"You will find more than one specter haunting your canyon, Merrick," Tara assured him in a deadly tone. "But I won't be riding herd on your cattle. I will become *your* constant shadow, and you will never forget the merciless crimes you have committed."

His head swiveled around to see the grim expression that settled into her exquisite features, and there was such venom in her words that Merrick found himself believing she meant what she said. But hers was not the first spiteful vow he had ever heard, and he had never been superstitious enough to believe spirits could interfere in earthly matters, especially his.

"Idle threats," he snorted arrogantly. "You have escaped disaster in the past, but before the night is out I will be well rid of you, and I truly doubt that I will hear from you again."

Tara glared daggers in his back as he led her up the trail to the mesa high above Palo Duro Canyon. She worked frantically at the ropes that bound her wrists. She would not become Merrick's third victim, she vowed to herself. She would ensure that Merrick paid for his crimes if it was the last thing she ever did. Tara gulped hard at that thought. Riding to the mesa with Merrick could very well be the last thing she ever did, if he had his way . . . and Merrick Russel usually did. . . .

A bemused frown creased Sloane's brow when he squinted in the darkness, seeing nothing in Tara's tent but an empty bedroll. Where the devil had she wandered off to this time, he muttered under his breath as he crept around the side of the unoccupied tent. He was going to have to stake that inquisitive imp down to something with roots to keep her from prowling around after dark. Dammit, she could get herself into trouble if she was out snooping around as she had been the previous night.

Another possibility occurred to him and he pivoted around to aim himself toward Julia's tent. When he drew back the flap to see if Tara might have been doing something as harmless as visiting with Julia, she gasped at the sight of the ominous figure who filled the entrance of her tent.

"What are you doing here?" she snapped curtly as she snatched the quilt around her neck.

"Where is Tara?" Sloane questioned impatiently.

"In her tent, I suppose," Julia growled. "But I want you nowhere near her. You have caused her quite enough distress."

Sloane did a double take. "What the hell are you talkin' about?" he demanded.

"I am referring to the despicable way you have used her," Julia bit off. "She is not some trollop from Tascosa, and don't think I don't know what cowboys do when they set foot in that wild town." Julia was just gathering steam. She had spent the day stewing and had every intention of marching to Tara's tent to spout a lecture, one similar to those Tara had delivered to her when she had thought herself in love with this handsome, hard-hearted devil. "You have your nerve, Sloane Prescott! Tara is a gently bred lady, and her grandfather would make mincemeat of you if he knew you had been cavorting with his granddaughter. He insists on marrying her off to a man she doesn't love. If you had one shred of decency, you would realize you could do no better than Tara and make her your wife, if only to spare her the agony of wedding that stuffy aristocrat her grandfather has selected for her. You owe her that much, after you have . . ." Julia fumbled for the appropriate words to describe his inappropriate behavior. She was not too naive to know Sloane and Tara had been engaged in something more intimate than conversation when she had intruded on them at the riverbank the previous night. "After you have compromised her virtue." Julia wagged her finger at Sloane, who was having considerable difficulty keeping a straight face during the verbal lynching. "And to think I saw promise in you," she sniffed distastefully. "It seems I am a lousy judge of character, because I am not at all sure you have any!"

"Julia, I . . ." Sloane began in self-defense, only to be cut off by Julia's low growl.

"I am not finished yet," she assured him hotly. "Tara could have any man she wanted if she were allowed the freedom of choice, and she might have offered her heart to you, but would you accept it?" She didn't await his response, plunging on before Sloane could wedge in a word. "No, you just forced yourself on her, taking unfair advantage. You have stripped her of her dignity, and when her grandfather learns of it, you will be sorry. I promise you that! He will have your head mounted on the mantel in his study as a reminder to any man who might consider toying with his granddaughter."

"*Now* are you finished?" Sloane inquired as he arched a dark brow and reassessed the strawberry blonde, who seemed to have matured overnight. She was not as self-centered and vain as she had once been. She had considered someone besides herself. Sloane's opinion of his cousin rose several notches after she had raked him over the coals, even though she hadn't said anything that hadn't buzzed through his head a thousand times since he had found himself irresistibly attracted to that stunning silver-blonde with the amethyst eyes.

"I suppose I am," Julia grumbled grudgingly. "But if I think of anything I might have forgotten to mention, I will let you know."

"Do, by all means," Sloane drawled, his baritone crackling with amusement. "But before you recite another soliloquy, I think it's fair to tell you I'm in love with Tara."

"You are?" Julia croaked in disbelief, her mouth gaping wide enough for a family of sparrows to roost in.

"And I intend to tell her so if and when I find her," Sloane grumbled as he spun on his heels to continue

377

his search.

Julia stared bug-eyed as Sloane disappeared into the darkness, and then she melted into a smile. Sloane *was* every bit the man she had fancied herself in love with, and if anyone could convince Ryan O'Donnovan that Tara had found a worthy mate all by herself, Sloane could. After all, he was his own man, and even her father had never been able to master him. There were not many men in Texas who could boast of that feat, she reminded herself as she snuggled into her bedroll and pictured Sloane and Tara as they had been the previous night. What a striking couple, she mused. They were as different as dawn and midnight, but there was a rare quality in both of them that had drawn them together like two moths consumed by a flame.

Chapter 24

A troubled frown etched Sloane's brow after he had made a careful search of the camp. He had the uneasy feeling something was amiss. Tara was nowhere to be found, and neither were Merrick and Cal . . . A feeling of dread sizzled through every nerve and muscle in Sloane's rigid body. Merrick was planning something dastardly. He could feel it in his bones. His keen gaze swept the moonlit canyon and he pricked his ears to the sound of hooves rumbling in the distance.

"Damn," Sloane muttered as he swiftly strode over to retrieve a mount. Merrick was moving the cattle. He must have realized Tara knew of his plans, and Merrick intended to . . .

Sloane's heart flip-flopped in his chest as he gouged the steed and reined him to the north. Merrick would see to it that Tara met with an untimely death, claiming she had been accident prone since the moment she found herself out of her element, Sloane mused acrimoniously. Confound it, why hadn't he sent Tara back to her father for protection? She would have been safe from Merrick's clutches. But no, Sloane had allowed that distracting beauty to dissuade him from sending her away. He had already lost everyone who had meant anything to him, and now he stood to lose Tara to the very man who had taken his family from him.

379

Pulling hard on the reins, Sloane brought the winded steed to a skidding halt. His sharp whistle pierced the night air and he waited an impatient moment before sending a second call, which was answered by the white stallion's whinny. Sloane hopped to the ground and strode toward the moon-eyed steed that could find his way far better in darkness than daylight. The stallion had been grazing north of the camp until he heard his master's call, and he came prancing to Sloane like a puppy in search of affection.

Sloane absently patted the stallion's powerful neck and then hurriedly untied the dummy from his back and donned the incandescent poncho and ghastly hood himself.

As he swung onto Diablo's back, he scanned the rising precipices of Palo Duro, searching for a shortcut to take him to the elevated mesa. As Sloane pressed his knees to Diablo's flanks the white stallion lunged into a gallop. The steed laid back his ears, his nostrils flaring as if he sensed his master's apprehension.

Sloane allowed the surefooted stallion free rein as he thundered toward the canyon wall to pick his way along the treacherous path that led to the mesa. With one mighty lunge, Diablo scrambled up the loose sandstone and set his feet on level ground to dart after the herd Cal Johnson had driven from the box canyon south of camp. Sloane swore he would run the calves right over Merrick if Tara wasn't with him. It would be a fitting end, Sloane told himself as he gouged his heels into Diablo's ribs and leaned against his neck to pursue the skittish herd that trotted ahead of him.

The color drained from Merrick's weather-beaten features when he saw the phantom rider appear, as if the specter had spirited straight up the towering walls of Palo

Duro to give chase.

"The Night Rider comes to claim his bounty and your malicious soul," Tara taunted as the horse and his master flew across the mesa at incredible speed.

John Simpson sucked in his breath when his wide eyes anchored on the incandescent specter that circled the stampeding herd, his poncho billowing about him as if his shapeless body were equipped with wings. "He's going to drive them right over us!" he screeched as he reined his steed around and frantically searched for cover.

For a moment Merrick's mind stopped functioning. He could only sit and stare at the apparition that had hounded his every step, remembering the hissing vow Tara had made as they climbed to the mesa. His eyes blazed with fury as they followed the phantom's swift flight across the grass. Perhaps his brother's vengeful spirit *had* come to claim his soul, he thought, feeling suddenly sick. The white stallion's shrill whinny caught in the wind as it stretched out to race beside the flighty calves, veering them to the east the split-second before they swallowed up the threesome in their dust.

Merrick sat in a trance as the silver stallion bounded to a halt and reared, his powerful hooves thrashing the air, his eyes wild, his nostrils flaring as if he were about to begin breathing fire.

When the stallion and his formidable rider leaped forward, advancing on them like an avenging knight upon his white charger, Merrick's heart catapulted to his throat to strangle him.

Tara's goading laughter served to bring him back to his senses. "Your dreams are beginning to crumble about you. When my father and grandfather have proof of your underhanded dealings, the Diamond R will no longer be yours," she assured him as she wormed her hands free of the rope and flung it at him.

Merrick raised his arm to strike her, but Tara pressed

381

her knees to the steed's flanks, causing the startled gelding to bolt forward. Merrick very nearly toppled from his saddle when he tried to keep a firm grasp on Tara's reins, but he quickly recovered, dragging himself back into an upright position, cursing as the taut reins were yanked from his hand. His temper snapped as Tara darted away to carry the information to her father, the man who had spent three years sniffing his tracks like an inquisitive bloodhound.

Like a madman Merrick charged after Tara, racing along the crumbling rim of the canyon, itching to get his hands on the young woman who could shatter his dreams.

"Merrick, for God's sake, no!" John screamed at the top of his lungs, but Merrick was deaf and blind to everything except his purpose.

Terror leaped through Tara when she braved a glance over her shoulder, seeing the murderous gleam in his eyes as he forced her closer to the precarious caprock of Palo Duro. Frantically, she leaned down to snare the dragging reins, but they were impossible to reach without falling off the runaway steed.

Tara held on for dear life as Merrick's swift mount moved along beside her, and she couldn't contain the bloodcurdling scream as he swerved toward her, attempting to unseat her.

"Merrick, no!"

John's voice seemed a thousand miles away, and Tara could hear it echoing about her as she struggled to cling to her frightened mount. But the plea had no effect on Merrick, whose stormy gray eyes spelled murder.

A gasp of horror escaped Tara's lips when she glanced up to see the canyon rim cutting into the plains, just ahead of her. Her steed attempted to veer to the left to avoid plummeting over the caprock, but Merrick granted him no space. Sickening dread flooded over Tara as the two galloping horses collided and Merrick pushed at her again.

Tara could see her life passing before her eyes as her mount stumbled on the dangling reins and then skidded on the loose rock on the lip of the canyon. Her terrified cry pierced the night as the horse lost his balance and fell off the ledge into the dark abyss of Palo Duro.

Sloane's heart stopped and he felt a part of his soul wither and die when Tara lost her battle with the madman who had forced her over the caprock and her trim silhouette disappeared like a diver plunging into a river of black. Sloane cursed himself a thousand times as he reined Diablo away from the stampeding herd and urged him toward the jagged cliff where Tara had valiantly struggled and gone down in defeat to the devil.

Although Merrick had thundered away to round up the startled herd, Sloane did not give chase. All he could think of was Tara and the horrible scene that flashed in his tormented mind. The silver stallion tensed when they neared the canyon rim, but Sloane dug his spurs into the reluctant steed's ribs, forcing him over the ledge and down the dangerously steep incline. Diablo tucked his hind legs beneath him as he skidded down the precarious slope. Sloane leaned back in the saddle until his back was practically pressed to that of his horse, minimizing the risk of being hurled over Diablo's head if he lost his footing. But Sloane didn't really care if he plunged to his death, not now, not if it meant living without Tara.

When Diablo found solid footing on a lower shelf of the canyon wall, Sloane's frantic gaze sped about him and he growled in agony when he spied Tara's lifeless body sprawled beside her horse. The dazed steed had drawn one bloodied leg up beneath him and stood beside his rider, stunned and disoriented after his harrowing slide down the wall of the canyon with nothing to break his fall but rough boulders.

Sloane could feel his pulse pounding in his ears as he forced Diablo to make his way around the jutting rocks. His tortured gaze anchored on Tara as he approached, praying she would rouse from her deathlike trance, that she would offer even the smallest sign of life, some dim hope that he hadn't lost her. But she lay facedown, sprawled on the jagged rocks motionless.

His trembling hands folded about her waist as he sank down beside her to draw her limp body to his, cradling her in his arms, soothing her as he would a small child who had endured a frightening nightmare. But this was one terrifying dream from which this sleeping beauty would never wake, he thought in anguish, his heart twisting in two as he clung to the rag doll that lay in his shaking arms. Sloane whispered words of love, words he had delayed too long in speaking. Now it was too late, he thought miserably. Dragging his ghastly hood from his head, he laid his cheek against Tara's. It was too damned late, his tortured mind screamed. Now Tara would never know she had taken the sun and moon with her when she left him. She would never know how deeply he had loved her, cherished her as he had no other woman before her. She would never know how he had come to need her, how he had basked in the warmth of her radiant smiles. He had felt unmatched stirrings in his heart when he had lost himself to the precious memories of their nights together. Their lovemaking had created its own wild, unique design. The passion they had shared would never come again, except in his bittersweet dreams.

Groaning in agony, his massive body shuddered as another tidal wave of grief crashed upon him. Sloane clutched Tara's lifeless body to his and absently stroked the tendrils of spun silver and gold that spilled down her back. God, how could he go on without her when he could be no more than half a man? His broad shoulders shook as he buried his head against her breast, engulfed by such fierce, soul-shattering emotion that he could barely draw a breath without choking on it. The pain of losing Tara cut like a knife, leaving his wretched soul to bleed. The agony that filled his heart was almost more than he could bear. God, he couldn't believe, didn't *want* to believe he had lost the only love he had ever known. Dammit, it wasn't fair!

"Merrick, you ruthless bastard, I swear you will pay with your life," Sloane gritted out, giving way to the boiling tears that scalded his eyes.

Now Sloane fully understood the indescribable anguish his mother had endured when Vernon had been taken from her. He knew the feeling of deeply embedded bitterness that had poisoned Carmelle. Nothing could stop the frustrated anger, the twisting knot in the pit of his belly. The sensations wretched his bleeding soul and spilled through his entire being. Sloane could not fathom how he could survive this throbbing sense of loss. It was like dying inside, bit by excruciating bit, and being forced to go on living without a breath of hope.

The hauntingly disturbing emotions that churned inside him tested his sanity, stretching it until Sloane feared it would snap. Perhaps madness itself was all that would save him. Maybe he would go out of his mind and block the tormenting vision of Tara's fall from his memory. It would be a blessing, Sloane breathed in raspy spurts, clutching Tara to him as if he never meant to let go.

The dam of barely contained emotions finally burst. A wave of hot tears flooded his cheeks and fell upon Tara's ashen face. Sloane made no attempt to restrain the tormenting emotions. Maybe a man wasn't supposed to allow his inner feelings to show, but Sloane permitted it, just once in his life. Tara had taught him to be gentle enough to care, compassionate enough to feel the sting of loss that crumbled his composure when nothing else had.

Sobbing deliriously, Sloane eased back against the rocks and pulled Tara's limp body onto his lap. As he rocked her in the cradle of his arms, he combed his trembling fingers through her hair. "Tara, *mi alma,* how I loved you. . . ." Sloane tilted her death-white face to his. Slowly, he lowered his head to place his quivering lips over her unresponsive ones. As the tears rolled down his rugged face, he blessed Tara with one last kiss, offering her a breath of life, a life that no longer had meaning when he was forced to endure it without her.

And then a piercing cry of tormented rage and abject frustration burst from Sloane's chest. The pent-up emotions that sought to destroy him rang through the dark valley, stirring all within their path. His soul cried out to Tara's, leaving the earth to shudder, releasing a grief that was too much for any man to bear in quiet mourning.

An eerie silence clung to the mesa. Merrick stared at the bluff where he had forced Tara over the side and then watched in disbelief as the Night Rider and his silver-white stallion plunged over the edge without breaking stride. When the bellowing cry, as cold and frightening as a banshee's loud wailing, echoed around the rim of the canyon, Merrick flinched uncontrollably. A strange, haunting tingle skidded down his spine as the doleful cry wrapped itself around him and sent a rash of goose pimples creeping across his skin. It took grim determination to get himself in hand after what he had seen and heard. And he could not help but think that now there would be two phantoms following on his shadow.

Hard gray eyes swung to the man who fidgeted beside him. "Take the herd to Harrold," Merrick ordered abruptly. "The Diamond R ranch hands will trail behind you."

John had practically swallowed his tongue, and it had taken him several minutes to compose himself. His entire body shook as if he were suffering an attack of the spasms. He had agreed to help Merrick for a share of the profits, but he had never expected anything like this! God, he was cavorting with a madman who would stoop to murder without giving it a moment's consideration.

"But what about the Winslow girl?" he chirped, like a sick prairie chicken. "What are you going to . . ."

"I have already made it known that she was accident prone," Merrick interrupted in a calm tone, too calm to reassure his wary conspirator. "Someone will find her body, and we can only assume that she wandered off during the night and took a fatal fall. There needn't be any other explanation."

"This is the last time I am taking your strays with my herd," John told him shakily. "I don't want any part in killing."

Cold chips of granite pierced John's peaked face. "You will do as I tell you, or *you* just might meet with an accident, my friend. I have come too far to be sold out by a squeamish coward."

John gulped hard as he backed his horse away and followed the herd toward his camp. No wonder Merrick was haunted by specters, he mused as he braved a glance toward the caprock, expecting at any moment to see the phantom float above the steep precipice to pursue the herd and the man who had proven himself capable of cold-blooded murder. John had once been skeptical about the existence of an apparition that kept a constant vigil on Palo Duro, but no more. What he had seen with his own eyes had convinced him. Mortal men did not appear from nowhere and then dive off canyon ledges, at least none he had ever met!

A demented smile pursed Merrick's lips as he watched Cal and Jesse drive the cattle across the mesa. The deed was done. He had disposed of Terrance Winslow's daughter. No one would step forward to accuse him of wrongdoing. After all, he had been asleep in his tent as far as all the rest of the cowhands knew. When Tara was discovered missing, he would aid in the search and grieve over the loss of his daughter's friend. And when Terrance came to headquarters ranting and raving, Merrick would have witnesses to swear that he could not possibly have been responsible. Terrance had no proof, nor would he ever have, he thought smugly. He always covered his tracks, Merrick reminded himself as he stared out over his canyon, *his* empire. He had built this kingdom with his own hands, and no one questioned his power. What he wanted was his for the taking, and nothing stood in his way. He was the cattle baron of Panhandle Texas, and those who dared to cross him never lived to relate their version of the incident.

Chapter 25

When Merrick heard the carriage rumbling toward headquarters he glanced up to see the mixture of fury and grief that rippled across Terrance Winslow's face. If looks could kill, Merrick would have been a dead man. Obviously, news had traveled fast and Terrance had gotten wind of the tragic incident on Mesquite Mesa.

Terrance could barely contain his emotions. He was like a keg of gunpowder burning on a short wick. When the news of Tara's death reached Clarendon, Terrance had been beside himself with grief and disbelief. It couldn't have happened, Terrance told himself over and over again during his ride to the Diamond R Ranch. But finally, the voice of reason reminded him that Merrick Russel was very capable of murder. Hadn't he disposed of his own brother because of greed? Hadn't he shot down Don Miguel in cold blood?

Gritting his teeth, Terrance had cursed himself a thousand times over for sending Tara into the jaws of hell to confront the devil himself. God, he had been such a fool for believing Merrick would never dare to harm Tara. He must have been out of his mind! Tears of grief misted his eyes and he choked on a wretched sob. Not Tara, his tortured mind screamed. Not his little girl!

These tragedies happened to other people and their families, not to him . . . not until now. Lord, how was he going to explain to Libby and Ryan? Terrance shuddered at the thought. He would be blamed for Tara's death, just as surely as if he had sent Tara plummeting over the rim of the canyon.

He would deal with Ryan and Libby later, Terrance told himself, gathering his crumbled composure. But for now he would deal with the ruthless, bloodthirsty bastard who had dared to take Tara's life. Terrance feared he would go mad before he could reach headquarters to confront Merrick. Never had he felt such a fierce, uncontrollable hatred for another man. His soul would surely burn in hell for the vengeful thoughts that were whipping through his mind. But it would be worth it, Terrance told himself, fighting back the sea of tears that threatened to flood over him.

Terrance had come with pistol in hand, prepared to avenge the terrible injustice. His purpose did not include allowing Merrick to explain Tara's *accidental* death. He knew it had been no accident, and no amount of talking could change his mind.

When Terrance stepped from his carriage with a pistol aimed at Merrick's chest, the color drained from Burns Dixon's face. Moving faster than he ever had in his life, Burns darted in front of Terrance, blocking his path.

"Get the hell out of my way," Terrance hissed. "Russel isn't going to get away with another murder, not this time, not my daughter's. I have come to do what someone should have done years ago."

Warily, Merrick backed away. He had expected Terrance's arrival, but he had not anticipated anything like this! Terrance had never been a violent man, and he rarely carried a pistol, even for his own protection. But now he was armed, and he looked blatantly dangerous. His face was skewed up in a cold, murderous stare, and his eyes rivaled a diamond's for hardness. And there was a hint of madness in his features, an expression of daring recklessness that spelled trouble.

"It was an accident," Merrick blurted out as Burns fought to contain Terrance. "I was nowhere near your daughter the night she perished. I didn't know she was dead until Sloane brought her body into camp. I swear it, Terrance."

"Lies. All lies!" Terrance screamed, attempting to push past Burns, who refused to budge an inch. "You murdering bastard! Did Tara recognize you as Don Miguel's murderer? Is that why you disposed of her? You'll pay for this, Russel, with no less than your own miserable life."

"Git a grip on yerself, Winslow," Burns snapped frantically, afraid Terrance would break loose and fire his revolver before anyone could stop him. "You don't stand a chance. Merrick will have his men gun you down."

Burns's hushed words gradually seeped into Terrance's haunted thoughts. His wild eyes swung to Burns's strained expression. "He killed my little girl." His voice cracked, his shoulders slumping as if the weight of the world had been dropped on his shoulders. It was all he could do to keep from crumbling in unrestrained grief.

"Facin' off against Russel ain't gonna do Tara no good," Burns insisted. "Believe me, Terrance, I know what yer feelin'. I've been there before. But this ain't the way to solve it." His narrowed gaze slid over his shoulder to see the tense look on Merrick's face, the dangerous way his hand hovered beside the revolver that hung on his hip. "Come pay yer respects to Tara. Her body lies in state in the parlor. You ain't thinkin' clear right now, Terrance. Come with me. . . ." Carefully, Burns eased the pistol from Terrance's trembling hand and propelled him toward the house. When Terrance allowed himself to be led peacefully, Burns breathed a relieved sigh. "This ain't the time for killin'. It's a time for grievin', just as Sloane is doin'. The two of you need each other right now."

When Burns and Terrance disappeared into the house,

Merrick relaxed, but only for a moment. His gaze circled the congregation of men. There was not one among them who seemed sympathetic toward his plight. Terrance's ravings had planted suspicion in their minds, and Merrick found himself wondering if any of the hired hands would have come to his rescue.

After several minutes Burns and Terrance emerged from headquarters. Like a tiger stalking its prey, Terrance closed the distance between them, still glaring murderously at Merrick.

"You haven't seen the last of me, Russel," Terrance assured him in a deadly hiss. "I would have killed you. But Burns was right. This is the time for grieving my loss. But mark my words. Your time will come. And when it does, I will shed no tears for your passing."

"I have several men prepared to swear I was nowhere near the scene of the accident," Merrick insisted, his chin tilting to meet Terrance's condemning glare.

"Don't you always," Terrance snorted contemptuously before spinning on his heels and stalking toward the carriage.

Casting one last embittered glance in Merrick's direction, Terrance popped the reins over the horse's rump and thundered down the road in the direction he had come from. There was a time for all things, Terrance reminded himself. Clinging to that vindictive thought, Terrance rode toward Clarendon, knowing he would be back to watch Merrick's Camelot crumble about him like pieces of a shattered dream. Merrick had dared too much. He would pay. Justice would win out, even when confronted with a man as selfish and ruthless as Merrick Russel.

Dressed in a gown of black, Julia hesitantly approached the parlor, her footsteps heavy, her eyes red and swollen from crying a sea of mournful tears since the day Sloane had discovered Tara's mangled body on the jagged rocks of the canyon. He had returned to camp with Tara's broken body draped over his saddle and a blanket wrapped tightly about her to conceal her battered features. Half-crazed with grief, Sloane would allow no one near Tara, vowing that no one but he would be forced to see the results of her tragic, painful death. Like a bereaved man marching in funeral procession, Sloane had led Tara's horse and broken remains away from camp, informing Merrick that he alone would make the arrangements for burial.

Julia had been beside herself with grief, but Sloane's reaction to the accident greatly disturbed her. She had never seen him so bitter and withdrawn. Sloane had refused to leave Tara since the moment he had found her crumpled body on the rocks. Even after she had passed into the spiritual world, Sloane would not leave her alone. Like a guardian angel, he remained beside the rose-covered coffin while visitors filed into the room to pay their last respects to her. Julia's heart went out to Sloane, knowing he had never been able to profess his love for Tara before she died. And now, as if he were paying penance, Sloane lingered by the closed casket, grieving over his loss, harboring the love he had waited too long to claim.

Sloane was a changed man, and Julia seriously wondered if he would be the same again. He brooded and mourned, as if his prayers might still be answered. Julia couldn't blame him for being wretched with grief, but she feared his behavior would strip him of his sanity. It seemed he was intent on punishing himself, forcing himself to go on living long after the essence of his being had shriveled and died the day he found Tara's lifeless body.

Mustering her courage, Julia peered into the parlor, watching the dim candlelight cast dreary shadows on the slumped form of the man who sat beside the casket. Her

393

tear-rimmed eyes circled back to the tapered candles that had nearly burned themselves out, knowing Sloane would rise to replace them, refusing to leave Tara alone in the dark.

It was with great effort that Julia approached the brooding remnants of the man garbed in black. "Sloane, you really should rest," Julia murmured as she focused misty eyes on Sloane's chiseled features that had not changed expression for two long, agonizing days. "Why don't you go home for the night. There is nothing more you can do for . . ."

"I'm not leavin' her." His grim blue eyes swung to Julia momentarily and then shifted to the opposite wall, as if he were staring back through the window of time, captured by memories of that past that seemed to torture him as painfully as the tragedy he was forced to endure. "I'm never leavin' her again," he said brokenly. "If I had found her that night I went lookin' for her, this wouldn't have happened."

"Sloane, listen to me," Julia begged as she knelt before him, forcing him to meet her pleading gaze. "Tara wouldn't have wanted you to grieve so. She would have wanted you to remember the good times you spent together and to go on with your life, to cherish the sweet memories, not allow them to destroy you."

"I have no life without her," Sloane ground out bitterly. "And I will stay with her until the end. It is the least I can do . . . all I can do."

"I will keep the candles burning while you return to your cabin and tomorrow you can . . ." Julia tried to offer.

"No," Sloane growled gruffly. "There will be no tomorrow. There is only darkness now that she's gone and *I . . . am . . . not . . . leavin' . . . her!*"

His tone was so harsh and grating that Julia winced and then heaved a defeated sigh as she rose to full stature. It broke her heart to see such a strong, stable man so overwrought with grief, but it was apparent that his ill-fated love had made him tremendously vulnerable. He intended to torture himself because he had not been allowed to show his love, a love Julia was certain could come only once in a lifetime for a man like Sloane who had always kept to himself and never allowed anyone to become truly close to him, not the way Tara had. She had worked miracles with this rough-edged cowboy, who had never shown emotion until she had walked into his life and brought him a warmth and happiness he had never experienced, would never enjoy again.

"Can I bring you something to eat or drink . . . anything?" Julia questioned, slanting him a rueful smile, the best she could muster at the moment.

"No, nothin' . . . thanks." Sloane sighed as he massaged the tense muscles in the back of his neck. "I just want to be alone. . . ." He jerked his head up, his eyes narrowing mutinously on Merrick, who lingered by the door.

For a brief moment their gazes locked, Sloane's burning a hot blue flame, Merrick's cold and controlled. Sloane could feel his body going rigid with barely contained fury. God, how he loathed the sight of this murderer, a man without a conscience, a man who had built his empire with blood. How could Merrick stand there so calm and collected before the casket, knowing it was his own hand that had sent Tara plunging into the jaws of the canyon? Because he had killed and killed again, uncaring that he had made human sacrifices to keep the land and title he had claimed, Sloane thought bitterly.

Silence hung like a partition between the two men, a tension so thick it could have been sliced with a knife. Merrick had learned, too late, of Sloane's affection for Tara. Since they had returned to headquarters, Sloane had been distant and remote, his occasional glances hostile and accusing. Merrick knew Sloane held him responsible. But he reminded himself that Sloane was overwhelmed with grief and that he hated the world and everyone in it at the moment. He was blaming everyone for Tara's death.

"Will you join us for supper?" Merrick questioned quietly.

"No."

Sloane's gruff voice made Julia jump as if she had been stung. Her eyes darted back and forth between the two men, sensing Sloane's odious regard for her father, who had always lacked compassion. But then, her father had never been a sentimental man. Nothing seemed to touch him, just as nothing had touched Sloane until Tara was taken from him. She had considered Merrick and Sloane to be much alike, except that Sloane was now capable of deep feeling. Tara had taught him that. She had changed him, stirring him as no other woman had.

"Then we will leave you alone to grieve," Merrick whispered as he gestured for Julia to follow him.

When the door closed behind them and their footsteps faded in the hall, Sloane stood up. He strode over to bolt the double doors that had been flung open wide for Terrance and the procession of ranch hands who had left the herd to pay their last respects before rejoining the drive to Harrold. Then he walked over to replace the dwindling candles in the gold candelabrum in the distant corner of the parlor. His tasks completed, Sloane sank back into his high-backed chair and leaned over the casket. His long tanned fingers brushed over the huge wreath that was adorned with dozens of colorful roses and greenery that he had woven with loving memories.

"Comfortable, *mi vida?*" he whispered ever so softly.

"Actually, it's a bit stuffy in here," came the hushed reply. "Move the roses away from the air holes. The sweet aroma is strangling me."

The first smile anyone had seen on Sloane's frozen features in days broke his sober countenance and he laughed out loud. "That is a rather odd remark for a dead woman to make," he mocked lightly.

"How would you like to spend the day staring at the walls of this pine box and listening to your friends speak of you as if you were no longer among them?" Tara sniffed distastefully and then sneezed when the strong scent of the roses overwhelmed her.

"This was all your crazy idea," Sloane reminded her flippantly. Jerking up his head, his eyes flew around the room. If anyone barged into the parlor, he would swear Sloane was *crazy* for carrying on a conversation with a coffin. Assured that he had not been overheard, Sloane glared at the pine box. "You were the one who dreamed up this insane notion. I would have handled this in an entirely different manner."

"You would have cut Merrick to pieces without waiting for a confession," she insisted as she squirmed to find a more comfortable position in her narrow cubicle. "Then we still wouldn't know for certain that Merrick was responsible for Vernon's death. I have given the matter careful consideration, and this seems the most effective method of dragging the truth out into the open."

Sloane heaved an exasperated sigh. Tara was right, and he knew it. If she had permitted it, he would have ridden back into camp that very night and torn Merrick into bite-sized pieces with his bare hands.

"Open the lid," Tara requested. "I'm beginning to develop a severe case of coffin fever."

After setting the extravagant wreath of flowers aside, Sloane lifted the creaking lid to meet Tara's impish grin.

"That was a touching scene between you and Julia. *'I have no life without her? There cannot be a tomorrow?'*" Tara mimicked in a melodramatic voice as she sat upright and impatiently waited for Sloane to lift her from her temporary resting place. "For a moment, I actually thought you cared."

A wry smile skipped across Sloane's lips as he scooped her up and set her on her feet. "You told me to sound convincing," he reminded her glibly.

A curious gleam flickered in her eyes as she surveyed the handsome raven-haired rogue who towered over her. He had treated her differently since the moment she had roused from her near brush with death. He had been fetching and heeling like a lackey attending a queen. No doubt, the shock of thinking she had perished had rattled him, and he had not fully recovered from the incident.

Tara wasn't certain how she *had* managed to survive the terrifying fall, but she credited her steed with saving the both of them. If the horse hadn't found his footing in the nick of time, they both would have plummeted all the way to the floor of the canyon. But the gelding had miraculously kept his balance, and Tara had clung to him like an extra set of skin until he had collided with the boulder on the ledge, finally stopping his downward motion. But then she had been jolted loose when the horse came to a screeching halt, and the jagged boulder had come at her at incredible speed, knocking her senseless.

She had climbed back to reality, rousing to find herself in Sloane's protective arms. When her eyes fluttered open, she wasn't certain which of them was more surprised to see she was alive. Tara could have sworn she had seen a misty haze in his eyes, and even now she couldn't help but wonder if Sloane truly did feel something for her. He had been so relieved to find she had survived that he immediately set about to inspect her bruises and scrapes, many of which still discomforted her.

Once he had assured himself that she had suffered no internal injuries that might have been aggravated by movement, he had pulled her up beside him and vowed to storm back to camp, giving Merrick what he deserved—a bullet in his hard heart. But Tara had convinced him that she was the one who deserved to have revenge on Merrick and that she intended to handle him in her own way. Reluctantly Sloane had consented, and they had set about to plan Merrick's downfall, one that would begin as soon as her father arrived with the sheriff in tow.

When Sloane bent to press a light kiss to her lips, Tara melted in his powerful arms. It was his image that had floated about her as she struggled against impossible odds, she reminded herself as she surrendered to his potent embrace. The thought of never sharing his kiss or enjoying his skillful caress again had kept her clinging to the saddle, even when she doubted she would live to see another sunrise. But she had, and Sloane had been waiting on her hand and foot, carrying out her wishes to set the trap for Merrick.

"Come," Sloane whispered as he dragged his lips from her soft, responsive mouth. "Burns has prepared something special for us."

"Phantom stew?" Tara teased as she followed Sloane out the window.

"Your wit has been dulled by your prolonged stay in yonder box," Sloane smirked as he lifted the windowpane and then agilely contorted his body to slide to the ground.

Tara frowned thoughtfully as she watched Sloane slip outside. Before the attempted murder, she had been determined to confide the truth about the past to Sloane when Burns had refused to enlighten him. But now she was beginning to understand why Burns had harbored the secret these past years. Perhaps Burns had been right after all. Perhaps what Sloane didn't know was better left alone.

"Are you coming?" Sloane whispered impatiently, dragging Tara from her thoughtful contemplations.

Tara nodded mutely and then eased her bruised hip onto the windowsill, grimacing when she put weight on another sensitive spot.

"Still a mite tender?" Sloane questioned as he carefully lifted her into his arms and then strode swiftly toward the back of the house.

"Every bone and muscle screams in pain when I move," Tara confided.

Her reminder made Sloane ease his grasp for fear of causing her further distress. Although he had been stung by the fierce desire to make wild love to this she-cat who seemed to have been blessed with nine lives, he had refrained. He ached to clutch her to him, to lose himself in her silky arms and ease the tormenting thoughts that had plagued him as he rode down the steep, treacherous incline of Palo Duro. But after finding her so bruised and battered, Sloane had restrained himself. The time would come when he could prove his love and openly confess it, *after* Tara had frightened Merrick within an inch of his life, as miserable and rotten as it was.

When Tara had informed Sloane that she had heard stories of train robbers stuffing themselves in coffins to be carried onto the railroad and that she planned to employ the technique of rising from the dead to scare the wits and the confession from Merrick, Sloane had stared at her as if she were addle-witted. He was sure the fall had scrambled her brain. But no amount of argument had dissuaded Tara from her scheme. After giving the idea careful consideration, Sloane had agreed the shock of seeing another ghost rise from the casket might be the one and only way to rattle a man as cold and callous as the boss of the Diamond R Ranch.

After they had returned to headquarters, Sloane had attempted to send a message to Terrance informing him of their plans. But the rumors were already buzzing around Clarendon. Terrance had come like an avenging god, prepared to drop Merrick in his tracks. Thankfully, Burns had intercepted him and guided him into the parlor to allow Sloane and Tara to explain what they had in mind for Merrick. Terrance had been greatly relieved

400

that his worst fears had not materialized before his eyes. His appearance had been a convincing one, Sloane mused. Terrance had been raving like a madman, assuring Merrick that he too believed Tara had perished from the fall.

After giving his not-so-dead daughter a loving squeeze, Terrance had followed Sloane's request to meet the sheriff before he arrived from Clarendon. They were to return at the appointed time to witness the eerie confrontation when Tara and Sloane planned to outfox the fox. But even as the pieces of the scheme fell into place, Sloane still had difficulty overcoming his apprehension. They were dealing with a man who was capable of murder, one who rarely cracked under pressure. Merrick had stopped at nothing to build his vast cattle empire, and Sloane gave him full credit for being as cold and hard as granite. But the devil's luck had finally been depleted, Sloane reassured himself, determined to believe it. Merrick wouldn't walk away proclaiming his innocence this time. He was a doomed man, and his hours were numbered.

"Is something troubling you?" Tara queried, leaning back to peer into Sloane's rugged face as he carried her around the corral and aimed himself toward the back of the mess-house.

"I wish this night were over," Sloane said, and then glanced down into Tara's bruised, but bewitching features, mesmerized by the way the moonlight kissed her satiny cheeks. His thoughtful frown mellowed into a rakish smile. "And then I would like to have you alone until dawn."

Her perfectly arched brow raised acutely and then slid back to its normal position. "And what would we do, dark phantom, thunder around the caprock howling like banshees?" she teased, hoping that was not at all the case and that his straying thoughts were following the same track hers had taken, detouring in a most arousing direction.

His smile broadened in roguish anticipation, revealing even white teeth. "I think I'll let you endure the suspense of wondering what I have in mind for you, *mi alma*," he said with a wink as he deposited her behind a sprawling cedar tree and then spun on his heels to fetch their meal.

Tara inhaled a breath of fresh air to rid her senses of the sticky-sweet smell of roses. Soon Merrick would be exposed as the fraud and conniving scoundrel he was and, hopefully, Sloane would know the answer to the question that had long tormented him. A troubled frown knitted Tara's brow. She prayed Sloane would be considerate of Julia. This night could prove devastating for her. Tara hated deceiving Julia, but under the circumstances, there was simply no other way to entrap Merrick. Julia would be caught in the middle, and there was nothing Tara could do to prevent it. Julia didn't really know her father, and when she learned the bitter truth it would come as a terrible blow, one Julia might have refused to believe if she were not allowed to hear the proof.

When Sloane strode back to her, balancing the tray and a satchel under one arm, Tara relieved him of the delicious-smelling stew and then sank into the grass to enjoy their feast.

"Mmmm . . . Burns has outdone himself. Remind me to compliment him," she said absently as she lifted the lid from the steaming porridge and let the appetizing aroma invade her rose-clogged senses.

"Thank you," Burns murmured as he stepped around the cedar tree to flash her a grin. "Yer lookin' well for a lady in yer condition," he snickered as he drew a heaping basket of sourdough biscuits from behind his back and squatted down to offer Tara one. "I don't believe I've ever seen a livelier corpse. Merrick ain't goin' to trust his eyes when he sees you starin' back at him."

"I only hope the shock works like a truth serum," Tara murmured before biting into the warm biscuit.

"Don't forget to send Diablo on his run after Terrance and the sheriff arrive," Sloane instructed Burns. "We intend to give Merrick the full effect of haunting spirits converging on him."

"I won't forgit," Burns grunted as he struggled to his feet. "You've reminded me ten times already."

As he waddled away, Sloane folded his tall, brawny frame beside Tara, reminding her of a jungle cat crouching to rest. Tara could not disguise the expression of love in her eyes. The emotions were close to overflowing, but she reminded herself this was not the time to become distracted. She needed to concentrate on her task. When she confronted Merrick she needed to be in full command of her senses. Although she loathed Merrick Russel, she also respected his craftiness. It would never do to live with the false security that one could snare that clever weasel and keep him trapped indefinitely. Anything could happen, and she had to be prepared. She and Sloane would have the element of surprise on their side, and Tara prayed it would give them an advantageous edge.

Tara and Sloane ate in silence, each one grappling with their apprehensive thoughts. When they had finished their meal, Sloane set the tray aside and leaned over Tara, forcing her back to the plush grass carpet.

"Don't try anything reckless," Sloane cautioned as he cupped her bruised chin in his hand, demanding that she meet his somber gaze. "You have already taken far too many risks as it is. There is no way of knowing what Merrick might do, and if he resorts to violence, climb out the window. Terrance and the sheriff will be there waiting."

"I intend to be careful," Tara assured him as she brushed her fingertip over the dainty gold locket that hung about her neck and then blessed Sloane with a confident smile. "And you will be there. . . ."

"I wouldn't allow you to follow through with this crazed scheme if I weren't," he insisted. "Merrick is too unpredictable when he completely loses his temper." His sensuous lips feathered over hers, giving her strength, bolstering her courage. "Just don't play the martyr." He nibbled at the corner of her mouth, loving the taste of cherry wine in her eager kiss. "I endured nine kinds of hell that night on the mesa, and I'm not certain my pounding heart could survive another fright as devastating as my last experience. I would prefer to have you alive than to hear Merrick's confession."

His kiss deepened, the pressure of his mouth becoming more demanding. His fingers delved into the cascade of silver-gold and then curled behind her neck, tilting her face to his devouring embrace. Tara could only respond as the floodgates of passion opened and all the pent-up emotions threatened to burst loose like a raging river. She could feel herself letting go of reality as his roving hand traveled over each curve and swell of her body, sensitizing her nerves, leaving her craving far more than a kiss and caress.

Suddenly, Sloane jerked back and scowled to himself. What the hell was he doing? Tara was still bruised and tender from her fall, and they had several matters to attend to before Terrance arrived. And here he was, sprawled in the grass like a love-starved idiot who had no other care in the world.

"Come on," Sloane growled as he hopped to his feet and carefully drew Tara up beside him. "First things first."

A sly smile pursed her lips as she allowed Sloane to lead her through the darkness. He *had* been thinking what she was thinking, Tara thought delightedly. He wanted her, and a midnight ride around the canyon would be the farthest thing from his mind when they had completed their task.

Chapter 26

After Sloane drew the pasty concoction from his satchel and brushed it on Tara's face, working meticulously to give her a pale, chalky appearance with just the right amount of ghoulish shadows around her eyes and mouth, he drew a white gossamer robe from the bag and offered it to her.

Tara peeled off her plain cotton gown, much to Sloane's delight, and then stepped into the white silk chemise with its outer covering of transparent muslin. The sheer fabric flowed down her arms and hips, giving her a shapeless appearance. When she moved, the gossamer cloth fluttered about her, billowing slightly in the gentle whisper of wind that flooded through the open window.

Sloane stepped back to survey the transformation in the pale candlelight and then nodded approvingly.

"Well, how do I look?" Tara demanded as she raised her arms as if she were casting a devilish spell and then pirouetted on tiptoe, allowing him to view his creation from all angles.

"Positively dreadful," Sloane assured her with a wry smile. "If I didn't know you were mortal I would be quaking in my boots."

"Why, thank you, sir," Tara drawled as she retrieved Sloane's garb from the pouch and tossed it to him. "We

405

will make a ghastly pair. Merrick will find himself surrounded with phantoms and specters, more than he cares to count."

"But he will count them, one by one," Sloane murmured as he dragged the hood over his face and then pulled on the incandescent poncho that distorted his muscular physique and made him look less human.

Scooping up their discarded garments, Sloane stashed them in the pouch and then snuffed out all but one candle before moving silently to the door to leave it standing ajar.

Soon Merrick would adjourn to his study, as he did every night after he had taken his meal, Sloane calculated as he strode back to Tara. Only a few ranch hands remained at headquarters. The rest had returned to the trail, grumbling about Burns turning his chuckwagon over to an inexperienced cowboy who had offered to try his hand at the culinary art.

No doubt, this was the first cattle drive Merrick had missed in all his thirty years at Palo Duro. But for appearances' sake, he had sacrificed the journey to play the role of the bereaved host, Sloane thought bitterly.

After Sloane and Tara had positioned themselves behind the thick drapes that hung on either side of the window, they waited several impatient minutes before they heard the rustling below them. Tara poked her head around the drapes to see her father, Burns, and the sheriff crouching beneath them.

Terrance jerked back when he spied the hideous figure looming above him. He gasped for breath and clutched at his chest to keep his heart from leaping out, and it took a moment to compose himself after he came face to face with the startling wraith.

"My God, child. You'll scare Merrick to death before he can utter a word," Terrance croaked.

A mischievous grin stretched across Tara's deathly

pale lips when she viewed the three men's reactions. She was reasonably assured she would have at least the same dramatic effect on Merrick.

Before Tara could respond to her father's comment, she heard Diablo's shrill whinny echo through the canyon, and she stepped back into concealment, awaiting the moment Merrick would enter the room to meet his Waterloo.

The sound of hooves pounding the ground caused Merrick to bolt from his chair. He squinted in the darkness, frowning warily as the silver-white stallion galloped around the corrals and then darted past the mansion . . . without his phantom rider. The sight had an unsettling effect on Merrick, as if the riderless steed carried some ghastly message. Never once had he seen the stallion without the apparition floating on his back, and it seemed odd that on this night of all nights the specter would not come by means of his white charger.

The frown carved deep lines in his face when he heard the crash in the parlor. Instinctively, Merrick moved toward the sound as the stallion's hoofbeats melted into silence and the mansion became deathly quiet.

Merrick's wide eyes flew to the open window, watching the drapes billow in the cool breeze that rushed into the room bringing with it the chill of death. Nonsense, Merrick scolded himself as he shrugged off the eerie sensation and pulled a tight rein on his superstitious thoughts. His leery gaze swung to the candelabrum that sat in the far corner. Only one long, tapering candle cast its flickering light on the casket that stood in the middle of the room. Odd, he mused. Sloane had never allowed the candles to burn out, but tonight only one dim flame lingered in the silent room, and Sloane's chair sat empty for the first time in two days . . . except for the bandanna

407

he had tied over Tara's mouth and the rope he had used to bind her hands.

A feeling of dread settled on Merrick's shoulders as he lingered at the door and then staggered back when a corpselike specter materialized from the shadows and the scent of roses drifted toward him in the evening breeze. Merrick's face whitewashed when he spied the gold locket that hung around Tara's pale neck, and he found himself frozen to the spot. He couldn't breathe. He couldn't move. He could only stare aghast, his eyes popping as the apparition floated closer to take its place behind the rose-draped coffin.

"The time of atonement has come." Tara's low, throaty voice made Merrick's hair stand on end.

He was seeing and hearing things! Merrick assured himself, but he didn't believe it. He had been hounded by his brother's ghost and a legend that wouldn't die for a score and ten years. Why should he doubt this disembodied spirit? Tara had vowed to return to haunt him, and now she had!

One pale hand folded around the heart-shaped locket that brought a sea of forbidden memories flooding over Merrick, causing Merrick to sway as if he had been knocked about by a tidal wave. A fiendish smile rippled across Tara's lips as Merrick gripped the door facing to keep his balance.

"Did you think to escape your brother's curse, Merrick?" Her whispering voice rang with intimidating accusation. "He awaits you. He has sent his silver steed to bear your damnable soul."

"No!" Merrick shrieked, his heart thudding against his ribs as if it meant to beat him to death, fulfilling the apparition's prophecy.

"You must pay for your brother's murder, just as you must serve your eternal sentence for mine, Merrick," Tara insisted, her voice deadly calm as she dragged out

408

the words in a chanting monotone. "Was it worth this agonizing end that awaits your sinful soul? Your brother's restless spirit has kept constant vigil on this canyon, waiting to claim retribution, just as you took his life with your hands."

"He would have destroyed the dream," Merrick frantically protested as Tara waved her arms, murmuring incantations like a spell-casting witch. "He had to be sacrificed. He stood between all I ever wanted, the ranch, Carmelle. . . ."

"But she would not have you, knowing you had taken your own brother's life, the man she loved, the man you despised because he was everything you could never be. . . ." Tara opened the locket, holding it before him to reveal the faded photograph. "You felt no regret, did you? He was your own flesh and blood, and still you killed him."

"I couldn't let him split the herd," Merrick blurted out as he retreated another step from the haunting specter. "And he wouldn't listen to reason."

"So you started the stampede and cast the blame elsewhere," Tara finished for him. "But the fault lies with you, and you bear the mark of a murderer. I can see the guilt in your eyes. You have killed not once but thrice to protect your secret. Your guilt led you to Don Miguel, but the locket and its forbidden truth eluded you."

"Chavez intended to dig up the past." The words tumbled off his tongue as the Night Rider emerged with another cold breath of wind, his phosphoric cape glowing in the flickering light. "He would have destroyed all I had built in this vast wilderness. I had to protect myself."

"But who will protect you from me?" Sloane's muffled voice rumbled in the uneasy silence. "Carmelle made me promise to drag the truth from your lips, but even that is not enough. . . ." He yanked the ghastly hood from his head to glare murderously at Merrick, who would have wilted on the floor if he hadn't grabbed the back of a nearby chair for support. "May you burn in eternal hell!" Sloane growled vindictively.

Merrick had been struck by one devastating blow after another and he was in a state of shock. His gray eyes were as round as saucers, his jaw sagging from its hinges as he stared at Sloane.

Tara gasped when Sloane cocked the hammer of his revolver and drew back his poncho to aim the weapon at Merrick's heaving chest. "No!" she pleaded with him. "You can't kill him."

His piercing blue eyes never left Merrick's peaked face. "Can't I?" There was deadly venom dripping in his voice. "He killed my father and my grandfather. And this miserable bastard tried to kill you. He made Carmelle's life a living hell," he gritted out between clenched teeth. "Killing is too good for him, but I have no other means of retribution at my disposal."

Sloane's words devastated Merrick, and what little color remained in his weather-beaten features immediately waned. "Carmelle's son?" he choked out, his heart hammering so furiously that he could barely draw enough breath to speak.

"Vernon Russel's bastard son," Sloane sneered disdainfully. "I couldn't even claim my rightful name. You stripped me of that privilege, as well as the right to know my own father. It should have been you who perished in that stampede, not him."

"Sloane, no!" Tara screamed at him as he raised a steady arm and took careful aim at Merrick's pounding heart.

There was only one thing that would stop him, Tara thought frantically. The secret Burns had spared him would daze him momentarily, before he could put a bullet in the man who had been as cold and ruthless as the devil himself.

"Carmelle led you to believe Vernon was your father. But it was a lie," Tara hastily told him. "Vernon was your uncle, Sloane. Merrick is your father. You can't kill your own father!"

Sloane froze, his head swiveling to Tara, his eyes wide with disbelief. "No." He couldn't believe it, didn't want to believe it.

"Tell him, Merrick," Tara insisted, her narrowed gaze nailing Merrick back against the wall. "Tell him what happened when you went back to the mission at Valquez."

"I wanted to marry Carmelle, but she wouldn't have me," Merrick blurted out, revealing the truth he had harbored for over thirty years. "I was the first man she had known. At least he couldn't take that away from me."

"Oh my God!" Julia gasped. She had heard the crash and had come to investigate. After learning the bitter truth, she pulled herself together and then stepped around the corner, her face as pale as Tara's after Sloane had smeared the pasty concoction on it.

Merrick's shocked gaze swung from his tormented daughter to his illegitimate son. The instinct to flee overwhelmed him, and he spun on his heels to bolt through the door, practicallly knocking Julia off balance in his effort to escape the harsh, accusing glares that were directed at him. When he dashed onto the porch, his wild, hunted eyes landed on Terrance, Burns, and the sheriff, who had stepped around the corner of the mansion to block his path. He was trapped! Everyone knew the truth! His world was crumbling down around him like an avalanche!

"You're through, Russel." Terrance glared at the despicable man who had brought grief wherever he had gone. "The Diamond R Ranch is no longer yours. Your investors are calling in the loan, and we will find someone more honest and capable of running this ranch while you

411

are rotting away in prison."

Merrick glanced behind him, seeing the hurt and dis-
illusionment in Julia's eyes, the hatred and disgust in
Sloane's. The child of the only woman he had ever loved
loathed the sight of him. Carmelle had spit in his face and
vowed revenge when he had forced himself on her.
Carmelle—the raven-haired beauty who had returned
years later with the promise that one day he would be
punished for his unforgivable sins—had seen to it that
his dream was shattered into a thousand pieces. Merrick
was devastated, stunned, disoriented. The shocking
events of the evening had riddled his senses, and no
matter what direction he faced, haunting specters from
the past rose to haunt him.

Blinded by the tormenting visions, Merrick flew down
the steps toward the moon-eyed stallion and vaulted into
the saddle, intent on running for his life. He gouged his
boot heels into Diablo's flanks, but the steed knew only
one man as master and he fiercely objected to the
commands of the man who had dared to mount him.

Cursing the contrary steed, Merrick slapped Diablo on
the rump, sending him charging up the winding path that
led to the caprock of Palo Duro, but Sloane's sharp
whistle brought the steed to an abrupt halt. Merrick
scowled as he jerked on the steed's reins, forcing him to
continue along the winding slope or have his head twisted
against his back. Merrick's frantic gaze flew over his
shoulder to see Sloane in fast pursuit, and he kicked
Diablo in the ribs, demanding that he move.

The battle between man and beast became one of raw
wills when Sloane whistled again and Merrick struck the
white stallion on the side of the head in sheer des-
peration. Diablo reared, screaming like a panther in
the night as he pranced on the precarious ledge, determined to answer his master's call.

Merrick's terrified voice rang through the canyon as

he was thrown from the precipice and plunged down the vertical wall where there was nothing to break his fall. The path he had chosen in his haste to escape had been too steep and treacherous, and now there was nothing to spare him from the inevitable.

He had held nothing sacred and had seen no sacrifice too great as a means to his end, and the magnificent canyon he had claimed as his own had, at last, claimed him in final payment for his inexcusable crimes.

And then a deafening silence hovered inside the pastel-colored walls of Palo Duro, a silence finally broken by Julia's heart-wrenching sobs. She clung to Tara, shedding tears for the man she had called her father, a man she had never really known, a man driven by such greed and desire for power that he could find no place in his heart for love, except for the obsession for the one woman he couldn't have.

When Sloane walked his horse back to the quiet group and dismounted, Julia flew into his arms. "I'm so sorry. . . ."

While brother and sister clung together, Sloane's remorseful eyes lifted to stare at Tara, watching the unrestrained tears trickling down her pallid cheeks. Words wouldn't come. They were lodged behind the lump in Sloane's throat, Julia was the only family he had left, the sister he had never realized existed, born of a man Sloane had spent his entire life loathing and plotting to destroy. It took several minutes to come to grips with the chain of events that had led him to the truth, but there was still a rash of unanswered questions that tormented Sloane.

"Yer ma made me promise never to tell you who yer real father was until you had made him pay for Vernon's death," Burns explained solemnly. "I was there the night Merrick took Carmelle from the mission and forced himself on her. He was tryin' to convince her to become

413

his wife, promisin' her riches beyond her wildest imagination. Carmelle was no match for him, and she hated Merrick for what he'd done. She was too bitter to love again, and when she learned she would bear a child, she swore it would be her son who wrote the final chapter of her ill-fated love for Vernon and his brother who had taken destiny into his own hands." Burns paused to stroke the white stallion's muscular neck and then stared in Tara's direction, offering her the explanation he had refused to give her when she had prodded him. "Carmelle came to the ranch years later . . . after Merrick's wife had died. Sarah was a good woman, but she had never been able to make Merrick happy because he still wanted the one woman he could never have. Carmelle tried to force Merrick to admit he was responsible for Vernon's death, but he wouldn't admit nothin', and he tried to persuade her to stay with him, promisin' to compensate for her years of loneliness, and for his. But Carmelle would have no part of him, and she swore she would never let Vernon's memory die. She vowed the day was comin' when Merrick would pay for his crimes. To her, it only seemed fittin' for Sloane to destroy his own father and avenge the bitterness and hatred she'd harbored for Merrick." Burns heaved a heavy sigh as his solemn gaze swung back to Sloane. "Forgive her, Sloane. She loved Vernon and she never got over losin' him. Merrick spoiled every chance she had for happiness, and she was determined to see him pay. She made me promise to keep the legend alive and never to let Merrick forgit his brother. There wasn't one cowboy who passed through here who didn't know the rumors that surrounded the phantom of Palo Duro and how the specter came to be. That's why I stayed on with Merrick, to please Carmelle. She made me swear it would be her son, a man who grew up without his rightful name, who claimed her revenge once she had gone to join Vernon. I loved

Carmelle too much not to do her bidding. We all loved her, but it was Vernon she wanted." Burns dropped his head and then spared Julia a quick glance. "I'm sorry, child. It didn't seem right that you should be caught in the middle of this lifelong feud, but fate ain't always fair to its innocent victims. You and Tara was hurt by Merrick's ruthlessness. He was the keeper of dreams, ones so powerful that they finally consumed him," Burns murmured as he turned to lead the silver-white stallion to the corral.

As the somber congregation filed into the house, Sloane grasped Tara's hand to detain her. "Thank you," he whispered softly.

Tara frowned bemusedly. Why should he thank her for tearing his world to pieces? She would have allowed him to live with the lie, she thought dismally. All she had accomplished was making him more miserable when she had attempted to prevent him from murdering Merrick.

Sloane slanted her the faintest hint of a smile. "Thank you for stopping me before I lost my head. After what Merrick tried to do to you, I wanted him dead, by my own hand."

"I couldn't let you do it," Tara breathed tremulously as tears misted her eyes. "Like it or not, Merrick was your father. I hesitated in telling you what I had learned, but I couldn't stand by and watch you shoot him." Trembling fingers unclasped the locket and lifted the photograph from its resting place. "Your mother left you a message on the back of the picture."

God forgive the lie. I would have given the world if you could have been Vernon's child instead of Merrick's.

Sloane read his mother's handwriting and then sighed heavily at the bitter irony of the truth. While he stood

415

lost in thought, Tara turned away, deciding it best to leave him alone for a few minutes.

"The sheriff asked me to ride to Harrold with him to retrieve the herd Merrick filtered into Simpson's cattle. When I come back, you and I are going to have a long, private conversation," he assured her softly.

Tara's heart leaped in anticipation. There was so much she wanted to say to Sloane, to bring all truths into the open. Emotion clouded her vision as he strode toward her, lingering below her on the steps so that, for once, she could look straight into those fathomless pools of blue. And then, without a word, his mouth slanted over hers in a strangely tender kiss, one that offered the gentleness Tara had once demanded of him. But now it wasn't enough. She craved the taste of fire and longed to be consumed by the flames. It had been an eternity since she had slept in his protective arms, and she hungered for the passion she found in this man's caress.

How could she endure the week without him when one day was much too long to survive without the feel of his sinewy arms pressing her to the hard, masculine contours of his body? Tara ached to profess her love, to run with him into the darkness and prove to him that he held the key to her heart and soul. They had suffered through hell together, and she yearned to explore the boundless horizon of heaven in the unending circle of his arms.

"I'll miss you," she whispered as he reluctantly released her and backed away.

His cobalt-blue eyes twinkled with amusement as he blessed her with one of those charismatic smiles that always melted her heart and left it dripping on her ribs. "Will you now, ma'am?" he drawled lazily. "I thought perhaps in a week's time a sophisticated lady like yerself might forget this backward cowboy ever existed."

His lighthearted tone and teasing smile were contagious, and Tara struck a pose on the stoop like a regal queen making her dramatic exit from court. "If I find that to be the case, humble knave, I shall count upon you to find the proper way to refresh my memory."

"Proper?" He pounced on her choice of words. "What I'm thinking could more aptly be described as risqué debauchery in some social circles, madam," he growled seductively.

"I am impressed with your fluent command of the language, sir, and I am intrigued by your suggestion." Tara slid him a provocative smile as she considered his masculine physique, leaving the bold implication that she liked what she saw and would not be opposed to seeing him in far less. "I will anticipate your return, and I can only hope it proves to be as stimulating as you suggest."

Sloane was pleasantly surprised by her remark and the seductive way she sauntered toward the door. Damn, he would have given most anything if he could have postponed the journey to Harrold, but he couldn't delay. Merrick's investors deserved to receive their fair share of the profits from the misplaced herd, and Cal Johnson and John Simpson had to be bound over for custody after their part in the swindle. Sloane had taken on the job and he was obligated to see it through to the end.

Reluctantly, Sloane ambled to the corral to retrieve the white stallion and join the sheriff. His gaze drifted back to the shapely silhouette at the door of the mansion and he cursed himself for not telling Tara how much he cared about her. Coward, he berated himself. Never once had he murmured those three words, and each time he attempted to speak them, they seemed to strangle him. He was only waiting until the time was right, he assured himself. Once this matter was settled, he and Tara could come to terms with their whirlwind marriage.

Would she accept him for what he was and be content

to remain by his side? She had said she wanted a true marriage or none at all, but never once had *she* said she loved *him*, he reminded himself, his confidence drooping a notch. Perhaps if she had professed to harbor some deep feeling for him, he would not have been so reluctant to blurt out *his* confession. He had never been quite certain where he stood with that high-spirited minx. At times he thought she cared about him, but sometimes she became so furious with him that he would have bet his best saddle she despised him.

Well, at least, he would have a week to formulate his thoughts and select some romantic setting for their private interlude, he told himself. He would make it impossible for her to refuse the marriage and his love. He would sweep her off her feet and portray the gentleman she wanted him to be. Clinging to that positive thought, Sloane followed the winding path to the caprock of Palo Duro and focused on the eastern horizon, whimsically wishing he were coming instead of going and that his white stallion would sprout a pair of wings to hasten his journey.

Chapter 27

Ryan O'Donnovan eased back in his seat, checked his timepiece, and then impatiently drummed his fingers on his knees. His gaze swept the flat plains of West Texas as he heaved an annoyed sigh. He had waited well over a month, expecting at any moment to see his lovely young granddaughter trudging meekly up the steps to apologize for her foolishness and beg his forgiveness for traipsing off to Texas. But to his dismay, he had heard not one word from Tara. After listening to Libby recite a list of a thousand catastrophes that might have befallen her, Ryan had decided to fetch Tara home, away from Terrance's influence. No doubt, she had demeaned herself by associating with that contrary father of hers, Ryan thought disgustedly. There was no telling what type of rehabilitation would be necessary after Tara had lived under the same roof with Terrance!

After adjusting his spectacles, Ryan peered over at the blond-haired man who had insisted on accompanying him on this uncomfortable journey. Joseph Rutherford sat staring out the stagecoach window, his thin hair whipping in the breeze. He looked out of place on the sprawling plains, Ryan mused as he squirmed to find a more comfortable position for his aging bones.

"I still cannot fathom why Tara would set out across this godforsaken country," Joseph sniffed distastefully as he flicked the dust from the ruffled cuff of his shirt. "We have a great many arrangements yet to make for the wedding, and by the time we return to civilization time will be short." His pale blue eyes swung to Ryan and his flaxen features puckered in a frown. "I fully intend to chastise her for being so inconsiderate."

"My granddaughter has always been a bit impetuous," Ryan said. "And her misguided loyalty toward her father has her chasing childish dreams. I suspect she intended to remain for the entire summer, only to defy me."

Joseph's frown carved deep lines in his face as he studied the gray-haired man who had been his father's business associate and was now his. "I'm counting upon you to be firm with her, Ryan. She has been gone far too long as it is. It annoys me to have my friends taunting me, insisting that her reasons for leaving St. Louis stemmed more from avoiding me than seeing her father. I will take no more ridicule." Joseph straightened his cravat and then glanced back out to view the wide-open spaces of Texas. "And I hope that investigator you hired has succeeded in exposing Russel. I'm beginning to think this cattle investment you and my father sank our money into is a losing proposition."

"I expect Mr. Prescott has the situation well in hand," Ryan assured him, slightly annoyed that Joseph had voiced nothing but complaints since they had boarded the train in St. Louis. "I would not have hired him if I didn't consider him capable." A sigh of relief tumbled from Ryan's lips when he spied the settlement of Clarendon on the western horizon. "Mr. Prescott may be rough around the edges, but he struck me as being a very persistent man." He gestured toward the first sign of human life they had seen in miles. "I hope we can find suitable accommodation in Saints' Roost, but I don't have high expectations for this backward encampment."

Joseph craned his neck to see the jagged silhouette of

Clarendon breaking the wide horizon and then grunted disdainfully. "Your detective does not impress me. After all, he has been pursuing this case for almost a year. For all we know, he may have given up his investigation long ago." He resettled himself on the seat, his nose wrinkling in dismal anticipation of arriving in another outpost on the edge of civilization. "I trust our stay in this dust bowl will be brief and fruitful. No doubt, Tara has been appalled by the lack of suitable companionship to be found in Clarendon."

A wry smile brimmed on the old man's lips. Tara would probably be so elated to see both of them that she would insist they return on the afternoon stage to Harrold. She might have endured the drudgery of Saints' Roost to spite him, but Ryan was reasonably confident she would voice no complaints about returning home where she belonged.

Clinging to that positive thought, Ryan fastened his green waistcoat and impatiently waited for the stage to come to a halt.

Tara wiped the perspiration from her brow and then began pounding her mallet on the wooden block as she sailed it across the type in her father's newspaper office. She had proofread her father's articles and intended to surprise him by having the paper prepared for print by the time he returned from the Diamond R Ranch. But no matter how many hours she labored, she could not put Sloane out of her mind. She kept remembering that warm, teasing smile that had played on his lips the night he had left for Harrold. The tender glow in his blue eyes when he had whispered good-bye lingered in her thoughts, even after a week. The mere thought of him brought her a sense of security and contentment, and Tara was prepared to swear that, in Sloane's case, absence made the heart grow fonder. She missed him terribly, and she thrived on the hope that he had been miserable without her, as well. How she longed to speak of her love and request the chance to give their marriage a sporting chance. But was it love or lust he felt for her? Tara sighed heavily as she locked the forms in the chases and struggled to carry her heavy armload to the printing press. Sloane was right, Tara mused as she set the chases in the bed of the hand press and snatched up a can of ink. They *were* going to have a long talk when he returned. Tara had to know where she stood with Sloane before she went stark raving mad.

The creak of the door stirred her from her silent reverie and she glanced up to see Ryan and Joseph approaching like an invading army. She half-collapsed against the printing press, the color gushing from her cheeks. Sweet merciful heavens! The last person she wanted to see before she and Sloane came to terms was her supposed fiancé. And the second-to-last man she wanted to face when she was still standing on shaky ground with Sloane was her grandfather. Damn, of all the rotten luck!

A disapproving frown plowed Ryan's brow when he adjusted his spectacles to see his granddaughter garbed in western attire, her cheeks and hands smudged with ink. "My God! Don't tell me Terrance has you manning his presses while he sits in his parlor sipping tea, that lazy lout," he snorted disdainfully.

Joseph shambled toward her, staring bug-eyed at the comely blonde. She reminded him of some heathen out of a Wild West show in her gray Merino skirt and flimsy calico print blouse that he wouldn't have allowed his servants to wear in his presence, much less his fiancée. His disbelieving gaze flooded over her scuffed boots and then ascended to her tanned face. Her silky hair was drawn back and trailed over her shoulder in a reckless braid.

"Tara, where on earth did you dig up that garb?" Joseph squawked in disgust.

Her chin tilted to a proud angle as she wiped the ink from her fingertips and then tossed the stained rag aside. "This is the customary apparel for Texans, and I have decided to become a citizen of this state," she declared.

Ryan's penetrating gaze narrowed on his defiant granddaughter. This was not the type of reception he had anticipated. Tara seemed to appreciate looking like a ragamuffin and behaving like a heathen.

"Joseph and I have come to fetch you home," he assured her in that stern, commanding tone Tara had come to know all too well.

"We have wedding plans to make," Joseph chimed in. "What the devil has come over you? Have you lived too long with these barbarians?"

"Long enough to know that I can never be happy again in St. Louis," she told them flatly. "I am perfectly satisfied in Texas, and I have decided to stay . . . indefinitely."

Ryan clutched his heart, certain the palpitations were about to get the best of him. Libby had been right. Terrance had poisoned Tara! Retrieving his granddaughter from Texas would be comparable to the horror stories Ryan had heard about the return of white captives from Indian camps. Tara had been pressured into thinking the life style of these ill-mannered bumpkins was preferable to that of a wealthy aristocrat. Good God, he barely recognized his own flesh and blood! Terrance and his band of heathens had distorted Tara's thinking and had her dressing like one of them!

"Now you listen to me, young lady," Ryan barked as he wagged a bony finger in her rebellious face. "I will hear

423

no more of this ridiculous talk. You are coming home where you belong, and you and Joseph will be married as soon as proper arrangements can be made."

A wicked gleam flickered in Tara's violet eyes as she sauntered toward her grandfather and the spindly-legged blond who wasn't even half the man Sloane was. "That is quite impossible. You see, I have already taken a husband, and I have no need of another."

Ryan stumbled back against Joseph as if Tara had knocked the wind out of him with a punishing blow to the midsection. "What?" he squeaked.

Joseph propped the older man back on his feet, his face crimson with fury. "How dare you attempt to make me the laughingstock of St. Louis!" he raged. His snapping blue eyes were riveted on Tara, who did not cower beneath his contemptuous glare. "You agreed to become my wife, and by damn, you shall be." His eyes landed on Ryan who was still attempting to regain his shattered composure. "You had better back me on this, O'Donnovan. I want her marriage annulled. I will not be humiliated by my friends and associates. Our engagement was announced long ago, and I will not have it said that I lost Tara to some bowlegged cow servant from Texas!"

As usual, Joseph was more concerned with his unblemished reputation than he was with her, Tara thought as she studied her whining fiancé with disgust, her low opinion of the sap sagging several more notches.

"You heard Joseph," Ryan growled in agreement. "You will not remain married to a man you could only have known a few weeks." His agitated gaze flew past Tara to glare holes in the back door of the office. "Where is your father? I suppose he approved of this fluke marriage, just to spite me."

"Papa doesn't know about it." Tara could have cut off her tongue for voicing the truth. Ryan would be skeptical

424

of her marriage and even more suspicious when he learned it had been a secret wedding. Tara could tell by the look on her grandfather's face that her blundering reply had planted the first seed of doubt.

"No?" His narrowed eyes landed on her bare ring finger. And then it came, that leery, mistrusting expression that assured Tara that Ryan believed she had conjured up the excuse. "Very well, then can you at least produce a marriage certificate or this mysterious man you claim you have married as proof that what you say is true?"

"He is out of town and he has the papers," Tara muttered, noticing that the seed of doubt had begun to sprout and take root. She berated herself for handling the situation so poorly.

She wasn't dealing with a moron, she reminded herself. Ryan was as sharp as a tack. Joseph, on the other hand, had questionable intelligence. Unfortunately, she couldn't deal with Joseph alone. He and her grandfather came as a package, and Ryan would ensure that Joseph didn't lose his head and make the situation worse than it already was. Damn, this was turning out to be a miserable day!

"Next I suppose you are going to tell me that this new husband of yours has abandoned you," Ryan smirked. "If that is the case, then it is all the more reason for you to return to St. Louis." He gestured toward the back door of the office. "Pack your belongings, child. You are coming with us. You have lived so long among these heathens that already you've begun to dress like them and dream up the kind of tall tales for which Texans are notorious."

Tara was going nowhere with Joseph Rutherford, and certainly not to the altar! Her frantic gaze darted about the room and then she sprinted toward the front door, determined to return to the Diamond R Ranch where her father had stayed to sort through Merrick's files and keep Julia company until Loren returned to manage the ranch for her. But Ryan and Joseph intercepted her before she could dash to freedom.

"I swear it will take two months to undo the damage of your visit with your father," Ryan muttered as he herded Tara out the door, deciding to leave her luggage behind and board the stage before she escaped him.

Despite her vehement protests, Tara found herself shuffled down the street and stuffed into the stagecoach. She sat silently fuming as Ryan and Joseph wedged her between them, hardly allowing her room to breathe, much less throw herself out the window.

Despair closed in on Tara as she watched the settlement fade in the distance. She was leaving her soul behind. It was somewhere between Harrold and Palo Duro, tucked in Sloane's saddlebag. Lord, the days she had spent waiting for him to return had been pure hell, and now Ryan was putting greater distance between her and the husband he refused to believe she had married. Would Sloane breathe easier now that she was out from underfoot permanently? He had always said she belonged in St. Louis, and there she would stay if Joseph and her grandfather had any say in the matter. Tara groaned miserably when she landed on that depressing thought. Ryan would not allow her out of his sight until he had seen her wed to Joseph. And then what would she do? After all, a woman wasn't supposed to be married to two men at the same time. It seemed someone up there didn't like her, she decided as she gazed heavenward. Fate had frowned upon her, and she found herself in more trouble than she had dreamed possible. Never in her worst nightmare had she actually believed she would find herself strapped to stuffy Joseph Rutherford, but the dreadful dream was beginning to unfold before her very eyes, and Tara knew she could never endure Joseph's touch.

Heaving a discouraged sigh, Tara laid her head back against the wooden seat and stared at the blank wall. She was doomed. Sloane would soon have what he wanted—the Diamond R Ranch—and he would quickly forget her. She thought he had come to care about her in his own way, but it was not nearly enough to besiege her grandfather's mansion and take her back to Texas. *You will never see him again,* Tara told herself firmly. It was over and done. She would have to discreetly dissolve the marriage and become Joseph's wife as her grandfather demanded. Tara couldn't fight the both of them. Now she fully understood why Terrance had packed up and left St. Louis. He had not been able to overpower Ryan and Libby, nor could Tara ever hope to win against Ryan and Joseph. It was best that she close the door on yesterday and attempt to forget Sloane Prescott existed. And just how many years would that take, Tara asked herself. Too many to count. It was best not to think at all, she decided, and then stared blankly at the opposite wall of the stagecoach, forcing all thoughts of Sloane to the shadowed corner of her mind.

As the summer sun cast its last glorious rays on the walls of Palo Duro and then sank on the western horizon, Sloane drew his weary steed to a halt and peered down into the plush green valley. He had come to West Texas bent on revenge, a cynical man determined to obey Carmelle's dying wish, as if it would win him the love she could never fully offer her son. Only now did he comprehend why he had never been able to please her. Carmelle had seen something in him that she could never forget, the painful memory of a man she detested, a vengeance she could never appease. Her son had been a bitter reminder of her tormented past, and even the bond between mother and son could not stand the strain of her long-harbored hatred.

For more than a week Sloane had wrestled with the painful truth and had finally come to terms with it. Carmelle had intended the irony of Merrick's downfall to be a double-edged sword. Burns would have seen to it that Merrick learned the truth while he served his sentence for murder, forcing him to live with the knowledge that his own son was responsible for the collapse of his Camelot.

Sloane heaved a weary sigh as he pressed his knees to Diablo's flanks and urged him down the meandering path that led to the fertile valley below. He had covered so much ground in the span of nine days that both he and his white stallion could barely set one foot in front of the other without stumbling. There had been dozens of loose ends to wrap up before he could return to Palo Duro, and there were still several matters left unattended. The first order of business was to set Julia's mind at ease. Sloane had given her position serious consideration. As much as he had come to love this magnificent valley, he couldn't deprive Julia of the only home she had ever known. She had lost everything she held dear, and he didn't have the heart to send his half-sister away from headquarters.

When Sloane rapped on the door Julia appeared before him, wearing a rueful smile that lacked her usual bubbling enthusiasm. She murmured a quiet greeting and then stepped aside to allow him to pass. Sloane veered toward the study, hoping to see Tara dashing out to meet him, but he was met with an empty room and disappointment.

"Are you staying here alone?" he questioned as he plopped down in the chair behind the desk to retrieve Merrick's ledgers.

"This was to be the first night," Julia informed him as she eased her hip onto the edge of the desk to assist Sloane in sorting through the important papers. "Ter-

428

rance left this afternoon. He was helping me dispose of my father's . . ." Julia stopped short, her gaze dropping to avoid meeting Sloane's probing blue eyes. "We sifted through his personal belongings while Tara returned to Clarendon to file the deeds that I have had changed to include your name as well as mine." Her lashes fluttered up to meet his solemn gaze. "It is only right that you should share in whatever is left of the Diamond R when the investors have been paid."

"That isn't necessary," Sloane said quietly. "I have sold my grandfather's ranch near Palo Pinto, and I plan to buy out the investors if they will agree to it. The house and land will be yours. I only ask to lease enough acres to run a cattle herd that will provide a modest living."

Tears misted Julia's eyes. She deserved no generosity after what her father had done to Sloane's family, after he had been deprived of the luxuries she had taken for granted. "I cannot accept your terms. We are brother and sister, and we should share alike. If you persuade Terrance to sell his stock, the entire ranch will become your charge. It seems fitting and proper."

A faint smile brimmed Sloane's lips as he surveyed the attractive strawberry blonde, who had endured her own soul-shattering torment. Julia had matured quickly these past two weeks, and although bitter tragedy had befallen her, she had survived.

Sloane leaned across the desk to take her hand in his. "I would prefer to keep the ranch in the family," he said with a wink. "I think we should share the responsibilities of the Diamond R."

Julia fondly squeezed his hand and then sighed in relief. "I was hoping you would feel that way. And if Loren will still have me after I have behaved like a spoiled brat, I plan to accept his proposal." A wry smile touched her lips. "Would you think me too conniving if I threatened to have you fire him if he didn't accept his new position as my husband and business partner?"

Soft laughter rumbled in Sloane's massive chest. "I doubt that you will hear any complaint from Loren. The last time I saw him he was fidgeting like a caged cat, anxious to conclude his business and return to the ranch. You won't find it necessary to twist his arm or threaten him to get him to agree to a wedding."

Julia rose to her feet and pivoted on her heel. "I'll fetch you something to eat while you are going through the books," she offered and then paused at the door to cast him a humble glance. "I wouldn't have blamed you if you ordered me off the ranch without a penny after the misery you have suffered."

"Past is past," Sloane assured her. "My only desire is to make the Diamond R all it should be. Now, where is that food you promised? I haven't eaten since early this morning, and it will be impossible to sort through all these papers when my insides are gnawing at me."

When Julia flashed him a pleased grin and disappeared around the corner, Sloane slumped back in his chair to stare at the avalanche of papers stacked before him. He couldn't approach Terrance about selling out the investment stock until he knew what price would be fair and reasonable. And he couldn't approach Tara until he had concluded his investigation of Merrick's finances.

Damn, he couldn't get that bewitching minx out of his mind. The thought of Tara had been the driving force that had kept him moving this past week when he had very nearly collapsed from exhaustion. Each time his eyes attempted to slam shut and he was certain he couldn't take another step, her soft, compelling voice called to him from afar and her angelic face materialized before him. Impulse bid him to cast aside his obligation and seek her out, but logic urged him to complete the task he had begun.

And Sloane still found himself battling that mental

tug-of-war between duty and desire while he labored over the ledgers by candlelight, long past the midnight hour.

An anticipatory smile played on Sloane's lips as he swung from the saddle and tied Diablo to the hitching post in front of the newspaper office. It had taken him two full days to sort through Merrick's financial records and itemize the statement to present to the members of the Cattle Investment Corporation of St. Louis, but he had finally completed his business just as the ranch hands returned to headquarters.

Loren had been celebrating his upcoming wedding, and the entire canyon echoed with festivity as Sloane aimed himself toward Clarendon. During his ride he had carefully planned his first evening alone with Tara in weeks, and the mere thought of their romantic rendezvous aroused him. Lord, he was like a man strapped on a torture rack, having his limbs stretched out of proportion, his mind tormented by a vision of loveliness. He could think of little else besides taking that violet-eyed nymph in his arms and compensating for the endless nights he had been forced to spend without her.

Sloane's cheerful smile evaporated when he strode into the office to see Terrance slumped over his desk, looking as if he had lost his last friend and didn't have the foggiest notion where to begin searching for him.

"It's about time you got back," Terrance snorted grouchily and then threw down his coffee spiced with brandy. "What the hell took you so long?"

Sloane didn't appreciate having his head bitten off, but he overlooked Terrance's black mood, knowing the sight of Tara would counteract her father's sour greeting. He tossed the file of papers beneath Terrance's disjointed nose and down-in-the-mouth frown and then parked himself in a nearby chair. His gaze circled to the back

431

door of the office, hoping Tara would come barging in to interrupt them. But to his chagrin, the door didn't creak open to reveal her exquisite face.

"If you recall, I had a score of matters to attend to, and since Diablo didn't sprout wings, I was forced to ride instead of fly home." A mocking smile bordered his lips as he pushed his Stetson back from his forehead and shot Terrance a sideways glance. "You have thought of me as the Night Rider for so long that you seem to think I am capable of working miracles."

"I could use one about now," Terrance muttered before chugging another gulp of coffee. "Forgive me for being so curt. I am just out of sorts."

"It certainly seems so," Sloane chuckled, noting that Terrance still looked as if he had been chewing on a lemon rind. "But I think my report will lift your spirits. Cal Johnson has confessed that Merrick sent him to ransack your newspaper office. And for the first time in several years, your cattle investment has shown a profit." He tossed the money pouch on the desk, but the good news had no effect on Terrance.

"I'm glad to hear it," Terrance mumbled absently.

He certainly didn't act as if he were, Sloane mused. His wandering gaze strayed to the back door. Where the hell was Tara? "If you would prefer to discuss business later, I will return after you have come to grips with whatever has disturbed you," Sloane offered, rising to his feet.

Terrance choked down another swig of brandy-laced coffee and then slammed his fist into the top of the desk. "I would prefer that you take your pile of papers and personally deliver them to Ryan O'Donnovan. And I can tell you exactly where I would have you stash that file!" he growled resentfully. "That old buzzard sneaked into Clarendon and kidnapped Tara. While I was at the ranch with Julia, he carted her back to St. Louis with him." His voice rose until he was bellowing like a parade of banshees.

432

"What!" Sloane staggered, feeling as if he had had the props knocked out from under him. He prayed he had misunderstood Terrance, but he had the sickening feeling there was nothing wrong with his hearing.

Sloane's reaction stunned Terrance, who had not expected his business associate to be so dismayed by the news. "Why are *you* so upset?" he demanded. "She is *my* daughter," he snorted gruffly.

"And she is *my* wife!" Sloane blurted out, deciding to cast diplomacy to the wind. He had intended to break the news to Terrance gently, but this was no time for tact. But no matter how delicately he could have put it, it would never have come out right, Sloane realized. Their whirlwind marriage would come as a shock to Terrance no matter what, and flowery explanations couldn't ease the blow.

"What?" Terrance echoed as he vaulted to his feet to glare at Sloane. "When did you find time to court her and wed her with all the activity you've been involved in in the past two months!" he pressed.

"It was a short courtship," Sloane explained with a sick smile and then grimaced when Terrance glowered disapprovingly. "We were married in Tascosa and I . . ."

"Tascosa!" Terrance hooted like a screech owl. "What the devil were the two of you doing in that unruly town, of all places?"

"Delivering horses," Sloane calmly informed his raging father-in-law.

"So naturally you herded Tara along with you and married her," Terrance grunted sarcastically.

"Well, not exactly." Sloane heaved a frustrated sigh. This wasn't going well, and Terrance wasn't making it any easier as he glared at Sloane with scornful mistrust. "I was having difficulty keeping track of her. She tried striking out on her own in Tascosa, and got herself in trouble, so I married her."

"And you thought tying her in wedlock was the logical answer?" Terrance chirped as he wilted back in his chair and rolled his eyes toward the ceiling. "For a man who usually calculates his every move, you certainly have behaved irrationally where my daughter is concerned."

"I couldn't help myself," Sloane defended himself. "She happens to be a very attractive woman, and it seemed to be the best way to keep her under control, since she has the uncanny knack of getting herself into trouble."

A wry smile pursed Terrance's lips as he regarded the hard, calloused cowboy in an altogether different light. One of his main reasons for inviting Tara to Texas had been to have her meet this rough man who was towering over him. He had hoped the two of them would find a common interest and that Tara would be inclined to stay, but never in his wildest dreams had he expected Sloane to tote Tara off to Tascosa and secretly marry her. But then, not even a man like Sloane could resist his lovely daughter, Terrance thought smugly. And then that revelation led to an even more disturbing one.

"Christ!" Terrance croaked as he whipped open the desk drawer, rummaging through the papers to find the letter Ryan had sent him.

"What the sweet loving hell is wrong now?" Sloane grumbled as he watched the papers float about Terrance in disarray. Lord, the man was behaving strangely.

Terrance groped for his spectacles and held them before his squinted eyes as he blazed through the letter. "Tara's grandfather says she will be wed to Rutherford at the end of the month and that she has made her first and last visit to these barbarian plains."

"She can't marry him," Sloane ground out. "Tara already has a husband."

"Not for long," Terrance assured him as he allowed the letter to flutter down to take its place with the

434

disorderly pile of papers that were strewn about his desk. "Even if Tara is satisfied with the husband she has, Ryan will have it annulled." He eased back in his chair to scrutinize the raven-haired cowboy, who was seething in irritation. "Does she love you?"

"She didn't say that exactly," Sloane hemmed and hawed.

"Well, *exactly* what did she say?" Terrance questioned point blank.

Embarrassed red worked its way into Sloane's tanned cheeks, a rare occurrence for a man who was not easily rattled. How did a man tell his father-in-law that his wife was attracted to his body? For in truth, that was as close as she had come to confessing that she felt something for him, Sloane reminded himself. She had expected a commitment from him because it was right and proper, but dragging words of love from Tara had been as difficult as pulling teeth.

Terrance watched the uneasy cowboy balance on one foot and then the other, as if he were standing on needles and pins. Finally, Terrance lost his patience. "Well then, what about you? Do you love my daughter?" he demanded.

At least Sloane could answer *that* question with certainty. He looked Terrance square in the eye. "Yes, I do," he said simply.

"Does she know that?"

Terrance was giving him the third degree, and Sloane resented the barrage of questions, but he responded, just the same. "No, I haven't told her," he grumbled out of one side of his mouth.

"Why the hell not?" Terrance snorted disdainfully. "That is not the sort of thing a husband neglects to tell his wife, and by damn, it should have been a prerequisite for marriage!" His voice rose until he was all but yelling in Sloane's face.

"I had planned to," Sloane countered hotly. "I just haven't got around to it, but I . . ."

"You haven't got around to it?" Terrance repeated incredulously and then threw up his hands in disgust. "Did it ever occur to you that you might have gotten the cart before the horse? Sweet mercy, Sloane, someone should have taught you a few rules of etiquette. You don't just drag a woman off and marry her and forget to tell her you love her. What the devil is Tara supposed to think? Ryan will have her married off to Rutherford, and she will probably surmise that *you* prefer it that way. If she dared to tell Ryan about the secret wedding, he will see to it that she is legally free of her commitment to you." Terrance shook his head in dismay. "What a fine mess you've made of my daughter's life. Had I known you were so incompetent in handling your personal life, I would never have suggested Ryan hire you to sort out the dealings of the Diamond R Ranch."

The insult stung like a slap in the face, but Sloane grudgingly admitted he had it coming. "I shamefully confess you are right."

"But it is too late to do anything about it now." Terrance heaved an exasperated sigh. "Tara is on her way to St. Louis and Ryan won't let her out of his sight until he sees her properly wed. She couldn't escape him if she wanted to. If I know Ryan O'Donnovan, and I do know him all too well," Terrance added acrimoniously, "he will keep Tara tied to her bedpost to prevent her fleeing." He glanced up at Sloane, who wore an expression sour enough to curdle milk. "But you probably are relieved to have the marriage annulled, since you always claimed the strings of wedlock were much too confining. Indeed, I cannot imagine you loving my daughter enough to chase after her, since you didn't even bother to announce you had married her in the first place."

Sloane's piercing blue eyes riveted on Terrance. "For a

newspaperman, you certainly have difficulty getting your facts straight. You are mutilating the truth, and I do not appreciate being misquoted," he growled sarcastically.

Terrance leaned back in his chair and bit back a wry smile. He had purposely baited Sloane and he was delighting in casting out the line and watching this brawny cowboy tangle himself in it. "Then suppose you tell me how it is between you and Tara. After all, she is my daughter, and I have a right to know if you truly married her for love or if you have a discreet eye on her money."

Sloane's clenched fist pounded the desk, jarring the stick of furniture and everything near it, Terrance included. "Tara's money is the least of my interests!" he stormed back at Terrance. "I don't want her married to that sophisticated aristocrat, and I don't want her in St. Louis. I want her here with me! If she thinks she can scribble her signature on a piece of paper and sever the bond between us, she is wrong. We waded through hell together, and I expect to be granted at least one glimpse at heaven. I am not giving her up to some pompous gentleman with polished manners. I'll bet my right arm he can't handle Tara."

"And you can?" Terrance challenged with a taunting smile. "You won't be able to dominate her. She doesn't respond to sharp commands, but if you allow her free rein, she will run away with you." Feigning a thoughtful frown, Terrance eyed the powerfully built man from head to toe. "Come to think of it, I'm not certain you are man enough for her, either. Just look at all the scrapes she got into while the Night Rider was supposedly keeping a constant vigil on her."

The barb stuck like a well-aimed arrow, stabbing into Sloane's male pride, and his flaming blue eyes made mincemeat of Terrance's mocking grin.

"Your precious daughter isn't perfect either, Winslow," Sloane hurled at him, attempting to control his rising temper. But it was damned difficult when Terrance's jibes had him boiling like an overheated coffee pot. "Perhaps if you hadn't spared the rod and spoiled the child she wouldn't be so difficult to manage."

Now it was Terrance's turn to snatch up the gauntlet, and he was itching to slap it across Sloane's smirking face. "She was happy and well adjusted until Ryan began meddling with her. If she is contrary, it is *his* fault, not mine!"

"But you walked out on her when she needed a father," Sloane threw at him and then grinned when he saw the smoke rolling from the older man's ears.

"I was forced out," Terrance defended himself harshly. "You try your luck with that stubborn old buzzard and see how well *you* fare."

"I damned well intend to," Sloane assured him as he scooped up his file and marched toward the door like the cavalry charging into battle.

"What do you plan to do?" Terrance questioned him as he bolted from his chair to catch the door before Sloane slammed it shut and shattered the glass insert in his fit of temper.

"I am going to retrieve my wife from O'Donnovan's clutches," Sloane grunted as he aimed himself toward his horse.

"You can't shoot the old buzzard down," Terrance insisted as he hurried his step to keep up with Sloane's swift impatient stride. "St. Louis is too sophisticated for gunfights on Main Street."

Sloane slowed his pace when he realized Terrance had every intention of accompanying him to Missouri. "Are you sure you want to tangle with this vicious bulldog you have been ranting about?"

A wry smile pursed Terrance's lips as he ambled along

438

beside Sloane. "I wouldn't miss watching you and Ryan go at each other's throats for all the cattle in Texas. After the fur flies, I'm curious to know which one of you walks away in one piece."

"If this is your idea of lending moral support, I can do without it," Sloane muttered as he swung into the saddle.

"I would be doing you a disfavor by allowing you to think you can waltz into O'Donnovan's mansion and retrieve Tara without having a battle on your hands. Ryan always has his way, and he does not readily adapt to change. You'll need a suit of armor and a mighty sword if you clash with that iron-handed, rock-headed old goat."

Sloane frowned at Terrance's description of his nemesis. How the hell was he going to take what rightfully belonged to him without a full-scale war? Well, he would just have to work that out during their rail ride, Sloane decided. If Ryan O'Donnovan was as bull-headed as Terrance insisted, Sloane would need an army to storm the walls. There had to be a way to win this battle without firing a shot, he thought determinedly. He had just endured one lifelong feud, and it had left a bitter taste in his mouth.

Sloane swallowed hard when a discouraging thought stampeded through his mind. What if Tara had decided to wed Rutherford after all? What if she had decided that Rutherford could offer her what she wanted from life? She *had* thrown the man's name in his face from the very beginning, and she *had* insisted that her "fling" in Texas was no more than that. As a matter of fact, Tara had never once mentioned that she preferred to make Texas her home. She had enjoyed the visit, but she had said nothing about taking up permanent residence in Texas. Tara *did* care about him, Sloane mused less than confidently. But did she care enough to sacrifice the wealth and glamour St. Louis had to offer? Would she decide this was the best way to resolve their marriage, a marriage she had protested in the first place and then insisted they have annulled, since they had never lived as man and wife?

Doubt hounded Sloane every step of the way. What would he do if Tara no longer wanted him, if she insisted on having their marriage abolished? He couldn't fight Ryan, Joseph, *and* Tara. Sloane struggled with his troubled deliberations until he had worked up a monstrous headache, one broken by an image of silky hair of spun silver and gold and violet eyes that danced with lively curiosity and undaunted spirit.

He would make Tara love him, Sloane promised himself. And he would find some way to earn Ryan's respect. Perhaps a frontal attack was not the best approach. When in Rome, one must behave accordingly, he reminded himself. He would simply have to defeat Ryan O'Donnovan at his own game, sweep Tara off her feet, and make Joseph Rutherford look like the bungling idiot.

A mischievous grin rippled across Sloane's lips as he pulled his Stetson down over his eyes, crossed his arms on his chest, and eased back in his seat in the passenger car. He had some meticulous calculating to do during his rail ride.

A wary frown plowed Terrance's brow when he glanced over to see Sloane sprawled in his seat grinning like a weasel who had just feasted on a henhouse of plump chickens. Sloane was not taking the matter seriously enough to please him.

"You had best be plotting your moves, Sloane," Terrance lectured him in a grim tone. "I thought I had made it clear what you would be up against. Overconfidence could be your downfall."

"Relax, Winslow, I'm scheming," Sloane insisted with

440

a soft chuckle. "If you butted heads with the old goat and lost, you should have questioned your methods. The best approach is not necessarily to fight fire with fire, but rather with a bucket of water."

Terrance rolled his eyes in disbelief. Sloane was talking in riddles. Obviously the man had spent too long trailing cattle herds and the uplifted dust had filtered into his head to clog the cogs of his brain.

"I seriously doubt that throwing cold water in Ryan's face will accomplish anything," Terrance snorted sarcastically. "If that is your best ploy, we might as well ask the conductor to put us off in Dallas and walk back home."

Sloane snickered at Terrance's pessimism, but he didn't bother to elaborate on his plan. It was still in its formulative stage, and he hadn't quite worked out all the kinks. Terrance was left to sit and stew while Sloane plotted his visit to St. Louis. Even when Terrance's curiosity burned him to a crisp and he demanded to know what Sloane had in mind, he received nothing for his investigative efforts. As usual, Sloane was tight-lipped, and Terrance swore he could have pried more information from a clam than he could drag out of this taciturn Texan.

Chapter 28

A heavy-hearted sigh escaped Tara's lips as she stood before the mirror staring at her gloomy reflection. She had dressed in the stunning off-the-shoulder burgundy gown her grandfather had purchased for her, and she made a feeble attempt to paste on the cheerful smile he had demanded of her before locking her in her room to prepare for the upcoming engagement ball.

The O'Donnovan mansion had become Tara's prison since Ryan had snatched her from Saints' Roost and spirited her off to St. Louis. Tara had made two futile attempts to escape, but Ryan and Joseph had thwarted both of them, even her attempt to jump from the moving train when it decreased speed as it rolled into Dallas. Ryan had watched her like a hawk, and Tara had been allowed so little privacy the past few weeks that she had almost forgotten the meaning of the word.

She had given up hope of convincing Ryan that she already had a husband. He had turned a deaf ear each time she approached the subject. There was naught else to do but quietly have the marriage annulled when Ryan permitted her out of the house without breathing down her neck while he followed in her footsteps. And that *was* the best solution to her dilemma, Tara decided. Ryan would never allow her to return to Texas, and Sloane had too many irons in the fire to come chasing after her. Not that he would anyway. In truth, he was probably relieved to have her out from underfoot, since he had tried to send her away after he had impulsively married her. But he *had* begun to care about her Tara told herself. Given time he might even have . . .

Oh, what was the use of chasing whimsical dreams, Tara scolded herself. She couldn't continue to live on hope and the bittersweet memories of the past. Ryan was determined to see her wed to Joseph, and once he had made up his mind to something, nothing short of a miracle could deter him. She might as well accept her fate and learn to live with it, since she couldn't change the way of things.

Heaving a tremulous sigh, Tara rapped on the door to inform the waiting servant that she had completed her toilet, and then she trudged into the hall. She was unmoved by the gay music that echoed in every corner of her grandfather's sprawling fifty-five room mansion, on an estate that sat on eight acres on the outskirts of St. Louis. The grand salon, ballroom, billiard room, and dining hall were bulging with distinguished guests. Ryan had invited the gentility to join him in the celebration of his granddaughter's upcoming wedding, and he had spared no expense in preparation.

Strange, Tara mused as she wandered into the dining hall to pour herself a glass of courage to help her endure the evening. She felt none of the bubbling enthusiasm that should have accompanied such a festive occasion. Her heart was still imprisoned in a majestic canyon in Texas beside a murmuring waterfall that was capped with a ceiling of shimmering stars. She felt oddly discontent and out of place in the ornately decorated mansion adorned with gold and crystal chandeliers.

"Ah, there you are my dear." Joseph approached his fiancée like a strutting peacock on center stage, his voice drowning out the quiet conversation of the other distinguished guests.

Tara forced a civil smile as Joseph took her hand,

443

placed a light kiss to her wrist, and then flung his arm out in an exaggerated gesture, as if he were presenting his fiancée to a crowd that was standing a block away rather than in the same room.

"Our friends have refused to make use of the dance floor until we have the honor of the first waltz," Joseph informed her as he laid his hand to the small of her back and guided her into the entryway.

The congregation fell into step behind them like a processional trailing a prince and princess. The feel of Joseph's gangly arms about her and his spindly legs brushing against hers only served to remind Tara that no man could compare to Sloane, especially not stuffy Joseph Rutherford. It was with a heavy heart that she endured the first waltz and the swarm of guests who surrounded her to voice their congratulations on her upcoming wedding. Tara mustered a smile, but she was certain her face would crack before the evening ended and she could seek refuge in her room.

When she started to refuse the invitation to dance with one of Joseph's business associates, she caught her grandfather's warning glare and then reluctantly nodded her acceptance. Ryan had very nearly broken her spirit by hustling her from Texas before she had had the opportunity to speak with Sloane. The hopelessness of the situation drew heavily on her will to fight. It was unlike Tara to be complacent, but she was like a wild bird in captivity, lost and disoriented. And it was futile to rebel against her grandfather, Tara reminded herself as Joseph's young friend twirled her around the dance floor. Ryan was relentless in his efforts to see her wed to abundant wealth. By the end of the week she would find herself bound to two husbands, one of which she would have paid a king's ransom to avoid and the other for whom she would have given a king's ransom in exchange for his love. But Joseph would never allow her to leave him standing at the altar, and he would have posted guards outside her door to ensure that she didn't escape him if Ryan hadn't thought of it first. Tara had been so heavily chaperoned since her return to the mansion that her maid was instructed to attend her when she bathed or adjourned to her room, a room that resembled a prison to a woman who had formerly had the run of Texas.

The impulse to flee overwhelmed Tara once again, and she made her excuses to her dance partner, making a beeline for the terrace doors. But Joseph was watching her every move and intercepted her, propelling her along with him to meet several of his friends.

"Don't think to escape me tonight, my dear," Joseph gritted out through his tight smile. "You have already humiliated me once by traipsing off to that godforsaken dust bowl, and I will not tolerate another of your shenanigans." His pale blue eyes drilled into her. "Paste on a smile. I will not have my friends thinking I have yet to win your love and devotion."

"You haven't, you know," Tara said matter-of-factly. "All this pomp and circumstance doesn't change my feelings. You and I cannot have a happy marriage when I am in love with another man, and you are a fool to think otherwise."

His long, thin fingers bit into her arm as he bent closer to hiss in her ear. "Don't cross me, Tara. If I cannot have your love, I will at least find compensation in your grandfather's money. You have angered me twice. The third time I will not be so lenient with you," he threatened.

Tara would have challenged him if he hadn't brought her around to confront another of his friends. And so it went for another agonizing hour. Joseph stuck to her like glue, and Tara couldn't seem to move without her albatross strangling her with his spiteful attention.

"Cripes!" Sloane hooted as the coach rolled to a stop in

front of an extravagant mansion that reminded him of an emperor's grand palace.

It was apparent that cost was no object when Ryan O'Donnovan designed a home. Sloane's astonished eyes followed the massive rock walls and stone arches that surrounded the terraces that lined every side of the three-story monstrosity.

"Staggering, isn't it?" Terrance chuckled as Sloane plugged his eyes back in their sockets.

Sloane unfolded his tall, bulky frame from the coach and strode up the marble steps. Gathering his crumbling composure, he straightened his royal blue waistcoat, readjusted his silk top hat, and mentally prepared himself to meet Ryan O'Donnovan.

"Since you have been so secretive about your scheme and have not bothered to ask me for pointers, I only hope your plans are well laid," Terrance grumbled. "For the life of me, I cannot imagine what you expect to accomplish by barging in on Tara's engagement party."

Sloane didn't bother to explain. His thoughts had converged on his purpose, and he had no intention of failing. He had a great deal at stake, and he wasn't leaving until he knew where he stood with Tara. With grim determination, Sloane rapped on the door and impatiently waited for the servant to admit them.

"Mr. Winslow!" The gray-haired servant beamed at Terrance. "You are a sight for sore eyes, sir. I never thought to see you in this house again." Hudgens grinned wickedly as he gestured toward the billiard room. "The old man will split a seam when he gets a look at you."

"Then I suggest you summon his tailor, Hudgens," Terrance smirked as he ambled inside. "It would never do to have the sheik of St. Louis come unraveled in the midst of these festivities, especially since he considers this palace to be the mecca of society."

Sloane could not contain his grin. He could well imagine how Terrance and Ryan sliced each other to pieces with their cutting jibes. Terrance had already drawn his sword and was prepared to fence with his foe.

"Shall I inform Mr. O'Donnovan of your arrival?" Hudgens inquired as he took both men's hats and topcoats.

"I prefer to barge in unannounced," Terrance insisted as he marched down the vestibule. "Come along, Prescott."

Sloane's keen gaze drank in the extravagant furnishings and ornately carved trim that lined the walls and towering ceilings of the rooms they passed. This was the home in which Tara was raised? Why would she want to forfeit this to return to Texas? When that feeling of inadequacy crept over him, Sloane shoved it aside and moved deliberately toward the billiard room and the man he had met in Dallas the previous year.

Ryan O'Donnovan's face fell when the crowd around him parted like the Red Sea receding for the Children of Israel. Shock and dismay settled in his aging features as Terrance and his companion approached. Ryan's piercing eyes darted from the smug expression on Terrance's face to the tall, immaculately dressed gentleman whose long, confident strides quickly closed the distance between them. There was something familiar about the man, but it took Ryan a moment to place him. Once he had, he found it difficult to believe this was the same rough-edged cowboy he had met in Dallas. Sloane's tailored clothes complimented his lean, muscular frame and accented his tanned skin, and although Ryan was searching for a flaw, there was nothing about the man to criticize, except that he had waltzed in uninvited, and Ryan was quick to blame his rude son-in-law for that.

"Mr. O'Donnovan, it is a pleasure to see you again, sir." Sloane's rich, baritone voice was laced with bold certainty and his handshake was firm as he looked Ryan straight in the eye. He leaned close, as if to convey a confidential comment. "And may I compliment you on your fine taste in decor. I have had the opportunity to visit many distinguished homes in various parts of our country, but I find yours most impressive."

Ryan was not too nearsighted to notice the admiring glances Sloane was receiving from women and men alike. His bronzed skin and striking good looks had caught the crowd's attention from the moment he strode into the room. There was an aura about this powerfully built man. He projected the gracious, polished manners of a gentleman, and yet, there was a forcefulness radiating about him, a magnetism that shone like a torch in a blizzard. It set Ryan to wondering if Sloane had played the charade of a rough-edged cowboy the previous year to assure him that his investigator could handle the task expected of him.

"You will be pleased to know that I have concluded my investigation of your cattle investments, Mr. O'Donnovan, and I hope we will be able to discuss the matter at length. When time permits, of course," Sloane added as his gaze shifted to the other guests. "I would not think of interrupting you when you are in the process of entertaining your illustrious guests."

Terrance stood like a man transformed into a stone statue, his jaw gaping in disbelief. Gone were Sloane's southern drawl and plain-spoken English. The man was a veritable wizard! He had seen Sloane convincingly portray several charades, but he played the role of a worldly gentleman as if he were born to it. So that was his ploy, Terrance mused as he watched Sloane charm Ryan our of his silk stockings. It was to be subtle sabotage, Terrance chuckled to himself as he watched Ryan assess the darkly handsome gentleman brimming with charisma. If Sloane's past record was any indication of success, he would have the old buzzard eating out of his hand before the night was over.

Terrance cleared his throat to gain Ryan's attention

and then stepped up beside Sloane. "Although Mr. Prescott is a very busy man with diverse interests, he insisted that he come to St. Louis to formally close his investigation and present you with the profit of our cattle investment," Terrance explained in a polite tone, deciding Sloane's technique was far more effective than butting heads with the ram of O'Donnovan mountain.

The old man lifted a graying brow and then frowned bemusedly. "I hadn't realized you had other interests besides your investigative work, Mr. Prescott. What sort of business are you in?" Ryan pried as the crowd closed in around them, all ears turning to hear the dashing gentleman's response, especially the unattached young ladies.

His cobalt-blue eyes twinkled as Sloane slid Terrance a discreet glance and then refocused on Ryan. "My investments range from marketing wool and fine leather products to raising and selling prize horses," he hedged, taking the truth and twisting it just enough to impress Ryan. "Investigative work is just a fascinating endeavor which I undertake to sharpen my wits." A wry smile pursed his lips as he adjusted the expensive gold ring that was inlaid with diamonds and amethysts that encircled his little finger. "But recently I have become fascinated with collecting rare gems," he added nonchalantly, doubting that Ryan realized the priceless jewel to which he referred was his very own granddaughter.

Terrance camouflaged his snicker behind a sudden coughing spasm, knowing the marketing of fine wool and leather, to which Sloane had referred, were sheep and cattle on the hoof. Sloane was a clever rascal, Terrance gloated. He had turned Ryan every which way but loose, and they had only been within these castle walls a few minutes.

"I had no idea. . . ." Ryan mumbled bewilderedly.

Sloane shrugged nonchalantly, his royal blue velvet

449

jacket straining sensuously over his broad chest and powerful shoulders. "At the time Terrance contacted me to investigate your cattle investment, I saw no reason to divulge my other sources of income. I had already assumed the role of a common cowboy to establish my rapport in Texas," he explained. "I find private detective work an intriguing hobby, one to alleviate the boredom of idle wealth."

Ryan was impressed with Prescott, and the evidence showed as he gave Sloane the once-over, twice. "Perhaps you would be interested in investing as one of my stockholders. With your vast background, you might wish to . . ."

Sloane held up his hand to forestall Ryan and then addressed him with a wry smile. "I was thinking more along the line of *buying* your total investment in cattle," he informed his astonished host. "I have come prepared to make you a generous offer for your holdings in the Diamond R." His grin widened to display pearly-white teeth. "As I said, I have developed a penchant for rare gems and the *Diamond* R Ranch is among them." Sloane reached out to help himself to a glass of champagne as a servant with tray in hand meandered through the crowd. After taking a small sip, as if he were thoughtfully testing the stock of liquor, Sloane bent his gaze to Ryan. "But we can discuss our business another time. You have festivities in progress, and I wish to reacquaint myself with your lovely granddaughter. I had occasion to meet her during her sojourn in Texas, and I was terribly disappointed that I was unable to bid her farewell before she returned to St. Louis."

Ryan gestured toward the door. "I am certain Tara will be delighted to see you again," he insisted as he ushered Sloane toward the foyer, ignoring his unwelcomed son-in-law. "Come along, Sloane. We will see if we can drag Tara from her fiancé's arms. Joseph has monopolized

450

her attention for the better part of the evening."

"I trust you have selected only the most eminent and deserving man for our lovely Tara." Sloane frowned in concern. "I found her to be a very captivating young lady, one of incomparable charm and wit. I do hope her beau meets my expectations."

"Joseph Rutherford's family is a cornerstone of St. Louis," Ryan boasted. "He can well afford to offer Tara anything her heart desires."

"But is he man enough to hold her interest?" Sloane queried and then graced the comely brunette who was batting her big green eyes at him a roguish smile.

Although Ryan's spectacles were as thick as blocks of ice, Penelope Bronson's blatant interest in Sloane did not go unnoticed. Sloane had become the center of attention since he had set foot inside the mansion. One would have thought a gallant young knight had been introduced in court, judging by the way the young ladies were drooling over him. Finally, Ryan collected his straying thoughts and circled back to Sloane's questions.

"I am beginning to wonder if *any* man can hold Tara's interests," he confessed. "Since you have met my granddaughter, you must know that she is very rebellious and not easy to please. But, in time, I think she will come to realize that Joseph is a proper choice for her mate."

Sloane would have vehemently protested the point if he hadn't been so determined to play his role to the hilt. "She is your granddaughter, but were she mine, I would ensure that she had some fond attachment for her future husband," he brazenly suggested. "If I could not detect that lively sparkle in her eyes, that expression I have come to associate with the bewitching lass, I would not be quick to see her wed. It would be most distressing to see her delightful spirit and zest for life smothered by a loveless marriage. Tara would wither and die like a rose denied sunlight and nourishment."

The seed of thought had been planted in Ryan's head, and he found himself questioning Joseph's abilities to create such a stimulating situation for Tara. And then a fond memory from the past stirred in his heart. The vision of a lovely young woman, so like Tara, formed in his mind. Edith. Theirs had been a long and happy marriage. When he had lost Tara's grandmother he had locked those bittersweet feelings in his soul, and he had never stopped to consider that, with love, Tara would blossom and grow, just as Edith had.

"I have always considered wedlock to be an affair of the heart," Sloane went on to say as his observing gaze flooded over the voluptuous redhead who tossed him a beckoning smile and then sashayed into the ballroom. "Although I have seen my fair share of dazzling beauties, I search for a woman of depth, one strong enough to hold my constant attention and yet feminine enough to arouse my romantic interest." His meaningful gaze landed on Ryan. "Tara possesses those rare qualities that naturally attract men. I should hope Tara's fiancé feels such deep, binding emotion for your granddaughter, and that she, in turn, shares those fond sentiments for her future husband."

Sloane laughed softly as he gestured toward the dreamy-eyed couple who had wandered, hand in hand, from the ballroom, entranced, unaware that they were surrounded by a swarm of guests. "I hope to view the same contented smile on Tara's lips when I see her with her beau. I contend that love is what makes the world go around and money is only a means that offers two lovers a life of *over*abundant pleasure. Love can survive poverty and even tragedy, but it cannot thrive, even in the lap of luxury, unless husband and wife feel that natural attraction that is as ancient as time itself."

Ryan frowned curiously at Sloane's philosophical remarks. "Have you found the woman of your dreams,

Sloane? You speak like a man who has given the matter careful consideration."

A sly smile bordered Sloane's lips as he took another sip of champagne. "Forgive me for being so direct, sir, but I found the beginning of such an intriguing courtship with your granddaughter in the short time I knew her." He chuckled at the startled expression that was whittled in Ryan's features. "Although she informed me that she was engaged, I pursued her . . . and very relentlessly. My purpose for traveling to St. Louis is twofold. Not only do I intend to own the Diamond R Ranch in entirety, but I have come to make my intentions known to Tara." The smile evaporated from his bronzed features as he met Ryan's unblinking gaze. "If Tara is content with her fiancé, I will gracefully bow out to begin my search for another woman who possesses Tara's endearing qualities, if indeed there is one. But if Joseph Rutherford doesn't meet my expectations, I will not stand idly by and watch her walk into a marriage that cannot bring her happiness."

"You are a very straightforward man," Ryan speculated, raking the powerfully-built gentleman with piercing scrutiny. "I must assume you are accustomed to having what you want . . . on your own terms." His eyes narrowed as he continued to study Sloane. "But I must warn you that I also suffer from that damnable fault. It could very well be that you and I will clash."

Sloane raised his hand to toast his worthy opponent. "I have been forewarned that you are a man of integrity and firm determination," Sloane assured him as he gestured his raven head toward Terrance, who was propped against the door jamb, patiently waiting to see what direction Sloane intended to take with Ryan. "But no matter what the outcome, I think we both share a common cause—Tara's happiness." Sloane looked him straight in the eye. "That should be our first and foremost concern, don't you agree?" Penetrating cobalt-blue eyes held Ryan hostage. "Hear this and believe it. Tara has earned my respect and affection. She is a remarkable young woman, and if Joseph cannot make her happy, I demand the opportunity to try."

Ryan's graying brows shot straight up. "Do you think to march into my home and make such bold demands in the very middle of her engagement party? My God, you have incredible nerve," he snorted.

Sloane bowed before him, his smile so blinding and reckless that Ryan could not take offense, since Sloane had shown himself to possess the same strong traits Ryan claimed as his own. Ryan stood there dumbfounded as Sloane thrust the stemmed goblet into his hand.

"I will allow you to judge whose attention the lady seems to prefer. And, if in good conscience, you still maintain that Joseph is the better man, I will accept your decision. Fair enough?"

Ryan's pale eyes twinkled merrily. He could not help but admire Sloane's forthright manner and firm conviction. The man had not antagonized him as Terrance always had, but he was offering the type of challenge Ryan thrived upon. His calculating gaze took in Sloane's masculine physique and dashing good looks, and he found Joseph inadequate in comparison. Perhaps Joseph was a little too sure of himself. Life had been handed to the aristocrat on a silver platter, and maybe it was time he proved his worth, Ryan mused.

"Agreed." Ryan raised the goblet to return the toast. "You have my permission to pursue my granddaughter. We shall see how my selection of mates for Tara fares in the face of competition. I shamefully admit that is something with which I have not forced Joseph to contend."

As Sloane spun on his heels and aimed himself toward the ballroom, Ryan heard Libby's shocked gasp from

454

behind him. Libby had turned the corner to find herself face to face with the man she had battled to erase from her thoughts. But there stood Terrance, his face tanned, his eyes dancing with amusement, his wide smile making mincemeat of her emotions.

Employing Sloane's tactics and confident manner, Terrance strode forward and then bowed exaggeratedly before his estranged wife. "Time has been kind to you, Elizabeth," he murmured as his words whispered over her wrist. "You are still as lovely as the memory I have kept in my heart."

Libby's eyes rolled back as her palpitating heart hammered against her chest. And then, like a fragile flower left too long in the steamy summer sun, she wilted at Terrance's feet.

Ryan grumbled at his daughter's inability to confront her husband without fainting in a dead heap with all of St. Louis as witness. What lousy timing, Ryan grumbled to himself as he stepped over Libby to view Tara's reaction to Sloane Prescott.

"Clear the clutter from the hall, Terrance," Ryan ordered as he gestured to his fainthearted daughter who was still sprawled on the floor like a misplaced doormat. "I have better things to do than fetch her smelling salts."

As Ryan elbowed his way into the ballroom, Terrance scooped up his unconscious wife and carried her into the parlor to revive her. A mischievous smile played on Terrance's lips as he deposited Libby on the couch and then sank down beside her. This could prove to be a most entertaining evening, he thought to himself. Most of Ryan's parties were stuffy affairs that Terrance had always dreaded. But tonight was the first time Terrance had anticipated attending one of O'Donnovan's balls. It had all the makings of a chaotic fiasco.

Chapter 29

A look of boredom sat on Tara's pale features as she
sipped her drink and watched the elegantly dressed
guests twirl around the ballroom. Joseph had finally
deposited her at the refreshment table and had allowed
her a moment to rest her feet. Tara was thankful not to
have her spiteful fiancé breathing down her neck. He
was making a difficult situation very nearly impossible,
and Tara had counted to ten so many times in the course
of the evening in an attempt to hold her temper that she
had counted well into the thousands.

When Penelope Bronson fluttered up beside her, Tara
frowned curiously at the young girl's flushed face. She
looked like a bubble searching out a place to burst. "Is
something amiss?" she questioned the prissy brunette.

Penelope fanned herself before she swooned. "Amiss?
Hardly," she gushed. "I have just seen the handsomest
man I have ever laid eyes on." She sighed melodramatically and then wilted back against the wall, as if the mere
thought of Prince Charming had knocked the props out
from under her. "Oh, Tara, wait until you see him. He is
tall, dark, dashing. . . ."

Tara rolled her eyes at Penelope's description. She was
like the boy who cried wolf so often that no one would
believe him. Penelope considered everything in breeches
to be magnificent, and Tara had heard her voice that
same remark so often that she swallowed it with a grain of

salt. Penelope had wandering eyes, and she had been through so many beaux since her introduction into society that Tara was certain the comely brunette would never be satisfied to spend her life with only one man. Someone even more handsome would always come along to pique Penelope's interest. And if she ever did settle down to marriage, Tara didn't doubt for a moment that Penelope would be sporting several lovers.

"And you have your sights set on this handsome stranger," Tara speculated and then frowned in dismay when she saw Joseph pushing bodies out of his way to reach her.

"Come, my dear," Joseph cooed with mock sweetness. "I cannot bear to be without you for more than a few minutes at a time."

As Joseph drew Tara into his arms, she fought the wave of repulsion that flooded over her. Lord, if she could barely abide the feel of Joseph's arms about her, how could she endure having him sleep beside her in bed? The thought only distressed her further, and if she had any luck at all she would work up a splitting headache that would allow her the perfect excuse to return to her room. Being with Joseph only reinforced her belief that she was totally and helplessly in love with Sloane. Her heart cried out to him. Her soul ached for him, and she was certain her life with Joseph would be pure hell. She was doomed to be tied to a loving memory while she endured the rest of her life with a man who saw her only as a trinket, an object to confirm his position in society.

Sloane stopped short when his circling gaze landed on the breathtaking beauty in burgundy. Tara's skin had grown pale from lack of sun, but her face was no less exquisite, even with the sadness that was painted on her delicate features. His longing eyes flooded over the fashionable off-the-shoulder gown that exposed the creamy swells of her breasts and bare slopes of her arms. Her silver-blond hair was piled on top of her head, and amid the shiny curls was a tiara of sparkling jewels. The daring cut of her gown was adorned with artificial roses, and a sash of white satin accented the trim curve of her waist. Elbow-length gloves hugged her arms and gold bracelets surrounded each wrist.

A sigh escaped Sloane's lips as he watched Tara sail around the room in Joseph's arms. She looked like a princess from a fairy tale, a young woman of such abundant beauty that a man could be content to admire her from afar, spellbound by her sylphlike movements.

Finally, Sloane shook his head to shatter the spell and aimed himself toward Tara. He was damned well going to do more than watch this dazzling fairy princess from a distance, he reminded himself and then gnashed his teeth together as the comely brunette he had noticed earlier planted herself in his path.

The color seeped from Tara's cheeks and she half-collapsed in Joseph's arms when she saw the man Penelope had obviously been describing, since she was hovering about him like a bee in search of nectar. Tara's heart somersaulted around her ribs as her adoring gaze flooded over Sloane's virile form. He was garbed in the latest fashion, a blue tailor-made suit that complimented his sturdy physique. The white linen shirt accented his bronzed skin, and his trousers hugged the taut muscles of his thighs. Tara's knees went weak at the sight of him and she retracted every spiteful thought she had made about Penelope. The brunette had been right for once, Tara mused as her eyes radiated her pleasure. Sloane *was* the handsomest man anyone had ever laid eyes on.

She well remembered the feel of his hard male body pressed intimately to hers. His possessive embrace was like that of an agile jungle cat's, while being in Joseph's arms was like being held by a sickly canary. The comparison made her smile for the first time in weeks, and the expression remained intact as Sloane politely excused himself and pried away the clinging brunette who was draped on him.

When their gazes met and locked, Tara could feel the tidal wave of emotions sweeping over her. She didn't know how Sloane had managed to gain entrance to the ballroom and bypass her grandfather, and she didn't really care. Sloane was here! That realization made her heart leap with happiness.

"May I steal your lovely lady for one dance?" His remark was more demanding than questioning as he tapped Joseph on a bony shoulder and effortlessly pushed him aside. His flaming blue eyes never left Tara's exquisite face, a face that had filled his waking and sleeping hours since he had returned to Clarendon to find her gone.

Joseph puffed indignantly when approached by the bold stranger who curled his arm around Tara's waist as if it belonged there and drew her familiarly against him without waiting for permission.

"Now, see here," Joseph protested. "You cannot come barging in here unannounced and . . ." The words died on his lips as Sloane spun Tara around so he could stare over her head and down his nose at the frail blond gentleman who reminded him of a malnourished giraffe.

"The name is Sloane Prescott." His voice was low, but Joseph did not mistake the challenging undertone as he continued. "The lady is not yet your bride, and you hold her with so little authority that I thought she should know how it feels to be held in a *man's* arms, in case she was forced to settle for something less."

Joseph gasped at the insult, recovered his rattled composure, and then glared mutinously at the insolent intruder. The nerve of that rake! "Sir, I don't think you know to whom you are speaking," he smirked as he struck an arrogant pose and then flicked an imaginary speck of dust from his ruffled sleeve.

Wicked amusement danced in Sloane's eyes as he regarded the spindly-legged aristocrat who was so swollen with arrogant pride that he looked as if he might explode. "The question is *not* do I know to whom I speak, but rather, do I care? And the answer, quite frankly, is no," Sloane said blandly. "Now, if you will excuse me, I intend to devote my time and amorous attention to this bewitching gamin."

Another flabbergasted gasp bubbled from Joseph's narrow chest. "Gamin? How dare you refer to my fiancée with such disrespect," he spouted, glaring up at the raven-haired rogue who stood a half-head taller.

"I meant no disrespect," Sloane insisted as he curled his index finger beneath Tara's chin, his eyes glowing with lambent hunger as he stared at her heart-shaped lips. "Indeed, I only sought to compliment her spirit and marvelous sense of humor. How Tara can tolerate such a man as yourself is inconceivable."

Unable to resist the temptation, Sloane brushed his lips over hers, inwardly groaning as his kiss melted on her mouth like a thirst-quenching summer rain. A spark leaped between them, and Sloane momentarily forgot that he intended to leave several impressions with Ryan and his guests. All he wanted at the moment was to be alone with Tara, to appease a hunger that had been gnawing at him for as long as he could remember.

Joseph stood there fuming, steam billowing from the starched collar of his shirt. Where that impudent stranger found the gall to kiss his fiancée in front of God and all of St. Louis, insulting his manhood, was beyond him. That rake was making a spectacle of Joseph, and the thought had him flushing furious red.

"I refuse to allow you to take such privileges with my fiancée," Joseph sputtered.

"But the lady doesn't seem to mind," Sloane pointed out as he flung Joseph a taunting smile. "And, after all, *she* was the one I was kissing."

When Joseph attempted to step between them, Sloane twirled Tara around, and as her skirt sailed about them, he planted his foot just so. Joseph, who was not known for his agility, tripped over Sloane's booted foot and squawked like a chicken that was about to tumble from his perch. Although Joseph flapped his arms in an attempt to regain his balance, he met with failure and sprawled facedown on the dance floor.

With one powerful arm, Sloane grabbed Joseph by the nape of his waistcoat and hoisted him back to his feet. After drawing his silk handkerchief from his pocket, he brushed the dust from Joseph's breeches and then flashed him a patronizing smile.

"Have you been plagued with this stumbling affliction all your life?" Sloane questioned as he tucked his kerchief in his pocket and then slid his arm around Tara's waist to take up where he left off, holding her intimately against him.

Joseph was silently seething. Sloane had made *him* appear the blundering fool in front of the guests, while he arrogantly waltzed away with Tara, who seemed delighted to see her unwanted fiancé floundering like a fish out of water. Joseph pivoted on his heels, ignoring the snickers of the bystanders, and marched himself over to Ryan who was watching his granddaughter and Sloane Prescott sail around the room in perfect rhythm, staring into each other's eyes as if they were viewing a cherished photograph that had been tucked away for years on end. Ryan had never seen Tara so content. The smile that blossomed on her flawless features was worth a thousand words, and the color of roses that stained her cheeks reminded Ryan of another time and place, a time when he had made his intentions known to Edith's father.

Ryan had not allowed sentimentality to influence his thinking in years, but Sloane had tactfully reopened those tender memories. He had become hardened and

461

uncaring. He had been unsympathetic to his granddaughter's wishes, wishes he had overlooked in his effort to see her properly wed.

"How could you have allowed that arrogant, pestilent vermin in the front door?" Joseph ground out as he stormed toward Ryan.

"Are you referring to the illustrious Mr. Prescott, the man whom I hired to investigate, and quite successfully, I might add, and has shown us a margin of profit for the first time in years?" Ryan inquired as he dragged his eyes from the striking couple and anchored them on Joseph's flaming red face. When Joseph nodded affirmatively, Ryan's shoulder lifted in a leisurely shrug. "I found him to be every bit the gentleman, while you showed yourself to be a clumsy ox, tripping over your own feet in the middle of the dance floor."

"Gentleman?" Joseph crowed like an offended screech owl. He pointed an accusing finger at the handsome rogue who held Tara all too tightly to suit him. "He marched right up, stole Tara from me, insulted me, not once but thrice, and then planted his foot in front of mine! I demand that you have him thrown out of the house."

Ryan critically surveyed his young business associate in an altogether different light. Joseph had come tattling like a spoiled, cowardly child instead of confronting the source of his aggravation. The seed of thought Sloane had planted had begun to sprout and take root. Joseph had substantial wealth to back him, but he had always depended on others to carry out unpleasant duties. What would Joseph do when Tara exerted her rebellious nature and defied him, come running back to Ryan, demanding that he punish her for intimidating her new husband?

"Mr. Prescott has done nothing to offend me," Ryan insisted as his gaze strayed back to the couple who now had the attention of every guest in the ballroom. "If you find complaint with him, then it is your place to remove him from the premises."

Joseph's breath came out in a rush, as if Ryan had knocked the wind out of his sails. "I want nothing more to do with that impudent scoundrel," he scowled disgustedly.

"Are you afraid to challenge our bold guest?" Ryan's graying brows arched acutely as his gaze slid over Joseph, whose eyes darted to the awesomely built man who made two of him and lied through his teeth. "Certainly not," Joseph defended himself hotly.

"Then I suggest you prove it," Ryan challenged and then frowned thoughtfully when a previous incident popped to mind. "As I recall, you demanded that *I* keep *Tara* in line when she insisted that she didn't wish to become your wife. It leaves me to wonder if you are just beginning to show your true colors, Rutherford. Where is your backbone, man?"

He was without one, and he was becoming desperate. He had always relied upon assistance when he met with difficulty, and Ryan was refusing to aid him. Joseph was being made to look the simpering moron, and his mortification was singing his pride. Snatching the drink from Ryan's hand, he threw down a swallow of courage and then plowed his way through the crowd to prove to his future father-in-law and his guests that he was a man, not a two-legged mouse.

While Ryan and Joseph were debating Joseph's fortitude, or lack of it, Tara was melting in the circle of Sloane's sinewy arms, loving the feel of his masculine torso brushing suggestively against hers.

"Why did you come to St. Louis?" she questioned as she lost herself in the depths of Sloane's eyes.

A wry smile hovered on his lips as he drew her even closer to whisper in her ear. "I have come to collect payment for my investigative services and . . . to remind

463

you that you already have a husband."

His warm breath against her skin sent a fleet of goose bumps cruising across her skin. Tara leaned back as far as his encircling arms would allow, her expression sobering. "I tried to tell my grandfather that I was already married, but he wouldn't believe me, since I could not produce my husband, the wedding ring, or the marriage papers."

"Have you had the wedding annulled?" Sloane demanded as he guided Tara toward the terrace doors and ambled along the moonlit balcony.

"No, my grandfather has not allowed me out of his sight since he carted me home," she informed him bitterly, and then peered around Sloane's shoulders to see that Ryan and Joseph were still deeply involved in conversation. "And yonder stands my supposed fiancé. Do you honestly believe I would prefer that stuffy bag of wind to you, even if you wed me in a moment of madness?" Tara sniffed distastefully. "I would rather be whipped than find myself saddled to that shallow, overbearing aristocrat."

Sloane's grin stretched from ear to ear as he focused his undivided attention on Tara's luscious figure. "*Lo celebro mucho,*" he chortled softly and then traced the delicate line of her jaw, anxious to allow his lips to engage themselves in something more stimulating than conversation.

Tara suddenly bristled. She had no idea what Sloane had said, since he hadn't bothered to translate, but it annoyed her that he seemed to find her predicament amusing. He had probably come to watch her worm her way out of her difficulty without offering assistance. That rascal. Why couldn't he have marched up to Ryan, announced that Tara was his wife, and spirited her away from this mock celebration.

"You would not find the situation humorous if you were being forced to wed that scrawny dolt," Tara grumbled bitterly and then rolled her eyes in irritation when she spied Joseph shoving bodies aside as he stalked, stiff-legged, toward the terrace doors. "Speak of the devil and he appears."

Sloane pried his hungry gaze from Tara's soft, pouting lips and glanced sideways to see Joseph stomping toward them like a mad bull charging a matador. With one swift, agile move, he positioned himself between Joseph and Tara.

"You certainly seem to be in a huff this evening," Sloane mocked, choosing to go at his antagonist's throat with an annoying feather rather than a knife. "Is it another symptom of your stumbling sickness?"

Joseph had been stabbed with all the barbs he could stomach. He came apart at the seams, flying at Sloane with a doubled fist. But before he could land a punishing blow, Sloane's hand snaked out to catch his arm in midair, and then he ducked beneath Joseph, catapulting him over the terrace rail and into the shrubs below. He landed with a thud, but his temper was at a rolling boil. He scrambled to his feet and dragged himself up the rail, determined to land at least one blow after having been heaved into the bushes like a sack of flour.

Again, Sloane stifled Joseph's attempt to plant his fist where it didn't belong. Joseph squawked like a chicken that had its wing tucked behind his back when Sloane wrenched his arm up to his shoulder blades.

"Your manners are atrocious," Sloane scolded, his baritone voice crackling with laughter. "It is beyond me how Ryan could have selected you as the cream of the crop when your disposition is so sour that it could curdle milk."

Joseph was fit to be tied, and Sloane was doing just that, tying him in embarrassing knots. He was being publicly disgraced, and if he could have gotten his hands on a pistol he would have cheerfully blown this tormenting brute to bits.

A disappointed frown gathered on Ryan's brow as he was swept up in the wave of guests that flooded toward the terrace door to watch the tussle. Joseph was making an ass of himself. Only a fool would dare to match his strength against Sloane Prescott's, he mused as he watched Joseph's body being contorted into various uncomfortable positions. Sloane was the picture of brawn and muscle, and if Joseph wasn't clever enough to prey upon the man's weakness instead of his strength, he needed his head examined. Ryan had challenged Joseph to handle his own problems, but the blasted fool had only made the situation worse. What had he seen in Joseph in the first place, Ryan asked himself. Abundant wealth, he answered himself shamefully. He had been so determined to see Tara married into a family that was a pillar of society that he had overlooked one very important point. Joseph lacked character. No wonder Tara had difficulty pinpointing her reasons for disliking her fiancé. He didn't have enough personality to criticize.

Before Joseph lost his head and made another bungling attempt to oust Sloane from the party, Ryan wedged his way through the crowd of snickering onlookers to demand Sloane's attention.

"Perhaps this would be the proper time for us to discuss our business matters," he insisted, flinging Sloane a warning glance.

Sloane gave Joseph back his arm . . . or what was left of it after he had very nearly untwisted it from its socket. "I couldn't agree more," he concurred.

Sloane turned to bow graciously before Tara, who was having difficulty keeping a straight face. She felt the impulsive urge to laugh out loud at the distressed expression that was plastered on Joseph's waxen features as he attempted to recover the use of his right arm, which dangled at his side like a limp noodle.

"It has been a pleasure to see you again, my dear Tara," Sloane murmured as he raised her hand to brush

466

his lips across her fingertips and then broke into a rakish smile that was meant only for her. "Our night is far from over. Although your fiancé doesn't think I have a *ghost* of a chance of seeing you again, I shall return one way or another." His hushed words held a quiet promise, and Tara felt an arousing tingle race up and down her spine as he gave her hand a loving squeeze and then backed away.

She knew exactly what he implied, and the mere thought made her tremble with aroused anticipation. Tara did not think to question how and when. She knew Sloane would come to her like a phantom in the night to weave dreams about her. She could tolerate Joseph's annoying presence for a few more hours, knowing Sloane would somehow materialize from the shadows.

As the crowd dispersed and Ryan and Sloane strode toward the study, Joseph's painful grasp clamped into her waist.

"You are hurting me," Tara grimaced as Joseph roughly pulled her against him.

"Don't think you won't pay for humiliating me like this," he sneered maliciously. "You will soon become my wife, and I intend to see that you spend the rest of your days doing penance for this last disgraceful shenanigan."

Tara had seen Joseph lose his temper on occasion, but she was shocked by the glittering hatred she saw in his eyes. He had seemed harmless until his pride had been threatened. If looks could kill, she would have been roasting over hell's blazing fires. Joseph thirsted for revenge to ease his mortification, and Tara had the uneasy feeling that he would never release her from her grandfather's marriage pledge, even if Ryan had a change of heart. And that would take nothing short of a miracle, she mused dismally. Sloane couldn't fight Ryan and Joseph. They were too powerful. Sloane had found a way to defeat Merrick Russel, but it had taken months of meticulous plotting. Now time was short, and she wasn't even certain if Sloane cared enough about her to battle both men. *He* could quietly have their marriage abolished, walk out of her life, and return to Texas to manage the Diamond R while she became a human sacrifice to Joseph's fury. Lord, how did she always manage to get herself into such scrapes?

Despair hung over her like a looming cloud as Joseph shoved her back into the ballroom and forced her to dance in his arms. Her fiancé was not man enough to defeat Sloane in a confrontation, but he would deal severely with her. That depressing thought drew heavily on her spirit, and Tara did not trust herself to think or feel any emotion. She simply endured Joseph's suffocating nearness, dreaming of the moment her phantom would materialize from the shadows and take the dismal world away. She had to convince Sloane to help her. She just *had* to. Life without Sloane would be unbearable, but life with Joseph would be no life at all. He would make her miserable after she had shamelessly accepted Sloane's kisses and caresses. Humiliation and the thirst for revenge had a nasty way of distorting a man's logic, and Tara could tell by the way Joseph was glowering at her that his was becoming more entangled by the moment.

Ryan closed the door of the study and gestured for Sloane to park himself in the chair. "Apparently you were unimpressed with Joseph," Ryan surmised.

"I have to agree with Tara," Sloane remarked as he folded his tall frame into his seat. "What Rutherford lacks in fortitude, he also lacks in mentality. It is rare to find such a shallow man in a position of authority. I can only hope you make the important decisions for the both of you during business transactions."

Sloane was giving Joseph a verbal lynching, and Ryan found himself wondering if the young fool didn't deserve it. Joseph had behaved very badly in the face of adversity, squawking around the ballroom like a decapitated chicken. First he had come tattling to Ryan, and then he had, and most unsuccessfully, attempted to plant his fist in Sloane's face with the most eminent citizens of St. Louis watching.

"I admit that money talks," Sloane said flippantly. "But in Rutherford's case it is inarticulate. I consider the man educated past his intelligence." His sober gaze anchored on the aging gentleman who sank into his massive chair behind the walnut desk. "My opinion may be worth very little to you, sir, but I am very disappointed in Rutherford's showing. He cannot match Tara in wit, warmth, or spirit."

Ryan eased back in his seat, thoughtfully scrutinizing his straightforward, plain-spoken guest. "I will admit my candidate was less than stately this evening, but I cannot confidently say, after one night, that you are the man who can make her happy."

Sloane leaned forward, his features chiseled with grim determination. "I want the week," Sloane said deliberately. "I want the opportunity to see Tara, to test the bond that had just begun to grow between us while she was in Texas."

"And *if* perchance I decide to negate my commitment to Rutherford, and *if* Tara would agree to become your wife. . . ." Ryan's pale eyes probed into Sloane. "It *is* marriage you imply." His tone did not carry the inflection of a question. It was laced with firm insistence.

"Marriage is exactly what I had in mind," Sloane confirmed and then impatiently waited for Ryan to continue.

"What do you plan for my granddaughter? What kind of life do you intend to provide for her?" Ryan demanded.

The faintest hint of a smile rippled across Sloane's full lips. It would certainly not be as wild and harrowing as the experiences she had endured because of Merrick Russel, but he couldn't tell Ryan that, because the old man would have hit the ceiling if he knew all the catastrophes that had befallen Tara in Texas. "I want to take control of the Diamond R and make a home for the both of us in Texas," he said simply.

Ryan had been afraid he was going to say that. "I see . . . and if I offer our stock investment in the ranch at an even more reasonable price than you were prepared to pay for it, would you take your ranch and leave Tara here where she belongs?"

Sloane gnashed his teeth together and studied Ryan with tempered patience. *In St. Louis where she belonged?* Sloane inwardly smirked at the dainty, ladylike vision Ryan conjured up when he thought of his granddaughter. Tara had proven herself to be made of sturdy stuff. She was a survivor, one who had warded off assassins and overzealous beaux, Sloane included. She had suffered a snakebite, endured a near brush with stampeding cattle, and had withstood a fall into Palo Duro Canyon when anyone who didn't possess the nine lives of a cat would have perished. And Tara had, quite literally, come out smelling like a rose. Sloane had come to realize that Tara could survive and adapt to any situation, and it was a pity that he couldn't enlighten Ryan. But if Sloane began citing examples at this particular moment, just when he had wedged his foot in the door, he would find it slammed shut in his face. Ryan would never allow Tara out of his sight if he knew how often she had flirted with disaster.

"It is my opinion that Tara belongs in Texas . . . with me," he contradicted. "And I will not be bribed, not even if you donate your stock without asking me to pay a penny for it."

And Ryan had been afraid Sloane was going to say that, too. He breathed a frustrated sigh and slumped back in his seat, drumming his fingers on the desk while he met Sloane's unrelenting gaze. "I have graciously allowed you to compete with Rutherford, but you insist that winner takes all. What do *I* possibly have to gain? I am

470

very fond of my granddaughter, and the thought of her moving off to Texas disturbs me."

"Even if she assures you that is where *she* wants to be?" Sloane challenged with a daring smile.

Ryan had seen that magic sparkle in Tara's eyes, the living fire that flickered while she was dancing in Sloane's arms. He had never seen her so happy and content with any other man. But that realization did not improve his disposition.

"It greatly annoys me when reason is on *your* side, Prescott," he grunted, and then heaved a weary sigh. "Very well, you have the week to plead your case and to prove to me that you are the man who can continue to make my granddaughter happy." Ryan slowly shook his head at his generosity. "For the life of me, I don't know why I am even considering such a strange proposition the week before her intended wedding."

"Because you are a fair, just man who has his granddaughter's best interests at heart," Sloane complimented him as he rose to his feet to tower over the aging gentleman.

"You will receive considerable argument from my son-in-law on that subject," Ryan snorted resentfully and then blinked when another thought darted through his mind. "Good God!"

A worried frown plowed Sloane's brow as he watched Ryan scramble from his seat and bolt toward the door. "What is wrong?"

"I left Terrance in charge of Libby during her fainting spell. And I have seen nothing of them since Terrance scraped her up off the floor and toted her away." He threw Sloane a hasty glance as he sailed out the door. "Come by in the morning and brief me on your investigation."

Sloane followed Ryan into the foyer, his gaze straying back to the ballroom to see Tara held captive in Joseph's gangly arms. As if he had called out to her from afar, Tara glanced toward the door to see Sloane towering above the other guests. The gleam in his cobalt eyes held a promise that took Tara's breath away. Somehow she would convince Sloane to help her avoid this disastrous marriage, she told herself determinedly. She would prey upon his weakness, calling upon the lusting beast within him if she must. But she would find a way to persuade Sloane to assist her.

A deliciously mischievous smile pursed her lips, recalling how she had brazenly seduced him that night in Tascosa when he was determined to send her home. Yes, there were ways to deal with a man, ways more potent than force, she reminded herself and then grimaced when Joseph's bony fingers threatened to squeeze her in two.

"Must you drool over that insolent rake?" Joseph growled as he spun Tara around, deliberately placing himself in her line of vision so they couldn't send each other silent messages with their eyes. Tara's behavior was disgraceful, and Joseph seethed at the possibility of losing her to a man who had appeared from nowhere on the eve of his engagement party to disrupt his well-laid plans. "You are a fool to think Prescott wants you in a respectable capacity. More likely he would make you his whore and then leave you with only shreds of dignity and pride. He is the type of man who delights in coming between a man and his woman, merely for the sport of it."

The flicker dwindled in Tara's eyes as Sloane disappeared from view. "At least Sloane Prescott has the ability to accomplish such a feat," she hurled at him. "You have always been forced to *buy* a woman's affection. You don't have enough charismatic charm to fill a teacup."

Before Joseph realized what he had done, flesh cracked against flesh and his handprint blazed crimson red on Tara's cheek. Tara retaliated instinctively, but it was not

472

an open palm that flattened Joseph's sprawling nose against the left side of his face. It was a doubled fist, and the impact jarred Joseph's senses, leaving stars twinkling before his eyes. When Joseph staggered back, his mouth gaping in disbelief, Tara gave him a shove for good measure and watched in smug satisfaction when his storklike legs became entangled and he fell flat on his spineless back.

Without a word, Tara picked up the front of her skirt and dashed from the ballroom. Joseph prided himself in behaving like a proper gentleman, but even the rough-edged cowboy she had come to love had never laid a hand on her in anger. Beneath those expensive garments lurked another snake, and Tara detested those slimy creatures. She was *not* marrying Joseph Rutherford and that was the beginning and end of it. She would stay up every night during the following week to devise a workable solution, if need be.

Tara marched up the steps and slammed the door to her room with such force that all fifty-five chambers in the gigantic mansion rumbled as if besieged by an earthquake.

A sour frown etched deep lines in Ryan's face when he eased open the parlor door to find Terrance and Libby entangled in each other's arms.

"What the hell is going on here?" he bellowed.

Terrance eased away from Libby, who had colored seven shades of red after being caught dallying like a young, reckless lover. "Libby and I were just becoming reacquainted," Terrance explained.

"For what purpose?" Ryan jeered. "You won't be staying long enough for any type of reconciliation."

"We are still man and wife," Terrance pointed out as he rose to confront his indignant father-in-law.

473

"Legally, but not morally," Ryan argued as he glared holes in Terrance's starched shirt. "You abandoned your wife and child three years ago, and when you walked out, you forfeited every right you previously had in this household."

"I had no rights," Terrance snorted derisively. "You tolerated my presence, but you refused to acknowledge my position as father, husband, and business associate. Did it ever occur to you that your meddling might have caused the split in our family, not irreconcilable differences between Libby and me?"

The remark was like a blow to the midsection, and Ryan was unable to locate his tongue. Terrance took advantage of his father-in-law's speechless trance.

"Don't you think it tore my heart in two to leave the woman I loved and the daughter I adored? *Our* bickering was splitting my marriage apart, and I saw only one choice." Terrance let his breath out in a rush and reminded himself that he had not intended to instigate a shouting match with Ryan. They had suffered through their share of them, and Terrance did not wish to lock horns with the old goat when he and Libby were back on friendly terms. "Forgive me, Ryan. I don't want to argue with you tonight. I only want to be alone with my wife. Libby?" Terrance stretched out his arm, urging her to take her place by his side.

Casting her father an apprehensive glance, knowing he would not approve but unable to resist the man she had never stopped loving, Libby got up and moved gracefully toward the door. "Please make my excuses to our guests. Terrance and I would like to retire for the night."

Ryan watched in astonishment as husband and wife ambled down the hall and climbed the staircase, hand in hand. Muttering under his breath, he threw up his hands in a gesture of exasperation. The whole world had gone utterly mad and he was the only sane man left in it.

474

Sloane Prescott had barged in to make uncompromising demands. Joseph had behaved like a perfect idiot. His distinguished guests had swarmed around the terrace doors to watch the brawl like a pack of wolves hungry for the kill, and now Libby had taken her husband to her boudoir as if he belonged there!

His eyes lifted heavenward and Ryan expelled a defeated breath. "Where did I go astray, Edith? I only wanted the best for our daughter and granddaughter. Now I am considered a meddling old buzzard. I should wash my hands of all of them and let Mother Nature take her course. Then we shall see if they still complain about the way of things."

Giving way to that very thought, Ryan plopped down in a nearby chair and grabbed a cheroot. Perhaps he *should* sit back and leave destiny in charge. Well, he would make an attempt, he told himself. It might be interesting to see what course fate would take.

Chapter 30

Sloane scowled disgustedly as he eased another door shut on the second floor of the mansion. The way his luck had been running, he would never find Tara's room before dawn. He had waited until the guests had filtered from the house before scaling the stone column that led to the back terrace. After making his way along the balcony he had found himself lost in the many wings that jutted from the rock monstrosity, and he was beginning to doubt that he could reach Tara's room from the terrace. Ryan had probably locked her in a vault in the center of the mansion, making it impossible for her to exit or for him to gain entrance without storming through the front door and alerting the household to his presence.

Frustrated, Sloane picked the lock on another door, doubting that he would ever find Tara. But he swallowed his breath when his circling gaze landed on the seductive nymph who stepped from the shadows, allowing the flickering lantern light to frame her tantalizing figure.

Tara stood poised before him in a sheer negligee of lavender. The gossamer fabric left only enough to Sloane's active imagination to set it afire, and he found himself frying alive. The high thrust of her full breasts pressed wantonly against the alluring bodice of her gown, and the shapely curve of her hips was outlined beneath the soft, flowing cloth. Sloane groaned in agonizing torment, aching to caress what his eyes beheld.

A provocative smile pursed Tara's lips as she watched Sloane devour her with his flaming blue eyes. It was obvious that he liked what he saw, and his ravenous gaze assured her that her choice of clothing had drawn his undivided attention. Armed with the knowledge that she was having a devastating effect on him, Tara sashayed toward him as she slowly unfastened the tiny buttons on the scooped neckline, allowing the fabric to drift apart, revealing the inner swell of her breasts.

When she paused to view his reaction, Sloane crossed his arms and legs and propped himself against the doorjamb. "Mmmmm . . . don't stop now, *querida*. This is getting interesting." His cobalt-blue eyes feasted on her bare flesh, anxious to see every exquisite inch of her luscious body.

An impish grin curved the corners of her mouth upward as she took a bold step toward him. "Are you in the habit of frequenting a lady's boudoir, Mr. Prescott?" she questioned, her voice husky with desire. The mere sight of Sloane aroused her and her heart was fluttering so wildly that it felt as if a frightened bird was ramming into her ribs, searching for a means of escape.

Sloane pushed away from the door and strode over to plant himself in a chair. "No. As a matter of fact, my celibacy these past few weeks has resulted in both physical and mental anguish," he informed her as his hawkish gaze flooded over her alluring curves and swells. "Although I am a married man, my wife has so little consideration for me that she has taken a fiancé, and it leaves me to wonder if one man can ever truly satisfy her."

Perhaps Penelope Bronson suffered from that fickle affliction, but Tara did not. She knew what she wanted, and there was but one man who could appease her passions and earn her love. That particular rogue was now planted in the chair in her bedroom, and Tara was determined not to allow him to leave until she had made him fall in love with her, even if it took the rest of her life.

"You poor, deprived man," she cooed as she pulled the pins from her hair, allowing the curls to tumble about her in seductive disarray. "I will be only too happy to console you in your hour of need."

"Hour?" Sloane growled provocatively. "It will take far more of your time than that, *mi niña.*" One dark brow arched as his probing gaze undressed the shapely nymph who hovered just out of his reach. "Consolation was not what I had in mind when I stole into your room. . . ."

Sloane's thoughts derailed when she pushed the sleeve of her lavender gown off her shoulder. Lord, he had died and flown to heaven, he mused as the seductive gown slid lower on her breasts, exposing the soft, creamy flesh he longed to kiss and caress.

"If it isn't consolation you seek, pray, tell me how I can ease your suffering, sir!" she purred as she peeled the other sleeve from her shoulder, leaving her breasts dangerously close to spilling from the confines of transparent muslin and lace.

His guttural groan pierced the charged silence. He had caught fire and burned. If Tara continued to taunt him with that tempting body of hers, he was going to melt into a pool of desire, right on the seat of her velvet chair.

"Are you in some sort of pain, sir?" A mischievous grin traced her lips as she sauntered closer and then bent over him to brush her palm across his perspiring brow. Feigning concern, Tara withdrew to peer into his handsome face. "I do believe your temperature is rising. You must be coming down with some mysterious malady."

"I'm lovesick," was his self-diagnosis. "I have already told you my spiteful wife has left me starving for affection for weeks on end after she traipsed off with another man." One arm slid around her trim waist, drawing her onto his lap while his free hand slipped inside the gaping bodice to cup her breast. "I think bed rest can cure my affliction," he whispered as his moist lips captured one dusky peak, teasing it to tautness.

"Were I your wife I would never deny your needs," Tara assured him as she held his raven head to her breasts, loving the feel of his arousing kisses and caresses against her quivering flesh. "Were I your love, I would offer my heart and soul until the end of time and ensure that you wanted for nothing that love couldn't give."

The feel of her honeyed flesh beneath his roaming hands aroused him, the throaty whisper of her words gave him hope. And yet, he was losing interest in conversation. His body hungered for hers. He had been like a man stranded in a blizzard, craving the warmth of her, yearning to stoke the fires of passion and allow them to blaze out of control.

"God, Tara, I've missed you," he breathed hoarsely as his sensuous lips scaled the slope of her shoulder to capture her mouth.

He savored and devoured her eager response as his hands continued to roam over her satiny skin, stroking, arousing, weaving a spell so potent and tempting that Tara would have sacrificed her last breath for one interrupted night with him. A soft moan tumbled loose as his adventurous caresses wandered over her inner thighs, leaving wildfires burning in their wake. He was sweeping her into fierce currents of passion, towing her into the dark depths of desire.

Tara struggled to keep a grasp on reality, intending to offer every delicious sensation of pleasure back to him. Determinedly, she twisted away and then stood shamelessly before him as she let the lavender gown flutter into a pool around her ankles. She felt the heat of his gaze burning her naked flesh, saw the raw emotion glistening in his eyes. She wanted to unchain the lusty beast within him, to unleash the wild, reckless part of the man with whom she had fallen in love. She adored the dashing gentleman garbed in rich blue velvet who had walked back into her life that night, but she longed for that daredevil cowboy whose devouring kisses and bold caresses could send her spiraling among the stars.

And so she set about to uncover that tough Texan who bore the stamp of wild nobility. After urging Sloane to his feet, Tara pushed the velvet waistcoat from his shoulders and lifted deft fingers to work the buttons of his vest and shirt. As she turned slightly, the lantern light caught the discoloration on her cheek, and Sloane's blood ran cold.

"Did Rutherford do this to you?" he demanded as he curled his hand beneath her chin to closely inspect the bruise.

"Yes, but it doesn't matter," Tara assured him softly as she peeled off his shirt and tossed it into the pile of discarded clothes.

"It does to me," Sloane growled bitterly. "I want no man to lay a hand on you."

Her skillful hands skimmed across the dark matting of hair that trickled down his lean belly, causing Sloane's quick intake of breath. "Rutherford paid for his brutality," she insisted as her soft lips whispered across his chest. "I blackened his eye with my fist, and the last time I saw him he was lying flat on his back while my grandfather's guests waltzed all over him."

A low chuckle rumbled in his throat as his tension eased and he melted beneath her arousing massage. "You keep telling me you can take care of yourself, and by now I should believe it. But I want to take care of you, to fight your battles for you." Sloane cradled her exquisite face in his big hands and the smile died in his eyes. His rugged features were soft with emotion as he met her quizzical gaze. "I love you, Tara, *con toda mi alma*," he murmured, his voice ragged with deep-felt affection. His heart was in his eyes as he traced the delicate line of her jaw and the creamy texture of her cheek, memorizing every bewitching feature. "I don't care what sacrifices I have to make to keep you. I only know I can't let you go, not without relinquishing part of myself. You are what my dreams are made of, and without you life is empty."

Tara couldn't believe what she was hearing. How long had she waited to hear such a confession? So long that she had doubted it would ever come. Her heart swelled with such happiness that she swore it would burst. Oh, how she loved this lion of a man who had taught her the true meaning of love embroidered with passion.

Sloane eased the ring from his little finger and slipped the diamond-and-amethyst-studded band on her hand before bringing it to his lips. "This ring is far more appropriate than the simple gold band I purchased for you in Tascosa." He brushed his thumb over the jewels that were embedded on the ring. "The diamonds are for each night we spent together. And the amethysts are the boundless horizons I have seen when I gaze into your eyes. *En prueba de mi afecto,* I give you this ring, and with it goes my heart. It is yours for the taking, Tara, if you want it. . . ."

"If?" Laughter bubbled in her soul and gushed from her lips. Tara threw her arms around his neck and showered him with elated kisses. "I have wanted your love for so long that I have been unable to think of anything else," she assured him, her voice husky with emotion. "Oh, Sloane, you can never know how very much *I* love *you.* Words seem inadequate to express what I feel in my heart and soul."

A smile of roguish anticipation brimmed on his lips. Scooping her up in his arms, Sloane carried her toward the four-poster bed, which was covered with a lacy canopy. "Then perhaps you could *show* me how you feel about me."

Tara beamed seductively at the enticing suggestion when he tumbled with her to the satin sheets. "An excellent idea," she purred, stretching like a contented feline. Her soft feminine body brushed provocatively against his muscular torso. "But I hope you are in no rush to spirit off into the night. I intend to be very thorough when I count the ways I love you."

Sloane growled in response to her throaty remark, and then he moaned in pleasure when she set her hands upon him. She rediscovered every sensitive point on his masculine body. Tara had become a skillful seductress, and Sloane reveled in the rapturous sensations that spilled through him like an eternal spring channeling pleasure into every nerve and muscle beneath his trembling flesh.

He felt the sensuous outline of her mouth against his as her warm breath flowed into his. Her exploring hands wandered brazenly over his hair-roughened skin, drawing upon his strength, leaving him feeling as if he were sinking into the depths of the feather mattress. Her kiss deepened as she continued to work her sweet, tormenting pleasure on his flesh. And then the love flame that she offered in her embrace became the vital fire that burned within him. Sloane could feel the blaze consuming him, and he reached out to pull her supple body to his, unable to get close enough to the maddening sensations Tara had created with her kisses and caresses.

He was aware of the shapely softness that melted against his muscled length, the silky contours of her body forging to his, but still it was not enough to satisfy the wild, primal craving that had seized him since the first time he had held this bewitching nymph in his arms.

Again her hands made bold contact with the naked wall of his chest and then descended to trace the hard muscles of his thighs, transforming him into a quivering mass of desire. A groan of sheer pleasure rattled in his throat as she continued to weave her spell of sweet magic about him, leaving him oblivious to all except this wild, breathless need for her that bordered on madness.

Sloane could endure no more of her tantalizing torture. Like a lion rolling to his feet, he crouched above her, his cobalt eyes ablaze with barely controlled passion. His hands tunneled through her hair, tipping her head back. His hard, hungry kiss stole her breath from her lungs and then offered it back in a most arousing way. Tara clung to him, her trembling lips parting beneath his devouring insistence. His arms tightened about her as if he would crush her into him, but Tara didn't complain. She welcomed his fierce embrace, the solid male weight that moved against her. As his hips guided her thighs apart, Tara gasped in the wondrous pleasure of their union and rained kisses along his shoulder as he came to her and then withdrew, setting the tantalizing rhythm with which she swayed and then finally lost her grasp on reality.

He caught her cry of joy and pleasure within his mouth, his kiss savoring the sweet taste of her while his body delighted in total, exquisite possession. They were one, their hearts thundering at the same frantic pace, their souls soaring above each breathtaking plateau of pleasure to reach that ultimate pinnacle. And for what seemed forever, they skyrocketed around the perimeters of a universe that brimmed with such rapturous sensations that Tara was certain she could not survive the immense pleasure of his lovemaking. Again she caught her breath as ecstasy flooded over her, not once but again and again, leaving her suspended in feelings that defied description.

When Sloane shuddered above her, groaning as passion spilled, taking every ounce of strength with it, Tara held him close. One solitary tear of joy trickled down her cheek as she pressed her lips to the thundering pulsations on his neck. "I want it always to be like this between us," she whispered as she raked her fingers through his thick raven hair. "You fill up my senses and erase the emptiness that has plagued me since Grandfather forced me to return. You are my sun and moon, Sloane. Without you I only exist, in a dark, meaningless world."

"Now all we have to do is convince Ryan O'Donnovan that what we feel for each other is not a passing fascination," Sloane rasped as he propped himself on his elbows and then dropped another kiss to her heart-shaped lips.

"And how do you propose to do that?" Tara questioned as she yielded to his arousing embrace.

"I'll figure that out later," he murmured as his hands began to weave their exciting magic all over again. "But since *you* are such a suspicious minx, I think it best that I prove that what I feel for you is no passing fancy, and that there is no cure for this love I discovered a lifetime ago in Texas."

A soft sigh tumbled from her lips as his kisses and caresses splayed across her flesh, rekindling the fires that had only begun to cool. But now they blazed anew, feeding on a love that transcended physical pleasure and a passion that burned like the morning star, creating its own intense heat and flaming with blinding light to brighten the entire universe.

"Good God!" Ryan bolted straight up in bed, his eyes popping as he stared into the darkness. Sweet merciful heavens! How could he have been so stupid?

Grumbling under his breath, Ryan threw his legs over the edge of the bed, snatched up his robe, and grabbed a lantern to guide him down the dark hall. He had been lying in bed sorting through the events of the evening before the dawn of realization struck him like a bolt of lightning.

Without announcing himself, Ryan unlocked Tara's bedroom door and barged inside, intent on getting some answers.

"What the hell. . . ." Sloane muttered as a shaft of light shot across the room to disrupt what had been the first contented night's sleep he had enjoyed since he and Tara were wed.

Ryan froze in his tracks and glanced behind him, wondering how he could have veered into the wrong room. But this *was* Tara's room, not Libby's, he assured himself. When the dim light chased away the shadows, he squinted to see two heads protruding from the sheet. The blond one belonged to his granddaughter, and Ryan didn't need his thick spectacles to know to whom the other belonged.

"I see you have already made yourself right at home, Prescott," he snorted disdainfully as he watched his flushed-faced granddaughter pull the quilt up under her chin and Sloane tuck the sheet around his hips, leaving only his bare chest exposed to Ryan's scornful glare. "Why the hell didn't you tell me you were Tara's husband instead of letting me figure it out all by myself?" He squinted to see that the ring Sloane had been wearing earlier that evening was now encircling Tara's dainty finger. "I should have the two of you shot!"

"Would you allow us time to dress first?" Sloane questioned as a sheepish grin caught one corner of his mouth, tilting it upward.

Although they had been caught in a most embarrassing predicament, Sloane was relieved that the secret was out in the open. Now that he and Tara had come to terms with their feelings for each other, he seriously doubted that he would be able to disguise his love or manage to keep his hands off her.

After Tara found her tongue and regathered the composure that had come unwound when her grandfather burst in on them, she met his accusing stare. "I tried several times to tell you that I was already a married woman, but you refused to listen."

"You should have been more persistent," Ryan muttered as he flounced over to the chair and set his lantern on the nightstand.

"Well, at least you know that I cannot marry Joseph," Tara said, her voice soft as she peered over at the handsome rogue who was nestled beside her. "I am in love with Sloane, and he loves me."

"I should certainly hope so!" Ryan grunted caustically. "Otherwise I *would* have him shot and the two of you would have no business doing whatever it was you were doing before I barged in here." His gaze narrowed on Sloane, who looked like a meek, mild lamb after being caught bare-chested and redhanded. "Were you planning to make a habit of sneaking into my mansion in an improper manner?"

A rakish smile trickled across Sloane's lips as he dragged his eyes off his fetching wife and focused them on Ryan. "I was a desperate man," he defended himself. "You had taken something from me that I held dearer than life. A man in love cannot always be held accountable for his rash actions. If I am allowed entrance through the front door, I won't scale your mansion walls again."

Ryan couldn't help but grin. After his irritation had dwindled, he found the situation amusing. Tara breathed a relieved sigh as a smile settled on Ryan's features. She had expected her grandfather to be hopping mad, but that had not been the case. In fact, he seemed more compassionate and understanding of her needs than she had dreamed possible. Ryan had always been gruff, strict, and stubborn, but somehow he had changed. But whatever the cause of his sympathetic attitude, Tara was most thankful.

Her small hand folded over her husband's, her wedding ring glistening in the lantern light. "Joseph's abundant wealth cannot give me what I want most in life, Grandfather. In fact, all I could anticipate from Joseph is more of this. . . ." Tara turned the other cheek, exposing the bruise on the left side of her face.

A shocked gasp burst from him as Ryan peered at the

discoloration that marred Tara's exquisite features. "He dared to lay a hand on you?" he scowled contemptuously.

"Right in the middle of the dance floor," Tara told him. "Is that the type of man you expect me to endure for the rest of my life? Must I take a beating for voicing my opinion?"

Ryan heaved an annoyed sigh. "No, I do not expect you to fall beneath his whip. Rutherford has continued to disappoint me, and he has left me with no choice but to cancel the wedding arrangements—since you are already married and Joseph seems prone to brutal attacks." His gaze shifted to Sloane, his eyes twinkling in amusement. "You asked for a week to convince me that you were worthy of my granddaughter's love, but it appears we have resolved our differences in the course of the evening."

"Are you implying that we have your blessing?" Sloane questioned as he bravely laid his arm round Tara's bare shoulder and pulled her closer.

Ryan reached over to clasp Tara's hand in his. "You have my blessing, my dear, if you will forgive a silly old fool for being so uncompromising and thinking *his* way was the *only* way. Your husband tactfully reminded me that mutual affection cannot be bought and paid for. The gift the two of you can offer each other, that which Edith and I shared, is something money cannot buy."

Sloane shifted uneasily, wondering how Ryan would react to what he felt obligated to confess. "There is something I must tell you." A weak smile tripped across his lips. "I am not as wealthy as I led you to believe. The fine wool and leather to which I referred is *live* stock, and the precious gem that I intended to collect was Tara."

Ryan frowned when he realized he had been hornswaggled, but then, after giving the matter further consideration, he decided Sloane Prescott would never be a pauper. He was blessed with a strong inner force, and the charisma that naturally clung to him made him a leader among men. There were those who always stood out in a crowd, and Sloane was one of that rare breed. Prescott would ensure that he provided for Tara, seeing to it that she had everything she needed, and more.

"I do own half interest in the Diamond R Ranch," Sloane explained. "And I have sufficient funds to buy out the stock owned by the St. Louis Cattle company, but I am not worth as much as Rutherford."

Ryan studied the raven-haired man with thoughtful deliberation and then dismissed his confession with a careless shrug. "'Tis no matter. Your financial worth may not match his dollar for dollar, but you have something Rutherford obviously lacks—character. And I am sure you will see to it that my granddaughter wants for nothing." Heaving a weary sigh, Ryan hoisted himself from the chair and grabbed his lantern. "It is time I bid you goodnight and returned to my own room to contemplate what I intend to say to Rutherford when he shows his cowardly face tomorrow."

"It won't be difficult to recognize him," Tara smirked. "He will be the one sporting a black eye."

Ryan's head swiveled around to peer incredulously at them, Sloane in particular. "Did the two of you come to blows after he struck Tara?" he questioned, delighted with the possibility.

"If I had known what he had done, I would have done far more than blackened his eye," Sloane growled vengefully. "But I had already left for the night. Tara was the one who planted her fist in his arrogant face. It seems your instruction in self-defense has served its purpose."

Tara beamed proudly. Tara had given that two-legged rat exactly what he deserved. Nodding mutely, Ryan drew open the door and then quietly closed it behind him, satisfied that Mother Nature had not made a mess of things. Indeed, it seemed she had handled the entire affair far better than he had.

When they were alone once again, Tara turned in Sloane's arms, a sly smile playing on her heart-shaped lips. "Now that we have been rudely awakened, I find it difficult to fall asleep. What shall we do to occupy ourselves?"

"Would you be interested in learning to play mumbletypeg?" Sloane asked innocently. "It is a popular game among the cowhands."

"No, I think not," Tara murmured as her roving hand slid over his shoulder, circling each male nipple before trailing beneath the sheet to map the hard contour of his hip. "Have you another suggestion?"

"Perhaps a game of chess, then." His voice wavered when her bold fondling further aroused him.

"Intellectual stimulation is not at all what I had in mind," Tara assured him as her butterfly kisses fluttered over his pounding chest and followed the dark matting of hair that trailed down his lean abdomen. "Must I spell it out for you, Mr. Prescott?"

"No, Mrs. Prescott. That won't be necessary. I think you have made yourself reasonably clear. . . ."

He hooked his arm around her waist and pressed her to her back, aching to lose himself in the soft feminine fragrance that swarmed his senses. His long tanned fingers threaded through the waterfall of silver-blond hair as his mouth slanted across hers, tasting, teasing her with daring intimacy as his probing tongue traced the inner softness of her lips. And then his mouth abandoned hers to investigate every silky inch of her skin, worshipping each shapely contour of feminine flesh. His skillful deliberations were rewarded with her quiet moan of pleasure, assuring him that she craved his touch as much as he delighted in touching her.

His wayward hands wandered at will, stroking the taut peaks of her breasts, gliding over her trim waist and swirling over her thighs before retracing their tantalizing path to begin the same arousing process all over again. Growing flames of desire leaped across her quaking skin in the wake of his caresses, making her body arch to feel the imprint of his hard masculine body against hers. His warm tongue sent shock waves of pleasure spurting through her veins as it flicked at the roseate bud and then languidly moved to entice the other throbbing peak. He was feeding the craving, but he was creating a monstrous one, and Tara swore she would die from the want of him before he settled his powerful body over hers. The coil of longing that unfurled deep inside of her demanded appeasement, but still Sloane held himself at bay, arousing her with his kisses and caresses, assaulting her with sensations that became sweet, maddening torture.

Breathlessly, she cupped her hands on his face, bringing his lips to hers, drinking freely of the intoxicating potion of passion. And finally he came to ease the wild, ravenous hunger, to possess her, to love her as he had loved no other woman.

His knees nudged her legs apart and she welcomed his muscular weight, reveling in the rapturous sensations that flooded over her like a raging river that overflowed its banks. The slow, driving rhythm of his lovemaking took her higher and higher, until she had bridged the gap between physical pleasure and the all-engulfing emotions stirred by love. She was suspended in a world that knew no time and space, a universe swirling with undefinable sensations, so potent and soul-shattering that Tara was no longer certain if she were living or dying. But she didn't care. She would have surrendered her last breath to him if he had demanded it. He was her love, her reason for being, and he could send her gliding over pastel-colored rainbows to enjoy ineffable pleasures.

And then the wild, ecstatic sensations converged upon her with such intensity that it was like flying into the sun. The world split asunder and shards of penetrating light came from nowhere to shatter the dark world of churning emotions. All rational thought exploded in her mind as she followed the divergent sun rays into oblivion.

When Sloane groaned in ultimate pleasure and plunged into her, striving for unattainable depths of intimacy, Tara clung fiercely to him. Her nails dug into the hard muscles of his back as if she never meant to let him go, couldn't let him go. She was dazed and disoriented from her intimate flight. For what seemed forever, she waited for the sweet, tormenting sensations to fade and offer her back into the waiting arms of reality. But the heart-stopping emotions refused to relinquish their grasp, and she was rocked by yet another round of indescribable sensations as Sloane slumped against her, his ragged breath caressing her neck.

"Tara, *mi cariña*, do you know how very much I love you?" Sloane whispered against her velvety skin, his voice thick with deep emotion.

As he rolled away and gathered her in his sinewy arms, Tara pressed a tender kiss to his sensuous lips. It was a kiss that spoke of her love for him, an acknowledgment of his affection for her. They needed no words between them. Love spoke its own unique language.

A contented sigh escaped her lips as she rested her head on his sturdy shoulder. They had come the full circle, and Tara had found a love that would endure long past eternity. She would follow him to the ends of the earth and back again, brave the impossible to be near him. He was the essence of her being, her breath of life, and Tara knew there was no place she would rather be than in the unending circle of his arms.

Her tangled lashes fluttered against her cheek as Sloane cuddled her closer and then followed him into dreams. They were together again, running hand in hand along the sandy beach of paradise, basking in the warmth of boundless love that burned brighter than a thousand suns.

491

Chapter 31

It was with great reluctance that Sloane climbed from the bed following morning when the servant rapped on the door, informing him that Ryan was impatiently waiting for him to descend to the study for a private conference. Sloane would have much preferred to stay where he was, entangled in Tara's silky arms.

When Sloane veered to the right to join Ryan, Tara sailed out the front door, intent on riding about the estate and enjoying the freedom she had been denied since she had returned to St. Louis. Sloane watched the spritely nymph bound down the steps and skip toward the stables and he gritted his teeth, wishing he could accompany her. Resigning himself to the fact that he would be forced to explain his way through the pile of papers he had gathered from Merrick's ledgers, Sloane planted himself in a chair and blazed through the file at such incredible speed that Ryan insisted that he slow down. Mechanically, Sloane presented the financial reports at reduced speed, but he was chomping at the bit, itching to join Tara and take up where they had left off the previous night. Night? Sloane mused, biting back a rakish grin. It had been very nearly dawn before they had finally fallen asleep.

"Do you find something amusing about this mind-boggling list of numbers?" Ryan frowned when he glimpsed the half smile that had forced its way onto

Sloane's lips.

Sloane had been behaving strangely since he had arrived. He had fidgeted in his chair as if he were sitting on pins and needles, and his eyes kept straying to the clock on the mantel and then the window until Ryan had become dizzy just watching him. Had Ryan known Tara was gallivanting around the estate, he could have diagnosed the cause of Sloane's discomfort, but he assumed that she was still in her room, just as Terrance and Libby were.

Forcing a deadpan expression, Sloane concentrated on the ledger and rattled off an explanation while Ryan continued to regard him warily. After two hours, Sloane and Ryan had come to terms on the sale of stock in the St. Louis Cattle Company, and the Diamond R changed hands. They had just shaken hands to formally complete their transaction when an incessant rap at the door interrupted them.

Joseph grumbled in irritation when the door swung open and Sloane's ominous frame blocked the entrance of the O'Donnovan mansion. "I wish to speak with Ryan," he announced stiffly. "Kindly move out of my way."

A menacing smile thinned Sloane's lips, and it was all he could do to keep from putting a stranglehold on Joseph's skinny neck. Taking his own sweet time, Sloane stepped back and bowed mockingly before the dastardly ogre, who wore a silk morning jacket to conceal the yellow stripe that ran the full length of his spineless back.

"Do come in, Rutherford," Sloane requested in a tone that implied that he would have preferred to be staring at Joseph's departing back instead of his unwelcome face, which bore the black-and-blue stamp that perfectly matched the size of Tara's doubled fist.

Joseph didn't like the sound of his remark, and he cast Sloane a cautious glance before he wedged his way around the towering mass of brawn and muscle and

493

scampered toward the study like the weasel he was. Joseph was annoyed that Ryan had permitted the raven-haired brute in his house, especially at such an early hour. He had only taken his breakfast, and he didn't have the stomach to collide with Sloane Prescott before his morning meal had been digested.

When Joseph marched into the study, Ryan glared daggers at him. "How nice of you to drop by and save me the trouble of dragging you here to face a firing squad!" Ryan's fist hit the desk and the sound ricocheted off the walls, coming at Joseph from all directions. "You have proven yourself to be every kind of fool, Rutherford. I have babied you along for years, offered you my granddaughter's hand, and you seek to repay me by assaulting her in my very own house! How dare you raise your hand against her!" Ryan's voice was becoming higher and wilder by the second, until he was screeching in Joseph's bruised face. "I should coat you with tar and feathers, hang you by your boot heels, and *then* have you shot!"

"But she insulted me and I . . ." Joseph snapped in self-defense, only to be cut off by the low, threatening growl from behind him.

"And you deserved every degrading comment Tara might have possibly made about you," Sloane sneered contemptuously.

"Needless to say, the engagement is off." Ryan rose to his feet and stalked toward Rutherford, looking at him with disdain. "You have proven yourself unworthy of my granddaughter. The honor goes to Mr. Prescott."

Joseph wheeled around, furious red working its way up his face to tint the roots of his blond hair. "I suppose you are gloating over the fact that you made me look like a bungling fool," he hissed venomously.

"I didn't have to," Sloane hurled at him. "You managed that feat all by yourself."

"You won't get away with this." Joseph wagged a bony

finger in Sloane's face. "Ryan signed a contractual agreement and I intend to see that he . . ." His head swiveled around as he heard papers being ripped to shreds and he watched in dismay as both copies of the marriage contract drifted to the floor in a hundred jagged pieces.

"I will pull every share of stock from our cattle investment," Joseph threatened, desperately searching for a means to bribe Ryan into retracting his announcement.

"You have just sold your shares to Mr. Prescott," Ryan smirked and then watched Joseph's face whitewash. "Since I control ruling interest in the company, I have sold out."

"But you can't. . . ."

"Can't I?" Ryan lifted a mocking brow. "I have power of attorney in all our business dealings, as your father stipulated in his will. Even your own flesh and blood knew you didn't have a head for business . . . or anything else, for that matter," he added in a sarcastic tone that made the hair on the back of Joseph's neck stand on end.

"You won't get away with this," Joseph vowed maliciously. "I will find a way to save face while *you* lose yours! You will not make me the laughing stock of St. Louis."

"Oh, clam up, Rutherford," Ryan snorted derisively. "Tara was right about you. You are nothing but a pompous windbag."

Joseph staggered back as if Ryan had blackened his other eye, and mutinous thoughts whipped through his head. Leveling Ryan and Sloane one last glare, he yanked his top hat down around his ears, spun on his heels, and stormed out of the house.

Sloane watched the door slam shut behind Joseph and then cast Ryan a curious glance. "Do you suppose he intends to make trouble, even when he doesn't have a leg to stand on?"

"He isn't clever enough to make trouble," Ryan

assured him confidently. "Joseph's father was a very ingenious man, with an inventive mind, but he never devised a way to stuff an ounce of intelligence in that boy's empty head."

Relief washed over Sloane's bronzed features. He had endured enough trouble to last him a lifetime, and he prayed Ryan was right. He and Tara had just made a new beginning, and Sloane wanted nothing to spoil it. If Joseph Rutherford had any sense at all, he would set his sights on another woman and forget his engagement to Tara.

Sloane's pensive musings were interrupted by quiet murmurings in the hall, and he craned his neck to see Terrance and Libby floating down the steps, their arms entwined, their eyes locked as they conversed in secretive whispers. Amusement flickered in Sloane's cobalt-blue eyes as he propped himself against the door and waited for his father-in-law to glance in his direction.

Finally, Terrance dragged his eyes off his wife and settled then on the taunting grin that was plastered on Sloane's face.

"Have you seen anything of the old buzzard this morning? Libby and I have an announcement to make," Terrance explained.

"The old *buzzard* has taken roost in his study," Ryan snorted as he appeared beside Sloane and gave Terrance the evil eye. "Don't tell me. Let me guess. You and Libby have decided you cannot live without each other, and you are moving back to St. Louis." Ryan sounded as thrilled as a man confronting the possibility of having his home overrun by a swarm of pests.

"Not exactly," Libby murmured. "Terrance has convinced me to travel to Texas with him, just to see for myself what life is really like in the wide-open spaces."

"You are going to Texas?" Ryan hooted in astonishment. Libby *and* Tara in Texas? Ryan shook his head in disbelief. His world was crumbling down around his knees.

While Terrance and Libby explained their plans, Sloane glanced toward the window. A concerned frown etched his brow when he checked his watch. What had become of Tara? She should have returned by now, he mused. And then a knowing smile pursed his lips. No doubt she was thoroughly enjoying her newfound freedom and she had lost track of time. She would be back, Sloane assured himself. And when she returned, they would spend the afternoon in the privacy of their room, loving the day away . . . compensating for all the times he had ached to hold her in his arms and hadn't been granted the opportunity.

"Sloane?" Ryan tapped his daydreaming guest on the shoulder. "I don't believe you have been formally introduced to your mother-in-law." He gestured toward the attractive older woman. "Libby, this is Sloane Prescott, the private detective I conferred with in Dallas last year, the man Tara married during her sojourn in Texas."

Wide violet eyes just like Tara's swung to Ryan for confirmation. "And you have approved of this?" she questioned shakily. She had been so wrapped in her own world since the moment she had laid eyes on Terrance that she had temporarily forgotten she had a daughter. To learn that she was already married took the wind out of Libby's billowing sails.

"I have," Ryan grumbled as he sank into his chair. "Not that it matters. You have taken Terrance back, and Tara has secretly married. It appears that my opinion is of little consequence these days. This doddering old fool has been swept under the rug with the rest of the clutter."

"You have hardly been put out to pasture, Ryan," Terrance snickered. "It is only that each of us wants a hand in his own destiny. Is that so difficult to understand?" The wry expression that had claimed his

497

features mellowed as he strode over in front of the old man. "We only want to live our lives *our* way, even if we make a few mistakes along the way."

Ryan leaned back in his chair to study Terrance thoughtfully. "Perhaps I have been a bit too domineering," he conceded. "But all I ever wanted was . . ." The words died on his lips when a strange thump on the front door interrupted his train of thought. "What the hell was that?"

Sloane pivoted on his heel to investigate. When he returned, his face was twisted in a furious snarl. He stalked over to thrust the rock and the note that had been tied to it into Ryan's hand.

"I thought you said Rutherford was harmless," Sloane growled, his blue eyes blazing with fury.

Ryan adjusted his spectacles and then skewed his face into a hateful sneer as he read Joseph's ultimatum.

You need not bother searching for Tara. I have taken her with me, where she belongs in the first place. I am not canceling the wedding arrangements, and you will not be allowed to see Tara until she has become my wife. No one makes a fool of Joseph Rutherford.

"I said he was a moron," Ryan scornfully corrected. "But Rutherford has proven himself stupid enough to be dangerous."

"What are you two ranting about?" Terrance demanded to know.

"I told Joseph the marriage was off, and that Sloane was taking his place, but the ignoramus wasn't smart enough to deduce that Sloane was the man Tara insisted that she had married in Texas. Joseph has kidnapped Tara," Ryan muttered disgustedly.

"What?" Libby and Terrance echoed simultaneously.

"If the two of you hadn't spent the evening locked in-

498

the parlor you would have known what has been going on around here," Ryan snorted caustically and then jerked up his head, frowning bemusedly when Sloane wheeled around and stormed toward the door. "Where are you going?"

"I'm going to do what I should have done the first time I laid eyes on that cowardly bastard," Sloane ground out as his long, swift strides carried him into the foyer and out the front door.

"Oh, my goodness. My poor child. . . ." Libby swept her hand across her peaked forehead and wove to and fro like a willow swaying in the wind.

"Dammit, don't you dare faint," Ryan scowled as he gathered his feet beneath him and trailed after Terrance, who had already made a beeline for the door. "There will be no one around here to scrape you up off the floor. If you plan to travel to Texas with that prodigal husband of yours, you had better get your squeamish disposition in hand."

Libby snapped to attention like a private confronting his general, and then fell into step behind Ryan, bringing up the rear of the procession that was headed for Joseph Rutherford's estate on the opposite side of St. Louis.

Joseph steadied himself when he heard the crash of his front door as it wobbled on its hinges and then gulped when he heard the clank of spurs moving deliberately through the hall. His mouth gaped open when Sloane Prescott's powerful form halted at the entrance of the library to survey the cowardly weasel and his two henchmen, who stood on either side of the room.

Wide, apprehensive eyes flooded over the plaid shirt and leather vest that stretched across the broad expanse of Sloane's chest. Joseph's critical gaze flooded over Sloane's tapered waist, around which his holster and revolver hung. Denim breeches hugged his muscled thighs, and scuffed high-heeled boots equipped with spurs made Sloane seem more like a giant than a man. Warily, Joseph allowed his eyes to slide back to the chiseled features of Sloane's face, which were stamped with a grim frown. His Stetson was pulled down on his forehead, shading those flashing cobalt-blue eyes that could slash through a man like a double-edged dagger. Sloane Prescott looked every bit the calloused, rough-edged cowboy, standing there as big as Texas.

If Joseph hadn't called in his burly henchmen for the inevitable confrontation, he would have wilted and slid down the wall to land on the floor in a spineless heap. He had expected Ryan to come barging into his home, but nothing had prepared him for this awesome cowboy who looked as if it would pleasure him to tear Joseph into bite-sized pieces and feed him to a pack of coyotes.

"Where is Ryan?" Joseph smirked, gathering his courage and projecting an air of arrogance. "Surely you do not expect to come stalking into my home to do harm to my person with my friends here to protect me."

"Ryan and Terrance are waiting outside to glue you back together when I have finished tearing you apart," Sloane assured him in a cold, deadly tone that sent goose bumps trickling across Joseph's skin. His hard blue eyes drifted over Joseph's henchmen. The odds don't seem unreasonable . . . two and a half to one."

There it was again: that intimidating tone, and the cutting words that made Joseph bristle in irritation. He had been so furious when he stormed from the O'Donnovan mansion that he had been bent on revenge. When he had seen Tara wandering along the stream unchaperoned, Joseph had seized the opportunity to spite the entire O'Donnovan family and the insolent man who had been offered Tara's hand.

"You are wasting your time, Prescott," Joseph sniffed as he raked Sloane with a contemptuous stare. "I am keeping Tara with me until our wedding, and if you think you can get past my men, you are a bigger fool than I thought."

His taunt brought Sloane a step closer, his chest heaving, his fists clenched at his sides. But as Sloane stalked the blond-headed rat who had sought out the farthest corner and planted himself in it, his bodyguards approached his flanks. As they leaped at him, Sloane came uncoiled like an angry lion, his furious growl slicing though the tense silence, his fists flinging to catch one man in the jaw and the other in the belly. Both of them retreated a step, and Sloane lowered his head to charge at Will Perkins before he had the opportunity to brace himself. Sloane's powerful arms encircled his waist, squeezing Perkins in two as he slammed him into the shelves sending a row of books tumbling about them like a rockslide. A pained grunt erupted from Perkins's lips when he was mashed into the wall and pounded on the head by the falling books.

"Get him, Riley!" Joseph screeched, encouraging the other bodyguard to charge Sloane's blind side.

While Joseph stood shadowboxing in the corner, rooting for his bodyguards to hammer Sloane, Riley leaped on his foe and was caught in midair by a doubled fist. He dropped like a discarded punching bag, overturning the chair beside him, which, in turn, slammed into the end table.

It was as if a grizzly bear had been let loose in Joseph's elaborately decorated library. Tables and chairs had sprouted wings and were flying about the room and bodies were sailing through the air. Each time Riley and Perkins attempted to bring Sloane to his knees, he came at them like a wild beast, pelleting them with punishing blows before they could inflict enough pain to stifle the cowboy who knew how to handle himself against impossible odds.

"Watch out!" Joseph yelped as Riley crawled onto his hands and knees and then looked up in time to see another double fist coming at him at incredible speed.

A silly smile spread across Riley's lips as the blow knocked him senseless, and he sprawled on the floor in an unconscious heap, amid the broken furniture. Perkins gulped hard as Sloane whirled around, his eyes glistening, his mouth watering like a panther licking his lips in anticipation of the kill.

"Knock him down, Perkins!" Joseph ordered as he pranced in his corner, still shadowboxing with the air.

Perkins flung Joseph a withering glance and then raised his arms in surrender as Sloane stalked toward him. "Fight your own battles, Rutherford. I ain't stayin' around to see how this one turns out."

Joseph froze in fear as Perkins darted away with his tail tucked between his legs. Panic overwhelmed him when he glanced up to see the menacing smile that rippled across Sloane's lips. Frantically, he made a dash for his desk, fumbling to retrieve the derringer he kept in the drawer, but he halted in his tracks when he heard the click of Sloane's revolver splitting the silence.

"Don't try it, Rutherford, or you will give me all the more reason to blow your hand off the end of your skinny arm." His eyes narrowed on the spindly excuse for a man who had snatched Tara away from him. "Where is she?" he demanded gruffly.

Joseph's pointed chin jutted out. "If you kill me, you will never find her," he smirked.

From beneath the shadow of his Stetson, Sloane studied Joseph with piercing scrutiny. "Where is Tara?"

"I'm not going to let you have her," Joseph sneered spitefully. "All of St. Louis is expecting us to wed, and I won't be duped as a fool."

Sloane was losing his patience with Rutherford and his defiance. "When Tara told you she was already married before she left Texas, she was telling you the truth. I am her husband. Now, where the hell is my wife!" His voice

502

rose testily until he was bellowing in Joseph's face.

Joseph's jaw sagged on its hinges and then he quickly recovered to sneer at Sloane. "I'll see that you pay for this. Damn you, she was supposed to be *my* wife. Ryan promised her to me."

Sloane was getting madder by the minute. Impulsively, his hand snaked out to grab a fistful of Joseph's shirt, twisting around his neck and lifting him off the floor. "You aren't the first man who has tried to take her from me. One is dead and the other is in jail. Make your choice, Rutherford. Which way do you prefer to take your punishment?"

Crimson red swamped Joseph's face as Sloane twisted the shirt so tightly about his neck that he could barely draw a breath without choking on it. Impatiently, Sloane shook him until his teeth rattled.

"You are causing me to lose my good disposition," Sloane gritted out between clenched teeth and then slammed Joseph against the shelf, causing another row of books to topple from their perch like an avalanche.

And then Tara's terrified scream wafted its way through the mansion, and Sloane swore Joseph had buried her alive when the sound seemed to filter through the floor. His murderous blue eyes cut Joseph to shreds as he shoved him away as if physical contact with this cowardly weakling repulsed him. Sloane paid no heed to Joseph's startled squawk, nor did he glance back to see the unbalanced book shelf tilt away from the wall to come crashing down on Rutherford, pinning him to the floor. His ears were finely tuned to the sound of Tara's terrified voice, and he frantically searched for a means to take him to the basement of the monstrous house where she was being held prisoner.

Ryan shifted uneasily on his seat and then peered

503

toward the front door. He had listened to the crashing of furniture and loud squawks that erupted from the mansion for as long as he could stand. "I'm going in there," he announced as he bolted from the carriage.

"Sloane wants to handle this alone, and it *is* his right," Terrance reminded him. "If you doubt his abilities, you have sorely misjudged Sloane Prescott."

"Then I should at least like to sit ringside while he beats that foolhardy Rutherford to a pulp," Ryan insisted as he marched toward the front door, which was dangling from its hinges.

Terrance heaved an agitated sigh and climbed down to lift Libby out beside him. "We may as well go along. This won't be the last brawl you see if you accompany me to Texas."

When Ryan veered around the corner to the library he stopped in his tracks, his wide, disbelieving eyes circling the demolished room. One burly brute lay in a pile of broken furniture and Joseph was buried beneath a heap of splintered wood and ripped books.

"Good God!" he crowed as his gaze swept the disassembled room again, just to ensure that his eyes weren't playing tricks on him.

"Oh my!" Libby gasped and pulled up short when she spied what had once been an elegant library boasting an antiquary of expensive relics and volumes of valuable books. The room looked as if it had been ransacked by a devastating tornado, leaving not a stick of furniture in one piece or resting in its original place. Even the stuffed sofa of gold velvet was upturned and missing a leg.

Cautiously, Ryan cleared a path to Joseph, who was attempting to dig his way out of the clutter. "I hope you have learned your lesson," he snorted derisively.

Joseph was too dazed to speak. His head was spinning like a runaway carousel and he was seeing double. His gaze swung about the room and then he slumped forward, uncertain his wobbly legs would support him even if he managed to climb to his feet.

Tara's second bloodcurdling scream sent a shiver darting down Sloane's spine as he leaped down the steps two at a time to answer her frightened cry. He frowned bemusedly when her voice came from behind a solid wall in one corner of the wine cellar. Frantically, he moved his hands along the stone wall, trying to find the entrance. His fingertip brushed across the hidden latch and he pressed his shoulder to the wall, breathing a relieved sigh when the heavy door creaked and then swung open far enough for him to wedge in beside it.

Before he could glance around the narrow cubicle that had been lit with a single candle, Tara was in his arms, shuddering and sobbing in relief.

"There are snakes in here," she choked out and then gestured toward the wine rack that sat in the corner of the musty dungeon. A beady-eyed serpent slithered across a row of wine bottles, and Tara practically climbed up Sloane's muscular torso. "I hate those disgusting creatures."

A wry smile trickled across his lips as he scooped her up in his arms and inched through the narrow opening, cradling his shapely bundle against his chest. "Aren't you even going to offer me a kiss for saving you?"

Tara relaxed in his strong arms as he carried her through the dark cellar and up the steps. "Thank you, gallant knight, for saving me from distress." She looped her arms around his neck, drawing his head to hers to present him with a kiss that carried enough heat to melt his revolver into a pool of hot liquid and cause it to drip though the hole at the bottom of his holster.

Sloane swayed with the side effects of her potent embrace, his trembling anger replaced with desire.

"Lord, I love you, woman," he murmured against her honeyed lips.

"And I love you," Tara whispered back to him as she nestled her head against his sturdy shoulder and sighed contentedly.

She had been annoyed with herself for allowing Joseph to sneak up on her unawares and even more furious when he had stashed her in the secluded vault. But she had come apart at the seams when she saw several pairs of glistening black eyes peering back at her, and she had been unable to control herself. She had screamed at the top of her lungs, hoping Joseph would relent and let her out of the dingy hole he had locked her in.

When Sloane turned the corner to the library, Tara viewed what was left of the room with smug satisfaction until her eyes landed on Joseph, who had picked up his chair and then quickly dropped into it. There wasn't a scratch on that skinny oaf's face, except the one she had placed there the previous night. Sloane had demolished the room, but he had left Joseph unscathed.

Tara wiggled from Sloane's arms, picked up the front of her skirt, and stomped across the room to halt in front of Joseph. Her violet eyes snapped with fury as she stared down her nose at him.

"This is for closeting me with a den of snakes," she hissed as she swung her arm and punched him in his good eye, sending him swiveling around in his chair.

"Tara, for heaven's sake!" Ryan snorted disapprovingly.

"He had it coming," she snapped as she shook away the sting on her knuckles. "He knows I detest snakes and he locked me in the vault with them."

An amused smile rippled across Sloane's lips as he crossed his arms over his chest and propped himself against the wall to admire the feisty she-cat he had taken for his wife. His admiring gaze wandered over her curvaceous figure and wild blond hair. She was everything he had ever wanted. She was bright, witty, and beautiful, and she was bubbling with spirit. Sloane had the feeling his life would be anything but dull when he escorted this lovely misfit back to Texas.

"What was the name of the man who was forced to put his ranch up for sale in Texas?" Ryan questioned Sloane as he curled his arm around Tara's waist and led her away from Joseph before she felt the impulsive urge to rearrange a few more features on his whitewashed face.

"John Simpson," Sloane answered, wondering why Ryan had posed that question out of the blue.

Ryan nodded thoughtfully. "I want you to make arrangements to purchase that ranch," he said, and then peered over his shoulder at Joseph, who had collapsed in his swivel rocker. "Joseph and I are going to give you the deed to that particular section of land as a wedding present . . . aren't we, Joseph? It will be our way of compensating for the inconveniences and wishing you success in your future life together. Isn't that right, Rutherford? Or shall I turn Tara loose on you and let her finish what she has only begun?"

"It sounds like an excellent idea," Joseph said meekly.

"I thought you would agree. I doubt that it could be as costly as renovating your entire home after these two finished demolishing it," Ryan chuckled as he deposited Tara in Sloane's hands and then led the way toward the awaiting carriage.

"Madam. . . ." Sloane made an exaggerated bow before the wild beauty whose cheeks were smudged with soot and whose hair was a net of cobwebs. "I think we have done sufficient damage here. Shall we adjourn to your grandfather's mansion for a well-earned rest?"

Tara's amethyst eyes sparkled as she primly curled her hand around Sloane's proffered arm and stepped over the clutter in a most ladylike fashion. "And a cup of tea perhaps?" she inquired in a sophisticated voice that spoke of her gentle breeding.

But when her gaze locked with Sloane's, she knew what would be *his* cup of tea, and it was nothing remotely similar to pouring a steaming brew into a porcelain mug. A willing smile pursed her lips as she tossed him a saucy glance and allowed him to lead her from the house.

And that smile remained intact until Sloane escorted her to her room later that afternoon and barred the door behind him. Without further ado, Sloane shrugged off his leather vest and peeled off his shirt, his eyes gleaming with roguish anticipation.

"Well, ma'am, it seems we have tied up all the loose ends . . . except one," he said in that low, soft Southern drawl.

One dainty brow raised slightly as her eyes considered the hard wall of his chest and the crisp matting of hair that shaded his lean abdomen. "Oh? I cannot think of any matter we have left unattended," she insisted with mock innocence.

"Can't you?" Sloane growled seductively as he swaggered toward her and then let his hungry gaze drift toward the canopy bed.

"In broad daylight?" she teased, feigning surprise at the suggestive gleam she saw flickering in his cobalt-blue eyes, eyes that could look right through her to see that she had no complaint with what he implied.

Sloane reached up to work the small buttons that ran down the front of Tara's high-collared dress, one he fully intended to deposit in the garbage when he got her out of it. He detested its color and style, and he much preferred this shapely minx in her thin chemisette, bolero, and skirt. The image of her that he had carried in his mind while he rode the rails to Missouri was more arousing than this garb she had selected for riding. But then, he would have preferred her in nothing at all, he reminded himself as his hands slid around her trim waist and the soft, feminine scent of her warped his senses.

"Broad daylight or pitch darkness . . . it doesn't matter," Sloane rasped as his lips skimmed across her cheek to capture her mouth in a long, savoring kiss. "I'll love you at dawn, midnight, and every hour in between. . . ."

As the confining garments fell away, Tara surrendered to the feel of his hard, powerful body brushing intimately against hers, ached to lose herself in the never-ending circle of his sinewy arms. His ravishing kiss stole her breath from her lungs and then generously offered it back. His caresses swam over a sea of bare flesh, seeking out each sensitive point, kindling a fire that swept through her veins like a boiling river of unleashed desire. He tasted and touched her, worshipped her with words and kisses that chased all sane thoughts from her mind and sent them fleeing from the fire that burned her inside out. She was consumed by the passion he offered, overwhelmed by the love they shared as the world blazed up about them. And then he came to her, possessing her, being possessed. He became the flame within her, the eternal torch of love that could never be extinguished. She loved him, body and soul, and she reveled in the rapture that blossomed somewhere deep inside her and then spread through her entire being.

His name was on her lips as she showered him with adoring kisses and held him close as they soared past the twinkling stars on the most intimate of journeys to a universe that only lovers could touch without ever leaving the circle of each other's arms.

In the aftermath of love, Tara's moist lashes swept up to see the love glowing in his dark blue eyes. A satisfied smile grazed her lips as she traced her index finger over the sensuous curve of his mouth. "I'll go anywhere with you, Sloane. You are my world and everything in it."

Sloane chuckled softly and dropped a feathery kiss to her heart-shaped lips. His fingers combed through the tangled tresses of spun silver and gold that sprayed across the pillow. "And I'll build you a mansion in Palo Duro . . . beside the waterfall so we can hear the murmuring of the river outside our window each night when we fall asleep in each other's arms."

An impish grin caught one corner of her mouth as she stretched beside him like a contented feline basking in the sun. "That is very generous of you, but I think I will always prefer the secluded cave behind the waterfall to a bed. It is far more inventive and romantic. . . ."

The seductive gleam in her catlike eyes aroused him, but then, everything about this delicious vixen aroused him. "Take me there, *querida*, to our paradise beyond the silver waterfall. . . ."

As their lips met and their bodies touched they were transported back in time and space to a world bathed in moonlight, beneath a wall of sandstone that was draped with silver streams of a waterfall. The river's hushed murmurings intermingled with their soft words of love. And they were, as they had been from the beginning, wrapped in a dream of rapture and passion, finding themselves, their whimsical hopes, and wildest fantasies in the circle of each other's arms.

"I love you . . . *con toda mi alma*," Sloane whispered against her parted lips that melted against his like the spraying mist of a waterfall.

"And I will always love you," Tara whispered back as the strong, sinewy arms of love enfolded her.

Ryan O'Donnovan impatiently drummed his fingers on his knee and took another sip of his tea. He glared down at the four cups that sat on the silver tray in front of him and then peered up at the ceiling, hearing the soft laughter that trickled down the spiral staircase from the bedchambers above him. An annoyed frown plowed his brow as his eyes swung to the window to see darkness settling about his estate. It was becoming more obvious by the minute that his daughter and granddaughter were not coming down to join him in their nightly ritual of

510

sipping an after-dinner cup of tea and discussing the events of the day. There were bound to be more monotonous nights like this, Ryan thought disgruntled as he clanked his cup onto the saucer and pricked his ears, hoping he had heard footsteps in the hall. But he was met with deafening silence.

Well, if Libby and Tara were going to pull up stakes and march off to Texas, then he was damned well going with them. With all the dillydallying that was going on upstairs, he was sure to have any number of great-grandchildren to dote over in his declining years, he decided. And he was not about to be stuck in St. Louis. Maybe Texas wasn't so bad after all, he mused as he called to Hudgens to gather the unused cups of tea and cart them back to the kitchen.

Ryan climbed to his feet and strode toward the stairs, only to be assaulted by another round of contented laughter. "Ah, youth has a fetish for passion," Ryan chuckled to himself as he trudged up the steps and lifted his eyes heavenward." Never let them grow old," he murmured and then cast an approving smile toward each bedroom door as he ambled down the hall. "Let love keep them forever young."

A muddled frown gathered on Sloane's brow as he bent an ear toward the door, catching the quiet murmurings that drifted down the hall. "Did you hear something?"

Tara slanted Sloane a taunting smile as she drew his lips back to hers. "Are you searching for an excuse to interrupt what has every indication of becoming a very satisfying evening?"

"No, I only thought . . ." he started to protest.

"Don't think, just kiss me," Tara requested in a soft voice that was laced with inviting passion. "Too much contemplation can warp a man's mind, and I intend to ensure that doesn't happen to you."

His quiet laughter tickled her senses as he nuzzled his head against her breast. "It is comforting to know you have my best interests at heart. Who could ask for more than a loving devoted wife."

"Who indeed?" Tara agreed as she crouched above him, her wild blond hair forming a cape that blocked out everything that had any resemblance to reality. "Enough talk. Show me some proof of this love about which you boast."

"I already have, thrice!" Sloane reminded her and then chuckled at the mischievous smile that touched the corners of her lovely mouth. "How many times must a man make love to his wife before she is convinced of his affection? I am only a man, and I do have my limits."

"Only a man?" Tara whispered as her wandering hands made his male body rouse beneath her tantalizing caresses. "No, I think not," she objected. "No man, this. . . ." Her fingertips splayed across the naked wall of his chest and then languidly descended to map the hard, muscled contours of his hips. "But rather a dark, daring phantom who claims no physical limitations. Come, majestic specter, I have seen you fly along the caprock of Palo Duro like a winged centaur. Take me with you on your daring flight. . . ."

Sloane could no more refuse her husky request than he could control the rapturous sensations that coursed through his veins when she set her skillful hands upon him. When love commanded, he became what Tara desired. And together they soared along the precipices of pleasure, spiraling higher and higher until they had sailed above the clouds and looked down from their lofty perch, recalling each wondrous sensation that had sent them gliding over the pastel rainbow that led to paradise. And there they lingered, watching the wild violets swaying against a cobalt-blue sky where the vast horizon spanned into eternity.